THE MAN FOR THE JOB

"I simply don't have an armed escort under my orders now," Grierson said. "Hell, I don't even have a civilian scout. Practically everybody's out chasin' after Indians."

"Civilians!" Dinsmore said excitedly. "There's your answer, Colonel."

"Even if I wanted to," Grierson said skeptically, cocking his head at Dinsmore, "where would I get a civilian escort?"

"You leave that to me, Colonel."

"You know somebody?"

"Butler . . . colored fellow named Ples Butler. Hires out of Fort Scott off and on for Colonel Taylor. Ain't a better man ever stood in boot leather. Keeps a kid with him all the time."

"Mr. Dinsmore," Grierson said, "first you tell me the country's practically a death sentence for colored men, now you suggest I send two more out there. What makes you think they won't be killed too . . . if they're fools enough to go."

"Not these two, Colonel," Dinsmore said resolutely. "They'll not scare easy. Both of 'em go armed to the teeth, Texas style. They know what for. Used to be State Policemen down in Texas. And that's plum rough country. . . ."

Other *Leisure* books by Hiram King:
DARK TRAIL
HIGH PRAIRIE

Broken Ranks

Hiram King

LEISURE BOOKS NEW YORK CITY

A LEISURE BOOK®

June 2001

Published by

Dorchester Publishing Co., Inc.
276 Fifth Avenue
New York, NY 10001

ISBN 0-8439-4872-8

Visit us on the web at www.dorchesterpub.com.

Chapter One

Shadows of morning sun lay halfway across the alley between buildings when Lieutenant Nicholas Badger came out of the back door of the Liddell Hotel, where he had a storefront recruiting office. He was carrying a bulging brown envelope in his right hand, and had saddlebags slung over his left shoulder.

"All right, gather round here!" Badger called out.

The motley group of black men who'd been lounging around roused themselves, and came shuffling indifferently toward Badger. Since early that morning they'd been waiting in the alley behind the hotel out of plain sight of townspeople, as Badger had told them.

Lieutenant Badger was on a recruiting tour, had been for the past thirty days. Badger's commanding officer, Colonel Benjamin H. Grierson, had persuaded General Grant to assign Badger to his command and Grierson had promptly sent him off to recruit blacks to serve in the new Negro cavalry that was about to be established. Sporting his full

7

dress uniform, a row of bright Civil War ribbons on his chest, Badger had already recruited blacks in New York, Philadelphia, Baltimore, and Chicago.

Now, in St. Louis, Badger cast his eyes over the rabble gathering around him. They were all down-at-heels, shabbily dressed. No doubt looking for a better life than what almost two years of freedom had got them.

Nicholas Badger was five feet eleven inches tall, twenty-five years old. In his well-tailored dress blue uniform he was the perfect picture of health and vigor. He'd graduated from West Point, and when the Civil War came he'd reported to Union Colonel Grierson's staff as a shave-tailed second lieutenant just in time to go on Grierson's now-famous cavalry raid. During the raid Badger had impressed Grierson by his raw energy and drive. He had displayed uncommon boldness and leadership, volunteering to lead Company B when they had to storm Wall's Bridge spanning the Tickfaw River, the last rebel-held bridge blocking the regiment's safe entry into Baton Rouge.

Grierson knew he'd need all the competent field officers he could get in this great task of recruiting, equipping, and training a black regiment. Before Grierson had accepted the orders to form this black regiment, he'd insisted to General Grant that Badger be assigned to his command.

The black recruits drew up, Badger standing in the hollow of the rude horseshoe, scanning the dusky faces, wondering how in hell he'd let Colonel Grierson talk him into this. Wondering if Grierson, Grant, or the Army Department for that matter, really knew what they were getting into. Badger knew the huge gamble any white officer who volunteered for this duty was taking. This assignment could wreck careers. Stain lives forever.

"You too! Come on up here," Badger yelled out to a tall, dark recruit who hadn't moved, leaning casually against the hotel wall away from the others.

The recruit shouldered his body away from the wall, sauntered forward, walking slow and easy. He was six feet tall, had on faded blue jeans turned up at the cuffs, a dingy brown shirt, a brown felt hat battered to shapelessness, and black boots run down at the heels. Although dressed no better than the others, he had a look about him. Something in his quiet manner, something about the way he handled himself. Something in his eyes that would warn a man he was different.

He walked up aimlessly, stopped in back of the bunch, and stood spread-legged, looking indifferently at Badger, eyes expressionless, face blank.

"What's your name?" Badger asked. On his whirlwind tour Badger had signed up so many black recruits, in so many different towns, that faces and names were a blur to him now.

"Jerico," the recruit answered flatly.

"Jerico," Badger said, "when you're called, you come. On the double," Badger added with emphasis, glowering at Jerico.

"I could hear you plain as day where I was," Jerico answered.

"That don't matter," Badger said. "Just come when you're called. Now listen up." Turning his attention to the others, Badger continued: "All of you . . . listen up!" He paused, letting the murmuring die away. "All of you signed an enlistment contract," he stated, brandishing the brown envelope, "or put your mark on one. You're in Uncle Sam's army now. The same uncle that freed you is going to outfit you, feed you, and train you to fight."

Hours after the peace had been signed at Appomattox on April 9, 1865, a great many white men yahooed, threw their hats into the air, and promptly drew their mustering-out pay and went home to put their lives back together after four years of death and destruction.

Hiram King

By July the army had been drawn down from close to a million men to less than thirty thousand—a force the war department had come to realize was totally inadequate to meet the demands of reconstruction, homesteaders pushing west, railroad expansion, and frontier Indian trouble, trouble that had been left festering for four long years of fratricidal war.

Now the army needed more bodies. General Grant knew it. Home seekers and railroad crews out on the northern plains knew it. Sioux Indians under Red Cloud and an up-and-coming warrior named Crazy Horse were terrorizing settlers and railroad crews; Cheyennes under Roman Nose and Tall Bull were striking fear into the hearts of squatters, railroad crews, and anything else that moved on the Bozeman trail, a wagon road that branched northwest off the Oregon trail, cutting through traditional Indian hunting grounds, going to gold diggings in Wyoming. Merchants, miners, and immigrants on the southern plains and along the Santa Fe trail from Independence, Missouri, to Santa Fe, New Mexico, knew it too: Kiowas, Comanches, and Apaches were attacking merchant trains, scalping gold seekers, butchering sheepherders. Plus desperadoes, drifters, thieves, and men who'd cut loose from the army were robbing, killing, and rustling, and no peace officers within a hundred miles.

Frontier politicians were daily howling to the federal government for protection. Finally the war department was responding.

Now, Badger caught his breath, looking out over the last of the recruits he'd signed up in St. Louis. And Badger didn't like what he saw. This ragged mob didn't look like much. Just like the four previous drafts he'd shipped out to Fort Leavenworth. A bunch of ragtag, illiterate darkies. They'll never come up to standards, Badger thought, shaking his head sadly.

Badger's eyes came to rest on a tall, slim-faced recruit. "Bosie . . . Bosie Radford?" Badger asked, recalling the name of one of the very few newly liberated slaves who'd been able to sign his name.

"Yeah, suh," the thick-lipped man answered.

"Front and center," Badger ordered him.

Bosie shouldered his way forward, drawing up at Badger's side.

Bosie Radford was twenty-six years old. Five feet eleven inches tall, weighed about one-seventy. Had on an old beat-up Union campaign hat, a blue flannel shirt rolled up at the sleeves, and brown store-bought wool trousers. He'd come in on a freight train, but had walked some from Tennessee, where he'd heard the army was recruiting colored men for cavalry service.

Bosie had served almost two years in the Civil War along with close to two hundred thousand other black men. He'd served in the infantry. Had seen action at Brice's Crossroads in Colonel Bouton's Tennessee brigade and was there when Confederate General Bedford Forrest's cavalry routed Yankee General Sturgis's forces. General Forrest, a mostly illiterate former slave trader, had been so incensed at seeing colored men killing white men that he ordered his troopers to take no black prisoners, to shoot them down without mercy. Out of twelve hundred black men in Bouton's brigade, Radford was one among the few who'd escaped Forrest's wanton killing. He jumped in Tishomingo Creek, and swam across to safety. Three-quarters of the way underwater.

Radford had said as much to Badger when Badger asked about previous service, then wanted to know details. That's why Badger remembered Radford.

"I'm putting you in charge of these men," Badger said, stuffing the brown envelope into the saddlebag. Stiffening his posture, Badger drew up tall, announced to the rest of the recruits:

11

"All of you are going to Fort Leavenworth . . . Kansas. There's a train waiting down at the station. It'll take you as far into Missouri as it goes . . . Sedalia. From there the army'll send a detail to escort you. While you're on that train, Radford here's in charge." And he handed over the saddlebags to Radford. "You give 'im any trouble . . . any trouble atall," Badger repeated sternly, "and you'll answer to me." Badger ran his eyes over them, letting his words sink in. Then he asked mildly, "Any questions?" And he stood there, staring out at the blank, indifferent faces.

"When do we eat?" a short, slight-built recruit blurted out.

Badger's eyes lifted skyward, rolling to the back of his head. "Not again," Badger groaned. "You've asked me that three times already," he said moanfully. "Is eatin' all you think about?"

"You said we git three squares a day."

"What's your name anyhow?" Badger asked.

"Willie."

Willie Baker was nineteen. Five feet seven inches tall, he weighed one-forty at most. He had appropriated the last name of Baker. He was originally from the Mississippi Delta, but the war had ravished the Baker plantation he'd been raised on. When the war was over he'd found himself free but with no means of support. He'd hired on as a waiter on the Queenie, a Mississippi steamer. Not liking the boss, the work, or the river, he'd jumped ship in St. Louis, and found out he was worse off. No work. At least none to his liking. He ended up going to the storefront recruiting office advertised on handbills plastered up around the docks where blacks hung out looking for work.

And here he was. He had on the same clothes he'd jumped ship in: a waiter's dirty white jacket, sleeves reaching to the middle of his palms, a pair of blue seaman's jeans, and hobnail brogans.

"Well, Willie," Badger repeated patiently, "like I told you, you'll get three squares . . . in due time."

"When's due time, Augie?" Willie asked, looking at the recruit standing next to him.

"Due time is due time," Augie said, shrugging his shoulders.

Augie Lincoln was only seventeen, smooth-skinned and baby-faced, thin and had lied about his age to join up. He had come from St. Louis's docks too. That's where he'd met Willie when Willie first jumped ship and asked some dock scroungers gambling on the pier where work could be had. When they'd finished guffawing at Willie for asking such a stupid question, Augie rolled the dice, crapped out, swore under his breath, and started talking to Willie.

Come to find out, when Augie had been freed at fifteen he'd fled Georgia when the Freedmen's Bureau allotted his father forty acres and a mule. Augie could see hard work coming his way and wanted no part of it. So he left one dark night on a freight train heading north, making his way by stealing and working from time to time on docks, in saloons, in stables. Always around grown men.

But Augie had learned how to survive. Shooting dice, playing monte, stealing, Augie could hustle with the best of them. After a few senseless beatings and being hungry too many times, Augie realized he had no life. So when Willie mentioned joining the army, Augie decided that that wasn't such a bad idea. He went and found Jarbo, the man who'd beat him up last, on his knees shooting dice. Augie smashed a whiskey bottle alongside Jarbo's head, grabbed the money, and took off running after Willie, heading to the recruiting office. Augie had taken the last name Lincoln in honor of the assassinated president somebody had said set black people free.

"We ain't gettin' nothin' to eat," Willie said peevishly to Badger, "we ain't goin'. Is we, Augie?"

"It's too late to back out now," Badger said. "You've already signed up."

"We already et too," Augie said scoldingly to Willie. "Bacon and biscuits I bought with that money. Remember?"

"Hush up, Augie!" Willie snapped, jabbing Augie in the ribs.

Suddenly a man came running down the alley, shirttail flapping in the wind. "This where you join up?" he asked, coming to a running stop in back of the recruits, taking in great gulps of air, looking around for an answer.

"Yeah," Cecil said. "This's the place."

Cecil Hall was twenty-five years old, brown-skinned, and pimple-faced. Originally from Florida, he was five feet nine inches tall, and weighed no more than a hundred and forty pounds.

"Not if you expect to eat," Willie said huffily.

"I already et," the man said smugly, winking knowingly at Willie. Then looking up at Badger, he asked, "Can I join?"

"How come you want to?" Badger asked him. One of the stock questions Grierson had told Badger to ask all who applied, hoping for a patriotic answer, and sign up no one who didn't have a reasonable response.

" 'Cause I'm broke," the man answered honestly, smiling slyly. "Job played out," he added, looking around sheepishly at the others.

Antoine Battie snickered softly, then smiled handsomely.

Everybody started laughing.

Battie was twenty-six years old with a yellow complexion. Handsome, well put together. Jet-black curly hair. From New Orleans. He wore gray gabardine pants, a cream-colored ruffle-sleeved shirt, and black patent-leather low-top shoes. He had a shiny gold chain around his throat. And Battie was a self-made talker who would use ten words when one would do. Badger had had doubts about enlisting him in the all-black cavalry but Battie had convinced Badger that in spite of the high-yellow complexion and Creole name he was mostly colored. Born free, Battie was among the few who didn't have to choose a last name.

"I 'speck we all broke," Jefferson, a tall, dark, brooding man, said consolingly to him.

George Washington Jefferson was thirty-two, six feet tall, weighed at least one-ninety, and was heavy-handed. He had on a black flat-brimmed hat, a gray wool coat over a dirty-white wool undershirt, and faded jeans except in front, obviously where an apron had been.

His former master had named him George Washington, after the first president, for unknown reasons. Needing a last name, he himself had chosen Jefferson. So now he was officially on the army's rolls as George Washington Jefferson. Badger had personally recruited him as a blacksmith, finding him in his run-down, unprofitable blacksmith shop over in Clanton, Missouri.

"We ain't all joinin' just 'cause we broke," a tall, thin-faced man said sagely. His name was Hezekiah.

Hezekiah Skidmore was thirty years old, wore steel-rimmed glasses, and had an unlit corncob pipe clenched between his teeth. His gray tweed coat was coming out at the elbows. Hezekiah was from Helena, Arkansas, where he'd been teaching freedmen how to read, write, and cipher. In fact, he now had a burlap tote bag with the tools of his trade in it: three McGuffey Readers, a tablet of Big Chief writing paper, and a half dozen stubby pencils.

"If we had to have money to join up, I bet none of us could," Sam Manigo said, looking around at the raggedy, ill-fitting clothes most of them had on.

Sam Manigo was twenty-nine, five feet six inches tall and fat. He'd told Badger he weighed only about one-sixty. Badger guessed more like one-eighty and had told Manigo he'd have to lose some weight. Originally from Alabama, he'd wound up here after being stranded in Kentucky on his way anywhere north, putting distance between him and the South, where white people reminded him of the living hell that had been his life as a slave.

"I got money," Augie said brashly to Manigo. "Ain't I, Willie?"

"Hush up, Augie!" Willie said scoldingly. "You won't have none long you keep tellin' everybody."

Heads came around, eyes turned back to Badger, all the recruits wondering if he'd let the new man join up. They all knew the lieutenant had turned down others for one reason or another.

"You want to join the army because you're broke?" Badger repeated.

"Yeah, suh."

"Well, at least you're honest," Badger said. "What's your name?"

"Jake."

Jake McGruder was twenty-seven years old, a little bit better than six feet tall, lanky. He'd made his way here from Texas, where he had been working as a muckraker and roustabout in the stock pens around Fort Worth.

"You know him?" Badger asked Radford in a low voice.

"Seen him somewhere before."

"All right," Badger said to Jake, "you'll do. Come on up here."

"Yeaaahhh!" the recruits cheered out loud, some clapping derisively.

"What's that all about?" Badger asked, looking perplexed at Radford.

"I guess they seen him somewhere before too," Radford said seriously.

"All right," Badger said, facing around to Radford. "March 'em down to the station. I'll sign up McGruder and see he gets there."

"Yeah, suh."

16

"And, Radford," Badger added firmly, "you make sure they get on that train . . . all of 'em."

"Yeah, suh."

"Fall 'em in and march 'em down to the station," Badger said, stepping aside. ". . . Sergeant Radford."

"But . . . ," Bosie started, jerking his eyes around at Badger.

"Move!" Badger roared, interrupting him. ". . . Sergeant," he added out loud so they all could hear.

Bosie swallowed in his throat. "Fall in," he said casually to the men. "We marchin' to the train station."

Lieutenant Badger stood there looking at the black men milling around, forming themselves up. Finally they made four rude lines of various lengths and heights.

"Let's go," Radford said at length.

The recruits shuffled forward indifferently.

"Hold it!" Badger roared.

The formation lurched to a stop.

"That ain't no way to move a formation of men," Badger said scoldingly when he caught up to Radford's side. "You said you was in Bouton's Brigade, didn't you?"

"Yeah, suh."

"Didn't you drill any?"

"Some."

"Well, use what you learned! Now march these men the right way!"

"Yeah, suh." Radford had no desire whatever to be in charge. Reluctantly he faced forward, sucked in his breath, drew up tall as he'd seen Sergeant Norvell of Bouton's Brigade do. "Attention!" he ordered them.

The men braced up straight, stiff-shouldered, chests out exaggeratedly.

Bobo snickered at the seeming foolishness.

Bobo Jackson was twenty-seven years old, five feet eight inches tall, brown-skinned, and shifty-eyed. He had made his way here from Arkansas. He had a permanent scar along his ear and everlasting welts over his body where he'd been beaten unmercifully with the butt end of a riding crop by his former master at DeValls plantation.

Lieutenant Badger shot Bobo a stiff-jawed, disapproving look.

The snicker died away in Bobo's throat.

Radford screamed out, "Forward! March!"

The irregular ranks moved off disjointedly, Badger standing there watching them go, Radford tramping alongside somewhere in the middle of the moving formation.

"Get 'em in step!" Badger yelled after Radford. "Call cadence!"

"Left . . . ! Left . . . !" Radford said blandly. "Left, right, left."

They turned the corner out of the alley onto Main Street, disappearing from Badger's sight. Badger blew a sigh of anxiety, shaking his head dismally. Turning to McGruder, he asked offhandedly, "How old are you?"

"Twenty-fo'!"

"Come on inside, I'll sign you up. Can you write your name?" Badger asked, stepping through the back door of the hotel.

"Naw, suh," Jake answered at Badger's back. "I can make a plain X though."

Badger's shoulders sagged. "That'll have to do," he said wearily, and kept on walking toward his crude desk.

Down Main Street the ragged column went, moving disjointedly, like a great writhing python. Every white man on the boardwalk stopped what he was doing, looking, smirking knowingly. A man who'd just come out of Springer's Feed and Grain Store threw his sack of oats over into his farm wagon, and stood looking. "Won't you just look at that," he said more to himself than anyone else. "Army can't be that bad off," he added, wagging his head from side to side.

On the formation went, kicking up a moving cloud of dust behind it.

"Go back where you came from!" a white man yelled from in front of Vogel's Saloon. "You ain't fit for no army!"

"You won't fight, nohow!" another man yelled out. "Go back to pickin' cotton like you was!"

On they tramped, nobody in ranks saying a word. Everybody was uneasy, wondering what was going to happen next.

A pistol went off.

Every man in formation ducked involuntarily, flinched in his step at the sudden burst of gunfire.

Jerico was unnerved too. But only for a second. Jerico was an experienced fighter, and had been in some close-quarter gun battles already. Right now he had an old single-shot dragoon pistol hid out under his shirt. It was nothing, as guns went, but it'd kill a man just as dead as that Army Colt the man in front of the saloon had just shot off.

Jerico steadied himself, recognizing the situation for what it was.

The others? They were scared. As slaves, which all except one had been, they dared not know firearms. But they were none the worse for the scare. All except Rafer D. He'd come completely undone. Had burst from ranks and was running down Main Street, eyes searching frantically for a place to hide.

Everybody was watching him dodge from pillow to post. Finally he came to a sliding stop at a water trough, threw himself down behind it and peeped out.

Every white man on the street was guffawing at him. Rafer D. just knew the town was going to kill every black man in sight this morning. Badger had heard talk, and had mildly warned them that there might be trouble.

The tall, lanky, scar-faced man who'd been in front of the saloon, Woot Tally, was standing out on the edge of the boardwalk now, grinning. He'd fired his pistol into the ground as a lark.

Rafer D. Turner was twenty-two years old. Frail. Light-skinned with curly hair and a thin wisp of a mustache running along his upper lip. From Kansas. Rafer D. knew firsthand that John Brown and his sons from down by Osawatomie had forever stirred white blood when they brutally hacked to death three white men and a boy, and afterward tried to incite a slave insurrection. Rafer D. was scared witless because he knew no white man had forgotten about that. But a whole lot of Kansans were glad Brown had done what he'd done. Especially Doc Jennison, another abolitionist-minded Kansan.

Charles "Doc" Jennison was a slight, boyish-faced white man with abounding energy. He'd grown, up back East where he'd studied medicine and had evolved into a staunch, whole-souled abolitionist. He had come West to practice medicine, settling along the Kansas/Missouri border near Osawatomie, Kansas. Over the years he'd become embittered by the murders and outrages committed by Border Ruffians. Finally Doc could take no more, so he joined his neighbors in retaliation, crossing into Missouri, kidnapping and freeing slaves, killing and plundering slaveholders.

Jerico had been there. Doc had seen to that. Doc Jennison and his Jayhawkers had killed Corwin Walker and took Jerico and thirteen other slaves from Walker's plantation over by Lone Jack, Missouri, when Jerico was fifteen years old. The other slaves were family, so Doc took all the stock and the best wagons and sent them north. Jerico's family had been killed out already. Some said by Quantrill's outfit seven years before. So Doc had kept Jerico with him, mostly at Mound City just inside the Kansas border on Mine Creek.

None of the other recruits knew it but Jerico was a proven fighter. He'd been on raiding parties with Doc and his Jayhawkers. He'd also ridden with John Brown Jr.'s bunch a time or too. He was twenty-two now, and had seen killing beyond his years. Men pistoled to death, black and white, mostly white slavers. That's why Jerico had a pistol hid out. Word was out that two blacks had ridden with Doc Jennison and the Jayhawkers back then.

"Halt!" Radford yelled, breaking into Jerico's worry.

The formation came to a herky-jerky stop.

Radford took off, walking purposefully toward Rafer D. who was cowering behind the water trough. Slow realization was coming to the others, as it had come almost instantly to Jerico, that the shot had been fired only to scare them. They all started grinning knowingly at the cowardly way Rafer D. was acting.

All except Jake McGruder. Jake was mad, fuming. "I wish I had me a gun," he said bitterly.

"You know how to shoot?" Augie asked eagerly.

"Dang right I know how to shoot," Jake answered positively. "I hit what I shoot at, too."

Jerico made a mental note of Jake. He was somebody to remember.

"Git up from there!" Radford yelled at Rafer D. from where he was standing over the water trough, glowering down at him. "Ain't nobody shootin' at you!"

Rafer D. peeped out, nervously sweeping his eyes up and down the street. Satisfied that no danger was upon him, he got his legs under him, drew up clumsily to standing, grinning sheepishly at the others watching him.

"Don't never break ranks again," Bosie said sternly. "Now git back in there!"

Rafer D. lurched off, stumbling, Radford following after him.

Back at the formation Radford said consolingly to them, "That white man was just fooling around, tryin' to scare us."

"Wadn't no tryin' to it," Cecil said, grinning. "He did. Willie here almost ran over me."

"Scared you too," Willie said back to Cecil. "Scared us all. Didn't it, Augie?"

"Didn't scare me none," Augie said brashly. "I knowed what it was."

"You was scared," Willie said. "Just like the rest of us."

"I wadn't neither," Augie shot back.

"Aw, hush up, Augie," Willie said dismissively.

Rafer D. weaved his way back into formation, looking around sheepishly. Took his place, grinning like a Cheshire cat.

"Forward! March!" Radford ordered them.

"You shot, Rafer D.?" Cecil yelled up tauntingly from the tail end of the formation.

Somebody snickered from up front. Ike laughed out loud, then quickly clamped a palm over his mouth.

Ike Peeler was twenty-six years old, a dark, jovial man from Illinois, where he'd been performing in a traveling minstrel show and had acted a bit until audiences stopped coming and the money ran out. A black round-topped derby hat a size too small sat jauntily on his head. He was wearing black pants, a candy-striped shirt under a black vest too small for him, and brown and white patent-leather shoes.

"Quit laffin' in ranks!" Radford said scoldingly. "Just march."

On the column marched.

Behind them, Woot was still standing out in the street, spread-legged, fists clenched on his hips. He wore a Rebel kipi cap, his badge of defiance to the blue-shirted Yankees who now garrisoned the most lawless towns in Missouri, making sure that only right-thinking Union men got into power so the state could be reconstructed properly.

But Woot, and a lot more like him, had no wish whatever to be reconstructed. Even before war came, Woot had been one of Bill Quantrill's original bunch of border ruffians, along with David Poole, Bill Anderson, William

Gregg, and George Todd. And they had been a hard-handed, wanton bunch. They claimed to be out for revenge against wrongs done them by Jayhawkers, but that wasn't the whole of it. In spite of signing Union loyalty oaths, they were pro-slavery, southern sympathizers. And got caught at their deceit. So they simply went outside the law, calling themselves guerrillas. They cared not a whit for free-soil, abolitionist Kansans. In fact, one early morning they struck Lawrence, Kansas, like a prairie tornado, killing everything and everybody big enough to pack a gun. In less than an hour they shot down more than a hundred and fifty men and boys, and fired the town. The worst outrage the states had heard of at the time. Anyone suspected of being a Union man in Missouri was simply dead meat.

So now here was Woot, standing spread-legged in the street looking at the black recruits go, an ugly frown on his scarred face. Woot knew that the social change the Yankees were forcing on the country wasn't going to stick, would never stick if he had any say-so in the matter.

Woot turned in his steps, and started walking fast to his horse there at the hitch rail. Gathering up the reins, he swung onto the saddle, raked spurs across the flanks of the chestnut, and dug out, riding fast.

They all heard the rider galloping up behind them, drumming hoofbeats growing louder and louder.

"Keep your eyes in front of you," Radford admonished without turning his head. "Don't nobody look back. We ain't scared."

"Yes, we is too," Deese said playfully in a low voice.

"You scared, Rafer D.?" somebody asked teasingly.

"Don't run, Rafer D.," somebody else said tauntingly.

Deese giggled. A nervous, unsteady giggle.

John Deese was twenty-eight years old, a slim, long-jointed man from Iowa. A runaway from Virginia at the age of seventeen, he'd spent the last eleven years a freeman in Iowa, working odd jobs: chimney sweep, tailor's apprentice, street cleaner, and water-cart man.

It was all Deese and the others could do to keep from looking back. Battie was marching stiff-legged, hair on the nape of his neck standing up.

Presently Woot tore by, the chestnut throwing heel dust back over the formation. Woot rode so close Jerico could have reached out and touched him if he'd wanted to. Or put his one bullet in his back.

"I wish I had me a gun," Jake muttered. "I'd shoot that . . ."

At Jake's voice, Radford glowered across his shoulder in that direction—and saw how misshapen, deformed the formation was, everybody completely out of step. "Left . . . left . . . left, right, left," he called out, using what little drill training he remembered.

But it was no use. The formation looked like rabble instead of men going off to fight. But on they went.

A three-car rattletrap of a train was idly chugging away on a side track when they got to the station, the engineer leaning out the window watching them come, annoyed at being kept waiting. The conductor met them, and fell in step with Radford, asking, "You in charge of this bunch?"

"Yeah, suh," Radford told him.

"Load 'em on that car yonder." He pointed, indicating the last car, being provided free by the Missouri Pacific Railroad to the federal government to move troops and supplies out on the frontier. "And see that they stay there till I tell you otherwise," the conductor added sternly. "I don't want you people bothering the folks in them other cars."

Radford didn't say anything. He just kept on marching alongside the formation.

The conductor broke off, heading back to the locomotive.

Radford halted them at the stepladder of the last car, took up position at the steps, and motioned the first rank aboard.

"Go all the way to the back," Radford kept saying.

"Yeah, where you belong," somebody said and cackled out loud.

"After you, Sarge," Battie said mockingly when he came up to the steps, smiling deferentially at Radford.

"Uh-uh," Radford said. "You might go back to that whorehouse you came from," he added, running his eyes over the fancy silk shirt and velvet vest Battie had on.

"These," Battie said, hooking his thumbs in his vest pockets, beaming proudly. "These just old work clothes, Sarge," he added, stepping aboard.

They all got aboard and found seats. Jerico was almost the last one so he sat up front on the first bench seat. Radford entered the coach, looking around, counting in his head. Finished, he cocked his head undecidedly. Scratching at his jaw, he started counting again, this time pointing to each recruit. "There's supposed to be twenty-five of us," he said finally. "I count twenty-six. Somebody ain't supposed to be here."

"You can't count," Cecil Hall taunted.

"Sarge can't count! Sarge can't count!" Battie started chanting. As a lark they all picked up the chant: "Sarge can't count! Sarge can't count! Sarge can't count!"

Radford's lips drew into a pinched-off grin, embarrassed. He reached inside the saddlebags, took out the stack of enlistment contracts, started counting them.

Twenty-five.

"Y'all shut up!" Radford roared.

The chanting died away.

"Now, somebody ain't supposed to be here!" Bosie Radford said seriously. "Who is it?"

Jerico, sitting next to where Bosie was standing, shifted his eyes to a medium-sized man dozing on the last seat, shoulder slouched against the window. Jerico hadn't seen him before. And Jerico was a man to notice things. Quick to take in his surroundings.

Bosie's eyes followed Jerico's, and Bosie asked the stranger, "What's your name?"

No answer.

"You back there! What's your name?" Bosie demanded.

"Who want to know?" the man asked, his head coming around slowly, his cold brown eyes reaching out for the black person asking him something that was not none of his business.

"I do," Bosie said. "What yo' name is is all I'm asking."

"How come?"

" 'Cause he in charge," Hezekiah said mildly. Hezekiah didn't like disorder and confusion. A self-made teacher, he liked everything and everybody in good order.

"He ain't in charge of me," the stranger said sullenly. "And you neither," he added, shifting his eyes to Hezekiah. "None of you is," he added, running his eyes around the car.

"The lieutenant said—" Bosie started.

"I don't give a damn what the lieutenant—"

Just then Lieutenant Badger came through the door, Jake McGruder following after him.

"Lieutenant," Bosie said, "that feller back there . . ." He nodded toward the stranger slouched against the window.

"Oh," Badger said, "he's been on the train since early this morning. Came in last night . . . from Mississippi. His name's Hoby."

"Hoby what?" Bosie asked.

"Just Hoby," Badger answered, shrugging indifferently. "Says that's all he ever answered to."

"He wouldn't tell me nothin'," Bosie said. "Acts like he's mad at the whole creation. What's he goin' to use for a last name?"

"He said he ain't got one, and don't want one," Badger answered. "Said he was a freeman and he'd go without a last name before he took the last name of his former master. Says he hated him."

"Can he do that?" Augie asked, overhearing the conversation.

"Hush up, Augie," Willie said. "You ain't got nothin' to do wid it."

"Nothin' says he can't," Badger answered.

"How'd you sign him up?" Bosie asked.

"Just Hoby," Badger said.

Bosie looked slant-eyed across his shoulder at Badger.

Jerico glanced up at Badger too. Jerico had been in the same fix when he'd signed up. Fact was, Jerico had had only one name as far back as he could remember. Just Jerico.

"Army ain't particular," Badger said quietly to Bosie, shrugging his shoulders.

Jerico looked up at Badger again. That wasn't the way it had come out when Jerico had signed up. Jerico had told Badger his name was Jerico, and Badger had asked, "Jerico what?"

It had sounded to Jerico as if he needed a last name, so Jerico had started thinking. Doc Jennison had taken him and thirteen other slaves from the Walker plantation, so Jerico had said, "Walker."

So, for the first time he was using a last name, something that was unheard of to him, as it was to most of the others. Now he was Jerico Walker. He'd started to claim "Jennison" but he wasn't sure Doc would like that. Doc had always scolded him to be a man, stand on his own two feet, do his own killing, and such like. So Jerico had wanted to do nothing that might send Doc into a raging sermon, or worse.

"Hoby and Jake make twenty-seven," Bosie said to the lieutenant.

"That's right," Badger said, his eyes roaming over the black faces watching him, listening in on the conversation. Badger continued, talking louder now. "This train'll stop along the way but the less you get off, the better off you'll be. Don't go looking for trouble. The conductor'll let you know when you're supposed to get off. In the meantime, Sergeant Radford here's in charge. You'll do what he tells you to do. Anybody give him any trouble, any trouble at all, you'll answer to me. Any questions?"

Nobody had any questions. At least none they cared to ask.

"Good," Badger said, backstepping toward the exit.

"Do we git to eat along the way?" Willie yelled at Badger.

Ignoring the same question from the same recruit, Badger kept on backstepping, and dismounted the stepladder. Standing alongside the train, he waved the go-ahead signal to the engineer still leaning out the window, then took off, walking toward the station's telegraph office.

Chapter Two

Sitting at his headquarters desk at Fort Leavenworth, Kansas, Colonel Benjamin H. Grierson stared pensively at the telegram the orderly had just brought him from Lieutenant Badger.

Grierson looked up reflectively, his mind going back to that cold winter day in November, 1865, after the Grand Army of the Republic had passed in review down Pennsylvania Avenue at Washington City and he'd given up his rank of Brigadier General, Sixth Illinois Cavalry Volunteers, and had mustered out of the Union army.

Now seventeen months later, he was back. In the regular army at the age of forty-one. At General Grant's personal summons the tall, heavy-bearded, Scotch-Irishman had come into the regular army as a Colonel of Cavalry with Grant's promise that a quick promotion to his old rank would certainly be in order if he accepted the special orders being offered him.

Grierson had accepted and a month later orders had arrived at his home in Illinois. Grierson had been stunned when he read the orders: *You are hereby directed to raise, equip, and train a Negro cavalry regiment.*

Now Grierson lifted his chin, firmed his jaws, thinking about the great task ahead. He'd already raised his right hand and sworn he was taking this obligation without mental reservation or hesitancy. But there had been reservations all right. Still were.

He read Badger's telegram again, parsing every word carefully:

DRAFT QUOTA FILLED IN ST. LOUIS **STOP** RECRUITS FORWARDED ON MISSOURI PACIFIC RR **STOP** REQUEST YOU ARRANGE TRANSPORTATION TO FT. LEAVENWORTH **STOP** LT. BADGER.

Grierson lifted his steel-gray eyes, thinking, staring blankly out across the parade ground. Directly his eyes wandered over to the post's headquarters, Colonel Hoffman's office.

William Hoffman was thirty-six years old, portly, bald-headed, and stiff-necked. High-bred and well-born. He came from a wealthy New Jersey family, had graduated from West Point, class of '52, and had served in the Civil War without distinction in the commissary department. In May of '66 he'd switched his arm of service to the Cavalry Corps after hearing from his fellow West Pointers that advancement would surely be swift for cavalry officers certain to get posted on the Indian frontier where a man could distinguish himself.

So here was Colonel William Hoffman, commanding officer, Fort Leavenworth, Kansas. Hoffman was also the commander of the Third Regiment, all white troopers, mostly Civil War veterans. All here on the wild Indian frontier. Right where an officer seeking promotion wanted to be, except . . .

Hoffman wanted nothing to do with Negro troops. But Republicans in Congress, the Army Department, and General Grant, all wanted to enlist Negroes in the peacetime army. An idiotic idea, Hoffman thought.

Colonel Hoffman and a lot of others couldn't bring themselves to accept the thought of Negroes serving in the regular peacetime army. Hoffman had said as much when Grierson showed up at the post that first day with special orders from General Grant telling him to recruit, organize, equip, and train a regiment of blacks at Fort Leavenworth.

Struck by a thought, Grierson hastily folded the telegram, shoved back rudely from his desk, tucking the telegram in his shirt pocket. Across the parade ground he went, taking great strides.

"Come in!" Hoffman bellowed at Grierson's rap on the door. They were both colonels but Hoffman occupied the senior position as post commander.

"More recruits coming," Grierson said mildly, walking up, sliding the telegram across Hoffman's desk. "Request overland transportation with an escort detail."

Grierson was a swarthy, scar-cheeked man. He'd been kicked in the face by a horse when he was young but now the scar was covered over by a thick, sandy, spade-shaped beard. Although a patient, mild-mannered man, Grierson was tough, dogged.

He'd earned his reputation in the Civil War by leading a cavalry regiment from La Grange, Tennessee, clean through Mississippi as a diversionary tactic while Grant was crossing the Mississippi to lay siege to Vicksburg.

"Fine, Colonel," Hoffman said, lifting his eyes from the telegram. "But my orders still stand," he added bluntly.

"Colonel . . . ," Grierson said deliberately, leaning over, pressing his palms facedown on Hoffman's desk, "these troopers are to be treated like everyone else."

"Like everyone else . . . ," Hoffman repeated scornfully.

"Like men . . . ," Grierson said flatly. "You read my orders from General Grant."

"Colonel," Hoffman said patiently, lifting his eyes up at Grierson, "my orders are for you to bivouac your regiment on the south end of the post. Nothing has changed. Nothing will," he added arrogantly, smirking up at Grierson.

"That's pure swamp land down there," Grierson shouted, drawing himself upright from where he was leaning over the desk. "And you know it!"

"My orders still stand," Hoffman said coolly, averting his eyes, picking up the ink pen there on his desk, tapping it idly against his thumbnail. Bringing his cool blue eyes back up to Grierson's, he added insolently, "Any niggers posted here will be kept away from white men."

"General Grant know about this?" Grierson asked.

"That'll be all, Colonel," Hoffman said curtly.

Grierson looked down along his nose at Hoffman for a long minute, then turned, headed for the door. Halfway to the door Hoffman's voice stopped him. Hoffman said pleasantly, "Nothing I can do about General Grant posting niggers here, Colonel. But I'm still the commanding officer."

"For now," Grierson said solemnly, facing around deliberately.

Hoffman smiled wryly. Suddenly he went grim, said abruptly: "This whole idea is foolish! Preposterous!" he roared, rudely throwing aside the pen. "You can't make troopers out of them—"

"Them what, Colonel?" Grierson asked, cutting in.

"Them . . . ," Hoffman started, then caught himself. "Whatever . . . ," he added indifferently, shrugging. Then he added seriously, "One thing you ought to know, Colonel, I won't tolerate your buffoons disgracing white men. You'll keep them strictly away from my regiment."

"I've got to train them somewhere," Grierson said resolutely.

"That's right, Colonel," Hoffman snapped. "And by heavens you'll do it all on your own! Not a single white man on this post will have anything to do with your black regiment. You'll personally see that they're fully equipped, drilled daily, and go through post evolutions the same as the white regiments."

"My orders exactly from General Grant," Grierson said tersely. "I wouldn't be here otherwise."

"You think a lot of General Grant, don't you, Colonel," Hoffman said, leaning back in his cowhide chair, his head cocked at Grierson.

"A lot of men do," Grierson answered. "And not just army men either."

"Because he sent you on that horse trot through Mississippi?" Hoffman said mockingly. "Why, that whole chirade was nothing but a mere sally the eastern press turned into a daring raid," he scoffed. "Any shavetail fresh out of West Point could have done it."

"If that's all . . . Colonel?" Grierson asked contemptuously.

"That's all," Hoffman answered, coming forward in his soft chair.

Grierson turned and marched out of headquarters.

Grierson had sensed after his first meeting with Hoffman that he would get no cooperation whatever in training black recruits at Fort Leavenworth. Hoffman had shown himself to be pompous, arrogant, and rude. Tactless in his talk, devious in his ways.

Grierson had already heard Hoffman talk down to officers not of West Point. And he had seen how ruthless he was to his staff officers with a better war record.

Every officer in the cavalry corps who'd heard about Grierson's assignment knew that if Grierson successfully trained a Negro regiment he'd leapfrog in rank over a lot of high-toned West Pointers who looked down on him as crude, low-bred.

Hoffman didn't want Grierson or blacks to succeed in this endeavor. Didn't want him or blacks at Fort Leavenworth, period. He and a great many others would go out of their way to see that Grierson failed. Hoffman had a career to build. He had no time for some grand, idiotic social experiment.

The train chugged out of St. Louis's Union station. The recruits sitting on the edge of their seats, looking apprehensively out the windows. It was the first train ride for all of them except Radford and Hoby. They'd come in on one.

Around the edge of the levee the train crawled, skirting the town. Up a slight grade it went, slicing through a cut in the surrounding bluffs, then over a gorge spanned by a wooden bridge, and around the edge of a low hill. Finally the rails straightened out, snaking across flat prairie land broken here and there by ravines and gullies.

The whistle went off. A long, sorrowful wail.

Ten minutes later the locomotive dropped down into the mouth of a steep gorge bordered on both sides by low sandstone cliffs, mounds of dirt from the rail bed heaped up on both sides; a dense mixture of pine and oak trees covering the landscape.

Out of the gorge the locomotive came; into the gorge the last car plunged.

And gunshots erupted. Shots racketing through the gorge, echoing away across the prairie. A shattering volly of rifle shots. Bullets spattering against the side of the last car, splintering wood, thwacking into seat backs.

To a man the black recruits came clear of their seats, hitting the floor as one.

Jerico hit the floor just a split second before Radford did. Radford had been sitting on the outside next to him, but Jerico was sitting next to the window. Plus he'd been alert for trouble ever since they left the station. He knew the country a little bit; the people by reputation. He'd figured that if trouble was coming it'd be someplace like this where bushwhackers could do their work under cover.

The train kept on going. And behind them they heard high-throated quavering yells. Jerico and Radford both had heard it before. They knew it was the Rebel yell that was supposed to strike fear into a man . . . or nerve a Rebel for death.

The shots stuttered away to sporadic. Then stopped completely.

Out of the gorge the last car came, sunlight once again draping it. Out in open prairie again.

Along with the rest of them Jerico picked himself up off the floor, felt for the heavy pistol he had hid behind his belt. It was still there. He'd already made up his mind he'd not use it unless a life-or-death situation came upon him.

"Anybody hit?" Radford asked, a stiff set to his face.

Nobody answered.

The engineer wailed his whistle.

"You shot, Rafer D.?" somebody asked out teasingly.

Kalem laughed out loud.

Kalem Jones was twenty-two years old. From Georgia. A short stocky, heavyset bull of a youngster with bandy legs, legs as crooked as an Apache bow. Dull-looking, and as dark as any African night his ancestors had ever seen.

"What you laughin' 'bout?" Jake asked Kalem, glaring at him. "It wadn't funny."

"It was to me," Kalem answered, grinning stupidly.

"I wish I had me a gun," Jake said sullenly, brushing broken wood from his seat.

Across the prairie the train kept on chuffing. The last car carrying twenty-seven black men. They all were mostly footloose. All looking apprehensively into the future. Each man's hopes and dreams reaching out for a new life. None of them had a past worth talking about. Freedom was their new life and they wanted to make something of it. Was the frontier cavalry it?

On the train went.

Hours later, Jerico finally fell asleep like the rest of them. He'd listened to the others talk some, ragging each other good-naturedly, mostly Rafer D. He'd taken it all right. Silence had slowly crept over the car, everybody listening to the clatter of the rough rails, each man with his own thoughts. And doubts.

Suddenly Jerico was jounced awake. Coming upright in his seat, looking out the shattered window. The train was heading southwest, chugging along on rough nails, crossing over a war-scarred bridge, upright members still broken and blackened in places. This would be Elders Bridge. Spanning the Gasconade River. Jerico remembered the place. He'd been here once before with Colonel Anthony when Doc had been laid up with a bullet in his leg. Doc had given command to Anthony when Captain Lyon had called for reinforcements to intercept Rebel General Sterling Price, who was marching on Jefferson City, burning bridges and bending rails behind him.

On the train went, reaching out into land so flat a man could see unobstructed clean to the horizon. Since Jerico was last here, sometime around September of '65, he thought, the railroad had been repaired a lot. Price had had a seasonal habit of wrecking every railroad south of the Missouri River every spring before the Yankees came out of winter quarters. Both armies had had the predictable habit of taking to the field in springtime.

The train lurched around a bend near the spot where a natural cave had been cut into the rocks long ago by the rushing waters of the ever-changing Missouri River. Weird Indian paintings had been discovered inside the cave and Ned Bohanna had thrown up a tavern there, selling bad whiskey and rancid food. And spying for the Rebels. He was found hanged in September of '64. Some said Doc and his raiders did it.

Jake McGruder woke up. He'd felt the train lurch. Rubbing his eyes, looking out the bullet-shattered window on the left side. Wasn't much use in him looking out there though. As far as any man could see, it was the same: buffalo grass and stunted sagebrush. But that was deceptive. The land was broken all through by shallow gullies and ravines, spanned over by viaducts and wooden bridges. Some still showing charred uprights and burnt crossmembers from Price's spring raids. And Quantrill's too.

Jake was worried. Wishing he was safely back at the stock pens he'd left. Wishing he'd had nerve enough to bring that Springfield rifle he'd mentioned he'd left behind. Said he'd bought it from a feller named Dave Cowan, a Civil War veteran down on his luck and needing cash money to buy a good horse so he could move on in search of better prospects.

Jake ran his eyes around the jouncing car.

Everybody sleeping. Heads lolled to the side, swaying to and fro, bouncing with the motion of the train.

Jake leaned his head against the bullet-pocked window frame, resigned to his fate, whatever that might be.

Jerico? There wasn't anything he could do except be ready for whatever might come. So he leaned his head over and went back to dozing too.

Hours crept by. The train crawling along, heading west by a little bit north, chuffing across the flat prairie, looking like a giant worm crawling across a vast tabletop. The sun casting rectangular rays of light through the shattered windows.

When next Jerico opened his eyes and looked out the window, the train was crossing the Osage River, the rickety bridge still blackened in places where Rebel guerrillas had dynamited it in the spring of '64, plunging the center span into the water. It had been repaired but both ends were still black from fire smoke.

They were coming on to Jefferson City, a diabolical town before, during, and after the war.

Jerico straightened himself around, got alert.

The city of Jefferson was no mere settlement; it was the state capital. A big town, as towns out here went. Rowdy in its seedy sections, outright lawless in others. And the town was still partisan to a fault. The statehouse had been fought over in the early years of the rebellion. Yankee Captain Nathaniel Lyon and a volunteer German brigade had run Governor Jackson and his militia clean out of the state when Jackson tried to take Missouri out of the Union. The city yet remained a hotbed of partisan infighting. And what side a man had fought on during the war depended on who asked the question.

The train chuffed into the station just off the fairground, the same fairground where Governor Jackson's militia had been rounded up and marched off to prison, sparking a riot when they passed through town.

Now coming on to sundown the fairground lay quiet, somber. Wads of discarded paper scudding across in the slight breeze. A mangy dog was trotting across, heading west.

The train crept to a stop, the first car coming to rest alongside the station's platform so first-class passengers could conveniently debark.

The black recruits in the last car started stirring about, stretching, craning their necks out the windows, looking over the town.

"This where we git off?" Augie asked up to Radford.

"The lieutenant said the conductor'll let us know," Radford said, craning his neck, looking along the tracks up toward the station.

"Naw," Jerico said, "this ain't where we git off. This's just a regular stop. Train'll take on water or something."

"How much farther we got to go?" Radford asked, looking back at Jerico. Jerico had already told him he knew the country a little bit.

"We still got a ways to go," Jerico said. "A long ways."

The conductor came up the steps, stuck his head in the doorway, asked Radford again, "You the one in charge, ain't you?"

"Yeah, suh," Radford answered despairingly.

"Y'all just sit tight. Army's got somebody comin' to see after you." And he ran his eyes around the coach, looking as though he hated what he was looking at.

"How long we goin' to be here?" Radford asked him.

"Don't know about y'all," the conductor answered, "but the train'll be here an hour or so."

"A hour!" Battie muttered. "We got to sit here a whole hour doin' nothing? In a big town like this . . . ," he added, smiling at the prospects, panning his eyes out over the town.

"Don't let the town fool you," the conductor said soberly. "It's got nothin' for you. Anyhow, what you boys do ain't none of my business. I'm just tellin' you what I tell all the army boys comin' through here," he added sourly. And walked off.

"We stayin' on this train till the army comes," Radford announced out loud. Then looking across his shoulder at Jerico, he added advisedly, "no use'n us goin' lookin' for trouble."

Jerico didn't say anything. He knew that was sound advice.

A lot of beaten Confederates were straggling back home now. Guerrilla bands too. Disillusioned, bitter men. Homes destroyed and they without prospects. Few had admitted the war was about slavery; but most had come to see that's what it was all about.

The black man sticking out like a swollen thumb was a constant reminder of their ill-fated rebellion. The mere sight of a black man in some places sparked violence, set off killings in some men. Like Jim Jackson and his henchmen, and Warren Martin and his cutthroats. Riding the countryside over in Jackson and Cass Counties, killing and hanging colored men, terrorizing women and children. Driving colored widows and children out of the country, taking over what little land they had.

Defeated and destitute, some ex-Rebels were scrambling for a living now. Robbing banks, stagecoaches, trains; others taking over farms, homesteads, abandoned lands. Revenge seekers on the prowl. The whole population was unsettled, didn't know what to expect next. The only thing most white men were certain of was that they didn't want blacks on equal footing with them.

Staying on the train made a lot of sense.

Thirty minutes later, Battie and some of the others had got impatient. Wanting to be up and about. Battie was saying to Radford, "We ought to at least go look 'round."

"Yeah," Willie said. "Git somethin' to eat. Augie's got money, ain't you, Augie?"

"I won't have none if you keep tellin' everybody," Augie answered.

"Everybody already know," Willie retorted.

"I'll git off this train," Hoby said testily, coming upright in his seat. "Git somethin' to eat. I ain't scared."

This was the first time anybody had seen Hoby sitting up straight. Now he was saying brashly to Battie, "Let's me and you git off." Hoby stood up, faced around to Augie, said: "Gimme the money, we'll go git somethin' to eat."

Surprisingly, Hoby was bigger than he looked when he was slouched down in the seat. Standing up, he was close to six feet tall.

"My money go, I go too," Augie said stubbornly, looking up front toward Radford for approval.

"Don't matter none to me," Hoby answered.

"Willie go too," Augie added.

Willie cut his eyes up at Radford, looking for approval too.

"Y'all's doin'," Radford said carelessly. "I don't care."

"And you call yourself in charge!" Hezekiah said reprovingly, wagging his head disgustedly at Radford's lack of firmness.

"I ain't never said I was in charge of nothin'," Radford said. "The lieutenant's the one said I was in charge."

"You sho' don't act like you in charge," Hezekiah said. "Them younguns ain't got no business gittin' off this train. No tellin' what might happen to 'em."

"Nobody's makin' 'em go," Radford growled.

"Nobody's stoppin' 'em neither," Hezekiah said flatly. "If you had any gumption you'd go yo'self."

"I ain't said I had no mo' gumption than nobody else," Radford answered. "The lieutenant put me in charge on his own."

"Well then . . . you ought to go," Battie said. "That's what in charge means," he added sagely, and smiled.

They all looked at Radford, wondering what he'd do.

Radford had been scowling at Hezekiah; now he switched his eyes to Hoby; then shifted them to Battie.

Hezekiah was grim-faced; Hoby was somber-looking; Battie was smiling, amused.

"He's right," Jake said. "You ought to go. Only right thing to do," he added reassuringly.

"Wouldn't hurt you none," Jerico added quietly.

The tension drained away from Radford's face, looking around at the other recruits watching him. "All right," he said resignedly. "Augie, you and Willie stay here." Roving his eyes over them briefly, he added, "Me, Hoby, Battie, and Jerico here, we'll go git somethin' to eat." He paused, waiting for a reaction. There was none.

"Augie, give Hoby the money," Radford ordered.

Augie's hand went to his pocket, then hesitated, Augie looking at Willie, saying dejectedly, "See, Willie . . . I told you . . . tellin' everybody I had money."

"Don't worry," Radford said reassuringly, "I'll see you git it back." After Augie had forked over four dollars and change, Radford asked out loud, "Anybody else got any money?"

Nobody said anything.

"I got a few dollars," Jerico said.

"That'll do," Radford said. "Let's go."

So the four got off the train, and started walking toward the station.

It was coming on to sundown, long shadows stretching across the tracks they crossed over, heading for the block-house of a station up ahead, Battie talking animatedly. Saying, "Town like this got to have some pleasure."

"Women?" asked Hoby.

"They pleasure, ain't they?" Battie answered.

"Whorehouse?" Radford asked.

"Don't call 'em whorehouses," Battie said reproachfully.

"What else is they then?" Radford asked.

"Pleasure houses," Battie answered brightly, and grinned.

They stepped up on the wooden platform fronting the station.

Three white men were watching them. Gaunt, grim-faced men. Watching them out of cold, silent eyes, eyes that had seen too many smoke-filled battlefields. The first two were sitting on a bench alongside the station. Milas Soaper and Elmer Babcock. Both had on war-worn, mismatched Confederate army clothes.

The other man was standing slack-legged down at the end of the platform. Had on a Confederate gray felt hat, crossed sabers on the crown, and a dingy Confederate captain's uniform. An empty left coat sleeve dangling at his side.

They all three had fought the last two years of the war in Confederate General Bedford Forrest's cavalry and were just now making their way home, if such they had. Each man had belted around his waist an Army Colt revolver. The younger one, Elmer, had a rifle lying across his war bag. A good rifle. A Spencer seven-shot carbine that he'd taken off a dead Yankee cavalryman.

"Can I help you boys?" asked the agent, glancing up at them filing into the station.

"Lookin' to buy somethin' to eat," Radford answered.

"Buy somethin' to eat?" the agent repeated, lifting his eyebrows. "Y'all them fellers from the last car back there, ain't you?"

"Yeah, suh," Battie said before Radford could work his mouth.

"The conductor was supposed to tell y'all about them army rations," the agent said exasperatedly, coming from behind the counter. He stalked across the floor, went out the door, looked down the platform for the rations.

Nothing.

The agent turned to the two ex-Confederates sitting on the bench there next to the door, and said sarcastically, "I don't suppose neither one of you seen what happened to them army rations that was stacked up yonder?"

"Army rations?" Milas repeated incredulously, feigning surprise.

Milas was thirty-four. Had on a buttonless butternut jacket over a faded blue shirt and a kipi cap cocked cavalierly on his head. "Ain't seen a one," he added, wagging his head sadly. "You seen any Yankee rations, Elmer?" he asked, smirking knowingly at the younger man sitting next to him.

"Uh-uh," Elmer said. "I ain't seen Yankee rations since them we took from 'em at Chicamauga."

"There was rations left here," the agent said positively, turning back to Radford. "I seen 'em. Didn't the conductor tell you?"

"Naw, suh. All he said was the army was comin' to see after us."

"I got me an idea what happened to them rations," the agent said dispassionately in a low voice, cutting his eyes at the two shabby, run-down ex-Rebels.

Now nobody much cared about returning Rebels and guerrillas unless he had been one himself. They were low men on the totem pole now. Being blamed for trying to break up the Union, causing more than six hundred thousand deaths on both sides. No ex-Rebel could vote, hold office, or own more land than a small farm. The country was being run by men who had remained loyal to the Union, backed up by the federal army. The newly freed slaves had suddenly acquired all the rights and privileges that had once belonged to secessionists. It was a bitter cud ex-Rebels had to chew. And they felt downtrodden, put upon. They were surly, angry men. Touchy about almost everything.

"You accusin' us of takin' them rations?" Elmer asked, coming to his feet.

"Keep your shirt on, Reb," the agent said good-naturedly. "I ain't accusin' nobody. I'm just sayin' what was left there."

Just then the man with the missing arm came walking down the platform. He'd overheard it all. "Them Yankee rations are yonder," he said, nodding toward the south side of the platform.

The agent walked along the platform, looked over the side.

Crates had been broken open, rations eaten, the rest scattered about.

"I ordered it done," the one-armed veteran said to the agent when the agent turned around, started back. "I'm Colonel Long."

Peyton Long was thirty-two years old. Six feet tall, slight-built. Had lived through four years of hard fighting in General Forrest's Tennessee cavalry volunteers of the Army of the Tennessee, serving under Generals Bouregard, Bragg, and Johnston.

"These men," the colonel said, nodding toward the two enlisted men, "are honorable fighting men. I'll not see 'em go hungry. Not while niggers fatten up," he added, looking at Radford.

Long was a man who relished authority and sought responsibility. He wouldn't walk around what he saw as his high duty. Not even now with one arm missing.

"That's it," the agent said gravely to Radford, shrugging his hands apart helplessly. "Ain't nothing I can do about it. You're welcome to what's left."

They walked over to the side of the platform, looked down at what was left. They saw that the hardtack and salt pork had been partially consumed, the rest willfully scattered in the dirt.

Radford looked across his shoulder at Battie standing next to him. They all knew perfectly well what had happened.

Battie shook his head disdainfully, wanting no part of the dirty, exposed rations.

Radford turned aside too. They all headed back toward the station.

"You boys don't want 'em?" the agent asked when they came down the platform.

"Ain't nothing left fit to eat," Battie said. "Somebody had a feast, then ruined the rest."

"Slop is what you use to eatin', ain't it, boy?" Elmer asked deliberately. "Now you think you too good to eat after white men?"

"We came to buy," Battie said, smiling gently.

"Meaning we can't?" Elmer snapped, jerking up his rifle, bringing it around to bear.

Jerico's right hand inched up his thigh, crossed over his belt line at his side, then crept to the back of his shirt.

"Corporal!" snapped Colonel Long.

Elmer's body went slack. He lowered his rifle barrel carelessly.

"War's over," Colonel Long said mildly, looking over the black men contemptuously. "These boys gov'ment property

45

now," he said mockingly. "Yankee gov'ment property."

"So's a cavalry mule," Milas said gravely, "and I seen a many of 'em brain shot."

Just then Rafer D. came running along the tracks. At the edge of the platform he saw the confrontation, came to a running stop, his mouth working at words that didn't come out. A second or two Rafer D. steadied himself, and announced doubtfully, "Army's here."

"Where?" Radford asked.

"They comin'," Rafer D. said, flourishing a hand timidly, indicating behind him along the tracks.

"Let's go," Bosie said calmly, watching Elmer all the time.

"Let's go get somethin' to eat," Hoby said defiantly. "Like we started to."

"I heard that army man say rations was left down here for us," Rafer D. said, looking around for the rations.

"Somebody stole 'em," Battie said, looking at Elmer.

Elmer snapped. Threw his rifle around pistol fashion, finger inside the trigger guard.

Jerico shot him. The bullet smashing into Elmer's chest, tearing him off the platform, sprawling him out at Rafer D.'s feet.

Chapter Three

Rafer D. leaped back wildly, screaming like a scalded cat, eyes bucked at the body that had come to rest grotesquely at his feet.

Milas went for his pistol. Grabbing across his body for the Army Colt that was butt forward in a holster on the other side.

"Hold it!" a stiff voice ordered Milas.

Milas froze in his motion, jerking his eyes around at the commanding voice.

It was Major Holmes.

Major Emmett Holmes was twenty-five years old. About five-eight, solid-built. Had sandy-brown hair sticking out from under a blue campaign hat. First Sergeant Michael Shannon and Corporal George Swope were with him. They were all dressed in clean, neat-fitting Yankee blue uniforms.

"Leave the gun right where it is," Major Holmes ordered Milas. "There'll be no more shootin'. I'll handle this."

Milas shifted his eyes from the Yankee officer giving him orders to Colonel Long.

"All right, Sergeant," Long said advisedly. "The major's calling the turn."

Milas's hand went slack on his holster flap, then fell away.

"Sergeant Shannon . . . disarm him," the major ordered, indicating Jerico.

Shannon marched forward out of Jerico's direct line of fire, reached out, put a hand over the pistol's hammer, and wrenched the gun from Jerico's fist.

"You the one supposed to be in charge?" Major Holmes asked Bosie, going by the vague description he'd got back at the train.

"He said I was," Bosie answered softly, shifting his feet, his eyes studying the plank boards in the platform.

"He who?" Holmes asked sternly.

"Lieutenant Badger."

"Lieutenant Badger tell you to stay on the train?" Holmes asked, running his eyes up and down Bosie's body, sizing him up.

"Yeah, suh," Bosie said meekly.

"How come you didn't?"

"They wanted somethin' to eat."

"They who?"

"The rest of the men."

"You was put in charge, wasn't you?"

"Yeah, suh."

"Lieutenant Badger say you was a sergeant?"

"Yeah, suh."

"Sergeant Shannon!" Holmes barked out.

"Yes, sir!" Shannon answered up.

"He look like a sergeant to you?"

"Not even a pimple on a sergeant's ass, sir," Shannon said seriously.

The major smirked to himself. Putting back on his stern face, he told Bosie plainly, "Take these men back to the train and wait there for me."

"Yeah, suh," Bosie murmured.

At the major's words, Rafer D. bolted away, running down the tracks, eager to get away from the frightening situation that was before him. The others filed quietly off the platform, started walking down the tracks, Battie looking wonderingly back over his shoulder at the dead man.

When they were out of hearing distance, Hoby asked playfully: "Battie . . . how come you didn't tell 'im you was lookin' for a whorehouse?" And Hoby grinned at the thought.

"Yeah, Hoby," Bosie said, "how come you didn't tell 'im you was a freeman like you been tellin' me, and that you go wherever you want to."

"I ain't in charge," Hoby answered flatly, looking across his shoulder at Bosie. "If I was in charge, I'da gave him a piece of my mind!"

"You can be in charge," Bosie said seriously. "Anybody who want to can," he added despairingly.

Behind them, Major Holmes was speaking: "Colonel," he was saying, turning to the one-armed veteran. "Looks like there's been some misunderstanding here."

"I assure you, sir," Long said pompously, "there's been no misunderstanding. Insolence, that's what it was. Pure and simple."

"Now, Colonel . . . surely you don't think . . ."

"No other way to think, Major. Nigger coming out like that accusing a white man of stealing."

"Rations were broken into, Major," the agent said. "No misunderstandin' that."

Holmes smiled tolerantly, and said conversationally to Long, "Looked to me like the shooting was self-defense, Colonel. It look like that to you, Sergeant?"

"That it did, sir," Shannon said smartly.

"I demand an arrest," Long said.

"Arrest?" Holmes repeated. "You'd have to stay and prefer charges," he added, amused.

"That's out of the question, Major. Circumstances won't allow it. Surely your Yankee courts will accept the word of a gentleman."

Sergeant Shannon coughed noisely, clearing his throat, looking the other way out over the town.

"I'm afraid not, Colonel," Holmes said. "Law says a man's got a right to face his accuser. In case you hadn't heard, colored men got that right now. Same as you and me."

"In that case, sir," Long said properly, "I'll defer to your Yankee law." And he bowed slightly, mockingly.

"Like I said, I'll handle this," Holmes said.

"What about Elmer?" Milas asked, nodding toward Elmer's body sprawled out there in the dirt. "Law got anything to say about him?"

"Sergeant . . . ?" said Major Holmes, looking a question at Shannon.

"He'll be properly laid to rest, sir," Shannon answered promptly.

Just then the train's whistle went off. Two quick, impatient blasts.

"Train's got a schedule to keep, Major," the engineer yelled out the cab from down the tracks.

"Hold your water, Roy," the major yelled back. "I'll only be a minute more."

"Pleasant journey to you, Colonel," Holmes said to the Confederate officer even as he turned away, saying to Shannon, "Let's go, Sergeant."

Major Holmes, First Sergeant Shannon, and Corporal Swopes started walking along the tracks, heading back to the last car, where there was a great commotion going on: All of the raw recruits who'd been raised to a life of docility had heard the shot from up ahead. But nobody had nerved himself enough to get off the train and search out gunfire, a thing that all their lives they'd learned to dread.

As soon as Bosie and the others had got back, the first question had been yelled out facetiously: "You shot, Rafer D.?"

"I thought I was," Rafer D. had said. "But it was Jerico."

"Jerico shot?" Augie asked anxiously.

"Aw, hush up, Augie," Willie said scoldingly. "How could Jerico be shot when he's standin' right there!"

"Jerico's the one shot somebody," Rafer D. said. "A white man," he added breathlessly.

"A white man!" somebody said, astonished. "We in big trouble now!"

"What Jerico shoot 'im for?" Jake asked.

"He pointed his rifle," Rafer D. said excitedly. "He was fixin' to shoot somebody."

"I knowed it," Hezekiah said gravely. "Battie runnin' his mouth too much, I bet."

"They comin' after Jerico?" Kalem asked.

"Where'd he get the gun?" Jake asked.

"Nobody don't know," Hoby said. "First thing we knowed it was in his hand."

"I wish I had me a gun," Jake said.

"Y'all quiet down!" Bosie yelled to them. "Rafer D. don't know what all happened. He wadn't even there when it started."

"Jerico . . . what happened?" Hezekiah asked bluntly.

"Nothin'," Jerico said. "He was fixin' to shoot, so I shot him first."

"I'd a shot 'im too," Jake said seriously.

"What else?" Manigo asked. "What else happened?"

Bosie panned his eyes around the car. Met Hezekiah's.

"Tell it," Hezekiah said soberly. "You in charge, ain't you?"

"I wish I wasn't," Bosie stated.

"Well, you is," Hezekiah stated. "So tell it."

The car fell silent, everybody all ears. Bosie started telling them what had happened, everybody listening raptly, sitting quietly, eyes shifting from the speaker to Jerico. Bosie was almost finished when Major Holmes came through the door, panning his eyes around the car, counting heads, making sure Lieutenant Badger's full complement was onboard. He'd already sent Corporal Swope back to the storehouse to bring back some more rations.

"Sergeant Shannon," Holmes called out behind him, staring at Jerico.

"Yes, sir," Shannon answered smartly.

"Hand me that gun."

Shannon passed the gun butt first through the door.

Everybody was sitting on the edge of his seat, eyes on the major, wondering what he was going to do to Jerico for shooting a white man.

Holmes turned the gun over in his palm, looking pensively at it, lips pursed. Glancing up at Jerico, he said thoughtfully, "Army single-shot dragoon. Not many in use now."

"I had it a long time," Jerico stated.

"No point in me asking where you got it?"

"Naw, suh."

"Two years ago the army arsenal at Independence was broken into and robbed," the major said conversationally. "A shipment of brand-new dragoon pistols and ammunition was taken. Some said it was Doc Jennison and his Jayhawkers."

"Mighta been bushwhackers," Jerico said advisedly. "Bill Quantrill and his bunch. They was raidin' all over the country back then."

"It could've been them," Holmes said, nodding his head agreeably. Presently he flipped the gun over, looked under the butt. "Serial number's still here," he stated, looking a look at Jerico. Then he said musingly, "If Sergeant Shannon here was to check these numbers, you think they'd match with one of them stolen guns?"

Jerico knew that deeds committed during the war by both sides were gone by the boards now. Being overlooked by the army and what scarce law there was. Doc Jennison had told them all that when they had disbanded. But Jerico knew that that didn't stop a man from pushing his own particular brand of law. Expecially in his case.

"War's over now," Jerico said. "What was done back then don't go against you now."

"That's right," Holmes said agreeably. "But you just now killed a man."

"He was fixin' to shoot Battie."

"Can't dispute that," Holmes answered. "But the fact remains a man's dead and this gun's evidence," Holmes added, sticking the long-barreled pistol behind his belt. "Only reason I'm letting you go is you're in the army. I'll find you if I need you," the major added dismissively.

"Sergeant Shannon!" called out the major.

"Yes, sir!"

"Them rations here yet?"

"Yes, sir. Sitting right here, sir."

"Signal Roy then."

"Yes, sir," Shannon said happily, and started waving the go-ahead signal to the engineer still leaning out of the cab, looking.

Looking across his shoulder at Bosie, Holmes asked doubtfully again, "You the one in charge?"

"Yeah, suh," Hezekiah said before Bosie could speak.

"Yeah, suh," Bosie repeated halfheartedly.

"Train's pulling out," Holmes said to Bosie. "Get them rations in here and see these men get fed."

Momentarily the train lurched, crept forward.

Holmes backstepped to the door, swung down off the ladder.

The train chugged off even as Bosie was throwing the last of the rations through the door, Willie's eager hands already tearing at the bindings.

The train crept away.

"Now we got somethin' to eat, Willie," Bobo Jackson said. "You can stop whinin' like a crybaby," he added tauntingly.

Jackson was twenty-three years old. From Arkansas. Stood five feet eight inches, and weighed about one-fifty. Had shifty, uncertain eyes that studied the ground a lot.

"Yeah, Willie," Deke added, "and you can eat all you want. Ain't nobody goin' to stop you."

Deke Poole was twenty-eight years old. Six feet tall, weighed about one-seventy. Had a brown, ruddy complexion and gapped teeth in front.

"Willie ain't going to eat much," Bosie said tersely, "if these here army rations like the ones we et."

"Anythang's better'n nothin'," Willie said, breaking open a container. "Ain't it, Augie?"

"I don't know," Augie answered gravely, looking at the moldy green salt pork Willie had just opened up. The pork had been packed with salt in a keg that had been broken open during transit, the meat fetid now.

The train got up to speed, trailing a ribbon of smoke into the gathering darkness.

The whistle went off. A long sorrowful shriek.

Willie and Augie passed out the army's daily bread, hardtack, a three-inch-square solid cracker, hard as a rock and just as tough. Only one of two good things anybody would say about hardtack: It was better than nothing, or it was filling.

The tainted pork was left sitting in the aisle.

"That ain't nothin' but plantation sowbelly," Battie said scornfully. "It's got more fat on it than Manigo." And Battie grinned impishly, looking at Manigo.

"And just about as stinky too," Bobo said. They all busted out laughing.

"I ain't eatin' that like that," Manigo said.

"How come?" Battie asked in mock surprise. "You and that greasy sowbelly go together." Everyody started laughing again.

Except Hoby.

"Leave him alone," Hoby said ominously.

Battie looked across the aisle, saw Hoby was dead serious.

"He ain't botherin' you," Hoby said, looking Battie squarely in the eye.

"I was just makin' sho' he don't miss no meals," Battie said, smiling. "He look like he ain't never missed one yet," he added, grinning, looking around at the others.

"Leave him alone, I said," Hoby repeated gravely.

Silence came over the car. Everybody paying attention to the fight shaping up, wondering if Hoby was as tough as he acted.

"Aw, I was just kiddin'," Battie said, a serious look to his face now. "Manigo knows I was just kiddin'."

"Yeah," said Hoby, "like you was just kiddin' when you almost got yo'self shot back there."

"That wadn't my fault," Battie said.

From up front Bosie glanced at Hezekiah. And just as he had suspected, Hezekiah was watching him, wondering if he was going to intercede before blows were struck. "You in charge, ain't you," Hezekiah said, more a statement than a question.

"Yeah, I'm in charge," Bosie said grudgingly.

"Stop 'em then."

"I was fixin' to," Bosie answered. Stiffening his jaw at the unwanted task ahead of him, Bosie stood up, faced around, said out loud, "Willie, bring that pork back up here."

"I ain't messin' with that stinky stuff," Willie blurted out.

"I'm orderin' you to," Bosie said, and glanced at Hezekiah. "And I ain't tellin' you again. Bring that meat up here!"

Hezekiah nodded, smirking approvingly.

"That ain't meat," Cecil said. "That used to be meat."

Everybody started laughing.

Willie reluctantly got up out of his seat, crossed over to the smelly keg of pork, and with his nose curled up to the air, picked it up with his two hands, and carried it to the front of the car.

"Eat some, Willie," Deese said. "You always sayin' you hungry."

"Yeah, Willie . . . eat some," Bobo yelled out. "It'll make you fat like Manigo."

"That's enough!" Bosie said. "Anybody don't want to eat pork, don't have to."

"That meat ain't all that bad," Manigo said self-consciously.

"Eat some then," Battie said challengingly.

"I would if I had me a skillet and a good fire."

"You can cook that stinkin' stuff?" Augie asked.

"Hush up, Augie," Willie said.

"Only thing you can do with that rotten meat," Jefferson said honestly, "is bury it . . . real deep."

"I can cook it up good enough to eat," Manigo said factually.

"Ain't nobody cookin' up nothin' now," Bosie said. "We ain't got nothin' to cook with, and we ain't got no fire. Anybody got the stomach and the nerve is welcome to his fill like it is." Bosie sat back down, wearily leaned his head on the window frame. Next to him Jerico turned his nose away from the foul-smelling keg that had just been deposited in the aisle next to him.

The train plodded on through the darkness, clattering over rough-hewn cross-ties and imperfectly joined rails.

The men ate only the hardtack, munching on the jaw-breaker bread, ragging each other all the while.

Heading west, the rude Missouri Pacific rails reached out into sparcely settled, scrub-infested prairie land cut through by small streams, gullies, and ravines pocked with motts of cedar, hickory, and elm trees. Watercourses were marked by scrawny willows and scrub oaks.

From Jefferson City to Kansas City, the country all around was still recovering from the devastation of war, declared and undeclared. The people were still distrustful, suspicious, keeping mostly to themselves on scattered farms and ranches, living with memories of their dead, but consumed by the enormous task of rebuilding their lives shattered by armies of the North and South, plus guerrilla bands, Kansas Jayhawkers, Redlegs, and anybody else who had cared to take advantage of the chaotic situation before and during the war.

The train rolled on westward.

It lacked an hour before midnight when thunder muttered, then muttered again. From the northwest. Ten seconds later a gigantic stroke of zigzag lightning parted the black canopy of sky. Stray raindrops started pattering down. Thunder grumbled, then grumbled again. Raindrops started drumming. Big raindrops, like popcorn, cascading down, drumming on the train in a steady rhythm. And like a wounded buffalo seeking shelter the train lumbered down into the shallow valley leading into Tipton. Rattling over the hastily repaired trestle that Confederate General Jo Shelby had burned back in '63.

In the black of night, in an absolute downpour, the train limped into Tipton station.

There was a lit lantern hanging from the signal pole in front of the new station. Blackened ruins of the old log station hovering some forty yards down the tracks. Jo Shelby had burned it too.

Hiram King

The engineer saw the red light suspended out there in the slanting downpour. He eased the train to a rolling stop.

Two men quietly stepped down from the first car, and stood motionless alongside the tracks. One man had a rifle in his right hand and a war bag in his left. The other man had an empty coat sleeve pinned to his side.

The train pulled out.

The two men crossed over, started walking toward the new plank station.

Three other men quietly walked their horses from the shadows of the burned-out hulk of a station down the way. Through the slanting sheet of rain they came.

Thunder grumbled; lightning flared, illuminating the three riders. They all three had on yellow trail slickers, water dripping from wide-brimmed, bell-crowned hats pulled down tight on their heads. One man was leading two horses with empty saddles.

"Colonel?" the leader among them called out.

"That you, Frank?" Colonel Long asked out toward the soft thud of hoof-falls in mud.

"It's me, Colonel."

"Good," Long said. "We got work to do. You got some good boys with you?" he asked, straining his eyes across a blanket of rain into the darkness at the drenched horsemen.

"You bet, Colonel," Frank said as they came on. "Joe's here."

"Joe Dockum?"

"Yes, sir. Luman too," he added, nodding at the rider next to him as they drew up. "And that's Donnie . . . Donnie Pence back there. You don't know him but he'll do," Frank added appraisingly.

Frank Yoder was thirty-six years old. Medium height, average build. A tough, seam-faced, seasoned guerrilla fighter. They all three had been. Yoder had been with Quantrill but he'd ridden off with Todd and Woot when

58

Todd had had a falling-out with Quantrill and struck out on his own. But unlike Todd, who'd given up in May of '65 when things got too desperate, Yoder, Joe Dockum, and Luman Bigelow and some others hadn't quit. Like Woot, it simply wasn't in their nature to submit to the war's outcome, putting coloreds on their level. The Yankees might have won that war, but there were other ways to fight, Yoder and other like-minded men thought.

"Where's Elmer?" Dockum asked curiously.

"Dead," Milas answered up.

"How?"

"Shot."

"By who?"

"Some nigger back there at Jefferson City."

"Some nigger!" Yoder repeated, shocked. "How'd it happen?"

"Do y'all good to put on them extra slickers we brung," Donnie said to Long, interrupting the conversation, passing down to the colonel the reins to the led horses.

"How'd it happen!" Yoder asked again in a loud, impatient voice, even as Long and Soaper were retrieving the slickers tied behind the saddle cantles of the led horses.

"A bunch of niggers was scroungin' round at the train station," Long said, pulling on the slicker. "Elmer was aimin' to put 'em in their place. One of 'em had a gun hid out. Elmer never seen it. Never knowed what killed him."

"Damn!" Donnie said wrathfully. "Yankees prob'ly armed him," he added, and spat a stream of tobacco juice out into the rain.

"No prob'ly to it," Long stated, taking up slack on his reins, "they did." Long swung his horse around rudely, talking all the while: "Yankees making regular cavalry soldiers out of 'em too. We spent a lifetime beating 'em down, now the Yankees buildin' 'em up like white men."

"You right, Colonel," Yoder said grimly, bringing his horse about. "We sho' nuff got work to do."

"Let's git to it then," Long said solemnly, spurring his horse out southward away from the rails, heading out into an empty reach of dark prairie. The other five riders clattered after him, hoof-falls kicking back mud, dull drumbeats fading across the prairie.

Ahead on the slowly departing train two black men had seen it all. Jerico and Bosie. Jerico had been the only one who'd awakened when the train eased to a stop. He'd nudged Bosie awake when he'd heard the night riders talking. They both had watched it all, looking slant-eyed from the rain-streaked window.

"You figger trouble?" Bosie asked in a low voice so he wouldn't wake up the others.

"I'd bet on it," Jerico said softly. "That one-armed man didn't seem like the kind to live with what happened back yonder."

Bobo Jackson snorted out loud in his sleep, then turned aside.

The train's whistle went off, the Tipton station disappearing in their rear.

"How far's the next town?" Bosie asked presently, his mind thinking on where the white men would strike, if they were going to strike.

"I'd guess close to eighty miles," Jerico said.

"You reckon they'll stop the train between here and there?"

"Ain't no tellin'."

"You scared?"

"Naw."

"You got another gun or somethin'?"

"I wish I did have."

"What you goin' to do then?"

"Nothin'," Jerico answered, reclining back in his seat, "except get sleep."

Across the dark, lifeless rain-drenched prairie the train crept, making eight or nine miles an hour over the rough track. Inside, the car was pitch-black, quiet as a tomb. Every now and then somebody snored out loud, caught himself, and shifted position.

The next thing anybody knew, the rim of the sun was just nudging above the horizon. The train had stopped.

Jerico woke up first, looking around, surprised at how promising the day looked. There was not even a hint of the violent rainstorm of last night that had finally driven him off to a deep sleep.

SEDALIA. So the hand-lettered sign over the small train station said.

Bosie's eyes fluttered open. And unaccountably shifted to Hezekiah, the only man he felt was watching him all the time.

Hezekiah was still sleeping soundly.

Bosie inhaled and blew a low breath of relief. Panning his eyes around the car at the other men.

Everybody seemingly still asleep.

"Sedalia," said Jerico, sensing that Bosie had woken up. And Jerico started swabbing staleness from his mouth with his tongue.

"Seen anybody?" Bosie asked, remembering the night riders of last night.

"Nobody."

"You right," Battie said from back where he'd been awake all this time. "I ain't seen nothin' except sagebrush and a mangy dog."

Sedalia was a bleak, windswept settlement located on a slight rise in the prairie. It stood without sheltering mountains or even a sand hill. On the north side of the tracks where the sunbaked train station sat was the whole town: A bank, a two-story hotel, three saloons, a hardware store, and a livery. All plank buildings, sitting together yet all alone out on the prairie at tracks' end.

But men were going back to money-making endeavors now that the war was over. Even now there were plans to extend the rails into Kansas City. But that was in the future. For now the train had to circle around a switchback to make its return trip to St. Louis.

Yet the town had immediate possibilities. Already a Texas outfit had used the old Shawnee Trail to drive in and ship out a herd of longhorn cows. But for now the stock pens stood empty where they'd been hurriedly nailed up trackside off from the main line. And as future cow towns would be, Sedalia was wide open. Anything a man figured he could live through could be done or had in Sedalia.

Hezekiah snored out loud, and woke up. Fitting his horn-rimmed glasses back to his nose, he looked around, asking, "Where we at?"

"Sedalia," Bosie said.

"You better wake the others up."

"Ain't no hurry," Bosie said tersely, annoyed by Hezekiah's constant prodding.

"You in charge," Hezekiah said resignedly.

"Yeah," Bosie said sourly.

"Somebody's comin'," Battie said, looking out the window on his side.

"Who is it?" Bosie asked anxiously.

"How do I know?" Battie answered back even as Jerico jumped up, ran over to the other side of the car.

"It ain't them," Jerico said to Bosie, looking out the window.

"Them who?" Battie asked, perplexed.

"Them white men we saw last night," Bosie said.

"What white men?" Battie asked. "I didn't see nobody."

"You was sleep," Jerico said. "Like everybody else."

"Hey! Y'all wake up back there!" Bosie called out to the other recruits. "Somebody's comin'."

The recruits stirred themselves, each man nudging awake the man next to him, everybody looking around wide-eyed, wondering where they were and what was coming next.

Two men from the train station crossed over the tracks in back of the last car, heading for the door.

"Somebody's comin'," Bosie announced again.

"Who is it?" Augie asked Willie, rubbing sleep from his eyes.

"How do I know?" Willie answered. "Uh'm here with you."

The two men ascended the stepladder, came through the door.

The man in front, Henry Mallett, had a telegram in his hand, asking out loud, "Who's in charge?"

"He is," Hezekiah said, nodding toward Bosie before Bosie could answer.

"This's for you then," Mallett said, handing Bosie the telegram, adding, "Telegram says the army's sending a detail for you." Mallett roved his eyes around the car, making sure everybody heard what the telegram said, then added, "Says for you boys to wait here."

"Wait here!" Battie repeated disgustedly. "Ain't nothing here," he added, looking out at the bleak, uninviting town.

"Where we goin' to stay?" Augie blurted out, looking out at what Battie was looking out at.

"Right out yonder," said Jessie Stem, the other man who'd come up with Mallett. And Stem pointed.

They all looked out the window where Stem had pointed.

"Ain't nowhere to stay out there," Willie said.

"Yes, there is," Stem said, a pinch-lipped smirk on his face.

"Stock pens," said Jake disgustedly. "Army's puttin' us up in a stock pen!"

"Till they come git ya," Mallett said. "And if I know the army, ain't no tellin' how long that'll be."

The first white man who rode out of Sedalia that morning left with a smirk on his face, riding a fast horse, spreading word along his way that part of the nigger army that General Grant was putting together was stranded in Sedalia, holed up in the stock pen.

63

Chapter Four

At Fort Leavenworth, Colonel Grierson was overwhelmed. Close to five hundred black enlisted men that Lieutenant Badger had recruited had come in from every direction of the compass and by every mode of transportation. And were still coming in. Ragged, bedraggled, and bewildered. Looking for a life. All fit for duty, so the post surgeon was certifying after a cursory look-over.

Obeying Colonel Hoffman's orders, Colonel Grierson had bivouacked them on the swampy southern edge of the fort. Hundreds of army "A" tents dotted dry land bordering a stagnant, mosquito-infested creek. Living in war-worn tents that white regiments had turned in as unfit for service and Grierson had wangled. Strips of canvas, old coats, pant legs, willow and oak boughs provided shelter for men waiting for tents that Grierson suspected Hoffman was holding back.

Grierson had no staff. He was personally assigning the black recruits to companies as they straggled in in bunches.

Starting with Company A, sixty men to a company. A picked recruit assigned as company sergeant, responsible for the conduct and actions of the other fifty-nine men under him. Having just filled out the roster for Company I, Grierson was now waiting for more recruits to come in to fill out Company K. There would be no Company J. Looking at a company's guidon from a distance, I and J looked too much alike. Good or bad acts could be laid to the other company, as had been done in the late war. Grierson wanted no more of that.

White officers to staff the companies as Grant's directive had stipulated were another matter. At first no white officers had dared volunteer, especially if he had heard talk from West Pointers like Colonel Hoffman. But now even the lower ranks of the officers corps were scrambling for promotion. The Civil War was over. No longer could a man earn promotion by some daring feat performed in a battle against Rebels who just happened to come his way. Out on the frontier fighting Indians was where a man had to earn his bars and stars now. Or maybe in this new social experiment that a Republican Congress and General Grant had Colonel Grierson trying out.

So white officers looking for promotion straggled in. Staking their careers on what they could get out of black men with doubtful fighting ability and dubious military conduct. And they all knew wives, friends, classmates, congressmen, the president, the whole nation for that matter, were watching. And like Grierson and Badger, they also knew that if this thing blew up, their careers were over. Done with.

But they came anyhow. For their own reasons, good or bad.

Now, Grierson was sitting across his headquarters desk from Captain Gilford Dudley. Dudley had already talked with Colonel Hoffman at post headquarters where he had been escorted when he first reported in for duty. Hoffman had been dumbfounded when Captain Dudley, a fellow West Pointer, had told him that he had reported for duty with the black regiment that was being formed. Hoffman's warm smile and glowing talk had vanished. Without concealing his feelings, Hoffman abruptly dismissed the captain, calling him a misguided idiot. Just like the other seven white officers who'd reported in for duty with that baboon of a regiment.

But like the others, Captain Dudley was looking to make a name for himself. To break out of the pack of breveted Civil War officers who'd been broken back to their regular grade.

Dudley was thirty years old. Six feet tall. Well tailored. Two silver shoulder bars gleaming from a neat-fitting blue blouse. Pants creased nicely, plain leather black boots polished to a high gloss. Dudley already had had his personnel file favorably endorsed by General Sheridan, who was commanding the Department of the Missouri, which included everything west of the Mississippi River to the Rocky Mountains and from Red River to the Canadian border.

Grierson was silently going over Captain Dudley's personnel file spread out in front of him. Cunningly, Dudley had placed first in the file a favorable recommendation from Sheridan. Grierson read it quickly, turned it over smartly, and kept on reading.

"Confederate cavalry," Grierson said musingly, looking at the next page, making more of a statement than asking a question. And he lifted his eyes to the captain.

"Yes, sir," Dudley said smartly. "With General Forrest for two years." The war department had decided to enlist former Confederates who'd take the loyalty oath. Grant and Grierson knew from personal experience that the South had had excellent cavalrymen. And that the nation needed them now.

"General Forrest, huh?" Grierson stated with interest, eyes brightening from the memory that Forrest had outfoxed him and chased him clean out of north Tennessee. "He was a canny devil, that Forrest," Grierson added. "Never could get him where I wanted him."

"You wouldn't have liked it, sir . . . with all due respect," Captain Dudley answered, in spite of Grierson's great war record, which Dudley knew intimately. They'd barely missed clashing with each other when brevet Colonel Dudley had been leading a brigade of Forrest's cavalry that had chased after Grierson as Grierson was slashing through Mississippi. And it had been Colonel Dudley's brigade that had pounced on Grierson's rear guard back there at the Tickfaw River crossing, and Grierson had had to dash off with his main force rather than engage in a full-scale fight.

"Think Forrest's cavalry would've whipped us, do you?" Grierson asked curiously.

"We was in the saddle day and night looking to do just that, sir," Dudley said, remembering the arduous pursuit and Grierson's narrow escape.

"Wasn't my purpose to fight that day," Grierson said defensively. "My orders were to throw a scare into you Rebs, tear up railroad tracks, and ride."

"And you did it admirably, sir," Dudley said seriously.

Grierson glanced down at the captain's file, then looked up. Focusing his eyes on the captain, he asked seriously, "I suppose you know the nature of this regiment I'm organizing?"

"I do, sir. And Colonel Hoffman reminded me of it again."

"Colonel Hoffman's got nothing but scorn for this whole endeavor. I guess he told you that."

"He did, sir. Said it would wreck the army. Drive white men away."

"And you still want to volunteer for this regiment?"

"I figure I owe these men something, sir."

"How's that?"

67

"I was at Brice's Crossroads, sir," Dudley answered, referring to the fight in which black soldiers had been shot down without benefit of surrender. "What happened never should have."

"War's over and done with now, Captain."

"For some it is. But for men like you and me," Dudley said solemnly, "the war's never going to be over with."

Grierson shifted uneasily in his seat, moving his eyes back to the file, shuffled pages needlessly.

Dudley relaxed back in his chair, resumed talking conversationally, saying, "If this country's going to move forward, expand beyond the Indian menace, it'll have to convince men like Colonel Hoffman that colored men can soldier. God only knows what other proof they want besides what we seen already. Brice's Crossroads, Wilson's Creek, Fair Oaks, Fort Pillow, down in Florida. All hard, bitter fights that colored men acquitted themselves in admirably. But it'll take fair-minded white men to bring that to light, men like you . . . me, Mr. Lincoln."

"Lincoln's dead now."

"I know, sir. Now it falls to men like us, Colonel. And generals like Merritt, Forsythe, Hancock. Men who know 'em . . . men who've seen 'em fight."

"Them's mighty high-toned words, Captain," Grierson said. "You mean 'em?" he asked, thoughtfully stroking his unruly beard.

"That oath I took at West Point said something about duty, honor, and country. This's my country now."

"Never went to West Point myself," Grierson said lamely, closing the file, standing up.

"General Forrest didn't either, sir."

Grierson focused his eyes on the captain, giving him a probing look, then stated frankly: "I like your outlook, Captain." Grierson came around the desk, saying solemnly, "If this regiment's to succeed it's going to take men like you. It's going to be the devil of a job though. And right now I'm swamped." And Grierson looked at the hill of paperwork on his desk. "A good adjutant is what I need." Grierson cut his eyes at Dudley.

"I was hoping for a field command, sir," Dudley answered, shifting uncomfortably in his seat.

"You'd be second in command," Grierson said hopefully.

"A field command, sir, is what I'm really after. Company commander. What I spoke to General Sheridan about."

". . . And a promotion?"

"That too, sir."

"At least you're honest," Grierson said sourly. He thought the matter over briefly, stroking his chin whiskers all the while, saying more to himself than to the captain, "The war department knows the fix I'm in, staffing this regiment. If you was to put in, say . . . six good months' service as my adjutant, I'd see you get that promotion . . . or I'd give you a company and you can earn it the hard way." Grierson cocked his head at the captain, and asked, "That fair enough?"

"Where do I start, sir?"

"Right there," Grierson said, pointing at the blizzard of papers littering his desk. "Somewhere in there is a requisition. Find it, fill it out for overland transportation for twenty-seven more recruits and an escort."

Dudley got up, moved over to the scattered papers on Grierson's desk, started picking through them, asking, "Transportation from where, sir?"

"That's hard to say. Railhead's at Sedalia. My recruiting officer, Lieutenant Badger, didn't know it but the train's a chancy thing once it leaves Jefferson City. White people west of there don't feel the way you do, Captain. Most of 'em are still at war of a sort. They'd just as soon blow them colored recruits off that train as to see it run."

"I know the kind, sir," Dudley said mildly. "But I'll get 'em here . . . one way or another."

"I'm counting on you," Grierson said.

"The other recruits, sir?"

"Eight companies are already here. Two of 'em training some already. But we need more uniforms, weapons, and mounts. They're due in any day now. So says the post quartermaster," Grierson added dubiously.

"Colonel Hoffman's quartermaster?" Dudley asked.

"Yes. A Major Holmquist. Holmquist's a nice enough young man, dedicated to his duty and all. But like the others of his staff, Hoffman's got the major squarely under his thumb too. Promotion, you know," Grierson added scornfully, slanting his eyes at Dudley.

"I see," Dudley answered resignedly.

"Anyhow, it'll be your job to shake things loose over there at headquarters. We're lacking most everything."

"Including a commander for Company M," Dudley stated, looking cat-eyed across his shoulder at Grierson.

"You knowed?" Grierson asked, surprised.

"I heard, sir. That's why I went to see General Sheridan."

"West Pointers!" Grierson said in mock disgust. "You had it all figured, did you?"

"To the best of my ability, sir."

"Well, right now, you're my adjutant. Besides that, I've got a colored trooper, big mean-looking rascal, looking after Company M till the next officer shows up."

"You expect any more will, sir?"

"You West Pointers would be disappointed in me if none did."

Dudley smiled thinly.

"I'll be back shortly," Grierson said, pulling on his campaign hat. "I'm going to have a word with Colonel Hoffman."

"Not on my account, sir?" Dudley said anxiously.

"No, Captain. What Colonel Hoffman said to you, he's said to every officer that's reported in here. But that don't matter. We've got our duty to do," Grierson said, crossing over toward the door. "Don't we, Captain?"

"Yes, sir," Dudley answered, looking up from the paper he had been looking at. Struck by curiosity, Dudley asked, "If Colonel Hoffman don't want the colored troopers training with white troopers, exactly where do you train them, sir?"

"We manage," Grierson said. "Right now Lieutenant Hodges has Company A out across the prairie for target practice with carbines he managed to scrounge up. Most of 'em never handled weapons before so he's got to start from scratch. Same with the few side arms they've got.

"Captain Crawford's got Company B over on the mud-flats with some of the already broke horses we got, teaching them horsemanship. Equitation, he calls it. The rest of 'em are busy building stables, constructing barracks, and what-not."

"Not even barracks, sir!"

"Barracks are for white troopers. Colonel Hoffman wouldn't have it any other way," Grierson added distastefully.

Oh, I see."

"No, you don't, Captain," Grierson said plainly. "Not yet anyhow. But you will in due time," he added deliberately.

"Well, sir . . . it still seems you're making good progress."

"It'll be your job to speed things up, Captain. The quicker I get this regiment in the field, the quicker the nation will know about it. Besides that, winter and Indians wait for no man." Grierson faced back around when he was almost through the door, saying thoughtfully, "You know, Captain, the next white man who walks through this door I think I'll just make him our quartermaster."

"Dime to a doughnut he'll want Company M, sir."

"Quartermaster, Captain," Grierson said firmly. "Whether he wants it or not."

"And Company M, sir?"

"It'll just have to wait," Grierson said grimly.

"Yes, sir," Dudley answered dutifully.

Out the door Grierson went. Marching purposefully across the dusty parade ground. Stepped up on the boardwalk in front of Colonel Hoffman's open door, walked inside. The orderly sitting in a handmade chair there threw aside the picture magazine he was looking at, jumped up, and saluted.

"Tell the colonel that Colonel Grierson wishes to see him," Grierson said, returning the salute.

Shortly the orderly came back. Reported: "The colonel says he'll see you now, sir."

Grierson headed that way. Crossed over the threshhold to Hoffman's overly decorated office that disgusted him every time he came to see the post commander. Walls covered with the trappings of a great Civil War hero, which he wasn't. Regimental battle flags, Confederate battle flags, a great stuffed eagle at least four feet high, wings spread and a fish in its mouth, large framed pictures of Lincoln, Grant, Sheridan, and Custer on horseback.

"Come in, Colonel," Hoffman said amicably. "I was just about to send the orderly for you."

"Thought I'd save your overburdened orderly a trip, Colonel," Grierson answered facetiously.

"Very well, Colonel," Hoffman answered without offense.

"About them mounts—"

"That's what I wanted to tell you about," Hoffman said, interrupting. "They're here, Colonel. Saddles . . . bridles too."

"Where?"

"In the corral with the Third's mounts. I figured you'd want to cut them out and start mounted training as soon as possible. From reports I've been getting, it'll take a month of Sundays to teach your apes to sit a saddle," Hoffman added impishly.

"Them rank-broke horses we were issued don't help none. They're but one jump from being wild mustangs."

"Well," Hoffman said, chuckling, leaning back in his chair, "that bunch was bought without my knowledge from some colored half-breed Mr. Holmquist was misguided enough to contract with. You got a complaint how he fulfilled his contract, you're welcome to submit it right along with mine."

"If the next bunch is like the last, you can count on it," Grierson said.

"One other thing, Colonel," Hoffman said seriously. "The post will turn out this morning. Important visitor coming."

"General Sheridan?"

"No. General Custer."

"You mean Lieutenant Colonel Custer," Grierson said, offended. During the war it had rankled Grierson that Custer had drawn so much glory to himself. But like many other Civil War officers, Major General Custer had been broken back to his highest regular grade of captain. But now had been promoted to lieutenant colonel since serving out here on the frontier. But most everybody still fondly referred to him as General Custer.

"At any rate," Hoffman said dispassionately, "Custer's stopping over on his way to Fort Riley. And of course the post will render him appropriate military honors."

"You expect my men to turn out?"

"As a matter of fact, no. Your orders are to keep them away. I won't have them bringing discredit upon the command."

"I see," Grierson said reflectively. "Keep 'em out of sight. Doing stoop labor. That it, Colonel?"

"They're your regiment, Colonel. I should think you wouldn't want word to get out they're not up to par."

"I'm sure you wouldn't think of it, Colonel," Grierson said dryly. "Anyhow," he added mildly, "my regiment's got plenty to do besides standing at attention watching that snot-nosed Custer come parading in here."

"I'd certainly agree," Hoffman said. "And about that transportation and escort . . ."

"Captain Dudley, my adjutant, will turn in the proper requisition to Mr. Holmquist."

"Captain Dudley . . . your adjutant?" Hoffman was surprised. "Seemed a fine young man," he added seriously. "Well-to-do. Good family. He could've made a future with the Third Regiment."

"Guess he knew the company he'd be keeping, Colonel," Grierson said without emotion.

"Touché, Colonel," Hoffman retorted.

"Good day, Colonel," Grierson said, turning, walking away.

"Good day, Colonel," Hoffman said politely. "And, Colonel, I'll expect you and Captain Dudley to join me and my staff in front of headquarters for General Custer's arrival."

"Wouldn't miss it for the world," Grierson said, crossing the office. "And it's Lieutenant Colonel Custer," he added, and disappeared out the door, heading back to his own office, leaving Hoffman sitting there searching his mind for a thought.

Hoffman had every able-bodied man at Fort Leavenworth standing at parade rest in the hot forenoon sun, waiting for Custer and his Seventh Regiment to arrive.

It was almost noon when the gate sentry reported riders coming. The bugler blew. Every man snapped to attention. Mess cooks and government ghosts, stable hands who did their odorous work in snow-white dusters, were in full-dress uniforms for this special occasion. Standing shoulder to shoulder with regular troopers. Waiting to see the great General Custer. The man the country was glorifying in, and his fighting Seventh Cavalry, the tough Civil War veterans who were going to stamp out Indian depredations, sweep the plains of wild Indians.

Colonel Hoffman broke ranks from where he had been standing in front of his staff officers and Colonel Grierson, flanked by Captain Dudley. Holding on to the hilt of his gold-plated saber, Hoffman strode over to the post band, which had just now struck up the lively tune "Oh Susanna." Hoffman whispered something into the bandmaster's ear, did an about-face, started marching back to his position. Promptly the band stopped playing "Oh Susanna" and struck up "Garry Owens," the Irish barroom ditty that was Custer's favorite martial tune, Hoffman had found out.

Hoffman knew Custer was a favorite with the war department and the nation. From General Grant all the way down to the least private. And Hoffman wasn't a man to miss any opportunity to curry favor where he thought it might do him some good in the future.

Standing at attention, eyes focused straight ahead, the men could hear approaching hoof-falls as Custer's column of fours drew nearer and nearer.

Suddenly a rider burst through the gate.

It was Custer. Long yellow hair hanging limp at his shoulders from perspiration. Riding a long-striding bay horse, sitting the saddle expertly. Thongs on his buckskin jacket jiggling with the motion of his horse.

Custer had been pushing the Seventh hard all morning, coming in from the Platte River country where he'd been futilely chasing Cheyennes most of the month.

Custer's scout, Gaius Debow, who'd been riding ahead, had alerted Custer that Fort Leavenworth was turned out for him. And Custer wasn't a man to miss any opportunity to strut.

Custer wheeled his mount off to the side.

Through the gate the Seventh Cavalry burst. Tough, battle-tested Indian fighters, riding four abreast, boot-to-boot, guidon fluttering in the breeze.

With great dignity Custer nudged his horse out at a slow walk, joining at the head of the column, in time with the music.

Custer led the column around the parade ground with great pride, the band playing splendidly.

All eyes were on Custer, his big powerful horse stepping magnificently, caught up in the pomp of it all.

When Custer got directly opposite headquarters, Colonel Hoffman threw him a salute with his gilted saber that he'd withdrawn from the scabbard belted around the waist of his gold-braided dress blue uniform.

"Eyes right!" Custer commanded his regiment.

Every mounted man swiveled his head around on his shoulder, fastened his eyeballs on the row of officers standing at attention in front of headquarters.

Custer returned Hoffman's saber salute with a regal nod of his head, even as Hoffman deftly lowered his saber.

"Ready front!" Custer ordered his troopers.

They jerked their eyes back around.

The band playing on splendidly.

At the south end of the parade ground Custer reined his horse aside, sitting the saddle, watching his proud, highly disciplined troopers ride by, heading to the post stables to look after their jaded mounts.

When they were gone, Custer wheeled his mount, cantered up in front of headquarters, where Colonel Hoffman and his staff officers were waiting.

"Welcome, General," Hoffman said as Custer was dismounting regally. "Fort Leavenworth is completely at your disposal."

"Glad to hear it, Colonel," Custer answered seriously, shucking his great buckskin gauntlets. "It's been a hard campaign. We're in need of provisions and supplies."

"Come on into headquarters, General," Hoffman said, smiling, "and refresh yourself. We'll discuss your needs there."

"Fine, Colonel," Custer said.

"Dismiss the staff, Mr. Delvin," Hoffman said to Lieutenant Colonel Henry Delvin, his adjutant, even as he flourished a hand. Custer led the way Hoffman's flourished hand indicated.

Two hours later Custer and the Seventh Cavalry rode out of Fort Leavenworth. Colonel Hoffman standing at attention out on the boardwalk seeing them off.

Colonel Grierson was sitting at his desk across from the parade ground. Hearing the departing hoof-falls, he lifted his eyes, and saw the Seventh cantering past his door. When they were gone, he lowered his head, putting his attention back on the filled-out requisition that Captain Dudley had put on his desk for signature. Suddenly Grierson's head jerked up, his mind's eye going back to what he'd just seen. Grierson jumped up out of his chair, grabbed his hat, and bolted out the door. Across the parade ground he went on the double. He practically ran by the startled orderly, who managed to come to his feet just as Grierson burst into Colonel Hoffman's office.

Hoffman jerked his eyes up, unnerved, then caught himself, saying mildly, "Oh, it's you, Colonel. I was just going to send the orderly for you." And he laid his pen aside on the paper he had been hastily scribbling on.

"About them mounts for my regiment . . ."

"General Custer's got 'em," Hoffman stated, confirming what Grierson had suspected. Custer was a hard charger. Wouldn't spare men or horses if higher rank and greater glory was in sight.

"Damn Custer!" Grierson snarled under his breath, slamming his fist down on the edge of Hoffman's desk. It was just as he'd suspected. The Seventh had ridden in here on all bay horses. But had just now ridden out on horses of every shade. Horses that had been destined for Grierson's regiment.

"No help for it, Colonel," Hoffman said matter-of-factly. "Military priority," he added. "The Seventh's keeping to the field. Black Kettle's Cheyennes are on the move south."

Grierson's shoulders slumped.

"My regiment's going with him," Hoffman announced proudly. "The Third's finally going to see some action."

"You're taking to the field?" Grierson asked, surprised at the desk-bound colonel's willingness to go out on a scout himself.

"I am," Hoffman said firmly. "Every man of the Third that's fit for saddle."

"And my regiment, Colonel?"

"Your regiment'll have to wait, Colonel. The only personnel that'll be left here is Company C for garrison duty."

"But, Colonel, I need . . ."

"The army's aim is to put a stop to Indian depredations, Colonel. That's what I propose to do. Your orders are to equip and train a colored regiment. That's what I suggest you do while the Third's gone."

"Very well, Colonel," Grierson said patiently. "Here's my requisition for transportation and an escort for the rest of my regiment," Grierson added, thrusting out the form to the colonel.

"You'll have to see Lieutenant Spurlock. He's being left in charge of this post . . . as of"—and Hoffman looked down at the time he'd already written in the orders on his desk he was just now filling out—"fifteen hundred hours."

"The time Custer rode out of here . . . ," Grierson added.

"Exactly, Colonel," Hoffman said. "Officially the Third is now a part of the force that's going to bring Black Kettle and his band to heel."

When Grierson walked out of Hoffman's office he knew he was in a very tight spot. Fort Leavenworth would be stripped of what little support he was dependent on for material and supplies. Plus he had twenty-seven new recruits out there somewhere waiting for transportation and somebody to escort them to their base of training. Not one of them, as far as Grierson knew, had any inkling that western Missouri was as hostile to blacks as Indian country was to whites.

Across the parade ground Grierson went, heading back to his office, thinking over his next move. A great weight on his shoulders. Halfway across the parade ground he spotted Captain Dudley coming around the corner out of officers' row. Grierson angled over that way and they fell in step together. Dudley saying, "Did you hear, Colonel? The Third's taking the field against Black Kettle."

"I heard. The fort's going to be like a deserted hen roost come this time tomorrow."

"That ain't the worst of it, sir," Dudley added, "Custer's Seventh Regiment got every fit horse on the post."

"I know that too," Grierson said. "But we've got our duty to do, don't we, Captain?"

"Yes, sir."

"What did you find out about this half-breed colored man who's supposed to bring in more horses?"

"He's due sometime tomorrow, sir. The sergeant at the stables says he brings in twenty-five, thirty horses at a time."

"I want you to personally take delivery of them horses, Captain. Post yourself down at the corrals if you have to."

"Payment, sir?"

"Use army vouchers, credit, threats . . . whatever. Just make damn sure you take delivery of them horses."

"Yes, sir."

Dudley was surprised that Grierson kept on walking when they got to his office door. Dudley asked curiously, "And you, sir?"

"I'm going to see Lieutenant Spurlock about transportation and an escort. He's the post commander now."

"Since when, sir?"

"Since Custer rode out of here," Grierson said over his shoulder, and kept on walking.

"I just talked to Lieutenant Spurlock, sir," Dudley called after Grierson.

Grierson stopped, whirled around, asked: "What about?"

"About his Company C providing escort duty for us."

"What'd he say?"

"Said we'd play hell gettin' an escort after today. Every officer that's fit to ride and every wagon that's fit to roll is going on Custer's Indian campaign."

"Custer . . . ," Grierson said disgustedly, looking sourly at Dudley. "Every mother's son out here wants to fight Indians."

"You hit the nail on the head, sir."

"What nail, Captain?"

"Promotions, sir. Fighting Indians is how you get 'em now."

"Don't remind me, Captain," Grierson said, crossing over the threshhold to his office.

An hour before the bugler blew 0600 reveille, Fort Leavenworth had been a beehive of activity, everybody itching to take to the trail after Indians, whom they all had come to hate now. Not a single trooper of the Third Regiment took more than ten minutes to wolf down a breakfast of salt pork, biscuits, beans, and coffee. And ten minutes later every company officer had his troopers standing to horse on the parade ground, facing headquarters, where Colonel Hoffman's oil lamp had been burning ever since 0400 hours, when he had been awakened by the duty orderly.

At exactly 0630 hours, the usual time for breakfast call, Colonel Hoffman came out of his office, took the reins of his mount that the orderly held, waiting in front of headquarters. At exactly the same moment, every company commander yelled out the order: "Troopers . . . mount up!" And as a unit, six companies of cavalry swung into the saddle with Hoffman.

Lieutenant Spurlock, standing there in front of headquarters, threw Hoffman a salute. Hoffman returned the salute, and swung his horse away, walking him toward the gate. And assembled out around the flagpole, the regimental band struck up the heady tune, "The Girl I Left Behind Me."

Almost simultaneously, company commanders bellowed out: "Company! Forward! Column right, ho!" And they wheeled out, holding their horses in strict formation, moving to the cadence of the music.

Every man not actually on duty was outside, standing at parade rest, watching them go. Grierson and Dudley in front of Grierson's office. Lieutenant Spurlock in front of regimental headquarters, his eyes teared over. Spurlock sorely wishing his company was in that formation that was heading out the gate. In his mind's eye he could see the glory . . . and possibly promotion . . . the other company commanders were riding toward, leaving him and his company behind.

When the tail end of the regiment cleared the gate, Spurlock turned away, headed toward Hoffman's garish office. His own office for now. The weight of command responsibility heavy on his shoulders. Including the ticklish task of placating but frustrating Colonel Grierson, as Hoffman had instructed him to do.

Chapter Five

Sedalia was hot already. Very hot. Heat waves making the dry prairie look like a corrugated sheet of rusty tin.

The black recruits filed off the train, gathering in a loose knot around Radford. Looking down the tracks at the town, a row of false-fronted plank buildings strung out along the rails that roundhoused back on themselves fifty yards or so beyond the last building, obviously a livery stable.

Jerico was the only one among them who'd ever seen the country before. And he'd seen it only vaguely when he was Jawhawking roundabouts with Doc Jennison. But he knew for sure this was dangerous country. Country that had been populated with slaveholders and their sympathizers. Border Ruffians, some of them had called themselves before the war. Sneaking across the border in daylight and at night, they'd made Kansas bleed. During the war they'd turned to guerrilla fighting and freebooting.

What a man was now depended on who asked the question, and of whom the question was asked.

"No use us goin' up there to town," Hezekiah said, standing next to Radford, squinting his eyes west up the tracks toward the stark buildings.

"Wadn't fixin' to," Radford answered.

"Back yonder is where we ought to go," Hezekiah said, nodding his head back toward the stock pen. "We'd be out of the town's sight back there."

"I was thinkin' that too," Radford answered, shifting his gaze toward the gate in the middle of the huge stock pen, two raised chutes extending out to the railroad tracks.

"Tell 'em then," Hezekiah said, more an order than a suggestion.

"I was fixin' to," Radford said, giving Hezekiah a dirty look even as he faced around. "No use us goin' up there to town," Radford announced to the men, panning his eyes around at them. "Might be trouble," he added, stopping his eyes on Battie.

"It wadn't my fault back yonder," Battie blurted out.

"I didn't say it was," Radford answered.

"Where we goin' then?" Jefferson asked. George Washington Jefferson was the oldest among them but he had no qualms about taking orders. He knew the nature of white people and wanted no trouble whatever. He was a working man, a blacksmith. The sooner he got to where he could make the anvil sing and the bellows blow, the better off he figured he'd be.

"We'll wait in the stock pen back yonder," Radford said. "Till the army come for us." Radford stood patiently, waiting for someone to kick up a fuss.

Nobody objected. So Radford said contentedly, "Okay, y'all follow me." And started walking that way.

"Follow you!" Battie said in mock astonishment. "Jerico's been gone."

"That's all right," Radford said seriously. "That stock pen ain't goin' nowhere."

They moved out, talking freely, sauntering along behind Radford, a loose-jointed, long-striding man, ambling along the gravelly railbed.

"Be a good time to practice marching," Hezekiah said, walking shoulder to shoulder with Radford. "You got to learn how to give the right orders to move a bunch of men."

"There's time," Radford answered gravely, and kept on walking.

"Them rations we left," Hezekiah said shortly, "we shoulda brought 'em."

"Go get 'em then," Radford answered tersely.

"I ain't in charge," Hezekiah said dismissively.

"Couldn't prove it by me," Radford retorted, turning around in his steps, yelling out: "Willie!"

"Yeah!"

"You and Augie go back and git them rations we left."

"I ain't touchin' that stinkin' pork," Willie shouted back. "I'll bring the crackers."

"They ain't crackers," Radford said, looking across his shoulder at Hezekiah. "They hardtack. Now go bring 'um."

"Whatever they is, I'll bring them. But I ain't messin' with that stinkin' meat."

"Me neither!" Augie exclaimed.

"I'll go get it," Manigo said mildly.

"And you can eat it too," Battie said, smiling. "All of it."

Willie, Augie, and Manigo turned around, and headed back to the train.

The rest of them turned into the wide space between the two chutes. Halfway down the fence rail, Radford stooped, ducked under the middle rail in one smooth motion. On the other side, Radford looked smugly back over his shoulder at Hezekiah, then kept on walking.

"Let's see you do that, old man," Jake McGruder said tauntingly, grinning at Hezekiah.

"Ain't nothin' to it," Hezekiah said. And grabbing the top rail, he vaulted himself cleanly between the two rails.

"Look at the old man go!" Battie said, impressed.

"Don't break your neck showin' off," Jefferson growled, throwing one leg over the middle rail, sliding through.

The rest of them climbed through the fence, and started walking, ragging each other even as they did so.

"Look yonder at Jerico," Deke said. "He's got the only shady spot around here."

Fifty yards away Jerico was stretched out in the far corner of the corral in the meager shade of a rickety lean-to some cowboy had earlier thrown up.

"He acts like he's too good to be around us," Jake McGruder said, more to himself than anybody else.

"Maybe he's scared," Rafer D. answered.

"Like you?" Battie asked teasingly.

"Not like me," Rafer D. answered. "I didn't kill no white man."

"Y'all hush up that kinda talk," Radford said scoldingly. "Ain't none of us scared."

"Them white folks won't follow us this far," Battie said doubtfully. "Will they?"

"I knowed some that would," Deese said positively. "Some of 'em like that."

They drew up around the tattered canvas lean-to where Jerico was stretched out in a strip of shade. They all could see there wasn't shade enough for even one more man, so they stood around slack-legged, looking across the corral out over the burnt prairie.

"Sarge . . . ," Hezekiah said out loud so the others could hear, "how much longer before we git there?"

"I don't know," Radford said, dropping down on his haunches in the angle of the corral.

"Two days," Jerico answered quietly, "if they send wagons."

"What if they don't?" Radford asked.

"Four . . . five days if we have to walk."

"I ain't walkin' nowhere!" Battie exclaimed, squatting on his haunches next to Hezekiah.

"You goin' to fly?" Hoby asked plainly.

"Naw. I ain't goin' to fly."

"Didn't figure you was," Hoby said. "The only flyin' you do is flyin' off at the mouth."

Jefferson grinned. Deese snickered.

"I told y'all," Battie said testily, "it wadn't my fault back yonder."

"Nobody said it was," Radford said seriously.

"Hoby's always talkin' like it was," Battie said.

"This's my mouth," Hoby answered. "I can talk out of it whenever I git good and ready."

"Jerico . . . ," Jake said softly, interrupting the argument, dropping down on his haunches next to Jerico.

"Huh?"

"Where'd you git that gun you had?"

"I had it," Jerico answered. "That's all you need to know."

"Everybody's got guns except us," Kalem said.

"Not everybody," Augie answered, "just some white people."

"I wish I had a gun," Jake said longingly. "I'd feel better out here."

"We'll git guns soon enough," Jerico said. "Knowin' what to do with one is what you got to learn."

Suddenly Battie went wide-eyed, clamping a thumb and forefinger over his nose, looking around. His eyes found Manigo, coming up, carrying the peck of meat. "Don't bring that stinkin' stuff over here!" Battie yelled out to Manigo.

Manigo stopped where he was.

"Don't come no further!" Battie shouted. "Put that stuff down right where you at!"

"Better yet, take it back further," Ike Peeler said, holding his nose too.

"Manigo says he's goin' to cook that salt pork," Augie said, walking up with the hardtack.

Manigo put the peck of salt pork down where he was, walking on toward them.

"That what you goin' to cook it in?" Jefferson asked, looking at the bent-up tin washbasin cows had obviously trampled and Manigo had picked up.

"It'll do after I straighten it out some," Manigo said. "All I need is some water."

"Somebody was to git some water," Jefferson said, "I'd make the fire."

"Where we goin' to git water out here?" Jake asked, looking around at the parched landscape.

"Up yonder," Hezekiah said, talking around the corncob pipe he'd just lit and was sucking to life.

"Up where?" Radford asked.

"That water tank up yonder," Hezekiah said, nodding up toward the town.

They all looked at the water tank hulking in the distance. And to a man they could see it would be a chancy thing for anyone to climb up the thin wooden ladder leading up to the top.

"Rafer D.!" Battie called out ominously. "You the littlest!"

"I ain't goin' up there!" Rafer D. blurted out from where he was sprawled next to the fence.

"Rafer D.!" Jake repeated mockingly. "The job's yours!"

"I ain't goin'!" Rafer D. repeated. "You can't make me!"

They all started laughing.

Except Hoby.

"He said he ain't goin'," Hoby said, "and nobody's makin' him go."

"I was only foolin' around," Battie said.

"Yeah, like you was only foolin' around back yonder," Hoby said angrily.

"I told you," Battie said plaintively, "it wadn't my fault."

"Nobody said it was," Radford repeated.

"This here freeman," Battie said sarcastically, "keep talkin' like it was my fault." And Battie's eyes flashed at Hoby. "I'm sick of it!"

Hoby drew his legs under him from where he was lying. "I'm sick of yo' big mouth too," he said, coming to his feet. "That white man didn't kill you, but I will. With my bare hands." Hoby was standing there spread-legged, fists clenched.

"Hoby . . . ," Radford said gravely, cutting his eyes at Hezekiah, who was watching him expectantly. "Let it drop."

"You tell him to stop pickin' on Rafer D.," Hoby said. "And shut up."

"Why don't you shut me up?" Battie asked, smiling wickedly.

Hoby went off. "I'll kill you!" he screamed, starting toward Battie.

"He's got a knife," Jerico said evenly, turning over for the first time, facing the action.

Hoby froze in his steps even as Battie's right hand went to his back pocket. And came out holding a bone-handled knife, the blade flashing as he brandished it forward.

Hoby's eyes bucked at the cold steel.

"Damn!" Jake said solemnly, bolting up to a sitting position.

Rafer D. jumped to his feet, drew back.

Suddenly Hoby felt sick at the stomach. Wishing he'd kept his mouth shut. He backstepped, picked up the piece of plank board that he'd seen Jefferson leave lying there when Jefferson had started making the fire.

"Y'all let it drop!" Radford snapped.

"Y'all do what he says," Hezekiah said solemnly. "He's in charge."

"That's right," Radford said. "I'm in charge. And I say let it drop. Right now!"

Battie slanted his eyes over to Radford. A hint of a smile came over his lips. Then abruptly the smile broke into a big handsome grin. "Sarge . . . ," he said to Radford, "I ain't goin' to kill him."

"I know you ain't," Radford said grimly. "Now put that knife away."

Battie shifted his eyes out at Hoby, standing spread-legged in front of him, Hoby's face contorted with anger, the club of wood cocked back menacingly.

Battie deftly flipped the knife, catching it by the blade, then slid the weapon back in his back pocket.

"Hoby . . . you and Rafer D. go git the water," Radford said resolutely.

Hoby moved his eyes off Battie, and started glowering at Radford.

"Rafer D. can climb up there," Radford added appealingly, "he's younger and littler than you."

Tension slowly drained away from Hoby's body, his jaw going slack. Abruptly he flung the club aside violently. "Come on, Rafer D.," he growled, turning in his steps.

Rafer D. retrieved the washbasin that Manigo had straightened out some and they started off, walking shoulder to shoulder. When they were some thirty yards away, somebody called out: "Hey, freeman!"

Hoby glowered back over his shoulder.

It was Battie. And he added playfully, "Don't let Rafer D. fall over in that water tank." And Battie smiled handsomely.

"Damn you," Hoby said gravely, and kept on walking.

"Don't start no more," Radford said advisedly to Battie.

"I ain't, Sarge," Battie said, lifting his hands in mock honesty. "I'm through with it," he added, reclining back on his elbows.

Things got quiet. Everybody lounging around or sitting on their haunches, talking in low tones, watching Manigo and Jefferson out at the fire where Manigo had started working at the peck of salt pork.

Directly, Battie raised up off his elbows, asking Jerico curiously, "How'd you know I had a knife?"

"Outline of it's plain as day on your back pocket."

Battie rolled his hip around, looking at his own back pocket, saying, "I don't see nothin'."

"Only shows up when you bend over," Jerico said.

"You noticed that?"

"I noticed."

Suddenly Jefferson bolted away from the fire, putting distance between him and Manigo, clamping off his nose at the smell of the rotting pork Manigo had just opened.

"It smells way over here," Deese said when Jefferson came up.

"Smells like somethin's dead," Jefferson said. "Anybody was to eat that stuff they'd be dead too," he added.

"It sho' stink," Bobo said.

"I smelled worse," Jake said reflectively.

"I'd like to know where," Ike Peeler said. "I ain't never smelled nothin' that bad before."

"Slaughterhouse," Jake said. "Back in Texas. On a hot day like this, blowflies all around, the smell's bodacious."

"Aw, you enjoyed every minute of it," Battie said playfully.

"Not hardly," Jake said. "That's why I'm here."

"I thought you was here because you wanted a gun," Kalem said.

"Yeah," Deese said. "How come you want a gun so bad . . . to shoot white people?"

"I'd just feel better if I had a gun," Jake said factually. "White men got 'em. How come we can't have 'em?"

" 'Cause you might shoot somebody," Battie retorted.

"That's what guns for," Jake answered.

"That's what they for, all right," Jerico stated. "None of us better not forget it neither."

"Yeah," Augie said. "We might have to shoot some Indians. Mightn't we, Willie?"

"Aw . . . hush up, Augie," Willie said. "We ain't got to shoot no Indians."

"They try to scalp me, I'll shoot 'em," Augie said.

"Augie, ain't no Indian alive want that nappy hair you got," Bobo said, and laughed out loud.

"What about Battie's?" Deese asked. "You reckon them Indians want his hair?"

"They'll take his hair . . . they'll take any hair," Bobo said.

"For what?" Deese asked.

"Battie's hair, they could plait it up and make a good horsewhip with it."

They all laughed. Bobo cackled out loud.

"What could they make out of your hair?" Battie asked Bobo, "a scrub brush?"

Everybody whooped.

Out near the fire, Manigo wasn't fazed by the smell. He'd dumped the tainted pork out on the crude cutting board he'd fashioned from plank boards laid out on the ground. And was standing there looking at it, his hands on his wide hips, sizing up what needed to be done.

Shortly, Manigo asked out to them: "Anybody got a knife?"

They all looked at Battie.

"Not for cuttin' that meat, I ain't," said Battie.

"Aw, let 'im use it," Ike Peeler said. "Cuttin' that stuff won't hurt it none."

"Yeah," Kalem said. "A while ago you was going to cut some black meat, now let old Fatback cut some hog meat."

Bobo snickered. Augie was grinning, elbowing Willie lying back on his elbows next to him.

"Well," Battie said to Kalem, "since you put it that way, I guess I can't refuse old Fatback." Battie got up, started walking toward Manigo, reaching for the knife in his back pocket all the while.

"Fatback," repeated Hezekiah, a faint smile on his lips. "Fatback," he said again, wagging his head, amused, glancing out at the short, rolly-polly, Manigo, sweating, shirttail hanging out. "Fatback fits him to a tee," Hezekiah added sagely, returning his corncob pipe to his teeth.

Battie came to a faltering stop halfway out to where Manigo was, an ugly crinkle to his face. Clamping his palm over his nose, he turned in his steps, yelled back over his shoulder, "Sarge! This stuff's real mean-smelling. You ought to come see it!"

"I ain't ought to come see nothin'," Radford yelled back. "Just give 'im the knife and leave 'im alone."

Battie faced back around, took a couple of tentative steps, then stopped again. Struck by mischief, he got the knife from his back pocket and with one quick flip of his wrist, sent the knife zipping through the air toward Manigo.

Manigo leaped aside, wide-eyed.

The knife stuck, quivering in the keg that Manigo had dumped the meat out of, only inches away from where Manigo's foot had been a split second ago.

"Damn!" Jake whispered solemnly, more to himself than anybody else.

"Did you see that, Willie?" Augie asked in disbelief.

"I seen it," Willie said, impressed too.

Battie stood there smiling at Manigo. "Don't cut yourself with it," he said, turning around, heading back to where the others were.

They were talking in low tones of admiration when Battie sauntered up, dropped down lazily on the ground next to Deese, winking knowingly at Augie, who was looking with envy at him, mouth still gaped.

"How'd you do that?" Augie asked.

"Easy," Battie said boastfully. "Ain't nothin' to it."

"Can you teach me?" Augie asked.

"Sure . . ." Battie said.

"What for?" Hezekiah asked sternly. "Ain't nothin' good can come of you teachin' these younguns how to chunk a knife."

"It ain't done me no harm," Battie said defensively. "And it's come in handy a time or two."

"You killed somebody?" Willie asked excitedly.

"I didn't say that," Battie said. "I ain't no knife fighters," he added, smiled knowingly.

"Hezekiah don't like that kind of stuff," Radford said teasingly. "He's a teacher but he don't teach foolishness like knife fightin'. That right, Hezekiah?"

"That's right," Hezekiah snapped. "I got no use for knife fightin' . . . or knife fighters," he added, looking slant-eyed at Battie.

"Who said I was a knife fighter?" Battie asked incredulously.

Radford was smirking at his own cleverness, prodding Hezekiah this time.

"You a schoolteacher?" Ike Peeler asked Hezekiah, hearing about it for the first time.

"He sho' is," Radford answered. "And he's just itchin' to start teachin' us. Show us how smart he is."

"From what I seen, a lot of you need teachin'," Hezekiah said, panning his eyes around accusingly without calling names.

"Can you teach me how to read and write?" Kalem asked seriously.

"You got a brain and some fingers?" asked Hezekiah.

"He got fingers, but brains . . . that's doubtful," Battie retorted, and grinned.

"I got brains," Kalem said.

"Then I can teach you how to read and write," Hezekiah said assuredly, reaching for the burlap sack with his teaching materials inside. "Willie . . . Augie, y'all come on over here too," Hezekïah said cheerily. "Learn somethin' that'll do you some good."

"Like knife fightin'," Battie said facetiously.

"Knife-fightin's for fools," Hezekiah replied.

Willie, Augie, and Kalem moved in around where Hezekiah was sitting next to the corral post, his back against the bottom rail.

"They comin' with the water!" Manigo called over to them from squatting near the fire where he'd already peeled and pared away the rotten parts of the pork.

They all looked out across the stock pen, watching Hoby and Rafer D. coming on, Hoby carrying the washbasin of water, talking all the while.

"Now what you reckon Hoby's talkin' to Rafer D. about?" Ike peeler asked curiously.

"Prob'ly braggin' to Rafer D. about how he's a freeman," Jake said. "And don't have to do what nobody say."

"He's got to do what the army say," Willie said, taking his attention away from where Hezekiah was showing them how to write alphabets. "Ain't he, Augie?"

"We all got to do that," Augie answered.

"That's right," Hezekiah said, "and he's got to do what Sarge here says. And you too. Now pay attention here. You got to put your mind on what you doin' and keep it there."

"We all got to take orders," Radford said.

"That freeman don't know what he's talkin' about half the time," Battie said sarcastically. "Watch 'im when he git a nose full of that stinkin' pork."

They watched as Hoby and Rafer D. drew up to where Manigo was standing by the fire. They saw Hoby set the water basin down, talking animatedly. Neither Hoby nor Rafer D. grabbed his nose; neither man seemed bothered by the smell.

They were mystified.

They saw Hoby squat down, pick up a piece of cut pork, and bring it to his nose, obviously checking for odor.

Hoby didn't react. It was as if the foul odor weren't even there.

They were stunned.

Hoby stood up, disbelief showing on his face; Manigo was smiling, pleased with his work. "Set the water on the fire," Manigo said. "I'll have it cooked in no time."

Rafer D. took off running toward the others, saying out loud, "Manigo cleaned it! It don't stink no mo'!"

"That ain't possible," Jake said solemnly.

"For real, it don't stink no mo'!" Rafer D. said breathlessly. "He cleaned it! He's gittin' ready to cook it!"

"I guess old Fatback knew what he was talking about," Hezekiah said, smiling to himself. "Let that be a lesson to you younguns," he added.

"What lesson?" asked Augie.

"Somethin' good can come of nothin'," Hezekiah said sagely.

"Yeah, even rotten meat," Deese said flatly.

"Knife throwing too," Battie said cheerily.

"Ain't nothin' good can come of knife throwin'," Hezekiah retorted.

"Ask Hoby," Bobo said in low tones, grinning, as Hoby drew closer.

"Hoby . . . ," Deese said conversationally, "Battie here's a knife fighter. He said he's gonna cut you to shoelaces if you keep messin' with him."

"Battie runnin' off at the mouth again," Hoby said seriously. "Behind my back."

"I ain't said nothin' behind your back," Battie said testily.

"You better not," Hoby said grimly. "Or I'll break your neck."

"You got a neck too," said Battie.

"I told y'all," Radford snapped, "let it alone."

"They ain't goin' to do nothin', Sarge," Bobo said teasingly. "They scared of each other."

"You shut up and stay out of it," Radford said.

Things quieted down.

Deke Poole, John Deese, and Cecil Hall had walked over to the far side of the pen, talking among themselves. The only other talking was that of Hezekiah's calling out ABCs. Willie, Augie, and Kalem struggling with pencil and scratch paper, trying to construct each letter. But they all were keeping a curious eye out at Manigo moving about the fire, doing whatever it was he was doing.

Thirty minutes went by.

An hour.

Jerico tipped his hat back from his face, rolled over, sniffing the breeze. Hezekiah stopped schooling his pupils, and started looking out toward the fire. Battie rolled over, faced out to where Manigo was.

Something smelled good. Mighty good. The aroma wafting in toward them on the breeze.

"If I didn't know better," Ike Peeler said, "I'd swear bacon was cooking."

"That's bacon, all right," Battie said, sitting up.

"Manigo said that's what that meat was goin' to taste like when he got done with it," Rafer D. said, raising up.

"I guess old Fatback knowed what he was talking about," Hezekiah said, " 'cause that's sho' bacon cookin'."

Rafer D. sprang to his feet, and ran out to where Manigo was.

They were watching as Manigo took a couple of pieces of cooked meat from the fire-blackened washbasin there, passed them to Rafer D. They were looking intently as Rafer D. drew the meat to his mouth and started chewing. Suddenly Rafer D. bolted away, came running back toward them. He drew up, talking excitedly around the piece of meat in his mouth, saying, "Sarge, Manigo said taste this."

And Rafer D. handed Radford the other piece of brown, crisp meat.

They all were watching expectantly.

Radford broke off a piece, put it on his tongue, started chewing slowly.

Radford's eyes lit up with delight. "It's good," he said, passing the other piece to Hezekiah.

Hezekiah put the bacon on his tongue, started chewing. A smile lit up his face. "Old Fatback knowed what he was doin'," Hezekiah said. "This's good."

Battie got to his feet, started walking fast out to where Manigo was.

Deese jumped up, started running after Battie, asking, "Where you goin'? You said Manigo could have it all. Remember?"

"I remember," Battie said, not breaking stride. "But I changed my mind." And Battie kept hurrying out to where the sweet smell of bacon was coming from.

In no more than ten seconds Manigo had a crowd around him, every man with his palm out, wanting some of the bacon they all had thought was too foul for man to eat or grave digger to bury.

They sat around and ate every morsel of the bacon. Talking animatedly, munching on the hardtack too. With Hezekiah's prompting, Radford saw to it that each man got a fair share.

It was way into the afternoon when things finally quieted down again, everybody talked out, bellies full. One by one they dozed off. Cecil Hall asked the last question of Radford that was on all their minds: "When you reckon the army's comin'?"

"I don't know," Radford answered forlornly, turning over carelessly.

"You think we'll be here all night?" Battie asked, thinking about the night riders.

"How do I know?" Radford said tersely. "Let's just get some sleep."

"Ain't nowhere to sleep," said Willie, looking out over the stark, exposed stock pen, remembering that Jerico had killed a white man.

"Sleep where you at," Bobo said.

"I'd sleep a whole lot better with a gun," Jake said solemnly.

"Ain't nobody goin' to bother us," Radford said doubtfully.

"You scared, Rafer D.?" Battie asked.

"Leave him alone," Hoby growled.

"Make me!" Battie snapped.

"Both of you . . . shut up!" Radford snapped. "And get some sleep."

They did.

Chapter Six

A dozen miles east of Sedalia six men were holed up in a run-down farmhouse in a shallow valley just east of the Lamine River. They had ridden in off the prairie and through the breaks the night before in a drenching rain, had shed their slickers and had got a fire going in the fireplace. Then they sat around drinking coffee, talking in subdued tones until almost daylight.

They were all displaced, unsettled men. Two were ex-Confederate cavalry men, veteran fighters. Of the other four, two had been Confederate guerrillas and two had been bushwhackers. They'd all been on the losing side in the late war and were now looking for ways to set things back to their liking, figuring out overt ways and means to resist the hated Blue Bellies and their nigger accomplices running the country now. They had one thing in common: Not a man among them was willing to accept the verdict the war had rendered.

"Frank . . . ," Peyton Long said conversationally from the crude table where he was fingering a deck of dog-eared cards with his one good hand. The other hand was still attached to the arm that had been shot away, buried somewhere around Shiloah Church.

"Yeah, Colonel?" Frank Yoder answered, lifting up the wide-brimmed hat from his dull, cheerless eyes as he lay back in a rude bunk over next to the wall.

"This Woot Tally you say General Forrest sent, he say where we supposed to meet this feller from Ohio . . . this so-called Grand Dragon?"

"Lone Jack, Colonel. Used to be our stompin' ground. That's where Woot's to meet us."

"Funny," Long said pensively, "nobody mentioned Lone Jack to me when talk came up about organizing Holdouts." Holdouts were beaten Confederates who were toying with the notion of carrying on the war guerrilla style. They had no desire whatever of signing a loyalty oath, becoming law-abiding citizens again. Holdouts saw only two choices: guerrilla warfare or covert action against blacks, as General Forrest over in Pulaski, Tennessee, was getting organized.

"Lone Jack wasn't even in the picture then, Colonel," Yoder said. "Most Holdouts roundabouts here headed to Mexico where Old Pap is." Here Yoder was speaking of sixty-one-year-old Confederate General Sterling Price who had been fondly called Old Pap by Missouri Rebels and bushwhackers he'd commanded. Generals Price, Kirby-Smith, Jo Shelby, and a lot more men—officers, enlisted, and civilians—had lit out for Mexico to join up with puppet emperor Maximillian.

"Any Blue Bellies at Lone Jack?" Long asked, laying aside the deck of cards he'd been shuffling, picking up the tin cup of hot coffee there.

"None, Colonel," Luman Bigelow said, sitting in a chair turned backward in front of the fireplace, staring at the empty fire-blackened coffeepot on the coals. "Not even patrols." Bigelow had been a bushwhacker. He knew killing well. And had no qualms about doing it, fair or foul.

"I say damn the Blue Bellies," Milas Soaper said, stretched out in the top bunk, his long legs crossed over each other, showing run-down boots coming out at the soles. "First thing we ought to do is put some niggers in their place . . .'specially the one that killed Elmer. Me and Elmer come a ways together." Soaper and Elmer had joined the Rebel army together back in '61 when Jayhawkers ran them out of the county for concealing weapons and horses for guerrillas.

"Orders are to organize Holdouts," Long said firmly. "That's what I am to do."

"Organize, hell," Bigelow said testily. "I say we kill out the niggers . . . and Blue Bellies too, if it comes to that. Take back our country . . . white man's country."

"Redeem our country," Yoder said. "That's what the general says our objective is."

"And bring the federal army down on us?" Long asked sarcastically. "That's exactly what we don't want. We got to be smarter this time."

"Colonel . . . ," Milas said, "I'm willin' to follow orders but I'm tellin' you straight out, that nigger what killed Elmer . . . he's a dead dog. Plain and simple."

"We'll get him," Long said reassuringly.

"Colonel," Joe Dockum said bluntly, "Woot said General Forrest's orders are no outright killin'."

"General Forrest ain't here," Milas growled. "We got to do things our own way."

"I'm with Milas," Donnie Pence said. "We was to kill off a few niggers, the rest'll scatter. Them Blue Bellies won't have nobody to protect then."

"What about General Forrest?" Dockum asked.

"What General Forrest don't know sure as hell won't hurt him," Milas answered.

"All right," Long said decidedly. "Tomorrow when we join up with Doyle and the boys in Sedalia we'll pay them darkies a visit before we head out to Lone Jack. What we got to do shouldn't take long if they still holed up in them stock pens like we heard they was."

"What if they ain't?" Milas asked. "What if the Blue Bellies done come for 'em?"

"Then we'll find 'em," Luman Bigelow said frankly, and raised his tin cup of steaming hot coffee to his heavy lips.

At Fort Leavenworth, eighty miles north and west of the run-down shack where the six ex-Rebels were scheming to redeem their country, as they saw it, the bugler blew reveille. Fifty-seven troopers of Company C rolled out of their bunks in the enlisted barracks, preparing themselves to go about the fort's daily routine, such as it was with the rest of the regiment out in the field.

South of the barracks on ill-drained swamp land, four hundred and twenty black enlisted men crawled out of their A tents and lean-tos, preparing themselves for another day of cavalry drills, drills that were strange, queer to most of them. The only thing they knew for sure was that they were working for the government with a promise of thirteen dollars a month cash money, and clothes and rations. The rest was up in the air.

Captain Gilford Dudley rolled out of his bunk too. If there was one thing Dudley wanted to do this day it was get charge of those horses that were supposed to come in early this morning.

Dudley dressed quickly, splashed a bit of water on his face, and hastily toweled it away. He combed his hair with his fingers, then buckled on his service revolver, pulled on his campaign hat, and rushed out the door.

And stopped dead in his tracks.

Looking across the boardwalk at him was a well-dressed, middle-aged civilian on the seat of a canvas-covered army wagon, obviously loaded with supplies, a saddle horse tied to the tailgate.

Dudley's eyes shifted from the man's spare, crow's footed face to the heavy supply wagon pulled by four stout mules. Dudley knew all manner of contractors and suppliers were swarming into the fort, looking to sell the army shabby goods and shoddy services of one kind or another.

"Name's Dinsmore," the man said when Dudley's eyes returned to his. "Jack Dinsmore."

Jack Dinsmore was fifty-two years old. Medium height, slight-built. A plainspoken, down-to-earth, hardheaded moralist. Nothing in his Pennsylvania upbring had let him rest easy while one slave was still held in bondage. He'd ridden with Doc Jennison ever since the Kansas-Missouri border trouble first started back in '54, and had been with him all through the Jayhawking days. And Dinsmore had done his fair share of killing and plundering. Had stayed on as Colonel Jennison's lieutenant when the Jayhawkers were formally mustered into the federal service as the Seventh Kansas Volunteer Cavalry Regiment.

Now Dinsnmore was Doc's ranch foreman and right-hand man. Doing what needed to be done to preserve their ill-gotten gains while Doc drank the best whiskey and played poker in the Exchange Hotel in Leavenworth City, wearing expensive suits, string-tied white satin shirts ruffled at the sleeves, and fancy boots. And looking over his shoulder for the law, or some citizen he'd wronged.

"What can the army do for you this early in the morning, Mr. Dinsmore?" Dudley asked impatiently.

"I'm looking for Colonel Grierson."

"Colonel Grierson," Dudley repeated, relieved. Dudley had no time for contractors just now. He wanted to get down to the horse corral immediately.

"The colonel will be right in there shortly," Dudley said, flourishing a hand through the open door behind him.

"You're welcome to wait. In there . . . or where you at."
And Captain Dudley was off.

Across the parade ground Dudley went, walking at double quick time, heading for the corrals, his mind working at what had to be done. He was coming out of the row of vacated enlisted men's barracks when a vague drumming sound came to his ears.

Dudley cocked his head without breaking step.

The sound grew, and grew some more, rumbling. Almost shaking the very earth underneath him. Dudley shifted his eyes out toward the west end of the fort where the sound was coming from. And he saw what he was hearing.

The horse herd! Coming at a run, driven by only one wrangler.

Dudley broke into a run, heading for the corrals to make sure the gate was open. Running out of the row of low-slung barracks, Dudley saw the corral gate was already open. A stable hand dressed in a white canvas stable frock standing by.

Dudley sprinted up to the corral, his breath coming hard.

The horses had already been penned.

The man in the frock saluted, saying to Captain Dudley: "Thirty, sir . . . I counted thirty."

"Good," Dudley answered, returning the salute. As if struck by a thought, Dudley asked, "The man who drove 'em in, you know 'em?"

"Yes, sir. That's Jimmy . . . Jimmy Bowlegs. I've took delivery of horses from him before, sir."

"Any trouble?"

"No, sir. Not unless you count rank-broke horses."

Dudley looked out over the corral at the half-wild horses, kicking and snapping at each other. He brought his eyes back to the stable hand in the white duster, government ghosts they were called, and asked conversationally, "What's your name, trooper?"

"Corporal Snell, sir."

"Company C?"

"Yes, sir."

"Corporal Snell," Dudley said with formality, "you are hereby relieved of duty here."

"I am, sir?" Snell asked, astonished at being relieved of stable duty by a captain.

"You are, Corporal. Report to Lieutenant Spurlock for further assignment."

"Thank you, sir," Snell said breathlessly, and took off at a doubled pace.

Dudley turned in his steps, watching the corporal go. Presently he faced back around, putting his attention on the obviously half-blooded black man who'd driven the horses in and was now cantering his long-legged pinto up toward him, holding the lead ropes to two mares that had been the bell mares for the herd.

"I bring thirty horses," the tawny-complected man said when he reined up in front of Dudley.

"Thirty," Dudley repeated musingly, looking up at him.

"You pay now," Bowlegs said in studied English.

"I no pay," Dudley said, mimicking Bowlegs. "The colonel pays." And Dudley pointed toward headquarters. "Army regulations," Dudley added, seeing Bowlegs looking disapprovingly toward headquarters.

"We go there," Dudley said when Bowlegs brought his steady, unemotional eyes back down to his.

Dudley could read nothing in Bowlegs's eyes. "We go?" Dudley asked inquisitively.

"We go," Bowlegs said without emotion, nudging his horse out.

Jimmy Bowlegs was twenty-six years old. Called Bowlegs to his face by those who knew him, and a lot of other names behind his back. Six feet tall, Bowlegs weighed a good two hundred pounds. Had on a calico shirt and a high-crowned hat, an eagle feather stuck in the rawhide band. Had on knee-high moccasins with blue army pants stuffed inside them, and a white cotton breechcloth covering the seat of the pants. A big government-issue Army Colt .44 revolver was holstered on his right side, and a Sharps 44-40 rode in the saddle boot. Part Seminole, Jimmy had been resettled west with his father and two hundred other survivors of Chief Osceola's warriors after a year of bitter, futile fighting in Florida's swamps.

Bowlegs yet had the look of wild country about him. Now his life was roaming the plains and prairies of high country, catching wild horses for sale. He'd just as soon sleep out in the open as under a roof; he'd just as soon eat raw meat as cooked; and he'd just as soon shoot at white men as ride around them. Fact was, Bowlegs would shoot at anything white moving on the open plains and prairies that belonged to Indians, as he and other Indians saw it.

Bowleg's guns didn't go unnoticed by Dudley when Dudley fell in step on the left side of Jimmy's pinto, heading back to headquarters.

Glancing up at Bowlegs, Dudley saw on his left side a skinning knife, blond scalp hair intricately woven into the knife handle and scabbard.

"Where you from, Jimmy?" Dudley asked casually.

"Here . . . there," Bowlegs said, and kept on riding.

At headquarters, Colonel Grierson had come into his office and had been startled by a civilian sitting on the crude chair over next to the wall, obviously waiting for him.

"Who're you and what you want?" Gierson asked, irritated at being disturbed by a contractor this early in the morning of a day that already had the promise of being distressing.

"Name's Jack Dinsmore," the man said when Grierson had crossed over the threshhold.

"You're mighty early, ain't you, Mr. Dinsmore?" Grierson said rudely, cooly eyeing the well-dressed civilian from over his shoulder, heading toward his desk.

"That captain of yours said I was welcome," Dinsmore answered.

"If you're looking to do business with the army, you're a day late," Grierson said, taking a seat behind his desk. "The fort's commanding officer is out in the field."

"I ain't rightly looking to do business with the army, Colonel," Dinsmore said, idly fingering his white, high-crowned hat.

"What's your business then?"

"Mr. Jennison sent me," Dinsmore said.

"Doc Jennison?" Grierson asked, shocked.

"That's right, Colonel."

"Well, I'm damned," Grierson said. "The way I hear it told, Doc's the last man to want to do business with the army."

Anybody who'd lived in or passed through the territory in the last fifteen years knew Jennison had been the leader of the Jayhawkers, and classified as a killer and a thief. Even now there were lots of unanswered questions being asked about Doc's vast land holdings and prime stock. Property it was whispered he'd taken from southern sympathizers and secesh after running off some and killing out the rest.

"You got it all wrong about Doc, Colonel," Dinsmore said affably, smiling wanely. "Doc's a changed man."

"You didn't ride all this way to tell me that."

"You're right, Colonel," Dinsmore said agreeably. "Fact is, Doc's heard about the trouble you're having provisioning that regiment of yours. He sent over some surplus army supplies his regiment had on hand when they disbanded. He figured you could use 'em right about now."

"He did, did he?" Grierson asked, his interest now piqued. "What's his concern?"

"His concern's about them recruits you got stranded in Sedalia."

"What makes that his concern?"

"Well . . . Doc's kinda partial to one of 'em. Jerico."

"How come?"

"Jerico used to ride with Doc and me. Jerico and Jack Mann was the only two colored fellers what did. Doc and me, we kinda raised Jerico. So when Doc heard about this colored regiment you was puttin' together, Doc sorta steered Jerico into it. Doc always figured coloreds could do their own fightin'. And Doc don't like to be proved wrong."

"Can't say he's wrong on that score," Grierson said. "Army'll do 'em better than the way I seen some of 'em. Once this Jerico and the rest of 'em gets here, I'll make troopers out of 'em."

"That's what Doc's worried about. Him getting here. In case you hadn't heard, Colonel, from here to Sedalia was nothing but secesh country. Overrun with bushwhackers and guerrillas till we cleaned 'em out. Now they're back. And there's dead to prove it. The country's still hostile territory, enemy territory for any colored man, woman, or child. You got twenty-seven colored strangers out there that some white men would just as soon shoot at look at."

Grierson looked slant-eyed at Dinsmore, wondering how he knew that practically half a company of his regiment was stranded, as lost to him as if they'd dropped off into a deep well somewhere.

Finally Grierson said resignedly: "I guess Doc also knows that Colonel Hoffman and the third's marched off with Custer. Leaving me with no transportation and escort."

"Doc never figured on that. I thought the fort looked awfully deserted this morning."

Just then Captain Dudley walked in, Bowlegs following in his footsteps, carrying his saddle gun in his right hand as was his habit.

"Horses here, Colonel," Dudley announced. "Thirty. Jimmy's here to collect his pay."

"Well, if it ain't Jimmy Bowlegs," Dinsmore said pleasantly, interrupting. Doc Jennison and Dinsmore knew who was in the horse-stealing business. They'd been in it too, before, during, and, some said, after the war.

"You bring horses too?" Jimmy asked Dinsmore.

"No," Dinsmore said, "Doc ain't in the horse-selling business no more."

"You know him?" Grierson asked Dinsmore.

"Everybody knows Bowlegs," Dinsmore said. "He's the best wrangler and horse thief from the North Platte to the Rio Grande."

"Doc buy horses?" Bowlegs asked seriously, looking at Dinsmore through devilish brown eyes. "I bring pretty damn quick."

"Doc's got plenty a horses," Dinsmore said. "At least he had plenty before you turned up," Dinsmore added facetiously.

Dinsmore twisted around in his chair, faced Grierson, saying: "Colonel, seems to me Jimmy here's the answer to your transportation problem."

"How's that?"

"He's under contract to deliver horses. Why not in Sedalia? There's four, five, maybe a half dozen McClellan saddles in that supply wagon I bought. Enough rigging to go along with 'em. Them that don't already know how, can learn to ride on the way here."

Grierson's eyes sparkled at the thought. He looked at Dudley. It was a thing they hadn't thought of.

"I no take horses to Sedalia," Bowlegs stated flatly. "You pay now."

"Doc would be mighty appreciative," Dinsmore said to Jimmy.

"How much he pay?" Bowlegs asked.

"Now just a minute," Grierson said rudely, interrupting. Catching himself, he continued with authority: "The army pays thirty dollars a head for every sound horse delivered. That right?"

"*Sí*," Jimmy said. Jimmy's talk switched from English to Mexican, from Kickapoo to Apache and even sign language. He'd lived for four years in a poverty-stricken Kickapoo village down in Nacamiento, Mexico, riding with renegade Mescalero Apaches, raiding and plundering across the Rio Grande in Texas where the border had been thinly guarded during the war.

"The army'll only take delivery of them horses at Sedalia. And that's final," Grierson stated firmly. Feigning disinterest, he picked up the writing pen on his desk, started writing something.

"You pay more," Bowlegs said. "I take to Sedalia."

Grierson lifted his eyes, looking at Dinsmore for an answer.

"Forty dollars a mount," Dinsmore said.

"Forty-five," intoned Bowlegs.

Grierson looked across his shoulder at Dudley.

Dudley shrugged indifferently.

"Doc's worried," Dinsmore stated.

"Doc's not payin'," Grierson stated. "Army is."

"Could be he would," Dinsmore said seriously.

"Okay," Grierson said decidedly to Bowlegs. "The army'll pay you for delivery to Sedalia."

"Provided you start them horses to Sedalia today," Dudley added.

"You pay today," Bowlegs said.

"Captain Dudley," Grierson said with authority, handing over a requisition, "take him to Mr. Holmquist. See that he gets paid what's comin' to him."

"Yes, sir."

Grierson and Dinsmore watched as Captain Dudley led Bowlegs out the door, Grierson taken aback by how heavily armed the half-breed was, saying to Dinsmore, "I gather he's a man expectin' trouble."

"He is, Colonel. Spends most of his time in wild country. He's only a step removed from a savage. But a man of his word. He'll get them horses to Sedalia or die trying. That's settled."

"Mr. Dinsmore," Grierson said uneasily, "nothin's settled until them recruits get here. From the way you talk about the country they got to come through, they'll need nothing less than an armed escort."

"That's what Doc was thinkin' all along, Colonel. He figured the army would have gumption enough to provide one."

"Country's that bad?"

"You'd have to have knowed the country before the late war. It was nothin' but a land of slave-holding secesh, bushwhackers, and guerrillas. Ever since Doc came to Kansas in fifty-three he's spent his life kidnappin' slaves and settin' 'em free. Now that they're free, he'll spend the rest of his life and wealth seein' that they get a fair shake."

"Giving back some of what he stole?" Grierson asked. "That it?"

"Call it what you will, but Doc's like that," Dinsmore said. "There's no explainin' it until you consider he's spent time with Quakers."

"I simply don't have an armed escort under my orders now," Grierson said. "Hell, I don't even have a civilian scout. Practically everybody's out chasin' after Indians."

"Civilians!" Dinsmore said excitedly. "There's your answer, Colonel."

"Even if I wanted to," Grierson said skeptically, cocking his head at Dinsmore, "where would I get a civilian escort?"

"You leave that to me, Colonel."

"You know somebody?"

"Butler . . . colored fellow named Ples Butler. Hires out of Fort Scott off and on for Colonel Taylor. Ain't a better man ever stood in boot leather. Keeps a kid with him all the time."

"Mr. Dinsmore," Grierson said, "first you tell me the country's practically a death sentence for colored men, now you suggest I send two more out there. What makes you think they won't be killed too . . . if they're fools enough to go?"

"Not these two, Colonel," Dinsmore said resolutely. "They'll not scare easy. Both of 'em go armed to the teeth, Texas style. Same as you seen Bowlegs. They know what for. Used to be state policemen down in Texas. And that's plum rough country from what I hear."

"You figure they're enough to scare off an attack?" asked Grierson, looking over at Captain Dudley, coming through the door. "Only two armed men."

"Three armed men," Dudley answered, overhearing the conversation. "Jimmy's got to come back with them."

"What happened?" Grierson asked.

"Them rank-broke horses in that bunch Jimmy just brought in," Dudley said, crossing over to his desk. "Paymaster ain't payin' for 'em till they gentle-broke."

Dinsmore looked a look at Grierson; Grierson looked a look at Dudley; Dudley said to them both: "Lieutenant Spurlock's doin'. Colonel Hoffman's orders."

"And Jimmy?" Grierson asked apprehensively.

"He's about as satisfied as his kind will be," Dudley answered.

"Money right?" Dinsmore asked.

"As right as Spurlock said it's goin' to get."

"How right's that?" Grierson asked.

"Forty dollars a mount," Dudley answered.

The few black men who were out on the sparsely settled frontier were conspicuous in their movements, talked about in their absence. If a man went in their general direction it didn't take long to find any one of them.

Dinsmore had been all his life a pugnacious character, not one to hang back in the face of challenges, threats, or provocations. He was a known fighter, someone who'd take it to you. Back in '63 when Quantrell had crossed the Kansas border and burned down Lawrence, Doc Jennison, Dinsmore, and John Brown retaliated across the Missouri border within the hour, striking Little Santa Fe with a vengeance. They figured the Missouri raiders had come from that place or through it, and whichever one it was didn't much matter.

Dinsmore crossed his heavy supply wagon over the Kansas River on Jesse Stem's ferry, crossed the border a mile below Little Blue River, and was at Pleasant Hill an hour after high noon.

Dinsmore had lashed his team getting back to Leavenworth City, and had broken in on Doc's poker game, telling Doc how Colonel Hoffman had left Grierson empty-handed out at the fort. Without transportation and with no escort, how the army was fooling around chasing itself while Jerico and the other stranded recruits were at the mercy of ex-Rebels and riffraff, and all.

"Damned army," Doc kept saying, threatening to resurrect the Jayhawkers. When Dinsmore had finished, Doc gave orders as to what he wanted done, adding emphatically, "You see to it!" Doc was het up, the way he was sometimes back in the old Jayhawking days when something had gone awry and Dinsmore, his second in command, had to personally see to it.

Now, Dinsmore pulled to a halt at Jack Winters's saloon, went inside, ordered a beer, and asked the right question of Winters:

"Seen Butler lately?"

"Pony Butler?" asked the walrus-mustached Winters, "or nigger Butler?" Most everybody out here had a nickname of a kind, for better or worse.

"Nigger Butler," Dinsmore repeated grimly, looking cat-eyed over the rim of his stein of beer at Winters.

"Last I heard," said Winters, carelessly wiping a dirty white rag across the rude bar top, "he was working the old Barlowe place."

"Just south of Sni Creek?"

"Yeah," said Winters. "You don't find him there, he's dead."

Dinsmore was shocked. The mug of beer fell away from his lips, landing with a heavy thud on the bar top, Dinsmore keening his eyes at the bartender, looking for an explanation.

"Butler said he and that kid was goin' to make a going ranch out of that place," Winters said casually. "Or die trying," he added, smiling wryly at his own wit.

"Thanks," Dinsmore said wryly, sliding a two-bit piece across the bar. And walked out through the batwings.

An hour Dinsmore followed the wagon road north out of town and across the prairie before he caught sight of the belt of timber that marked the bottomland. He left the wagon road, cutting across the rolling prairie, making a beeline for the belt of trees.

Ten minutes later Dinsmore pulled his heavy wagon into the dooryard of the old Barlowe place. On the wagon seat, Dinsmore tilted his high-crowned white hat back on his forehead, panning his eyes around, looking over the two-bit layout.

The shack was log-built. A two-room, dog-run affair as was common on the frontier. Had a rude rail and rider corral running off in back of it, leading down toward a creek of stagnant water. On the south side of the house was a hay barn, a door hanging off one hinge.

Dinsmore brought his head around at the sound of a ringing voice swearing bitterly, coming from down by the creek.

Dinsmore shook the lines, nudged the team forward. Drawing closer, Dinsmore saw the bare-chested, unarmed black man who had been doing all the swearing.

It was Ples Butler.

Dinsmore pulled to a halt just as Butler twisted around in the saddle at the sound of jingling trace chains.

Butler saw who it was. He undid the rope from the horn of his saddle, from where he had been swearing at the obstinacy of a huge deadfall he was trying to drag out of the water, clearing the creek of dead trees and branches deposited there by heavy seasonal rains.

Butler threw the rope aside, gigged his horse over to a deadfall, and retrieved his gun belt from a branch, hooked it over the saddle horn, then rode up the grade toward the wagon where Dinsmore was waiting.

Ples Butler was thirty-nine years old. A tall, slim-built, dark-complected, bony-faced man with skin sun-hardened like cowhide. A tough, solemn-natured man who'd been strengthened by hard times, and toughened by passing years. Smiles rarely crossed his face.

Dinsmore knew perfectly well that Ples and Fate were desperate for cash money like everybody else. He also knew that mundane ranch work was not of either man's nature or liking. Mostly they could be found out of doors somewhere, scouting, tracking, or freighting for the army out of Fort Scott.

"I don't envy you the work you got," Dinsmore said charitably when Ples reined up at the wagon, Dinsmore panning his eyes over the island of dead trees and branches that Ples had been working to remove.

"Fate wiggled out of it," Ples said grimly. "One of us had to do it though."

"Where's Fate anyhow?" Dinsmore asked.

"Down yonder," Ples said, nodding, "makin' up chink mud. Cabin's drafty as hell and leaks like a sifter," Ples added disparagingly. "What brings you?"

"Doc's offerin' work. If you can break yourself away."

"Depends," Ples said seriously.

"On what?"

"What the job is . . . and how much it pays," Ples said, slumping over in the saddle, stacking his palms on the saddle horn.

"You know Doc ain't short with wages. But the job's in Sedalia."

"Sedalia?" Ples repeated, straightening up in the saddle. "Me and Fate heard about them army recruits stuck over there. They come out yet?"

"Not yet, they ain't," Dinsmore said. "And they ain't likely to unless somethin's done."

"Like what?"

"Get this supply wagon through to 'em."

"My way . . . or the army's way?"

"How you do it is up to you."

"And the pay?" Ples asked.

"Regular freightin' wages," Dinsmore said, reaching into the inside pocket of his coat. "And Doc sent this." Dinsmore came out with a folded bundle of bills, and handed them up to Ples.

Ples riffled through the thin bundle of bills, getting a rough amount in his head. Drawing the Army Colt revolver from the holster on his saddle horn, he twisted around in the saddle, and fired a shot in the air. Straightening back around, he holstered his pistol.

"What was that all about?" asked Dinsmore.

"That'll bring Fate."

"You'll do it then?" Dinsmore asked.

"Don't see why not," Ples said, looking back sourly at the mountain of logs and branches he'd be getting away from. "Let's go up to the house. That's where Fate'll be."

Dinsmore wheeled the wagon around and walked the team toward the house even as Ples gigged his dun horse over, retrieved his shirt from hanging on a dead branch, and caught up alongside Dinsmore's wagon.

Ples had shrugged on his shirt, and they were halfway to the house when drumming hoofbeats of a running horse came to them. Suddenly a rider materialized, coming toward them, leaning over in the saddle, blistering the breeze.

It was Fate.

Fate knew that shot meant trouble or quitting time. And it didn't much matter which.

Fate Elder was nineteen years old. Chocolate-complected. Five feet nine inches tall, weighed no more than one-fifty. An active, alert youngster. Had on faded Levi's jeans, a black cotton shirt, and brown run-over-at-heel boots. Ples and he had done lawman duty for the Republicans two years ago down in Texas where they both were state police officers, and had had a run-in with the Texas Rangers. They'd taken off their badges and ridden out of the state without wages rather than be disarmed as new Texas law said all coloreds must be. They'd been on the move ever since, riding wild country mostly, sometimes in the Indian Nations.

Fate swung his horse into the dooryard, and spotted Ples riding leisurely alongside a wagon.

Fate swore under his breach, checked his horse down to a trot, pushed his low-crowned black hat back on his forehead, and came on. "What'd you shoot for?" he asked when he swung his horse around Ples's side.

"Doc's offerin' work," Ples said.

"I know we hard up for cash money," Fate said, "but that don't rate no warning shot."

"That shot was to git you to heist your tail," Ples said.

"Doc got pistol work again?" Fate asked, looking across his shoulder at Dinsmore.

"Not this time," Dinsmore said.

"What kind then?"

"Freightin'," Ples said. "That wagon Mr. Dinsmore's drivin'."

"Take it where?" Fate asked, looking back over his shoulder at the heavy four-up wagon Dinsmore was driving.

"Sedalia," Dinsmore said, pulling the wagon to a halt in the dooryard next to a crude hitching rail.

"Sedalia?" repeated Fate, looking at Ples, then shifting his eyes to Dinsmore, dismounting the wagon. "From what we heard, the army's got colored recruits in a bad spot over there. And that's the same as pistol work."

"That'll be up to you two," Dinsmore said from the tail-gate of the wagon, unhitching his saddle horse. "All Doc's interested in is gettin' these supplies there."

"When?" Ples asked.

"The sooner the better," Dinsmore said, swinging into the saddle. "Jimmy left this morning taking army mounts to 'em."

"Jimmy Pockmark?" Ples asked, "or Jimmy Bowlegs?"

"Jimmy Bowlegs," Dinsmore answered. "Was I you," he added, taking up slack on the reins, "I'd catch up to him. Three of you got a better chance than two."

"Catchin' up to Bowlegs won't be easy," Ples said.

"Horses he's drivin'," Dinsmore said, "at least a dozen of 'em are rank-broke. He'll be slowed some."

"I still wouldn't count on catchin' up to Bowlegs," Fate said.

"Well, it's up to you," Dinsmore said. "And one more thing you ought to know. There's guns hid under the seat."

"Guns," Ples repeated.

"Yeah. Some carbines Doc had on hand. He don't want it common knowledge though." Dinsmore touched spurs to his horse, saying across his shoulder, "When you get back, come into town. Doc'll want particulars." And Dinsmore clattered off, Ples and Fate watching him go.

Chapter Seven

Jimmy Bowlegs wasted no time. Within an hour he was clear of Fort Leavenworth, riding open prairie country, the horse herd strung out on the run. With the two lead mares tied tail-to-bit, Bowlegs galloping his long-legged Mexican pony at the rear of the bunch, looking on his back trail every now and again.

Bowlegs knew the country. Half-blooded Seminole, he'd been roaming wild country ever since being resettled West as an infant with his father and two hundred others of Chief Osceola's band after Osceola had been killed and they'd spent a year of bitter, futile fighting in Florida's swamps.

Bowlegs knew firsthand that one man driving good horses in broad daylight in wild, open country was asking to be relieved of his horses.

For that reason, a mile south of the fort Jimmy swung the horse herd west. Two miles out he took a switchback and fell into Blacksnake Draw, a shallow gully draining south that few men knew about. Striking the narrows of the Kansas River at an ancient Kaw Indian village two miles above Jesse Stem's ferry, he waded the horses across, let them drink a bit on the south shore, then pushed them on at a brisk pace.

Four hours later at almost exactly the same time Jack Dinsmore was turning over the army supply wagon to Ples Butler, Bowlegs was plunging the horses over the sloping bank of Titcher's Gulch, a well-concealed slash in the prairie that in rainy season fed into the Little Blue River. Staking out his two lead mares, he simply bunched the others nearby on good grass, knowing full well they'd graze peacefully close to the mares.

A half hour more and Jimmy had his saddle gear stripped, his pony tethered to a branch of scrub oak he'd picked out up on the rim as a concealed lookout. More out of habit than anything else, Jimmy squatted on his haunches, motionless, chewing dried buffalo meat, gazing back on his back trail. And as far as his eyes could reach, he saw heat waves shimmering over a lifeless tabletop of flat prairie land broken here and there by unseen dry washes, gullies, and ravines.

The same shimmering heat waves Jimmy was looking across, Ples Butler was looking across too. A dozen miles south and east of him. And Ples was saying to Fate, "Not even a fool would drive horses this time of day in this heat." Ples twisted around the big red-checked bandanna he was wearing around his neck, mopped pocks of sweat from his face with the tail end of it.

"Jimmy ain't no fool," Fate replied, swinging down from his horse where they'd watched Dinsmore disappear up the trail.

"I'd bet money I ain't got he's close to water wherever he's at," Ples said, looking out across the distance.

"There's a half dozen places he could be," Fate answered, stepping a toe up on the wagon wheel, swinging aboard.

"I'd guess he's somewhere in Sni Hills," Ples said, glancing up at the sun, judging time. "Prob'ly along Sni Creek."

The Sniabar Hills were a series of hills seven miles wide and thirty miles long connected by broken, densely wooded valleys. Sni Creek, a shallow-running stream, meandered through the hills. The area had been the favorite haunts of Quantrill and his bunch. It was said that five thousand men could hide in there and an army passing through wouldn't know they were there.

"That's rough country," Fate said. "If he ain't there, we'd have to double back with the wagon."

Looking inside the wagon, Fate said: "Ples, you better come see what's in here."

Ples dismounted, came over, lifted the canvas flap, and looking across the tailgate, commented, "Mr. Dinsmore said army supplies and some guns."

"They army supplies all right," Fate stated, running his eyes around inside the wagon. "Uniforms, some old saddles, boots, a camp chest . . . guns hid under the seat here."

"Now that I think on it," Ples said, "it ain't surprisin'. I heard talk back at the fort that back in Sixty-three Doc was drawing regular army supplies for his Jayhawkers. Most folks figured he'd sold everything."

"I guess this's what he kept for hisself," Fate commented.

"Likely the part he wouldn't part with," said Ples.

"The wrong people was to find out what we haulin' we'd have trouble on our hands for sho'."

"Maybe not," Ples answered thoughtfully. "If we was to throw in with Jimmy drivin' them horses, a supply wagon wouldn't rate a second glance."

"Catchin' up to Jimmy's the thing," Fate said, jumping down from the wagon.

"You shouldn't have no trouble," Ples said.

"Me, by myself?"

"By yo'self," said Ples. "The way I figure it, you go on ahead, catch up to Jimmy out there somewhere in the Sni

Hills. Tell him to wait for me with the wagon. I'll head out as soon as I load our gear in here."

"Wait for you where?"

"On the Blackwater is as good a place as any."

"This don't seem right, Ples," Fate said somberly. "You comin' by yo'self with the wagon. Between here and the Blackwater ain't nothin' but trouble. There's men in them hills who'd kill you for the clothes you got on let alone for what's in this wagon."

"You figure to protect me?" Ples asked facetiously.

"Well, I could help some," Fate answered awkwardly.

"Can't dispute that," Ples said honestly. Ples knew Fate was good with the Army Colt they both wore. Fate knew it too, but took no swagger in it.

"Let's do it my way," Ples said patronizingly. "Since I'm the one who's liable to git killed." And Ples looked up cat-eyed at Fate.

"I didn't mean it that way," Fate said defensively.

"I know you didn't," Ples said seriously. "Now git to it."

"What'll I tell Jimmy when I find him?" Fate asked, mounting up.

"You tell Jimmy we earnin' wages just like he is. We both got a job to do and we can do it without somebody gittin' killed if we work together. Tell 'im I'll be along directly."

"What if he don't listen?"

"Shoot 'im," Ples said in mock seriousness.

"Awww, Ples, you know what I mean," Fate said, turning his horse away.

"I know what you mean," Ples said, his eyes twinkling at Fate's discomfort. "You just tell Jimmy to wait for me on the Blackwater," he added soberly. "Jimmy's half wild but he'll listen."

"Okay," Fate said, and gigged his horse out.

"Look after yo'self, boy," Ples yelled at Fate's back. Ples was thirty-nine years old; Fate was only nineteen. More out of habit than anything else, Ples always sent a word of caution with the youngster when they took to different trails.

Fate took the older man's words as sound, fatherly advice, which he had never known. He waved a careless hand back, then spurred his horse into a gallop.

It was in the middle of the afternoon when Ples shook the lines and clucked the mules out, heading northeast. He'd loaded their trail gear, penned up the only three range horses they owned, and had simply pulled the tie-latch shut on the front door of the run-down shack; they had nothing worth worrying about inside.

Ples knew it was lawless country he had to pass through. Homeless returning veterans, drifting men, men looking for better prospects, and just outright thieves and robbers were roaming the countryside. Looking for an easy living.

For that reason, and others, Ples had his seven-shot, lever-action Winchester propped next to him on the wagon seat, and a shell belt full of 44-40s, which his pistol also fired.

Across the prairie Ples went. Sun beating down, trace chains jingling, leather harness creaking, the big Missouri mules keeping a good pace pulling the heavily loaded wagon.

In an hour, judging by the sun, Ples fell into the regular wagon road that would lead a man to settlements east, and the Blackwater.

Ples had a good fifteen miles behind him when he felt the uneasiness. The uneasiness a man who knows trouble feels when trouble is about. Instinctively, he looked back over the tailgate for his unsaddled horse tied back there.

The horse was still there. Trotting along, head up, ears pricked, coned to the side. Alert.

Alert for what!

Now Ples knew that dun horse. He'd been riding him for three years now. And Ples knew there was no earthly reason for that horse to be looking that alert after trotting along back there peacefully for better than fifteen miles with one rest stop.

Ples craned his neck around the canvas cover on his side.

And there they were! Two white men. Riding jaded horses on his hindquarter where they couldn't be seen through the tailgate. And they both had the look of trouble about them. How many there were on the other side Ples dared not look to see, or to guess.

Ples glanced over at his rifle on his right side.

It was there, close to hand.

He twisted his head around, glanced back around the canvas again.

The two men were still there. Riding in the same location, perhaps thirty yards back.

It came to Ples that they must have ridden out of the thickets he'd passed back yonder off to the left. They'd likely watched him come on, saw who he was, and had ridden out after him the moment he had passed. Making no effort whatever to pass him by, which they could easily do riding saddle horses.

A tingly feeling crept up Ples's spine, hair stood up on the back of his neck. And for lack of any better response, Ples simply pulled up. Just stopped. On the notion that he'd force their hand. They'd have to ride on by or make a play.

They rode on by. Their horses at a walk. Three of them; two on Ples's side, one on the other side that he hadn't seen. All three looking back, one grinning slyly at Ples. Nobody said a word. But that wasn't cause for concern to Ples.

The uneasy feeling started to leave Ples; he started to breathe easier.

"Stand up, boy!" a rough voice suddenly commanded Ples from the tailgate.

Ples stiffened as if he'd been stuck in the back with a knife. Taken completely off guard.

Ples stood up slowly, his eyes instinctively sweeping past his rifle, then coming to rest on the man who'd spoken.

He was tall, thin, shaggy looking. Had a pistol pointed at Ples, and a cunning smile on his face.

"Pitch the rifle out!" he barked at Ples.

Ples pitched the rifle out, hearing muffled hoof-falls of the other three riders who'd passed him, coming back.

"Now git down!" the shaggy one ordered Ples.

The thought came to Ples that if he jumped down, maybe in midair he could get lead in the man holding the pistol on him. But what about the other three coming back?

Ples had been around. He knew killing. But he was nobody's fool. Any way he looked at it, they had the ups on him. There simply was nothing he could do.

Ples stepped a booted foot on the wagon wheel, braced himself on the brake, and jumped down.

"Shuck the gun belt!" the shaggy-looking man told Ples after Ples had landed and had gained his balance.

Ples did what he was told. Throwing the shell belt and holstered pistol over where his rifle lay.

"What's he haulin', Butch?" the leader of the three who'd ridden back asked the shaggy-looking one.

Butch Larkin was about six feet tall, rangy, unshaven. Had on a low-crowned black hat, straw-colored hair sticking out over big red ears.

"Look to me like army supplies," Larkin answered, holstering his pistol.

"You freightin' for the army?" the leader asked, looking at Ples.

"Yeah, suh," Ples answered, hoping they'd think twice before taking army supplies.

"He's lyin' through his teeth, Doyle," the man next to the leader said quietly. "Army wagon's marked. This'n ain't."

Doyle Streight was a little bit less than six feet tall. A clean-limbed, solid-built, square-shouldered handsome man. Well bred and educated, he had a keen nose, high forehead, thin lips, and clear, gray eyes. Had on a pinched-crown brown hat, black checked shirt with a black cotton vest over it, and charcoal-colored pants. He'd been one of the few competent officers on Confederate General Marmaduke's gilded, inept staff during the war.

"Charlie, did you see any army markin's on the other side?" Doyle asked the man who'd ridden by on the other side.

"Not as I recall," Charlie answered.

Charlie Sligo was part Kickapoo Indian. He'd fought with the only Indian General in the Civil War, Brigadier General Stan Waite of the Confederate Indian Brigade recruited by General Albert Pike down in the Indian Nation when the war was young.

"Look again," Doyle ordered Charlie.

Sligo gigged his horse around the tailgate, then spoke from the other side of the wagon: "Ain't nothin' over here." Sligo was strictly a southern man now. In his dress, ways, and thinking, he was every bit like his white saddle partners. Whatever the Civil War meant, it didn't mean blacks were on his level. And Sligo would do his part in seeing that they never would be.

Doyle looked appraisingly at Ples, as though he was making up his mind whether to kill him outright or give him a slow, painful death for lying to him. Struck by a second thought, Doyle said abruptly, "Joe, gather up his guns and get up on that wagon seat."

Joe Shaler was medium height, medium weight, ordinary-looking, but a cautious, calculating man who didn't like to take chances. "We takin' it?" he asked, dismounting even as he asked the question.

"He's got no more use for it," Doyle said, looking at Ples.

"What about him?" Larkin asked. "He's seen us."

"Naw, he hasn't," Doyle said. "Have you, boy?" And Doyle smiled wickedly at Ples.

"Naw, suh," Ples said. Ples knew they had him dead to rights. He also knew the less he said, the better off he might be.

"No use in us takin' chances," Sligo said, pulling his gun.

"Sligo!" Doyle snapped. "I won't tell you again. No killing niggers outright."

Sligo grudgingly holstered his pistol.

"What'll we do with him then?" Larkin asked.

"Nothin'," Doyle stated tersely. "Sligo, untie his horse."

Sligo rode around to the tailgate, unsheathed the skinning knife he was wearing, and slit the reins to Ples's horse. The horse jerked up, trotted off a way, and stopped.

"Doyle, this wagon'll slow us too much, won't it?" Shaler asked from the wagon seat, reluctantly taking up the lines. They all knew Doyle was a high-toned, self-centered man. And would occasionally go off like a bomb.

"The business we got in Sedalia," Shaler continued conversationally, "we ought to go on and see to it. What's in this wagon ain't worth the fuss," he added, looking over his shoulder at the bunch of used army stuff.

"What's in it ain't important," Doyle said mildly. "The wagon might be of some use to us for what we got to do. Now take it out!" Doyle commanded.

Joe Shaler slapped the lines, giddy-up'd the team into motion, and they pulled out. Ples standing there watching them go. Jaw tight, a dark, grim look to his face. And killing rage in his narrow, brown eyes.

But Ples knew he'd been lucky in a left-handed sort of way. Plus he was used to hardships, little respect, and white men with careless contempt. Once before, down in Texas he'd been caught dead cold by white draft dodgers hiding out in elm thickets and had been beaten within an inch of his life and left for dead. But they'd answered in the end. And just like then, Ples knew it was wise to keep quiet, stay alive, fight another day.

Striding purposefully, Ples started for his horse standing off a way, ears pricked, eyes walled at him. Speaking soothingly to the horse, Ples finally caught him up after he'd shied away a time or two. Gathering up the reins that had been shortened by at least two feet still tied to the wagon's tailgate, Ples swung aboard, and heeled out, riding barebacked, heading for the Blackwater.

It was coming on to sundown when Fate crossed Fire Prairie and struck Dogwood Gulch, which fed into Sni Creek, the only conceivable place close around where Bowlegs could water the horses.

Spurring his horse over the rim, he slanted down the slope of the gulch, then picked his way along the sandy bottom. Following the gulch a half mile or so, Fate pulled up, ranging his eyes ahead, his nose sampling the thin air for scent of wood smoke, his ears listening for sound, any sound.

Nothing.

Fate touched spurs to his horse, and moved off.

Crouched utterly motionless under the overhang of a low-spreading oak tree a little more than a hundred yards ahead of him, Bowlegs was watching Fate, had been ever since Fate came in off the prairie.

Now Jimmy glanced upwind where his horse herd was grazing peacefully on good grass he'd put them on no more than two hours ago after leaving the Little Blue. Jimmy rose up off his haunches, shifting his Winchester to his right hand, pistol fashion, from where he had had it cradled in the crook of his arm.

Moving on quiet feet, Bowlegs started walking toward the strange rider, weaving his way through scrub oak and blackjack.

The rider was coming on, moving cautiously, eyes searching ahead. Obviously a careful man, Bowlegs thought . . . or a scared tenderfoot.

Bowlegs smiled to himself.

They were no more than thirty yards apart when Bowlegs drew up, looking down in the gulch, rifle at the ready, finger on the trigger. Then Bowlegs recognized who the man was.

A hint of a smile tugged at the corners of Bowlegs's wide mouth; mischief playing on his youthful mind that harbored many bitter memories.

Picking up a clod of dirt nearby, Bowlegs laid himself out at the lip of the gulch. And just as Fate rode below him, Bowlegs rolled the clod of dirt over the edge of the gulch, stirring the weeds and sifting down a trail of dirt and pebbles.

Fate jumped from the saddle. Landing spread-legged, his pistol already in his fist, leveled up at the rim of the gulch where the sudden noise had come from.

"You dead already," Bowlegs called out mockingly from concealment above.

"That you, Bowlegs?" Fate called out from behind the stunted oak he was looking out over.

"Where Butler?" Bowlegs asked, standing up, revealing himself. Everybody knew that Butler was never far away if Fate was around.

"Good way to git yo'self killed," Fate said, rising to standing.

"Where Butler?" Bowlegs asked again.

"I'm by myself."

"You buy horses?"

"Naw," Fate answered, holstering his pistol. "Butler sent me."

"Where Butler?" Bowlegs repeated.

"The old Barlowe place."

"Butler buy horses?"

"Naw. He sent me to talk to you."

"What talk?"

"About us goin' along with you to Sedalia."

"Soon I go," Bowlegs said, glancing toward the west at the sinking sun. And Bowlegs cradled his rifle in the crook of his arm, started walking the rim of the gulch back toward his camp.

"Let's talk first," Fate said, mounting up.

"You talk . . . I listen," Bowlegs answered, and kept on walking.

Fate let his horse pick its way along the bottom of the gulch, keeping opposite Bowlegs walking the rim. Directly the gulch flared out into an alluvial fan that emptied into the Sni during heavy rains. And that's where Bowlegs's small camp was pitched, off to the side.

"You talk," Bowlegs told Fate even as Bowlegs was toeing dirt over the small circle of coals that he'd used earlier.

"Me and Ples takin' a wagon load of supplies to Sedalia," Fate said conversationally, dismounting. "Earnin' wages same as you."

"Where wagon," Bowlegs asked, gathering up his blanket roll.

"Back at the old Barlowe place. Ples bringin' it."

"Why you come here then?" Bowlegs asked, swinging his saddle blanket onto his horse tied there.

"I'm tryin' to tell you how come I'm here," Fate said impatiently.

"You talk . . . I listen," Bowlegs said, throwing his saddle on his horse.

"Why, hell, Jimmy!" Fate said exasperatedly, "I been talkin' but you ain't been listenin'."

"I listen," Bowlegs answered, tightening up his cinch. "You talk."

It took Fate at least thirty minutes more to lay it all out for Bowlegs. Still the idea didn't sit well with him. Bowlegs was used to being lone as a lobo; plus he wasn't disposed to linger. Expecially if he wasn't getting paid for it. Fate had finally told him, "Butler said for me to shoot you if you don't listen."

"I no die," Bowlegs had said. Fate hadn't known how to take that, so he'd let it lie.

It was pitch-dark by the time Bowlegs and Fate got the horses rounded up and started on the move east. By the lemon light of moon they rode, moving the horses out at a good pace, Bowlegs in the lead alongside his two lead mares, Fate bringing up the rear. Heading for the Blackwater and a junction with Ples Butler.

It was coming on to midnight when a dozen miles south of them Ples turned his horse off the wagon road and struck out across the prairie, taking a beeline that would intersect the course of the Blackwater off to his left. Every bone in his body ached from jouncing around on the barebacked beast.

A mile or so farther, Ples pulled up, slid down with effort, and started rubbing his backside.

Millions of stars twinkled down on him and a full moon glowed from above. A slight breeze tickled the prairie grass and whispered through the scrub oaks. Somewhere from the far-off thickets a coyote called.

Ples pressed a hand to his aching back, panning his eyes along the dark loom of tree line ahead, thinking.

Out here it was a chancy thing for any man to ride up on another man's night camp. How would he find Fate and Bowlegs without getting himself shot in the doing? He knew it wasn't likely Bowlegs or Fate would pitch a night camp that could be readily seen by friend or foe. Nor would they have a campfire ablaze at this hour.

The horses. That was the thing, Ples decided. Find the horses, and he'd find Bowlegs and Fate.

Ples grabbed two handfuls of horse's mane and swung aboard, moved out at a trot, angling his horse for the very beginning of the dark outline that was the beginning of the tree line.

At something like fifty yards away, Ples drew up again, studying the rank growth of vegetation vaguely visible in the moonlit night, scrub oaks, elm, stunted willows, and bramble.

Nothing moved; not a sound could be heard; his horse blew.

Nothing more.

And then it hit Ples!

Fate and Bowlegs expected him to arrive driving a wagon. A lone rider prowling around the horse herd this time of night was apt to get himself shot!

Ples threw a leg over the horse's withers, and slid down. Looping the reins over the horse's neck, he tied them together. With a gentle slap on the horse's rump, Ples said, "Go! . . . find your mates . . . or water."

The horse took off at a fast walk. Already the smell of something enticing in his nostrils. Ples followed after him, walking fast, almost trotting, across the slight depression that was the valley of the Blackwater River.

Suddenly the horse changed its course, broke into a gentle lope, angling higher up in the thickets marking the river's course.

And bang! A gun went off; a rifle shot.

Ples's horse screamed in pain, and went into a stumbling, drunken run; Ples flinched in his boots, then instinctively threw himself down on the ground, eyes reaching out into the haze of darkness, wondering where the shot had come from.

Bang! Another shot went off.

Ples's horse caved in in its tracks.

Ples scurried sideways on hands and knees, then scrunched down behind a small scrub oak, plastering himself to the ground, eyes probing ahead where the shots had come from.

Nothing moved. Not a sound could he hear.

Ples put his ear to the ground, listening, holding himself absolutely still.

Nothing.

A minute went by . . . two minutes.

Suddenly Ples heard running hoof-falls! No more than a hundred yards away from him. Departing hoofbeats, fading in the distance. Ples knew right off what it meant.

Bowlegs had got suspicious for his horse herd. Thinking horse thieves were trying to stampede them away, or maybe a wild stallion was trying to toll them in. And taking no chances, Bowlegs had rounded them up and had hit the trail.

Ples stood up, gazing forlornly after the sound of fading hoofbeats into the gathered darkness. His hopes fell, shoulders sagged. Presently he put his hands on his hips and swore softly, disgustedly, eyes still reaching out after the way the horses had gone.

"Butler, you dead already," a voice said quietly at Ples's back.

Ples whirled around, his eyes searching out the voice, his hand instinctively going to his hip where his pistol usually was.

"Jimmy!" Ples said, shocked. Looking at Bowlegs calmly sitting his horse there. "What in hell . . . ?"

Bowlegs had circled around, and had quietly come in off the prairie downwind. He'd been on night guard and all the time had seen the lone rider coming and had woken Fate. Fate had reassured him that Ples was coming with the wagon, not on horseback. So who was the rider prowling the prairie? That's when Bowlegs's suspicions grew. And Bowlegs wasn't a man to shilly-shally around, so he'd attacked, telling Fate to round up the horses and drive them out.

"Where wagon?" Bowlegs asked blandly.

"Why in hell you shoot my horse?" Ples asked angrily.

"Maybe your horse take my horses," Bowlegs said. "Maybe you take my horses," he added accusingly.

"Didn't Fate tell ya I was comin'?"

"With wagon," Bowlegs said bluntly.

"I ain't got the wagon," Ples answered gruffly.

"Where wagon?"

"Four men got the drop on me and took it. Took it like I wadn't nothin' but a ignorant field hand," Ples said disgustedly.

"White men?"

"Yeah."

Bowlegs smiled weakly to himself across the darkness. He'd heard stories about Butler. Word of mouth had it that Ples Butler was one of the few black men out here to be reckoned with. Now Bowlegs was amused that Ples had let somebody take his wagon.

"White man take Butler's wagon," Bowlegs said chidingly. "I hear nobody take nothing from Butler."

"Well, they did," Ples said irritably. "Four of 'em. And there was guns hid in that wagon, guns for them recruits."

"Maybe white man sell guns . . . wagon too. Maybe I buy guns."

"Naw, you won't. 'Cause I'm gittin' it back," Ples said resolutely. "If the good Lord spare me."

"Where's Fate, anyhow?" asked Ples.

"He go with horses. He not go far. You walk."

"I no walk nowhere," Ples said bluntly, mimicking Bowlegs. "You tell Fate what happened and send him back with me a horse."

"What's a matter you?" Bowlegs asked tauntingly, kneeing his horse out, "Butler too good to walk?"

"Butler not Indian like you," Ples said at his back. "You just send Fate back here with me a horse."

"No worry, I send you good horse," Bowlegs said, and galloped off.

Walking stoop-shouldered and dejected, Ples started ambling along in that direction. A lone man unarmed out on the broad prairie under a canopy of wide, star-strewn sky. Defenseless. Naked as a jaybird. But Ples knew deep down what he had to do. He'd have his chance. Somebody would answer.

Chapter Eight

Out on Cowskin Prairie in a shallow bowl of a depression is where Bowlegs caught up to Fate and the horse herd. Fate had the horses bunched, grazing just off from some heavy timber where there was good grass.

Bowlegs told Fate about Ples's trouble and Fate started back immediately with a led horse. It was close to three o'clock in the morning by the time Fate and Ples returned. Bowlegs was still awake, on night guard, when they came clip-clopping in.

"You still woke, Jimmy?" Fate asked conversationally. "I figured you'd be sleep by now." And Fate swung down, tied his horse to a low bush there.

"I no sleep," Bowlegs said. "I watch horses."

"Just a wonder he didn't start shootin'," Ples said facetiously, swinging down.

"Wagon come, I shoot," Bowlegs answered.

"I'll bring the wagon," Ples said. "When we git to Sedalia."

"How you know they was headed for Sedalia?" Fate asked curiously.

"Heard 'em say so," Ples answered. "Said they had business there."

"They don't figure you got nerve enough to come after them, then," Fate stated.

"They figure wrong," Ples answered. "Jimmy, when you moving these horses?"

"Daylight come soon. Daylight no good. You no sleep, we go now."

"I can't sleep," Ples answered. "Not after what's happened. Let's go."

Even as they choused the horse herd out, they all three knew they were riding to Sedalia and trouble. Probably a shooting fight. Fate especially knew it. Ever since they'd started riding together down in Texas, Fate knew Ples wouldn't stand aside for any man. A man abused Ples at his own risk. Not even known tough men could disregard Ples with impunity, like Texas Rangers Captain McNelly and Sergeant Armstrong. They both had tried without success.

Fate knew Ples would kill a man just for the rifle he'd had taken away. They both had paid two months' scouting wages to own the latest cavalry carbine they'd bought from an unscrupulous sutler at Fort Scott. And the supplies in that wagon they'd promised to deliver, well, that was more than reason enough. Fate knew there'd be killing for sure.

Struck by a thought, Fate asked the question that had crossed Ples's mind as they rode along in the dim light of coming morning: "Ples, you reckon there's law in Sedalia?"

"Ain't likely," Ples said. "Anyhow, like Colonel Taylor said, once we leave the fort, the law's what we got strapped around our waist and what grit we got in our craw."

"Maybe they'll let you have the wagon back once they see you ain't scared."

"Ain't likely," Ples said. "I'll have to prove it."

"What about them recruits?"

"Ain't their concern. They ain't got supplies now. If I don't git the wagon back they'll be no worse off."

"What you mean, if 'you' don't get the wagon back?" Fate asked incredulously. "You don't think I ain't goin', do you?"

"I never said no such thing."

"Well, you was thinkin' it."

"How long we been together now, Fate?" Ples asked pleasantly.

"Close to four years."

"Four years," Ples repeated. "And you can read my thoughts now?" he asked tersely.

"Well, not exactly, but . . ."

"Then don't tell me what I was thinkin'," Ples stated frankly.

"I ain't," Fate said, and gigged his horse away, saying, "I'll go tell Jimmy."

"Tell 'im it ain't his concern neither," Ples yelled after Fate.

Looking through the gray haze of daybreak from high atop the water tower where they'd come to fetch more water, Rafer D. was the first one to see the heavy farm wagon drawn by two draft animals come plodding down Sedalia's main street. "A wagon's comin' into town," Rafer D. said down to Hoby, who couldn't see it yet.

"You reckon it's the army comin' for us?" Hoby asked up.

"Don't look like it," Rafer D. said, dipping up the washbasin full of water. Rafer D. kept glancing up at the wagon without care until he saw it pass through town and cross over the tracks. "Its comin' out here," Rafer D. said excitedly. "Maybe it is the army."

Hoby turned in his steps, his eyes searching out and finding the wagon.

The wagon turned into the wide gate of the stock pen, between the two chutes. "Come down quick!" Hoby yelled up to Rafer D. "It's the army come for us!"

Jerico had seen the wagon coming too. "Radford!" he called out from where he was leaning on the top rail, watching the wagon advance. "Wagon's comin'." Jerico had been one of the first to wake up this early in the morning. After Hoby and Rafer D. had gone for the water, and Manigo had started the fire, the recruits had started waking up in ones and twos. For a time he'd been looking out over the prairie, and like the rest of them, wondering when the army was coming.

Radford rose to standing in the angle where he'd slept, and his eyes found the moving wagon.

"Who is it?" Hezekiah asked from where he was sitting down next to where Radford was standing.

"How do I know?" Radford answered.

"Maybe it's the army come for us," Hezekiah said hopefully.

"Ain't but one man," Battie said. "That ain't no army."

The wagon drew up next to the small fire that Manigo had built. Manigo standing there stiff-legged, speechless, watching the driver, who was running his eyes around the stock pen, sizing up what manner of colored recruits the army had enlisted.

The big heavyset driver stopped his eyes from moving when they came to Manigo, and he asked in a heavy German accent, "Who's in charge?"

"Radford!" Manigo yelled out, relieved.

Radford, with Hezekiah at his side, quickened his pace. They'd already started coming forward at Hezekiah's urging.

"He wants to know who's in charge," Manigo said as Radford and Hezekiah drew near.

"He is," Hezekiah said.

"I am," Radford stated, drawing up to the man in the driver's seat.

"Good," the big German said, his thick lip hairs almost concealing the movement of his lips. "I am Frank Hoerheimer," he added, thrusting down a heavy hand to shake.

Radford shook the beefy paw even as Hoerheimer continued with much zeal: "What you do, German people say dat's good!" Swinging down from the wagon seat, he continued, "We hear about you. I bring for you something. You see." He walked back to the tailgate, threw back the flap. "See! All for you. Dat's good."

Frank Hoerheimer was forty-one years old. Big, brusque, and stubborn. He'd left Germany for New York back in the early fifties and had been one of the first of many German immigrants to head West after hearing stories from Free-Soilers of how rich Kansas farmland was. On his way to Kansas, Hoerheimer had discovered that Missouri farmland was just as rich, so he'd settled there. The battle between Free-State and slave-state men had inexorably forced him to choose sides, and Frank had come down on the side of Free-State men. Rising to become a prominent citizen in his German community of Brunsfeld, Hoerheimer had raised a brigade when the war started, and had served as its colonel for two years. His brigade was among those that captured the remnants of Governor Jackson's state militia at the fairgrounds at Jefferson City, sparking a riot when the Germans marched the prisoners through town at bayonet point. Hoerheimer knew exactly what it took to equip and train fighting men.

"All for you," Hoerheimer said bluntly, indicating the provisions and supplies that Radford and Hezekiah were looking at in the back of the wagon.

Hoerheimer had a pile of stuffy-smelling moth-eaten uniforms, crates of hardtack, and various other odds and ends of army gear.

During the war the army's supply system would provide any known loyal man who could raise volunteers with whatever quartermaster supplies he asked for as long as he did some fighting. Especially if his outfit had made a public record with victories applauded in big newspapers.

Up front behind the driver's seat Hoerheimer had bushel baskets of garden beans, corn, and summer apples. And two sides of beef.

"You like?" Hoerheimer asked, watching Radford and Hezekiah, roaming their eyes over the provisions.

"We like," Radford answered.

"We sho' do like it, Mr. Hoer—" Hezekiah started.

"I am Frank," Hoerheimer said, interrupting, pointing a finger at his own chest. "Only Frank."

"We sho' do like it, Mr. Frank," Hezekiah resumed. "We'll unload right away. Won't we, Sarge," Hezekiah continued, looking at Radford.

"Quick as we can," Radford said tersely, looking sourly at Hezekiah. Looking over at the recruits who had gathered around, Radford ordered: "Augie, git up in the wagon and pass that stuff down. Battie, Cecil, Willie, y'all gather round here and take this stuff Mr. Frank brought us. Augie'll pass it down."

"He got any guns?" Jake McGruder asked, peeping over the tailgate, panning his eyes around inside the wagon.

"No guns," Hoerheimer said, shrugging his hands apart.

"I wish I had me a gun," Jake said solemnly.

"What for?" Battie asked. "You'd only shoot yo'self," he added, and smiled amusingly.

"You'll git one soon enough," Jerico stated.

"Fatback knows how to cook," Hezekiah said quietly to Radford, roaming his eyes over the sides of beef. "You ought to let him take charge of that meat."

"I am," Radford answered, "if you gimme time."

"Fatback!" Radford called out loud, "cook up this here food."

"Fatback!" Kalem Jones repeated. "Who's Fatback?"

"Manigo," Battie answered. "You see who's comin', don't you?"

"I'll help Willie," Augie said, and vaulted over the tailgate into the wagon.

"Look at all this stuff," Willie said in low tones to Augie, roaming his eyes over the wagon.

"Let's git us somethin' first," Augie replied conspiratorially. "What you want?"

"Gimme that shirt yonder . . . and that hat."

"Okay," Willie said breathlessly. "I'm gittin' the same thing."

"Hide 'em under the seat," Augie said excitedly.

Directly, Willie and Augie started passing out gear to the rest of them.

"Dot's no way," Hoerheimer said, seeing them blocking the tailgate even as they were trying to pass the gear out. Hoerheimer undid the rope holding the canvas down, and threw back the cover, opening up the side of the wagon. "Now dot's better," Hoerheimer said of his own work. And Hoerheimer reached over the sideboard, withdrew a pair of army pants. He looked them over carefully, then panned his eyes around at the recruits. "This one you try," he said, tossing the pants to John Deese. Deese held the pants up next to his body, judging for fit. The pants were at least half a foot too long, and looked half again too wide.

"Dot's no good," Hoerheimer said, wagging his head. "You try," he added, indicating Battie.

Battie held the pants up to his body and they were almost a perfect fit.

"Dot's good," Hoerheimer said, nodding. "You keep."

Willie and Augie tossed army stuff out of the wagon, each recruit yelling for, and catching, whatever he judged by sight would fit him, and swapping with someone else when the fit was ridiculous. Hoerheimer was leaning against the wagon, watching them having a jolly time outfitting themselves. Occasionally smiling with satisfaction at what he and his German community were contributing to the salvation of the colored man.

The wagon was quickly emptied.

"That's it," Willie said. "Ain't no mo'."

"Darr," Hoerheimer said, pointing back in a corner under the wagon seat.

"That's for me and Augie," Willie said, scrambling forward, retrieving the two blouses and hats that they'd picked out and had stashed there.

"Dot's it," Hoerheimer repeated.

"That's it," Radford announced, looking around at the few recruits who hadn't managed to garner anything at all that would fit, or who didn't want anything.

Like Ike Peeler. Ike had no wish to replace the show outfit he'd performed in for so long for mere pieces of army dress. "I keeps what I got on as long as I can," Ike had said.

And Manigo. He'd simply got left out. He was over by the fire, busy cutting meat. He saw no use in wasting time scrambling for pieces of army dress.

And Hezekiah. He'd whispered to Radford that it wasn't right for the man in charge to be clawing and scratching like that for a uniform they were going to be issued anyhow. The only right thing to do, Hezekiah had said, was to wait until the army issued them proper uniforms. And Hezekiah would wait too.

George Washington Jefferson? The big blacksmith was six feet tall and weighed close to two hundred pounds. Not a stitch of what Hoerheimer had in the wagon would fit him.

The sun had climbed higher and it was already hot when Hoerheimer mounted the wagon seat and took up the lines.

Now he was looking at Radford, saying: "Good luck to youse."

"Thank you, Mr. Frank," Hezekiah said before Radford could speak. "We 'preciate what you done for us."

"I am Frank," Hoerheimer said again, "only Frank." And shaking the lines, he clucked the team out, wheeling the wagon around, heading home.

None of the others had heard Hoerheimer's departing words. They were all looking wonderingly at what Jerico was looking at: Four white men approaching on the wagon road alongside the tracks. Three of the men were on horseback, the other one was driving a canvas-covered wagon.

"Maybe they the army come for us," said Kalem Jones hopefully.

"They don't look like no army," Bobo answered gloomily.

"They ain't," Jerico stated.

"Is that them night riders?" Battie asked Jerico. "You seen 'em."

"That ain't them, neither," Jerico answered, his eyes following the white men.

"What night riders?" Augie asked.

"Hush up, Augie," Willie said. "You don't know what they talkin' about."

"You don't neither," Battie said, "you was sleep too."

The three riders came on, the wagon following after them. Almost in front of the stock pen, one man caught sight of the rabble of shabbily dressed black men in mismatched army clothes standing around in the enclosure where beeves ought to be.

"Doyle," Butch Larkin said scornfully, "you see what I see?"

"I do now," Doyle Streight said, shifting his eyes off to the side where Larkin was looking. "But I don't believe it."

"Joe," Larkin called back, twisting around in the saddle, "you ever seen two-legged nigger beeves?"

"Naw," Joe yelled up from the wagon.

"Well, looka yonder then." And Larkin was grinning slyly, nodding his head toward the stock pen.

"I seen 'em now," Joe Shaler said from the wagon seat. "They look right at home."

"We ought to scatter 'em," Charlie Sligo suggested, an ugly sneer on his face. "Stampede 'em right back where they came from."

"Not now," Doyle said firmly. "We got business to take care of."

So they rode on by the stock pen, each man twisted back in his saddle, looking. Amused at whom the Yankee army was allowing to join up.

"I told you they wadn't the army," Bobo said when they had passed by.

"You ain't told me nothin'," Kalem replied. " 'Cause you don't know nothin'."

Jerico turned in his steps, headed to where Radford and Hezekiah were standing in the angle of the pen, eyes still following the white men riding into Sedalia. "They looked like trouble," Jerico said when he came up.

"Ain't nothin' we can do about it," Radford stated.

"Maybe the army'll show up this mornin'," Hezekiah said gloomily.

The morning wore on. The recruits lying around, or milling about, eating apples that few of them had tasted before. Every now and again a man's eyes would lift, searching out across the prairie, hoping the army would come before trouble did.

Fatback, as they all had started calling Manigo, was shaving off beef for roasting. Any man who had found a skewer, a stick, or a piece of fence wire, anything at all, had a strip of beef roasting over the fire. Ragging each other even as they did so.

Twice they'd stopped their frolicking long enough to watch two groups of white men riding into Sedalia. Each time hoping it was the army, and when the riders rode on by, they were relieved that it wasn't the night riders they all had now heard about.

It was around midmorning when word quickly circled the crude camp that more riders were coming. On the instant in groups of twos and threes they stopped what they were doing, started looking out across the prairie behind them. This time they heard the pounding hoofs of many running horses. Coming in off the prairie instead of down the wagon road.

They all gathered along the railing, watching intently, waiting anxiously. Thundering hoofbeats drawing ever closer.

But the horses were mostly riderless! Only three men mounted.

Jimmy Bowlegs was in the lead, Ples and Fate riding the flanks.

The horses described a wide loop into the V that funneled into the mouth of the stock pen.

On they came.

The drovers' features became recognizable: two blacks and a tawny-complected man riding a long-legged pinto in the lead.

"They colored," Hoby said in a low voice to Rafer D. standing next to him.

"Sho' is!" Rafer D. answered exuberantly. "Hey, y'all, they colored!" he yelled out excitedly to them all.

"We see 'em," Battie replied scoldingly.

"They got guns too!" Jake blurted out, seeing Fate's pistol on his side, Fate pounding leather alongside the galloping horse herd.

"Army ain't comin' for us," Jerico said musingly to Radford. "Them hosses for us to ride to the fort."

Word went quickly along the rail: them hosses for us to ride to the fort.

They stood silently, apprehensively, along the rail, watching the horses being expertly bunched in the far corner of the pen. They noticed with envy the confident, easy way the drovers walked their horses over toward them.

They were filled with esteem when the three riders swung down, loosely tied their horses off to the side, and started walking forward, Ples in his loose-jointed easy manner, Bowlegs with his Winchester in his right hand, and the six-shooter-wearing Fate with his easy swagger, his eyes panning around at the mismatched, shoddy dressed would-be soldiers, obviously no fighting ability among them.

They were awed looking at Bowlegs, armed to the teeth, blond scalp hair on his knife scabbard moving in the slight breeze.

"He's part Indian," Augie said in wonderment to no one in particular.

"Hush up, Augie," Willie whispered. "He might scalp you."

"You better go talk to 'em," Hezekiah said softly to Radford.

"I am," Radford said, moving off, Hezekiah coming with him.

"Which one of y'all in charge?" Ples asked when they met.

"He is," Hezekiah answered.

"I am," Radford stated.

"I bring horses," Bowlegs stated bluntly.

"What for?" Radford asked.

"For you," Bowlegs said. "You must ride to fort." And Bowlegs ran his eyes doubtfully over the shabbily dressed recruits lining the rail, watching them. "Or walk," Bowlegs added amusingly, his eyes dancing at the prospect.

Radford gave a perplexed look across his shoulder, met Hezekiah's equally perplexed look.

"This's Jimmy Bowlegs," Ples said, interrupting. "He don't mean to be blunt like that . . . he's just half wild. I'm Ples . . . Ples Butler. This here's Fate Elder."

"I'm Radford . . . he's Hezekiah."

They shook hands around, with the exception of Bowlegs; for reasons of his own he didn't shake hands with anybody, black or white.

"Army hired Jimmy to bring them hosses so y'all can git yo'sefs to the fort."

"I doubt if half of 'em can ride," Radford said, roving his eyes over the men he was put in charge of.

"I teach," Bowlegs stated.

"Can you ride?" Ples asked Radford.

"Some."

"What about you?" Ples asked, looking at Hezekiah.

"Some."

Ples looked across his shoulder at Fate; Fate shrugged helplessly.

"We better talk this over," Ples said. "Over some of them vittles yonder," he added, nodding his head back over his shoulder where he'd seen the cook at work, and was smelling the aroma.

They all five started off that way, and Ples asked the question of Radford that they all three had been drawn to: "Where'd y'all git all this army stuff?"

"A German feller gave it to us. Came in with a wagon load."

"Right nice of him," Ples said without emotion, panning his eyes over the oversize and undersize, mixed and matched pieces of uniform the men were wearing. "By the way," he added, "did you happen to see another wagon come in this mornin'?"

"Yeah. But they didn't stop, just looked mighty hard. Jerico said they looked like trouble."

"He was right," Fate stated. "Except they the ones got the trouble."

"That wagon had supplies in it for y'all too," Ples said.

"How come they didn't give 'em to us, then?"

"They wadn't suppose to. I was."

"What happened?"

"White men take wagon from Butler," Bowlegs said, amused.

"I aim to git it back," Ples answered.

"That's what the trouble is?" Hezekiah asked.

"That's what it is," Fate said.

"I help you," Bowlegs said seriously to Ples.

"Like Fate told you," Ples said, "it ain't your concern."

"I help anyhow," Bowlegs replied flatly.

"There was four of 'em," Hezekiah said, "and you ain't even got a gun."

"White men take Butler's guns too," Bowlegs said with relish.

"I'll git them back too," Ples stated factually.

Chapter Nine

They gathered around the cook fire where Fatback was stirring a pot of stew of his own making of garden beans, corn, and beef shavings.

"Smells good," Ples said, taking up one of the half dozen tin plates Hoerheimer had brought, along with a fire-blackened pot and other rusty camp utensils.

"Ain't no seasonin'," Fatback answered, "but it'll do." And Manigo slopped a ladleful of stew onto Ples's plate.

"Spoons?" Fate asked, taking up a plate, as did Radford and Hezekiah. Bowlegs simply unsheathed his skinning knife and under an ugly scowl from Manigo was cutting himself a strip from the chunk of beef roasting over the fire on a crude spit.

"Ain't nothin' to eat with," Manigo told Fate. "You'll have to make do."

"He's made do before," Ples answered, squatting on his heels, bringing the tin plate to his lips, slurping hungrily.

"It's good," he said seriously, looking at Hezekiah, and slurped again.

"Guess he knows what he's doin'," Hezekiah said. "He made that rancid pork taste like a feast. Ain't that right, Fatback?"

"I cooked before," Manigo said. "There was thirteen of us."

"Fatback, huh?" Ples repeated, running his eyes over Manigo's heavy body. "Name fits," he added.

While Manigo ladled out stew to the rest of them, Ples continued slurping, talking between slurps: "The man that paid us to bring that wagon . . . Mr. Dinsmore, he said it was on account of a kid you got here that Doc Jennison's partial to. Name's Jerico. Which one's he?"

"He's yonder," Radford said and nodded. "The one with the floppy hat on."

They all looked out at Jerico, a tall, lean-hipped youngster with faded blue jeans on, standing off to the side in the angle of the pen, quietly looking out over the prairie.

"He ain't said more'n two words since we left," Hezekiah said.

"He maybe scared," Bowlegs stated flatly, squatting on his toes, quietly chewing on half-cooked beef.

"He ain't scared," Radford replied. "He killed a man back yonder, a white man."

Bowlegs twisted around, looked again, as if he were seeing Jerico for the first time.

"He killed a white man," Fate said, "he got reason to be scared."

"I kill white man," Bowlegs stated, cutting off another hunk of beef. "I no scared."

"That's 'cause you half wild," Ples said. "You ain't got brains enough to be scared."

"Butler scared too," Bowlegs said. "White man take his wagon." And Bowlegs got up and walked away.

"Damn Wild Man," Butler grumbled at his back, Bow-legs heading toward his horses, where the recruits had gathered, looking at the beasts they'd all have to learn how to ride sooner or later.

Radford summoned Jerico over and they talked while eating. Ples telling Jerico, Hezekiah, and Radford how the wagon load of supplies Doc Jennison had sent had been taken from him. Jerico wasn't at all suprised Doc would do a thing like that.

Ples laid out his plan for getting the wagon back.

"There'll likely be killin'," Ples said finally, looking at Hezekiah, one of the oldest, and more educated-looking.

"Let 'em have the wagon," Hezekiah replied. "We can make do without it."

"I can't," Ples stated.

"What about us?" Radford asked.

"Ain't y'alls concern," Ples told him. "Jimmy's goin' to git y'all out of here."

"What about the army?" Radford asked doubtfully. "We 'sposed to wait for 'em here."

"Army ain't here now," Ples said. "You in charge."

"I know," Radford said dejectedly, looking sorry-eyed at Hezekiah, " 'cause somebody's always remindin' me."

"Mr. Butler," Hezekiah said respectfully, "Radford ain't got no trainin' yet. You ought to take charge . . . git us to the fort."

Ples looked at Fate; Fate shrugged, said honestly, "Make sense to me, Ples. We take that wagon back, the town'll take it out on these folks."

Ples rose to standing, panning his eyes around at the recruits gathered over by the horses, obviously listening to what Bowlegs was telling Willie and Augie, still awed by the wild-looking youngster, armed to the teeth and talking as though he knew everything.

"They'd have to take my orders," Ples said thoughtfully. "All of 'em," he added firmly, remembering the discipline problems he'd had with new men when he was on the state police force down in Texas.

"They will," Radford said.

"Except maybe Hoby," Hezekiah added.

"Which one's Hoby?" Ples asked.

"The one in full uniform," Radford answered, looking out where the men were gathered. From the stuff Hoerheimer had brought, Hoby had bullied his way into a complete uniform, including a misshapen campaign hat, and a pair of down-at-heels troop boots.

"Okay," Ples said resolutely, looking at Radford. "You go tell 'em I'm in charge from now on until we git to the fort.

"Fate, go tell Jimmy to quit his braggin' and come over here."

There was no grumbling when Radford went over and gladly told the recruits that he was no longer in charge, that Mr. Butler was now.

"What's the difference?" Battie asked to no one in particular just as Fate started back with Bowlegs.

"There'll be some difference," Fate said bluntly over his shoulder. "Ples ain't goin' to take no guff. Take my word on that." And Fate and Bowlegs headed back to where Ples and the others were waiting.

"I ain't takin' no guff neither from him," Hoby muttered, more to himself than anybody else.

"You ain't nothing but guff yourself," Battie said chidingly.

"There go your big mouth again," Hoby said. "I'm goin' to shut it yet."

"Try it!" Battie snapped.

"There's time," Hoby said. "Just keep on."

Around the cook fire they squatted, Ples refining his plan for getting the wagon back. Bowlegs chewing on another piece of beef he'd cut off when they first came up.

When Ples was finished, Bowlegs stood up, saying dismissively, "You bring wagon, I no shoot."

"See that you don't," Ples said dryly.

Hiram King

It was an hour past noon when Bowlegs paraded twenty-five raw recruits and thirty head of horses out of the stock pen, heading west out across the prairie. On Ples's orders Manigo and Jerico had remained behind. The rest had been split up into two groups; Radford leading thirteen men and fifteen horses in one column, and Hezekiah leading twelve men and fifteen horses in the other. Each one of them holding the lead rope of one of Bowlegs's lead mares. Bowlegs had cut up his lariat and had made lead ropes, and any recruit who wasn't scared of a horse had picked one he thought he could learn to ride later.

Hoby had been first to pick a horse; Jake McGruder was next. "I wish I had me a gun," Jake had said. "I'd be ready."

"Ready for what?" Battie had asked dryly. "To shoot yo'self?" he added wryly, smiling.

Willie and Augie had horses of Bowlegs's choosing. "You take," Bowlegs had told them, passing over lead ropes to two of his gentlest horses. "They good horses. No trouble . . . they take you good."

So west across the prairie they went. Twenty-five unarmed recruits and thirty unsaddled and unbridled horses, close to a dozen of them still half wild. In two ragged columns they moved; Bowlegs riding in the lead, heading to a place of concealment before the shooting started, as Bowlegs knew it surely must if Butler was to get the wagon back.

They'd been gone about an hour when Ples, squatting on his heels around the dying cookfire, looked out at Fate standing in the angle of the pen. Fate had been watching the irregular columns moving away from him until they had dipped down in a shallow depression, disappearing from his view.

Presently, Ples rose to standing, saying to Fatback, packing up camp gear: "When that wagon come, you move your tail. No foolin' around for nothin'."

"I'll be ready, Mr. Butler," Manigo said. Manigo had had his doubts ever since he'd found out he was to stay behind. Jerico had also remained behind. Right now he was atop the water tower where he'd resumed watching the town after he had informed Ples that he'd spotted the wagon down at the livery.

"Mr. Butler, what if you don't come back?" Manigo asked doubtfully.

Ples gave Manigo a dirty look, then said instructively, "You hear shootin' and don't see me comin', you forgit about this cook stuff and git yo'self outa here."

"Yeah, suh."

"And don't you stop till you catch up with the rest of 'em."

"I won't."

"Fate!" Ples yelled out.

Fate turned in his steps, and headed toward Butler.

"It's time," Ples said when Fate came up.

Fate whistled, then beckoned Jerico down from the tower; Ples picked up Fate's rifle propped there on the camp gear Manigo had stacked up.

"It's time," Ples told Jerico when Jerico joined them.

Side by side they silently walked to the three horses standing slacked-legged at the railing. They all three knew somebody might be walking his last.

They mounted up. Fate stepping a toe into the stirrup and swinging aboard, Ples and Jerico grabbing a handful of mane and jumping aboard. Ples on his barebacked dun horse, and Jerico on a barebacked, fairly gentle sorrel that Bowlegs had cut out for him.

They swung their horses, heading for the gate between the two chutes, Fatback standing by the dead cook fire, watching them go.

"I'll be ready, Mr. Butler," Fatback called out after them, more out of nervousness than anything else.

They kept on riding.

Hiram King

When they turned into the main street leading into Sedalia, Jerico broke the silence: "Mr. Butler . . . anything happen to you, I'll make sho' we git the wagon back."

"We will, Ples," Fate added resolutely.

"See that y'all do," Ples said gravely, and kept on riding.

Sedalia was an east-to-west-running town. And the livery, where the wagon was, was at the far west end.

It was midafternoon when Ples came clip-clopping down Main Street from the east, the dusty street bathed in brilliant sunlight, the sun slanting down into his face, shadows starting to stretch out. Ples Butler, a tight-skinned, slim-muscled, unarmed black man approaching middle age, long legs dangling over the sides of a fair-to-middling dun horse.

He didn't look like much. So the few people who were on the street paid him scant attention, except to wonder if he was lost, or maybe had come into town looking for stoop labor.

On Ples rode.

In front of the Lydell Hotel a man came to the door, looked out at Ples without care, then dashed out a pail of mop water, looked up again carelessly, then went back inside.

Ples kept on riding. Hearing tinny music coming from Chance's Saloon up ahead where half a dozen horses were standing limp-legged at the hitch rail. A mangy dog was lying in the rectangle of shade next to the water trough.

The saloon next door, Aubrey's, is where Ples saw their horses. The big, powerful gray that Doyle Streight was riding standing out prominently. When Ples drew abreast of Aubrey's, two buildings up from the livery, a man got up off the bench out front, and went inside.

Ples kept on riding.

The man who'd got up was Johnny Bray, and Bray was delivering word of Ples's coming. Bray had been inside Aubrey's killing time over beers with Doyle and the others and had heard Charlie Sligo bragging about the nigger they'd scared the wits out of, and how they'd taken his wagon.

And from what Sligo had said, Bray knew this was the nigger.

Bray said as much when he weaved his way over to the table where they were. "You don't mean it," Joe Shaler said incredulously. "He didn't look that thick in the head."

"It's him, I tell you," Bray said.

"Go see, Charlie," Doyle told Sligo.

Sligo shoved back his chair, got up, hitched up his gun, strode over to the batwings, pushed through, and stood on the boardwalk, looking west down Main Street. Seeing that black hat and brown canvas jacket, Sligo knew it was him. Sligo pushed back his hat on his forehead, shaking his head disbelievingly at the stupidity of the black man they'd humiliated and almost killed earlier.

"Its him, all right," Sligo said, back inside at the table.

Joe Shaler looked a look at Larkin; Doyle looked a look at Sligo; Sligo said: "You shoulda let me kill him in the first place."

"Maybe you'll get your chance yet," Doyle said, shoving back his chair, standing. "Let's go see what he's up to."

The rest of them got up from the table, and headed for the batwings. They pushed through, bunching up on the boardwalk, looking west, the way Ples had gone. And every man among them stood stock-still in his tracks.

It was Ples. Coming back, escorting the wagon. Jerico handling the lines, Fate riding at Ples's side.

Fate and Jerico had circled around and had come in in back of the livery. Ples hadn't come the back way because nobody bothered wasting breath trying to convince him to. Fate hadn't even hinted at it when he heard the plan.

Doyle and the rest of them were dumbstruck. They couldn't believe it.

"Well, I'm damned," Doyle said respectfully. "Maybe we low-rated this darky." And Doyle stepped down into the street.

"I told you I shoulda killed him," Sligo said, stepping down into the street too, Shaler and Larkin following him.

The wagon came on.

"They seen us," Fate said in a low voice to Ples, seeing Doyle and the others out in the street.

"Figured they would," Ples replied.

"We got the wagon," Fate said, "let's ride on out if they let us."

"They won't," Ples stated bluntly.

Up ahead, Bray asked curiously, "I thought you said there was only one of them?"

"Was when we took the wagon," Larkin replied.

"Ain't now," Bray said flatly.

Bray was looking at the Army Colt strapped around Ples's waist he'd retrieved from the wagon, along with his saddle. And Fate was holding a Winchester carelessly across his saddle bows and had an Army Colt on his hip too; Jerico had Ples's Winchester resting across his lap on the wagon seat.

"Don't matter how many they is," Sligo said. "They askin' for it too."

In front of Pinkney's Hardware, perhaps twenty-five yards away, Ples pulled up, Fate following suit, as did Jerico driving the wagon.

"Wait here," Ples stated calmly, bringing his horse around, dismounting on the far side. Dropping the dun's reins to the ground, Ples stepped away from the horse. And Doyle spoke:

"What you think you doin', boy?"

"Gittin' my wagon."

Doyle chuckled softly, derisively. "Forget the wagon. Go on back where you came from," he added dismissively.

"Wagon ain't mine to forget," Ples replied mildly. "I was hired to deliver it."

"Consider it delivered," Doyle said, smiling wryly at his own wit. "Now go on about your business."

"Can't," Ples stated gravely.

"You goin' to take it?" Doyle asked mockingly.

"If it comes to that," Ples stated. And moved his feet a little way apart.

Suddenly Doyle knew Ples was deadly serious.

Doyle looked meaningfully at Slico; Sligo grinned knowingly.

"Now you listen to me," Doyle said roughly. "Forget the wagon. Ride on outa here. Leave!"

"Can't," said Ples.

Doyle went exasperated, turning a shade whiter, going red around the lips. "Charlie . . . ," Doyle said gravely. "Do what you been beggin' to do."

Sligo grinned wickedly. Suddenly the grin disappeared. And Sligo went for his gun.

He never made it.

Ples jerked and fired. The bullet took Sligo chest-high on the left side, just as his gun was coming level. Smashing him sideways, bringing his pistol around.

Ples fired into his body again, striking him in the right side that had presented itself.

Sligo came up on his tiptoes, tottered there for a quick second, his pistol going off in the hard-packed earth even as his breath was leaving him, his body sagging to the ground.

Doyle and the rest of them were stunned, simply stunned, seeing Ples kill Sligo like that. They had no thought whatever that Ples would beat Sligo.

Now Sligo was dead. And they all knew that the old, black slouch they thought was a pushover could use what he was wearing. None of them had seen anything like this.

"Doyle!" Larkin blurted out, his voice high-pitched, his gun hand poised. It was more a question than anything else.

Doyle was speechless. Eyes wide, lips red, his mind working at what had just happened.

"Doyle!" Larkin screamed again anxiously. It was more a prompting this time.

Doyle's lips still couldn't form words.

Anxiety was eating at Larkin; he wanted to do something about what had just happened. Impatience driving him. He grabbed for his gun.

Larkin had no chance whatever.

Ples simply threw his pistol around and fired, even as Fate was bringing the Winchester around, firing.

It was a matter of opinion which bullet struck Larkin first. But there was no doubt it was the Winchester that swept his body back about four feet, spilling it heavily in the street.

Ples swung his pistol back around, pointing it at Doyle's belly.

Doyle was buck-eyed now, indecisive. His own pride, ego, and conscience fighting against his will to live.

Sensing Doyle's indecision, Ples yelled to Jerico, "Git that wagon out of here! Move!"

Jerico slapped the lines, and hawed the big Missouri mules out of there. And Ples's horse, ground-hitched as it was, took off right along with them! The cut reins flapping in the wind.

Ples swore in his own mind, still keeping his eyes and his pistol on Doyle.

"Let 'em go, Doyle," Joe Shaler said gently. "Wadn't much in that wagon nohow."

"Just army stuff," Ples added calmly, "for them recruits."

"That's all it was, Doyle," Shaler said consolingly. "Let it go."

Doyle was staring out at Ples, wondering if he could live with himself if he let this go. His temples twitching, the fingers on his gun hand spasming. Doyle knew there was nothing in the wagon except a few old guns. He also knew a dead man had no use for guns.

"Besides," Joe Shaler added soothingly, "we got business, remember?"

Doyle looked around at Shaler as if he were seeing Shaler for the first time.

"Yeah, we got business," Doyle said lamely.

Fate knew it was over when he heard that, and saw the way Doyle was looking. Fate nudged his horse over to where Ples was standing, and removed a boot from the stirrup, keeping his Winchester pointed at Doyle.

Ples swung aboard in back of Fate, and they cantered off, heading down Main Street toward the stock pen, Ples still holding his pistol leveled back.

In front of Aubrey's Saloon where the wagon was just now passing, two men had come rushing out through the batwings at the sound of the shots. Jerico threw a careless shot that way. They both dived back inside.

Not until they reached the hotel did Ples holster his pistol, saying to Fate, "Git a move on, boy!"

Fate booted the horse into a swinging gallop, riding double as they were.

They swung into the gate between the chutes, Ples ranging his eyes over Fate's shoulder.

"They gone!" Fate said into the wind.

The wagon was gone; Manigo was gone; the camp gear was gone.

"There's my horse!" Ples shouted. "Over there!"

Jerico had hitched Ples's horse there. The dun had come trotting up when Jerico rumbled up with the wagon to pick up Manigo and the camp gear.

Fate swung his horse over that way, and Ples slid down, ran over, and jumped into the saddle of his own horse.

Through the stock pen they rode.

Coming out the back way, they struck out across the prairie. Riding to catch up with the wagon and the fleeing recruits somewhere out on the prairie.

Against his wishes Bowlegs was seeking a place of concealment for the ragged bunch of unarmed recruits unable to defend themselves. And where that would be, only Bowlegs knew. "I find good place," was all Bowlegs had said. "I come back . . . kill white men."

"The hell you will," Ples had said. "You'll stay wid them."

"Okay," Bowlegs had said grudgingly. "I watch for you, then."

Ples and Fate set their horses to running in the plainly visible tracks of the departed wagon.

Out on Fire Prairie at something like a mile west of Sedalia, they caught up with the wagon. They galloped up alongside, and Ples signaled Jerico to pull up.

"How come you didn't follow the rest of 'em?" Ples asked, mildly irritated.

"Don't have to," Jerico replied. "I know where they goin'."

Ples looked at Fate; Fate shrugged helplessly.

"You know Jimmy's mind, do you?" Ples asked bluntly.

"Naw," Jerico said, "but if he's got a mind at all, he'll take 'em to the closest water . . . Tabor Creek."

Ples looked a look at Fate; Fate said, "Make sense to me."

Ples looked a look at Manigo; Manigo said, "No water, no eat."

"Make sense to me," Ples said dryly. "Let's go. Fate, watch our back trail."

Across the prairie they went, Fate dropping back about a quarter of a mile or so, every now and again looking back the way they had come.

The land they rode was of prairie grass, the sky they rode under was high, wide, and blue, streaked with thin clouds stretching like gauze.

Twice they crossed over a dry wash, one fairly new where recent runoff rainwater had scoured away all vegetation on its way to the Blackwater. The other one was of ancient times, vegetation having grown back.

They'd been on the move for perhaps two hours when Ples turned his horse, angled in to the wagon from where he'd been riding the point. Riding alongside the wagon, Ples asked over to Jerico, "This Tabor Creek . . . how much further?"

"A mile or so. We top that rise yonder," Jerico said and pointed. "You'll see the tree line."

"I'm goin' have a look," Ples said, looking that way. "You wait here for Fate, then y'all come on." And Ples wheeled his horse, and took off.

Ples galloped ahead, scouting his eyes over the land that had started to rise gradually, meeting the horizon far off in the distance.

Suddenly a rifle went off.

A spout of dirt lifted up just in front of Ples's horse, and a bullet whined off.

Ples jumped from the saddle, landing feet first, and went belly-flat, keening his eyes out through prairie grass in the direction the shot had come from.

It was Bowlegs. Walking from over the rise, leading his horse, his Winchester in his right hand.

Ples got up, swearing under his breath, and caught up his horse.

"Why in hell you do that, Wild Man!" Ples asked when Bowlegs walked up.

"No wagon . . . I shoot," Bowlegs said bluntly.

Ples could read nothing in Bowlegs's eyes of whether he meant it or not.

"You knowed damn well it was me," Ples said acidly.

"I know," Bowlegs said. "Where wagon?"

"It's comin' yonder," Ples said and nodded.

Bowlegs looked out across the prairie and saw the wagon.

"You kill white men?" Bowlegs asked, looking approvingly into Butler's eyes.

"Two," Ples stated. "For no good reason."

"Wagon good reason."

"Maybe . . . maybe not."

"Somebody follow you?"

"Naw . . . not yet they ain't."

"You good man, Butler," Bowlegs said matter-of-factly. "Maybe next time I no shoot."

"Yeah, well, maybe next time I'll shoot you."

"I no die," Bowlegs said, swinging onto his saddle, nudging his horse out. "We wait there for you," he added across his shoulder, pointing his Winchester, indicating Tabor Creek. And Bowlegs rode off, leaving Ples standing there holding his reins.

Chapter Ten

They caught up with Bowlegs and the recruits on Tabor Creek shielded by heavy timber, Jerico having to fight his way through with the wagon.

Tabor Creek was mostly dry now. Blackjack, stunted willow, and bramble marking a steep gully with a narrow channel of slow-moving water in it, bordered by perhaps thirty yards of cracked mud. At the edge of the timber was good grass, and that's where Bowlegs had the horses bunched; and had the recruits in camp at the edge of the cracked mud.

Questions were on everybody's mind when they rode in. Ples and Fate tied their horses where a half dozen other recruits who'd picked horses had them tied on a short picket line that Bowlegs had used his last length of rope to stretch between trees.

Jerico parked the wagon on flat ground at the edge of the cracked mud.

Word quickly passed through camp that Ples, Fate, and Jerico had had a gunfight back there at Sedalia, and that two white men had been killed. Questions started to be asked in low tones, then out loud. Augie was speaking for them all when he asked Willie: "They comin' after us?"

"How I know?" Willie answered. "I'm here with you."

"They comin'," Jake said assuredly. "I'd bet on it."

"You ain't got nothin' to bet," Battie quipped, smiling devilishly.

"Wadn't nobody talkin' to you," Hoby snapped, irritated at Battie's constantly smarting off.

"Wadn't nobody talkin' to you neither," Battie shot back.

"You keep runnin' off at the lips," Hoby said, "I'm goin' to mash 'em for ya."

"You do and I'll gut you like a swamp frog," Battie said, more a promise than anything else.

"Both of y'all ought to shut up!" Radford said advisedly.

"Don't none of us know if they comin'," Hezekiah said calmly. "We better be on the lookout, though," he added, looking at Radford.

"I ain't in charge no mo'," Radford replied. "Mr. Butler is."

Hezekiah looked over to where Ples was talking to Fate, Bowlegs, and Jerico, standing together. "You ought to go over there," Hezekiah said, "hear what Mr. Butler's sayin'."

"I was fixin' to," Radford stated, and walked off.

Hezekiah fell in step behind him, and together they went that way. Followed by Battie, Jake, Hoby, and some others, all wanting to hear what had happened, and what was likely to happen next from Mr. Butler, as they all had started calling him.

When they walked up, Ples had his back to them, watching Bowlegs and Jerico riding out, going to keep an eye out on their back trail as Ples had ordered them to do. Jerico carrying Ples's rifle.

"Anybody else here know how to handle a gun?" Ples asked, facing back around, panning his eyes over the motley gathering of recruits, most of them dressed in a mismatched assortment of civilian and army clothes.

"I can," Radford said. "And Jake here . . . I think," Radford added, looking skeptically at Jake. "He's been beggin' for a gun."

"He's goin' to need one," Ples stated. "They'll come huntin' for us. And ain't no tellin' how many.

"What about you?" Ples asked, looking at Hoby. "I hear you itchin' to fight."

"I ain't itchin' to do nothin'," Hoby said testily. "Battie the one."

"Both of you goin' to git your chance," Ples said firmly. "Fate, git up in that wagon and pass out them guns."

"I want one," Augie blurted out.

"Hush up, Augie," Willie said. "You don't know what to do with no gun."

"I can learn," Augie replied.

"All of you goin' to learn," Ples stated gravely.

Fate mounted the wagon, opened the crate, and started handing down rifles—Spencer carbines, seven-shot, magazine loaded.

Radford was the first to get one, looking at it curiously. It was different from the muzzle-loading Springfield that he'd had at Brice's Crossroads. Jake was next to get a weapon, grinning from ear to ear.

"Now what you goin' to do with it?" Battie asked.

"Shoot," Jake replied unconvincingly, the grin leaving his face. It had suddenly struck Jake that this was serious business, killing business.

Fate passed out twelve carbines and some cartridges. Ples saw to it that Battie and Hoby each got a rifle. Now Hoby was the only man in the bunch fully outfitted, except for a side arm.

"Give Rafer D. one!" Battie said chidingly.

"Yeah, give me one," Rafer D. said.

"You know how to shoot?" Ples asked, surprised.

"Naw, suh. But I can learn."

"Give him one," Ples said to Fate. "Anybody who wants to learn, rates teachin'."

"Only one more left," Fate told Ples.

"What about you?" Ples asked George Washington Jefferson, the oldest man there, hanging back.

"I'm the blacksmith, Jefferson said, smiling proudly.

"Blacksmiths git killed too," Ples said flatly. "Take it."

So fourteen recruits had carbines, including Willie and Augie.

When Augie had been issued one, he'd said, "Give Willie one too."

And Willie hadn't objected.

Now they were all standing around, some eyeing the weapon distrustfully, as Rafer D. was . . . or ogling it proudly, as Jake was. However, nobody was anxious to show off his marksmanship. But Ples knew he had to find out right now who could shoot. He started giving orders: "Fate, them that got a gun, take 'em down in the gully yonder and show 'em how to load, aim, and fire. Let me know if any of 'em can hit the broad side of a barn.

"Bobo, you and Deese finish unloading this wagon.

"The rest of y'all that's got a picked hoss, see to it. Git 'em to water, then put 'em on grass somewhere. He run off, you better catch 'em 'cause you ain't gittin' another one.

"Fatback, git this wagon ready to roll.

"Hezekiah . . . let's you and me talk."

Moving away from the wagon out of earshot of Manigo, Ples and Hezekiah began talking, Hezekiah saying even as they walked away, "You figure they'll come, don't you?"

"They'll come," Ples said. "Only question is, can we stand 'em off?"

Suddenly a stacatto racket of shots erupted from down the gully where Fate had started them practicing firing.

Hezekiah looked that way, saying, "Guns like strangers to most of 'em. You think they'll stand and fight?"

"They'll have to," Ples answered. "Or git shot down runnin'."

"Well," Hezekiah said resignedly, "they knowed when they joined up there'd be killin'."

"Did you?" Ples asked, looking squarely at Hezekiah, an educated-looking man, wearing horn-rimmed glasses, looking out of place out here.

"Didn't figure it'd be this soon," Hezekiah replied. "But I seen dead before."

"And you didn't figure to be one of 'em, did ya?" said Ples. "Well, you might be this time."

"Man can't die before his time," Hezekiah said, and smiled weakly. "What'd you want to talk to me about?"

"When they come at us, ain't no tellin' what'll happen. It'll be up to you to git the rest of 'em outa here . . . across that creek there. And keep goin'. There's a town due west of here, place called Lone Jack. Keep clear of it. There's more trouble there than out here."

"I could stay," Hezekiah said. "Guns ain't no stranger to me."

"Maybe not . . . but they gonna need somebody. I figure not one of 'em know how to pour piss out of a boot yet."

"I 'speck not," Hezekiah said agreeably. "It'll take time."

"We ain't got time," Ples answered.

"What about them out yonder?" Hezekiah asked, nodding his head in the direction Bowlegs and Jerico had ridden out across the prairie.

"I ain't too much worried about them," Ples answered. "That half-wild Indian will see anything that moves. We'll git a warnin' when they comin'."

"And you?"

"I'll stay behind. Put up a fight out yonder somewhere with them that can shoot."

"Might not be many," Hezekiah said doubtfully.

"We'll see," Ples said, looking back down the gully, hearing the sounds of gunfire.

The practice firing down in the gully died off.

Ples drew his pistol, and fired into the air.

The sound racketed down into the gully where the recruits were kneeling in a line, taking turns shooting on Fate's command at branches, stumps, and rocks across the creek.

Rafer D. jumped up to standing, his eyes going wide, yelling excitedly, "They comin'!"

"Where!" asked Augie, jumping to his feet, looking around wide-eyed.

Every man among them came to his feet, looking around at Fate for an answer.

"Ain't nobody comin'!" Fate yelled. "That was Ples. He wants us to come in."

"How you know?" Augie asked skeptically. "They might be comin'."

"I know 'cause that's the way me and Ples always do," Fate said.

"That's y'all signal?" Kalem asked stupidly.

"Sort of," Fate said.

"See, Willie," Augie said delightedly, "they got a signal. Me and you ought to git us one."

"Aww, hush up Augie," Willie answered. "Mr. Butler said this's serious business."

"This's serious business, all right," Fate said. "Now let's go see what Ples wants . . . and tote them guns pointed to the ground . . . or in the air," Fate added rudely, warning them again.

"You hear that, Rafer D.?" Battie said chidingly. "This's serious business . . . don't git scared and run like you did before."

"You oughta not talk, Battie," Hoby replied mildly. "The way you shoot, you better run. You sho' can't hit nobody."

"I bet I can hit you," Battie said, grinning impishly.

"You point that gun at me," Hoby replied seriously, "and I'll break your head."

"Both of y'all shut up!" Radford snapped, turning around in his steps where he was walking in the lead with Fate. "Ain't nobody pointin' no gun at nobody, and ain't nobody breakin' nobody's head."

"You ain't in charge no more, Sarge," Cecil Hall said tauntingly, grinning.

"I know I ain't," Radford replied, "I'm just tellin' 'em. And point that gun to the ground . . . or in the air," he added, looking at Willie walking with his carbine canted at Jake's back.

"See, I told you, Willie . . . ," Augie started.

"Aww, hush up, Augie," Willie said. "I ain't goin' to shoot nobody."

"You accidentally shoot me," Jake said seriously, "I'm goin' to shoot you back."

"All y'all just shut up about shootin' somebody . . . and keep walkin'!" Fate said exasperatedly. "You want to shoot somebody, you'll git your chance."

They kept on walking to where Ples and Hezekiah were, each recruit carrying his piece in a manner of his own choosing, ragging each other as they went. Battie asking facetiously, "Rafer D. what you goin' to do if them white men shoot at you?"

"Shoot back," Rafer D. replied seriously.

"You must be goin' to shoot on the run," Deke said, " 'cause I know you'll be runnin'."

"What about you, freeman?" Battie asked Hoby.

"Shoot back too," Hoby answered, ". . . and my name ain't freeman."

"You keep saying you a freeman like that's your name," Battie retorted.

171

"I don't care what I keep sayin', that ain't my name."

They drew up in front of Ples and Hezekiah down by the wagon where Fatback was hitching up the team, preparing to move out.

"Any of 'em any good?" Ples asked Fate.

"Ples," Fate said, "you ain't goin' to believe this, but Rafer D.'s the best shot in the whole bunch."

Ples looked a look at Fate, an unbelieving look.

"He is," Fate said solemnly. "He hit everythin' I pointed out to him, hit it dead solid."

"You sho' it wadn't luck?"

"Ain't that much luck in the world," Fate replied. "He can shoot good. Ain't that right, Radford?"

"That's right," Radford said. "He shoots good. Real good."

"He do, huh?" Ples said wonderingly, running his eyes over Rafer D. from head to toe, seeing a frail, thin-shouldered kid of twenty-two weighing no more than a hundred and ten pounds soaking wet.

"You handled a gun before?" Ples asked Rafer D.

"Naw, suh. But wadn't nothin' to it. I just pointed at what Fate told me to, and pulled the trigger. I always had good eyes."

"Good eyes, huh," Ples said, looking skeptically at Rafer D.

"I don't know what he got," Fate said, "but he can shoot real good. Ask him," Fate said in a rush, looking around, and pointed at Jefferson.

"He can, Mr. Butler," Jefferson said. "I sho' ain't never seen nothin' like it."

"All right," Ples said to Rafer D., "stand aside over there," and Ples pointed off to the side.

"Anybody else any good?" Ples asked Fate.

"Him," Fate said, pointing at Radford, "he can shoot pretty good . . . and him too," he added, pointing at Jake.

"You two, git over there too," Ples told them, pointing to where Rafer D. was standing.

"What about big mouth here?" Ples asked, nodding at Battie.

"Well . . . ," Fate said, "he got his troubles . . . bad eyes, I guess."

Hoby snickered; Ike Peeler giggled; Kalem Jones grinned stupidly. They all had seen the clumsy way Battie had handled his rifle, and the shots he'd fired way off the mark.

"Battie couldn't hit his hip pocket with both hands," Bobo Jackson said, grinning.

Ples shot Bobo a disagreeable look, then asked Fate: "What about him?" indicating Hoby.

"He ain't up to it neither," Fate answered.

"I can shoot better'n Battie," Hoby said defensively. "At least I hit some of what I aimed at."

"You ain't hit no more'n I did," Battie said defiantly.

Ples eyed them both disdainfully, saying with mock disgust, "And you two want to fight!"

"Wadn't me," Battie said. "Freeman's the one who want to fight all the time."

"You the one," Hoby said, "pullin' that knife on me."

"Next time, I'm goin' to slit your throat," Battie said matter-of-factly.

"All right!" Ples said exasperatedly. "Both of you'll git your chance. Right now, I need a horse holder," he added, panning his eyes around at them.

"I'll hold 'em," a voice cried out.

Ples's eyes found the source of the voice. It belonged to the little kid who'd had on the drooping hat and a seedy brown cotton shirt but now had on a battered campaign hat and a blue army blouse that he'd taken from Hoerheimer's wagon. Augie, Ples had heard them call him.

"Okay, you'll do," Ples said.

"Me too," Willie chimed in, standing next to Augie. "I

can hold hosses." Willie had on a big campaign hat too, with crossed sabers in front, and a blue uniform blouse.

"All right . . . you too," Ples said, since he'd always seen them together anyhow. "Git over there with the rest of 'em."

Turning to Hezekiah, Ples continued, saying firmly, "The rest of 'em is your'n. You in charge, savvy?"

"Mr. Butler . . . ," Hezekiah started, looking cat-eyed at Radford, who'd overheard the conversation.

Radford had a satisfied smirk on his face, seeing Hezekiah put in an uncomfortable position of responsibility as he'd been in.

"I savvy," Hezekiah said lamely.

"Y'all git your hosses and come with me," Ples told the picked men. "Anybody ain't got a hoss, just pick one. We'll sort 'em out later."

They walked away, each man heading for his picked horse, if such he had. Augie and Willie, running in the lead, anxious to get going. Ples standing there shaking his head at the unbridled, headstrong youths, rushing headlong into the unknown. Unable to realize the danger that lay ahead. Just as he'd done when he was their age.

"Fate," Ples said, "git me one of them Spencers and some cartridges."

"Where's your Winchester?" Fate asked.

"Jerico's got it out yonder with Jimmy."

Fate looked slant-eyed at Ples, knowing Ples didn't like anybody using his guns.

"He said he could use it," Ples volunteered. "And the way I figure it, he's gonna need it."

At that instant, Ples looked up at the picked men coming back mounted, Rafer D. walking stoop-shouldered alongside them without a horse, his head hanging dejectedly.

"How come you didn't git yo'self a horse like I told you to?" Ples asked out to him.

"I did, Mr. Butler," Rafer D. answered. "But Battie took it from me," he added. "He says it's his'n, and ain't no mo' broke ones."

"That's just like Battie," Hezekiah said. "Acts like he's somethin' special . . . like he's the cat's meow."

"He do, huh?" Ples said musingly.

"Been like that every since he showed up."

"Wadn't he the one in charge?" Ples asked, nodding at Radford riding by.

"The lieutenant said he was," Hezekiah answered.

"Did he think he was?" Ples asked seriously.

"He didn't think nothin'."

"Well, he wadn't nothin', then," Ples replied. "Man got to think he's somethin' before he's somethin'," Ples added sagely. "He'll learn," Ples continued, twisted around in his steps, watching Radford and the others riding up out of the gully.

Just then Battie came walking his horse down the gully, fixing to cross the creek.

"That the hoss you had?" Ples asked Rafer D.

"Yeah, suh."

Ples took off, walking fast, almost running. He intercepted Battie at the edge of the cracked mud, and with one quick motion reached up, grabbed Battie's shirtfront, and snatched him from the saddle, throwing him in a rolling heap into the mud, his carbine flying out of his hand.

Battie came to a skidding stop, and when he did, Ples was hovering over him. Grabbing him by the shirtfront, Ples whacked him alongside the noggin, a glancing, open-handed lick.

Battie kicked a foot out, lashing out at Ples's legs.

Ples sidestepped the blow, slapping Battie alongside the head even as he did so, saying rudely, "You think you tough?"

Battie didn't answer, just kept on kicking, flailing his two feet wildly at Ples.

Ples held fast to Battie's shirtfront.

Everybody was standing there watching, tight-lipped, solemn. Nobody saying a word.

Ples lashed Battie again, then again, asking wrathfully, "You think you bad?"

Battie stubbornly refused to answer, tucking his head down into his shoulders, absorbing Ples's blows, suffering the humiliation of the others watching.

Ples flailed him again. Then some more, flogging him about the head, asking roughly, "You think you bad?"

Battie still didn't answer.

None of them had any sentiments for Battie. They all saw him as a smart-mouthed dandy without care. But now they all felt Ples was being too hard on Battie, taking it too far. None of them wanted this. Not ever for Battie.

Ples raised his open palm once more.

"Mr. Butler!" Radford called out from up on the rim of the gully.

Ples's hand paused in midair.

"That's enough!" Radford said.

Ples's eyes found Radford, and held there.

They all were waiting, expecting Ples to turn on Radford.

"Battie's goin' to mind," Hezekiah said tentatively to Ples.

Ples lowered his upraised hand, brought his eyes around, looking at them.

"He'll mind, Mr. Butler," Jefferson said earnestly. "We all will."

Ples threw Battie away from him, scowling at him, jaw tight.

"Ples . . . ," Fate called out from over by the horses, intentionally drawing Ples's attention away from Battie.

Ples looked over at Fate.

"That Spencer you wanted is on your saddle."

Ples relaxed, shifted his stance, panning his eyes around at the rest of them, calming himself down.

Suddenly Battie's right hand went for his hip pocket.

"Look out, Ples!" Fate shouted.

Butler whirled around just as the knife cleared Battie's pocket, the blade flashing.

Ples's booted foot came off the ground, the toe raking across Battie's wrist, knocking the blade free. And all in the same movement Ples smashed Battie's jaw with a balled-up fist, driving him down in the mud.

Ples stalked over, picked up the muddy knife, and threw it twenty feet away, sticking it in the ground on dry land. The instant the knife stuck, Ples's pistol jumped into his hand, and he fired . . . then fired again. The gunfire startling every man among them.

Battie's knife was no more.

"Ooww-wee!" said Bobo Jackson breathlessly, awed at Ples's speed and accuracy.

"Damn!" Augie said.

"Hush up! Augie," Willie said quietly.

"Did you see that?" Augie continued excitedly.

"Hush up!" Willie said again. "Mr. Butler might git you!"

Ples's first bullet had shredded the knife handle, the second bullet smashing the blade into a crude U shape.

Ples looked around sullenly at them, saying:

"Anybody else got a sneak-thief knife better keep it outa my sight . . . or be ready to use it," he added gravely.

Nobody said anything. Nobody had expected Battie to try a thing like that.

Ples holstered his pistol.

"We ready to go, Mr. Butler," Hezekiah said, breaking the moment.

"Go, then," Ples shot back, looking at Battie hauling himself up out of the mud, his silk shirt and velvet vest ruined.

"Battie," Hezekiah said, "git in the wagon with Fatback, and let's go."

Battie stumbled that way, his muddy hands held away from his body to keep from muddying up his fancy pants too.

"Not by a damn sight!" Ples snapped. "You ain't gittin' in no wagon."

Battie came to a stumbling stop.

"You comin' with me," Ples said. "Out there," and he nodded out across the prairie, ". . . out there where there's goin' to be killin', like you want to do."

"I don't want to kill nobody," Battie mumbled.

"That ain't the way I heard it," Ples said. "Now git another hoss and git out there!"

Battie looked pleadingly at Hezekiah; shifted his eyes questioningly at Radford; then switched them defiantly on Hoby.

Hoby shifted his stance, bracing himself spread-legged, fists down at his side, trying to buck up Battie.

Battie got the hint. He straightened himself around, and drew up tall, looking bravely at Ples. For a quick minute he looked squarely at Ples, then stalked over, rudely snatched up his carbine, and marched out of the mud onto dry land, head held high.

Deke Poole met him, passed over to him the reins of a half-broken sorrel that he'd picked for himself, saying, "You can have him, Battie . . . I'll git me another one."

Battie looked around at the others watching him.

"Take 'im," Hoby said encouragingly. "That hoss's about as hardheaded as you is, anyhow."

Battie's lips distended slightly, as if they wanted to peel back into a grin; John Deese smiled weakly; Cecil Hall ducked his head, hiding a grin.

Battie took the reins, looking at them as if he were seeing them for the first time. He mounted up, and rode off to join the other picked men up on the rise.

Ples came out of the mud leading the horse he'd snatched Battie off of. He walked the horse over to Rafer D. and, tossing him the reins, asked, "You shoot good, don't you?"

"Yeah, suh," Rafer D. answered.

"Next time somebody take a hoss from you, shoot 'im," Ples said without care, and walked off, heading toward his horse where Fate was waiting.

Rafer D. mounted up awkwardly, and cantered the horse off up the sloping bank, holding on to the saddle horn, bouncing in the saddle like the novice he was, heading to where the other picked men had gone. Jake, Willie, and Augie waiting attentively, sitting their horses.

They'd seen it all.

They watched Ples mount up, and spur out, Fate riding a little bit behind him. At the top of the gully, Fate split off, cantered over to where the other picked men were, watching Ples's back move away from them out across the prairie.

"He all right?" Radford asked when Fate drew up.

"He ain't yet," Fate said, "but he will be."

"Your big mouth is what done it," Jake said to Battie.

"Wadn't his mouth," Fate said.

"What was it, then?" Jake asked.

"He took that hoss from Rafer D.," Fate said. "Ples don't like to see nobody pushed around."

"It was my hoss," Battie said. "I picked him first."

"Mr. Butler said just git a hoss," Rafer D. replied. "And we'd sort 'em out later."

"Wadn't no sortin' to do," Battie answered. "It was my hoss."

"I warned you," Fate said to Battie. "When Ples tell ya somethin', he don't like to tell ya again. Now let's go catch up," Fate added.

They swung their horses out, Fate in the lead. Radford saying to Battie, "Mr. Butler said you was comin' with him. You better go catch 'em."

Battie looked skeptically across his saddle at Radford.

"Just don't say nothin' to him," Radford added. "Just do like he says."

"You'd save yo'self a lot of trouble," Fate retorted over his shoulder.

"Save hisself a lot of whuppin' too," Jake added, grinning, riding next to Battie.

"You shut up, Jake," Battie said, "before I whup you."

"You wanna whup me," Jake replied, "you better bring somethin' to eat 'cause it's gonna take you all day. You ain't got no knife now."

"I don't need no knife for you," Battie answered.

"How come you pulled it on Mr. Butler, anyhow?" Augie asked innocently.

"You shut up, runt," Battie snapped, and heeled his horse out after Ples.

Across the prairie they went, everybody riding silent, watching Ples's back out in front of them.

They left Augie's question unanswered. Nobody knew why Battie had done that. Not even Battie himself.

Chapter Eleven

Five miles east of Tabor Creek six men came galloping their winded horses in off the prairie, and fell into the wagon road leading into Sedalia.

They were uncurried, rough-looking men. Obviously had ridden a long way, and had been in a hurry to get where they were going.

The tall, slight-built man with his left coat sleeve pinned up where an arm was missing stood in his stirrups, ranging his eyes ahead to Sedalia's lone stock pen.

"Seems they gone," Peyton Long yelled into the wind at Frank Yoder, galloping his horse next to him. "Nothin's stirrin' in that stock pen."

"The town'll know what happened to 'em," Yoder shouted back.

They galloped on by the stock pen, checking their horses down to a walk just at the edge of town.

"Where you reckon they at, Colonel?" Luman Bigelow asked Long when they were in front of the train depot.

"We'll ask around," Long said.

"Wherever they at," Milas Soaper answered grimly, "I aim to find 'em. I ain't forgettin' Elmer."

"Ain't none of us forgettin' Elmer," Long replied. "But we got other business."

Word had spread throughout Sedalia and all around of what had happened. Everybody knew that two dead white men at the hands of colored men wasn't the end of it. A posse would surely be put together . . . or a lynch mob.

They passed in front of the Lydell Hotel, drawing stares, six rough-looking men. All wearing side pistols and all except the one-armed man with a saddle gun riding in the boot. Nobody in town doubted they'd come a-running after hearing word of what had happened.

At the sight of a big handsome gray horse and four others hitched in front of Aubrey's Saloon, Long swung his horse over to the hitch rail, the others following suit.

"Colonel Long?" Johnny Bray asked from where he was sitting on the bench out front where he always loafed, picking up gossip.

"I am," Long stated.

"Doyle's inside. He's been expectin' you since this mornin'."

"Well, we're here," Long said. "You in on this too?"

"Not as anybody could tell," Bray said, and grinned, glancing slyly at the other five men fanned out behind Long.

Bray had no stake in the matter. The war was over. He was about the business of putting his life back together, not about joining a covert war. But he knew he was in a town where he had to go along, or get out. He was going along.

"Where's them darkies we got word was holed up in the stock pen?" Milas asked. "We didn't see nobody."

"They lit out," Bray answered.

"Army come git 'em?" Bigelow asked.

"Naw," Bray said. Bray looked around as if the sidewalk had ears, then said quietly to Long, "You better go on inside, Colonel. You'll want to hear it from Doyle."

Long looked a puzzled look at Yoder, meeting Yoder's equally perplexed look.

They crossed over the boardwalk, and pushed through the batwings, Long's eyes searching the place.

"Colonel Long?" asked Doyle from where he and Shaler were sitting over beers. Doyle didn't know the Confederate Colonel Woot Tally had told him to expect was one-armed, but he recognized the uniform Long was wearing.

"You boys git yourself a drink," Long told Yoder and the other four. And Long kept walking over to the table.

"Where's Elmer?" Shaler asked when Long came up. Shaler knew Elmer from guerrilla days, and Shaler knew, like himself, Elmer wouldn't harbor any intentions whatever of being reconstructed by the Yankees swarming all over the country. Shaler had also heard from Woot Tally that Elmer was with the bunch that was on the way in to organize.

"Elmer's dead," Long said, drawing up a chair.

"Where?" Shaler asked, glancing sideways at Doyle.

"Jefferson City."

"Damned Yankees!" Shaler said bitterly.

"Damned niggers," Long retorted.

Doyle almost came out of his chair, his face turning a shade whiter; Shaler's jaw tightened, and he went purple around the ears.

"We had trouble here too," Doyle said gravely.

"With organizing?" Long asked anxiously. "The Yankees found out?"

"Not that," Doyle said. "Something else. Something no decent white man wants to stomach."

"Let's hear it," Long said, more a command than anything else.

Doyle laid out the whole story about their taking the wagon as a lark, and colored men coming into Sedalia to retrieve it, leaving two white men dead.

Colonel Long had listened patiently. When Doyle finished, Long said instructively:

"The general's orders are to organize. That's what we've got to do."

"What about them?" Doyle asked. "Somethin' ought to be done," he added, his eyes instinctively going to Long's empty coat sleeve.

"Don't let that fool ya," Long said positively. "Somethin'll be done." Glancing over toward the bar where his five men were drinking beer, talking among themselves, Long asked, "How many men you got lined up?"

"Just what you see . . . me and Joe here. Bray's out front, but he's doubtful."

"Them niggers . . . they armed?"

"Three I seen. Them that was in the stock pen I can't say."

Long shoved back his chair, stood up, saying succinctly, "We ride in ten minutes."

Long walked over to the bar where his men were lined up and ordered himself a beer. Took a deliberate sip, and calmly set the mug down on the bar, his lips puckered in mild agitation.

"Trouble, Colonel?" asked Yoder.

"Nothin' we can't handle . . . on our way to Lone Jack."

"What kinda trouble is it?" Joe Dockum asked innocuously, taking a sip from his beer.

Long gave the men the shockingly disgraceful news of Charlie Sligo's and Butch Larkin's deaths at the hands of black men.

"First there was Elmer," Donnie Pence said grimly, "now this. Colonel," he added solemnly, "I'm tellin' ya, we got to lay some niggers down over this."

"We will," Long stated.

"When?" Milas asked.

"We ride in five minutes," Long replied.

"That's five minutes longer than need be," Yoder said, returning his mug to the bar top. "I say let's git to it."

It lacked perhaps an hour before sundown when eleven heavily armed, vengeful white men rode out of Sedalia. They rode for a variety of reasons, depending on which man the question was asked of. Not least of their reasons was negligent disregard for the fighting ability of the colored race.

In two bobtailed columns they rode, as was Colonel Long's cavalry training and wont. They expected few repercurssions over killing some insolent niggers. The Yankees weren't everywhere to protect them. It was simply a matter of satisfying their own judgment of what needed to be done.

At the edge of town they wheeled into the stock pen and roared out the back where the rail-and-rider fence had been polled down. Taking to the prairie trail that the straggling recruits had left, and that Hollis had come across out on the prairie on the way into Sedalia.

Hollis Sleman and Bud Hacker, tough, veteran Indian fighters, had ridden into Sedalia late this afternoon looking for a fight when word of what had happened reached them where they had been holed up in the prairie breaks south and a little bit west of Sedalia.

Hollis was a lean, rawboned, hawk-nosed man. Was wearing a fringed, slick-worn buckskin shirt, now greasy from the wild table meat he'd been killing and skinning with the big Bowie knife hanging from his shell belt on the other side of his Colt .45 pistol. His high-crowned black hat had a turkey feather slanted back rakishly in the wide leather band.

Bud Hacker was medium-built, and ruddy-faced. Had on faded jeans, a blue frame-fronted shirt, a bell-crowned gray hat, and a big red bandanna tied around his neck. A blue-black brush of whiskers almost hiding his lips.

Hollis and Bud had drifted down into the country from Fort Kearny in the North Platte country. They'd been derisively known as Galvanized Yankees: Rebels who'd been captured and paroled on their sworn oath they'd not fight anymore against the Union cause.

In the case of Hollis and Bud, they'd been in on John Hunt Morgan's spectacular raid from Tennessee deep into Union-held Ohio. Morgan's raiders had been broken up and scattered crossing the Ohio River, where Hollis and Bud had been captured. They'd been paroled and shipped off to Fort Kearny on their sworn oath they'd help guard the Indian frontier against Northern Cheyennes, who were raising hob. Hollis and Bud promply defected to Red Cloud's band, fighting against blue-clad, yellow-legged Yankee cavalry troopers as they had been doing with Morgan.

Hollis and Bud were two tough, seasoned men of wild country who'd seen it all. And had done their share of killing whenever and wherever it was called for, or suited their purpose.

They both had done some bounty hunter work. And Hollis rightfully had the credit of being a first-rate tracker.

Across the prairie the eleven men galloped, Hollis riding out front like the tracker he was, leaning out over his saddle reading sign.

Three miles west of the stock pen, Long spurred up next to Hollis, saying, "Hollis, this trail you leading us on, I don't see no wagon tracks."

"Nobody told me there was a wagon in the bunch," Hollis answered, checking his horse down to a walk.

Long brought the double column to a stop.

"Somethin' wrong, Colonel?" Doyle asked when he drew up.

"That wagon ain't travelin' with this bunch," Long answered, looking ahead on the trail.

"If there was a wagon," Hollis answered, "it left tracks. And if it left tracks, I'll find 'em."

"They musta split up," Doyle said, "expectin' to be followed."

"Hollis," Long said, ranging his eyes ahead, "we'll sit here a spell . . . you and Bud find them wagon tracks and put us on 'em."

"I seen wagon tracks south of here," Bud answered, overhearing the conversation. "Not more'n a couple hours old, I'd guess."

"That'd be them, then," Doyle said.

"Let's git to 'em, then," Long said, and gigged his horse out, ordering: "Move out, Bud!"

Bud tore out, riding in the lead, Long's empty coat sleeve standing out prominently.

Bud piloted them across the prairie until they came across the wagon tracks he'd spotted earlier. They fell into the tracks, Bud scouting his eyes ahead on the trail leading over the next rise.

Just beyond the rise Ples, Fate, and the others reached the dry wash where Jerico had stopped the wagon earlier. Ples sitting his horse, looking out across the prairie for sign of Bowlegs and Jerico.

Suddenly a shot rang out. Racketing away across the dry prairie.

Rafer D. flinched in his saddle.

"They comin'!" Augie cried out.

"Hush up, Augie!" Willie said.

"That'd be Bowlegs," Ples told them. "Fate, y'all stay here. You," he added, looking at Battie, "come with me.

"You too," Ples told Augie, and Ples swung his horse away down the wash.

Battie looked doubtfully at Radford; Augie looked apprehensively at Willie.

". . . To hold the hosses," Willie said encouragingly.

Radford nodded agreeably.

Battie and Augie nudged their horses out and fell in behind Ples, heading south down the dry wash where the shot had come from.

They found Bowlegs a hundred yards or so away, lying belly-flat at the lip of the wash, looking out across the prairie, eyes steady, body motionless. Bowlegs didn't even break his gaze when they came galloping up on him.

"You see anything, Wild Man?" Ples asked. "Or was that shot meant for me?"

"They come," Bowlegs said.

Ples dismounted and, moving in a crouch, took up a position lying next to Bowlegs, ranging his eyes out across the prairie, asking, "Where?"

"There," Bowlegs grunted. "Dust. Birds fly away." Bowlegs slithered back from his position, and rose to standing.

"Where you goin'?" Ples asked, looking a queer look at Bowlegs.

"I make big surprise," Bowlegs said delightedly. "They follow wagon tracks. I lead them here, you maybe make big surprise too," he added, walking toward his horse.

"Where's Jerico?" Ples asked.

"There," answered Bowlegs, nodding north up the wash. "He make big fight too.

"You no shoot till I shoot," Bowlegs said instructively, and mounted up. "Me, you . . . make good fight, Butler." And Bowlegs clattered off down the wash, obviously circling around to come in on their flank.

Ples ran over, retrieved his saddle gun, and threw Augie the reins, saying, "Shootin' starts, you hang on to these hosses." Scurrying back to the lip of the wash, Ples trained his Spencer out over the landscape, saying facetiously to Battie, still sitting his horse there in full view: "Was I you,

I'd git down from there. Unless you lookin' to git shot," he added tersely.

Battie practically jumped out of his saddle, carbine held clumsily in his hand. He passed the reins over to Augie, ran over and sprawled out next to Ples, canting his rifle out across the prairie, eyes wide, heart pounding.

Ples knew Battie was unnerved. He looked over at him, obviously scared witless in his first shooting fight, his face glistening, his eyes wide.

"You ain't scared, is you, boy?" Ples asked, making light of Battie's fright.

"Yeah, suh," Battie answered, swallowing back the lump in his throat.

"You got a right to be," Ples said calmly. "There's white men comin' to kill ya. That gun in yo' hands says you got some say-so in the matter."

"Yeah, suh," Battie answered, dropping his eyes down at the strange thing in his hands.

"Just keep steady," Ples said. "Do like Fate showed you."

"Yeah, suh," Battie answered weakly.

Warily they advanced in the wagon track, Bud and Hollis riding in the lead, ranging their shrewd, experienced eyes ahead. Struck by a thought, Bud pulled up, ran a palm over the nape of his neck, saying to Hollis, "There's trouble up yonder. I can feel it in my bones."

"Yeah," Hollis answered uneasily, panning his eyes ahead from left to right of the wagon tracks going over the rise.

"What's the matter?" Long asked, reining up alongside them, the column following suit.

"If I recollect, that wash's just ahead yonder," Hollis advised them. "If there's trouble, that's where it'll be."

Long scouted his eyes ahead where Hollis was looking.

"Trouble, Colonel?" Doyle asked mildly.

"Hollis figures there's trouble ahead . . . ambush maybe."

"I wouldn't argue the point," Doyle said, ranging his eyes ahead where the tracks disappeared over the rise.

"Hollis," Long said, "You and Bud ride . . ."

A Winchester went off.

Bud Hacker left the saddle. Dead. A bullet through the windpipe.

Another shot went off.

Hollis's horse screamed, leaped into the air like a scalded cat, came back to earth, and caved under, Hollis leaving the saddle head over heels.

Another unseen shot cracked from up on the rise.

Long heard the ugly whine of a bullet pass by his face.

"Anybody see where that came from?" Long shouted.

"I didn't see nothin'," Doyle answered.

Another shot rang out.

A bullet peeled leather from Yoder's saddle horn.

Their horses got skittish, every man among them holding tight to his reins, the horses fighting the bit, pitching and bucking.

Another shot went off.

"Don't break!" Long yelled. "Hold your saddle!"

Bowlegs fired again.

Hollis!" Doyle screamed, looking for an answer from Hollis, climbing onto Bud Hacker's horse that he'd caught up.

"This way!" Hollis yelled, unsheathing his saddle gun, slapping spurs to his horse, heading off toward the puff of blue smoke he'd seen waft up from over the rise.

They all dug in their spurs, reaching back for their saddle guns. And that's exactly what Bowlegs wanted. To draw their attention to him. He fired again from his kneeling position, and in the next instant he was in the saddle, bullets whizzing overhead. Wheeling his horse, he took out, riding parallel to the wash where he knew Ples and the others would have good shots at his pursuers.

Ples had been watching the whole show from down in the wash.

"Git ready!" he yelled to Battie.

"They comin'!" Augie blurted out.

"They comin'!" Ples repeated. "You just hang on to them hosses!"

"Mr. Butler . . . ," Battie started, his voice breaking.

"Don't worry 'bout hittin' somebody," Ples said, "just shoot, boy! Shoot like hell . . . and keep on shootin'."

"Yeah, suh," Battie answered, raking his tongue over dry lips.

A hundred or so yards up the dry wash, Fate, Radford, Jake, and Rafer D. had taken up fighting positions at the sound of Bowlegs's first shot, Willie holding the horses. They had heard more sporadic shots, and then had seen Bowlegs come racing down off the knoll, riders chasing after him. Fate had put two and two together: Bowlegs was drawing them in front of their guns.

Now, at the sound of gunshots from close up, Fate knew the time was at hand.

Question was, would these raw field hands sprawled out next to him hold up under fire?

Fate looked across his rifle to his right, sizing up the untested newcomers over there: Radford. A man of some fighting experience, he'd heard. Something about Brice's Crossroads.

Jake. Tall, skinny. Lying almost on his side. Looking nervous. Beads of sweat pocking his face. But he'd been one of the first to grab one of the Spencer rifles. And had showed he could use it some, against stumps and things. Would he use it against men? White men? Shooting back at him?

Fate and Ples were credited with being among the very few colored men who'd killed white men and had lived to hear it told. Of course there had been John Lott and Toby Clark back in Texas. Where were they now?

Fate shifted his eyes to his left: Saw Rafer D. About his own age, Fate thought. Lying flat on his belly. Obviously

191

scared. But he could shoot good. Could he nerve himself to shoot a man?

Fate's attention was drawn to running hoofbeats out across the prairie.

"Don't start shootin' till I shoot," Fate told them.

A quick minute passed, the silence ominous. A slight breeze stirred the prairie grass. A shred of cloud drifted by, throwing them momentarily in shadow.

"Radford . . . ," Rafer D. said quietly.

"Yeah?"

"You ever kill anybody?"

"Had to," Radford answered. "Or I'da been killed."

"I never killed nobody," Rafer D. said somberly, his voice trailing off.

"We got to stand up for ourselfs now," Fate said, "or they'll kill us, like Radford said."

"Just shoot like you was shootin' back there at the creek," Radford said encouragingly. "Play like them white men just like them stumps you was knockin' over."

"Main thing is," Fate added, "shoot back at 'em. We make 'em think there's a bunch of us, maybe they'll leave us alone."

"These bullets don't fit!" Jake blurted out exasperatedly, his trembling fingers still fumbling at loading.

"They fit," Fate said calmly. "Just take your time."

"Do like I showed you," Radford added encouragingly. "They'll fit."

"Git hold of yo'self," Fate said, seeing Jake's hands trembling like a leaf in the wind. "Think of somethin' else."

"I can't," Jake said irritably. "This gun just don't feel the same now."

"You the one don't feel the same," Radford said scoldingly. "You got to shoot. Now git ready!"

Ples and Battie could hear drumming hoofbeats now. Close, real close.

And then, there they were!

In plain view. Galloping in a bunch. Bowlegs riding at least a hundred yards in the lead. And Bowlegs was fogging it, his pony's ears laid back, Bowlegs twisting back every now and again, throwing shots at the riders chasing him.

Suddenly they were in Ples's field of fire.

"Shoot!" Ples yelled at Battie.

Ples fired. Squeezing the trigger slowly, deliberately, aiming at the man he recognized from back in Sedalia, the one with the black checked shirt on.

Doyle came clear of the saddle, landing awkwardly. Rolled over, then went motionless, a bullet in his left lung. His horse running on with the rest of them.

Battie fired. A jerky, closed-eye shot that kicked up a spout of dirt way short of the galloping horsemen.

Ples fired again. Aiming at another man he'd seen before.

Joe Shaler's horse went down in a heap of flailing hoofs, tail, and hide.

Hollis swung his rifle and fired a quick shot at the puff of smoke he'd seen blossom out over on his left.

A bullet whined pass Battie's left ear, clipping grass between him and Ples, thudding into the earth on the other side of the wash.

Battie's head jerked down out of sight.

"Keep on shootin'!" Ples yelled at Battie. And lifting up, Ples fired again, screaming at Battie, "Aim higher!"

They were almost directly in front of them when Ples fired this time.

Luman Bigelow left the saddle. Dead. A bullet through the ribs on the left side.

Battie jerked off another shot.

God alone knew where the bullet went.

Donnie Pence and somebody else fired, aiming where Hollis had aimed.

Battie's head fell from sight at the ping of bullets chewing up earth in front of his face. Cringing back into the dirt, he turned his face aside, eyes closed.

"Git up from there and shoot!" Ples yelled at Battie, all the while searching for a target of his own.

The riders were past them now, only their backs visible. Ples fired; Battie fired at about the same time.

Donnie Pence slumped forward in his saddle, hanging on precariously, struck by a bullet high on the shoulder.

And then they were gone. Out of range.

"Let's git back!" Ples yelled, running for his horse. Snatching his reins from Augie's grasp, Ples jumped into the saddle. Off he spurred, saying to Battie and Augie, "come on! They'll need us!"

At the sight of the riderless horse that overtook him, Long looked back over his shoulder. And saw another riderless horse that had sheared off; and saw Donnie Pence lagging behind, slumped over in the saddle.

"Hollis!" Long screamed.

Hollis had no thought whatever of breaking off the chase after Bowlegs.

And Hollis led them directly into the field of fire of Fate's group.

"Shoot!" Fate yelled. And they all fired.

Fate's bullet was an ugly buzz across Hollis's hatband; Jake's bullet hissed across his shirtfront.

Radford's bullet was a nasty whine going past Long's ear.

Rafer D. was the last to fire.

Milas Soaper hung in his saddle a quick minute, then dropped, dead.

Rafer D.'s eyes went wide and his body went limp, head falling down onto his rifle in his hands, overcome at killing his first man.

"Hollis!" Long screamed again.

Hollis slowed down, then veered away, snapping off a

quick shot in the direction from where he'd seen the puffs of smoke flare out.

The sudden explosions of gunfire and zinging lead coming in startled the half-wild horses Willie was holding on to. They started prancing and snorting, tugging against the reins.

"Hold them hosses!" Fate yelled at Willie.

Willie set his weight back on the handful of reins, feet dug in.

One horse reared, lashing out wildly, wanting to be away.

Another horse bolted up, drawing the reins through Willie's fist; another one reared, hoofs lashing out.

A slashing hoof caught Willie across the arm. Willie dodged away, letting go of the remaining reins just as Fate came running up to a stumbling stop.

But it was too late. All five horses were off, heading up the wash, running and kicking.

Fate stood there, glaring after the horses, Willie standing off to the side doubled over, holding his arm.

"I couldn't help it," Willie said meekly. "I almost got kicked."

"I oughta kick you myself!" Fate said angrily.

Just at that instant, Ples came galloping up the wash.

"Our hosses!" Fate yelled to him, pointing. "Go catch our hosses!"

Ples didn't have to be told. He'd seen the horses stampeding up the wash, stirrups flapping in the wind. He knew gunfire had unnerved them and they had broken loose from Willie as theirs had almost done from Augie.

Ples spurred on after them even as Fate was yelling to him.

A half mile or so Ples rounded a slight bend in the wash, and pulled up short, ranging his eyes ahead.

It was Bowlegs. Had three led horses trailing behind him,

still tossing their heads against the bit. Behind Bowlegs rode Jerico. Leading two equally unruly horses.

"Butler . . . you lose horses?" Bowlegs asked mockingly when they drew up.

"I didn't," Ples answered. "I'm ridin' mine."

"Maybe I sell to army again," Bowlegs said.

"Your business," Ples said, nudging his horse up next to Jerico's. ". . . And the army's," Ples added, stretching a hand out for his Winchester Jerico had in his hand. Jerico passed it over and Ples gave him the Spencer he'd been using.

"I told you, we make big fight," Bowlegs said. "Where you go now?"

"I agreed to take 'em to the fort," Ples said. "That's where I go," he continued, mimicking Bowlegs. Ples swung his horse, asking Bowlegs all the while, "What about you?"

"I agreed to break horses," Bowlegs replied. "I break horses."

"Yeah, well, you better git to breakin' or you'll be back at the fort too," Ples said, and heeled his horse off back down the draw. Bowlegs and Jerico following with the five led horses.

Fate was standing in the middle of the wash when they drew up and dismounted, Ples running his eyes around at the whole bunch of them.

"He shot?" Ples asked, looking at Willie holding his arm.

"Naw," Fate said. "Hoss pawed him a little bit."

Ples walked over, removed Willie's palm, looking at the bruise.

"Ain't nothin' wrong with you . . . hoss holder," Ples said with mock scorn.

"What ails him?" Ples asked, looking at Rafer D. sitting with his head down, holding his forehead in his palms.

"Shot his first man," Fate answered.

"If I know the army," Ples said, "there'll be more."

"I shot one too," Battie said boastfully.

Ples gave Battie a dirty look.

"We make good fight," Bowlegs said approvingly.

"You think they'll come back, Mr. Butler?" Bosie asked.

"Maybe," Ples said. "Maybe not."

"Next time we make better fight," Bowlegs said.

"It'd suit me if there was no next time," Ples replied.

"Butler scared," Bowlegs said chidingly.

"Let's git," Ples said, mounting up. "We got to catch up with that wagon and the rest of 'em."

They mounted up, and Ples led the way out of the wash, riding to catch up with the other recruits.

Hollis had led them out of range back out across the prairie, getting away from the angry bullets that had been seemingly coming in from every direction.

Behind them they had heard a Winchester chattering, sending in still more hot lead all around them.

That had been Jerico farther up the wash. Jerico knew it was unlikely he'd score a hit at that distance, but he fired anyway.

When they had got out some distance, Long pulled them up, looking around at his thinned ranks.

"Who's out there?" Long asked, more of himself than anybody else.

"I don't know," Hollis said. "But it was more'n them three Doyle said came into Sedalia."

"Where is Doyle?" Long asked.

"Dead," Dockum answered. "I seen 'im go down."

"What about Shaler?" asked Long.

Everybody looked around, missing Shaler for the first time.

"Yonder," Hollis said, pointing out across the prairie.

It was Shaler. Walking toward them.

They spurred off, heading for Shaler.

Standing in the hollow of the rude horseshoe the riders made around him, Shaler was holding his bruised shoulder, searching his mind for an answer to the question Long had asked: "Who's out there?"

"Only three I knowed was armed," Shaler answered.

"Three, hell," Frank Yoder growled. "It was more like three dozen."

"I'd guess six or seven," Hollis said. "We was to pitch right into 'em, I figure they'll break."

"Not them three what rode into Sedalia," Shaler replied seriously.

Long panned his eyes around at the remaining men, turning over in his mind the men he'd already lost.

"Doyle's dead," Long said finally. "That wagon wadn't worth it. Besides that, our orders are to organize."

"That's what I told Doyle," Shaler said. "But he wouldn't listen. Wadn't nothin' in that wagon but a few guns."

"Guns!" Long repeated incredulously.

"Doyle never figured—" Shaler started.

"Doyle's dead now," Long said grimly, interrupting.

"Besides that," Hollis said, looking back at the way Bowlegs had gone, "we still ain't seen no wagon."

"It ain't the wagon," Donnie Pence said ruefully. "It's them niggers," he added. And Pence grimaced from the bullet wound high on his shoulder.

"I say we forgit 'em," Yoder said sullenly. "At least for now. Donnie here needs a doctor."

"Probably ain't a doctor within fifty miles of here," Hollis retorted.

"Maybe not," Yoder answered. "But Donnie still needs seein' to."

"All right," Long said impatiently, "we forgit 'em for now."

"Lone Jack?" Yoder asked suggestively.

"Lone Jack," Long repeated, swinging his horse away.

Chapter Twelve

It was nearly dark when Bowlegs, Ples, and the others topped out on a low hill and pulled to a stop from where Bowlegs had been guiding them along the trail of bent grass left by the wagon's wheels and by shuffling feet. Bowlegs scouting his eyes west along the seven-mile stretch of woods and bramble off to the right, looking for sign of the wagon and the other recruits.

"They are there," Bowlegs said positively, pointing at a faint break in the rank growth where the foliage had obviously been disturbed.

"I'd guess so too," Ples stated, seeing the same thing. Turning in his saddle, Ples motioned Radford forward.

On the way here Ples had done some thinking about what had happened back there. He knew the shooting fight had been a poor showing on the recruits' parts: Battie cowering away at the mere spat of bullets; Willie and Augie unable to manage the horses; not one of them able to defend himself, let alone someone else. Ples knew they all had a lot to learn if they wanted to make it in the army.

Ples and Fate had been mostly drifting since they left Texas rather than disarm as all colored men had been ordered by law to do. They'd done odd jobs in and around half a dozen army posts from Texas to New Mexico to Kansas. Ples knew these men didn't measure up to what they'd seen, and stories they'd heard. He also knew the whole country was watching, wondering if colored men could make good soldiers. And if they didn't, the whole country would blame the entire colored race. And Ples knew better.

Thirty-nine years old, two bullet holes in his body, and few prospects in sight, Ples knew his life was behind him. But what about these youngsters? Looking to be cavalrymen. And Fate? Judging by his own past, Ples knew the army was a future worth having. And he'd made up him mind to help them gain it.

Ples interrupted his own thoughts when Radford guided his horse up alongside him.

"Yonder," Ples said, pointing, "is where the rest of your men at."

"My men?" Radford asked. "You in charge, ain't you?"

"I am for now," Ples said, "but you'll be before long. You might as well start learnin' now before you start gittin' somebody killed."

Radford looked back apprehensively over his shoulder at Fate.

And could read nothing in Fate's expression.

"You ride in there," Ples continued, "and find the rest of 'em."

"Ples . . . ," Fate said tentatively, "they got four of them carbines wid 'em. Somebody'll likely start shootin' at anything that moves in the dark."

Ples and Fate both knew a man didn't ride into another man's night camp without good reason. And only then at his own risk. But Ples waved a silencing hand at Fate, and kept on talking, telling Radford: "They your men. You got to learn 'em . . . learn to chance 'em or not. Just go in real slow and easy."

"Mr. Butler . . . ," Radford started.

"Just foller them wagon tracks," Ples said instructively.

"What if they start shootin'?" Radford asked seriously.

"They start shootin', you done it wrong. They don't shoot, you done it right."

Radford looked along the wagon tracks for a long minute.

"Just put your mind to it," Ples said encouragingly. "You'll do all right."

Radford drew up straight in the saddle. Stiffening his jaw, he heeled out.

Fate looked a critical look at Ples.

"Only way he'll learn," Ples replied flatly.

A time or two Radford looked back uneasily, Fate's words rattling around in the back of his head: "Just do what Ples tells ya to."

Jerico, Battie, and the others were slouching in their saddles, watching apprehensively as Radford rode off, wondering if that would be the last they'd see of him alive. None of them said anything though; nobody wanted Ples's temper to go off again.

Then Ples himself started getting second thoughts. These recruits' destinies had somehow become his own. And Ples wanted no part of foul-ups.

"Jimmy . . . ," Ples said quietly.

Bowlegs gigged his horse up alongside Ples's.

"Circle round yonder," Ples stated, nodding, "and see he don't git hisself shot."

"I teach," Bowlegs replied.

"Naw, you won't," Ples answered firmly. "Let him do it. Let him hoe his own row. Only way he'll learn."

Bowlegs looked again at Radford riding off, then returned his eyes to Ples, saying, "I see to it." And Bowlegs galloped off.

Ples stepped down out of the saddle, watching Bowlegs heading out to the north. Dropping down on his haunches, Ples looked out contemplatively at the rest of them, wondering how in hell he'd let himself become involved in this. "Y'all might as well git down," Ples called out to them. ". . . Dismount," he added self-consciously.

They all clambered down out of their saddle, Battie practically falling out of his.

Fate walked his horse up to where Ples was. Jerico rode up with him, asking, "You figure them white men'll come after us?"

"Not tonight, anyhow. They won't give up, though," Ples added matter-of-factly.

"What about the army?" Fate asked. "You figure they comin'?"

"If they was, they'd have been here by now."

"You mean we got to take 'em all the way to Fort Leavenworth?"

"Don't see no other way," Ples answered, staring off. "They'd never make it on they own."

"What about the ranch we was to start?"

"It can wait. I wadn't born with no ranch. I can make do without one for a spell longer."

"I thought you—"

"Ranch'll keep," Ples said curtly.

Fate looked a queer look at Ples. Fate knew Ples had had his mind set on squatting on and fixing up the old Barlowe place. Had been dead set on settling down. He'd said as much. Often.

Galloping off north, Bowlegs had swung west and had struck the line of trees. Pushing his way through, he fell into a dim game trail, and followed it south where he knew the recruits would be.

Bowlegs was a man of wild country. Could follow the most obscure trails, and could read sign as an educated man could read books.

Now in enveloping darkness, he drew up, his eyes probing ahead, his ears reaching out for sound.

Nothing.

He dismounted, tied his horse to a low-hanging branch, then on quiet feet, moved off quickly, knowing he had to find the camp or the lookout, if such there was, before Radford spooked somebody.

Some twenty yards along the game trail, Bowlegs paused in his steps, listening into the darkness. Hearing night sounds: A wood rat scurrying across dry leaves; an owl hooting longingly into the slight breeze tickling the leaves. Bowlegs froze in his tracks. His nostrils reaching out, sampling the breeze.

Wood smoke!

It took Bowlegs only seconds to discern the faint but distinct odor of burning blackjack wood, and even less time than that to determine the direction the odor was coming from. And in the next instant he was off, moving silently, swiftly in that direction, his eyes probing the darkness ahead.

Concealed in the dark loom of a big blackjack tree, he drew up, listening into the night.

And that's when he heard it: the faint sound of movement, somebody or something rustling bushes.

Bowlegs sneaked forward, moving in stages, flitting in and out of shadowed darkness under the trees.

Suddenly a figure loomed up, just in front of him.

It was Hoby.

And just at that moment the swish of hoofs through grass caught his ears. And Hoby's too.

Hoby jerked around, his rifle coming up, leveling out.

In one quick lunge Bowlegs was on Hoby, his pistol smashing against Hoby's noggin, sending him sprawling forward.

Hoby crashed down in the bramble of bushes he'd been concealed in, the rifle falling away from his hands.

"Hoby!" Jefferson called out excitedly, hearing the sudden thrash of bushes and the abrupt thud of Hoby's body hitting the ground. ". . . was that you?"

"You no shoot," Bowlegs replied evenly.

"Jimmy . . . ," Jefferson called back, obvious relief in his voice. "That you?"

"It's me."

Jefferson came running, dodging in and out of bushes and brambles, making his way to where Bowlegs's voice had come from. Jefferson drew up, breathing heavily. "You sneakin' round here in the dark like that, I coulda shot you," he said bravely.

"You dead already," Bowlegs replied flatly.

Jefferson's eyes suddenly flared wide at the sight of Hoby lying unconscious in the bushes, Bowlegs down on his haunches, watching him like a guard dog.

"What's happened to him?" Jefferson asked, wide-eyed.

"He fell down," Bowlegs said without emotion. "You go there," he added, nodding to where the sound of hoof-falls had come from. "You no shoot though. Bo-see is there. You take to camp. I get Butler . . . then we come."

Jefferson looked around distrustfully at the menacing surroundings blanketed in darkness. "What about him?" he asked, stalling, looking down at Hoby's sprawled body.

"I bring," Bowlegs said. "You go."

"What if it ain't Radford out there?" Jefferson asked skeptically.

"He is there. You listen for sound of horse walking. You find."

Bowlegs kept his eyes on Jefferson, moving off hesitantly, slightly crouched, head sweeping from side to side, obviously scared.

"Maybe Radford shoot you," Bowlegs said tauntingly.

Jefferson froze in his steps.

Bowlegs smirked at his own prank, then said seriously, "You go. He no shoot."

Jefferson moved off heavy-footed, noisily, disappearing from Bowlegs's sight into gathered darkness. Directly, Bowlegs shifted his eyes to Hoby, still out like a light. Bowlegs unholstered his pistol, pointed it to the air, deliberately thumbed back the hammer, and fired a signal shot.

Bowlegs had but one intent in mind, but his one shot made other things happen: Jefferson almost jumped out of his skin out there in the darkness surrounded by looming trees casting spooky shadows; Radford no more than forty yards downwind from Jefferson bolted out of the saddle and scampered behind the nearest oak, leveling out his rifle; out across the prairie, Ples and the others heard the shot. Ples lifted his eyes toward the sound, then rose to standing; back at the wagon, Hezekiah and his group were jolted into motion, congregating around the wagon, everybody wide-eyed with apprehension.

"That you shootin', Jimmy?" Jefferson shouted back into the darkness.

"I shoot," Jimmy answered.

"At what?"

"You no worry. I signal Butler. Now you go find Bo-see."

Radford had heard it all on the thin night breeze.

"I'm over here," Radford called out from the darkness. "Don't shoot. I'm comin' where you at."

Out across the prairie where they'd heard the shot, Augie was asking, "You heard that, Willie?"

"I heard," Willie answered.

"You reckon Radford's shot?" Augie asked.

"How I know?" Willie answered. "I'm here with you."

"That was a pistol shot," Ples stated instructively, almost offended at this new display of their lack of even rudimentary knowledge of firearms. "Bowlegs's pistol . . . our signal."

"See, Willie!" Augie said in awe. "They got signals."

"Aww, hush up, Augie," Willie replied disgustedly.

"Let's go," Ples called out. "Mount up."

Back at the wagon, Hezekiah was trying to gain some

semblance of order, preparing to defend the camp, if need be. "Who all's got a gun?" he shouted out.

"I got one," John Deese said, looking down at the strange thing in his hand that might put him in danger, get him killed.

"Me too," Bobo Jackson admitted quietly.

"Deese!" Hezekiah said, "git up to the front of this wagon! Bobo, you take the back! Anything move, shoot! The rest of y'all git down out of sight . . . and be quiet!"

Deese and Bobo took up positions, Hezekiah looking out over Deese's shoulder.

It was quiet. Nobody moving. All ears peaked.

Seconds passed. Directly Deese cocked his head, said in a whisper, "I thought I heard somethin'."

"Me too," Hezekiah answered. "Git ready."

Deese raised his rifle carelessly, his quivering finger on the trigger.

"Hezekiah!" a voice called in out of darkness. "Hezekiah . . . it's me. Don't let nobody shoot!"

"Jefferson?" Hezekiah called back.

"Yeah . . . and Radford."

Hezekiah patted Deese on the shoulder. Deese's head slumped forward, nervous tension draining away from his body. His finger falling away from the trigger, the rifle drooping in his hands, even as Hezekiah was saying, "Y'all come on in . . . ain't nobody goin' to shoot."

Jefferson and Radford made their way to the rude camp, picking a clear path through thickets and bramble. They drew up to the tailgate of the wagon dimly lit by a circle of light cast by Fatback's dwindling cook fire, everybody standing back watching them.

"Who shot?" Kalem Jones asked.

"Bowlegs," Jefferson answered.

"At what?" Hezekiah asked.

"At nothin'. That was a signal for Mr. Butler and them to come on."

"Where they at?" asked Cecil Hall.

"Waitin' out yonder," Radford said. "Mr. Butler figured if we all came in at once, y'all mighta started shootin'."

"We ain't that stupid," Hezekiah retorted.

"Speak for yo'self," Radford said, remembering that Jefferson had told him that Hoby was about to shoot him until Bowlegs hit him over the head.

"We heard shootin' back yonder," Cecil Hall said. "Anybody hurt?"

"Naw," Radford said. "We drove 'em off."

"They killed two of 'em," Jefferson said, repeating what Radford had told him.

"They comin' after us," Kalem said plainly. "I know white people."

"What they botherin' us for?" Cecil Hall asked innocently.

"Just 'cause we colored," Hezekiah answered.

"Like Mr. Butler said," Radford added, "if we don't fight back, they might kill us."

"All of us?" Kalem Jones asked, astonished.

"You dead already," a voice said from beyond the fringe of firelight.

It was Bowlegs. He'd quietly guided his horse up without being heard. Had Hoby riding behind his saddle.

"You no listen good," Bowlegs said solemnly, "maybe you all die."

Hoby slid down, walked into the firelight. Fingering the lump Bowlegs had put alongside his noggin.

"What happened to you?" Deke Poole asked.

"He fell down," Bowlegs said flatly.

"Where's Mr. Butler and them?" Hezekiah asked.

"They come pretty quick," Bowlegs answered.

"How they know where we at?"

"Butler know," Bowlegs said. "Butler look . . . listen good. Not like you," he added disdainfully.

Ten minutes later Butler led the rest of the men into camp. Everybody lolling around, eating more hard bread and stew that Fatback had hastily thrown together. They had been talking gravely of what might happen to them if Mr. Butler for some reason didn't show up. Now Butler was here.

Ples and the others dismounted somberly, silently. All eyes on Ples, everybody wanting to hear details of what had actually happened back there.

"They was after us!" Augie kept saying. "Tryin' to kill us!"

"Hush up, Augie!" Willie said. "Mr. Butler don't like talk like that."

"Talk like what?" Augie replied innocently. "It's the truth. Rafer D. shot one of 'em. Knocked him clean out of the saddle. Mr. Butler did too. And Battie too . . . I think," he added doubtfully.

"Ain't no think to it," Battie said proudly. "I killed one of 'em."

"Killin' ain't nothin' to crow about," Ples said sagely, running his eyes around the camp. Ples had heard the bragging talk on the way here. And he knew it for what it was—false courage. These men, boys really, had a lot to learn.

"Fatback!" Ples called out loud.

"Yeah, suh!"

"You got anything fit to eat?"

"Yeah, suh. I saved you some."

"Bring it," Ples said, loosening the cinch on his saddle. "All of y'all listen to me," Ples said, still undoing his saddle gear, "you figure you had trouble today, tomorrow'll likely be worse."

"They comin' after us," Kalem Jones said ominously, more to himself than anyone else. "Ain't they, Mr. Butler?"

"They'll come," Ples said positively, throwing his saddle gear down. "Take my word on it."

Ples was lying back in the crook of his saddle, thinking, waiting for Fatback to fetch the food when Jerico and Fate came up, Fate talking, saying: "Ples, Jerico's got somethin' he thinks you ought to hear."

"Say it then," Ples answered, looking at Jerico. "I ain't goin' to bite your head off," he added sarcastically.

"I didn't mean it that way," Fate said apologetically.

"I know he ain't goin' to bite my head off," Jerico said plainly.

"You don't know nothin'," Ples said gruffily, "none of you do. Now, you got somethin' to say . . . say it."

"I told you," Jerico said, annoyed, looking at Fate. "Mr. Butler don't listen. I ain't got to tell him nothin'."

"Now you listen, boy," Ples said, coming upright from the crook of his saddle, "you got somethin' to say, say it."

"Tell 'im!" Fate snapped at Jerico.

"Well . . . ," Jerico started halfheartedly, ". . . them white men that jumped us . . ."

"What about 'em?" Ples asked anxiously, leaning forward, his interest piqued.

"Jerico thinks they headed to Lone Jack," Fate cut in.

"I knowed that," Ples said. "Ain't nowheres else within thirty miles they can go." Ples relaxed back in the crook of his saddle, shifting his eyes from Jerico to Fate and back again. Ples knew Fate knew the country roundabout as well as he did.

"Ples," Fate said exasperatedly, "Jerico here knows the town. Knows the people there."

"They'll come tonight?" Ples asked, looking with renewed interest directly at Jerico.

"I can't say for sure," Jerico said. "But I wouldn't be surprised. Mr. Butler, you don't know that town like I do. Lone Jack was the worse secesh town round here. There's been killin's. On both sides. We'd kill, and they'd come huntin'. They'd kill, and we'd go huntin'. That's the way it was out here."

"Who you mean *we?*"

"Redlegs," Fate cut in, "Jerico says him and Jack Mann rode with the Redlegs."

"Redlegs?" Ples asked.

"Jayhawkers," Jerico answered.

"Jayhawkers," Ples repeated incredulously. "They was all white men."

"All except me . . . and Jack sometimes," Jerico said. "Doc Jennison took us. He said it was only fittin' we fight for our own freedom. Stand up and be men."

"Doc Jennison?" Ples asked. "The man what sent them supplies?"

"Yeah, suh."

Ples looked off. Then looked again at Jerico. Looked hard. As if he were seeing him for the first time.

"You killed before?" Ples asked Jerico.

"Yeah, suh."

"White men?"

"Yeah, suh."

"In Lone Jack?"

"Yeah, suh."

"Not only that," Fate said, "he killed a white man on the way here . . . back there in Jefferson City."

"Army know?" Ples asked.

"Yeah, suh. Said they'd know where to fine me if they wanted me."

Ples swore under his breath. "They more'n likely comin' then. Maybe tonight."

"Either that . . . or before daybreak in the mornin'. That's the way they was."

Ples looked a look at Fate.

"I told you," Fate said to Jerico. "Ples listens . . . sometimes."

"What we goin' to do, Mr. Butler?" Jerico asked.

Ples looked off, thinking.

"We ought to ride into Lone Jack and . . . ," Jerico started.

"Git Radford over here," Ples said calmly, interrupting.

"I thought you was in charge," Jerico said, looking a question at Fate.

"I am," Ples stated. "For now. But I ain't in the army. Y'all is. Git Radford over here. He ought to hear . . . before somebody start gittin' killed."

"Mr. Butler," Jerico said doubtfully, looking over toward the campfire where they all were, "you ain't figurin' on takin' none of them into Lone Jack, is you? They'd give us more trouble than they would them . . . maybe one of 'em git killed."

"I know that," Ples answered. "That's how come I want Radford here. He's the one got to answer to the army. All of you do. But they got to learn," Ples added, nodding toward the rest of them, "just like you had to."

Just at that time, Bowlegs rode in on his long-legged pinto, leading a bunch of horses. The four with saddles used to belong to Bigelow, Soaper, Hacker, and Streight, men who'd been shot from the saddle back there out on the prairie; the first three dead, the latter shoulder-wounded. Bowlegs had retrieved their horses after they had joined his own hidden-away rank-broken bunch, as loose horses will do.

Bowlegs had arrived in camp like a shadow. And had sensed that something was brewing when he saw Ples, Fate, and Jerico talking quietly off to the side. Bowlegs didn't say a word, shifting his eyeballs from one man to the next, and reaching out his ears. Knowing perfectly well the white men hadn't given up the fight, Bowlegs was intent on hearing what was to be done, if anything.

"Good horses," Bowlegs announced casually, swinging a leg over his saddle horn, sliding clear of his saddle. "Maybe you take trade," he added, looking at Jerico, remembering that Jerico had told him earlier the horse he had been riding wasn't to his liking.

"I no take trade," Jerico said, mimicking Bowlegs.

"Maybe you take," Bowlegs said, tossing the reins of Streight's handsome gray to Fate.

"Mine'll do," Fate answered flatly.

"No sweat," Bowlegs replied evenly, repeating what he'd heard white soldiers say around various forts he'd been in and out of. "Maybe I give to Augie. He make good ride."

Bowlegs tied his own horse's reins on the saddle horn, as most men out here didn't do, talking conversationally as he did so, saying, "Butler, I think you make big talk. What you talk?"

"Jerico here figures them white men comin' tonight."

"They come," Bowlegs said without emotion. Taking his Winchester from the saddle scabbard, Bowlegs walked over, squatted on his haunches in the rude circle where they were, his eyes following Jerico, walking off to fetch Radford. "White men alla time come," he said, more to himself than anybody else. "Butler know," he added, shifting his eyes to Butler.

"I know," Butler replied. "Maybe not tonight though."

"Butler look . . . listen good," Bowlegs said, "but maybe not learn so good. Maybe I teach Butler too," he added, smirking at Fate.

"Like hell, Wild Man," Ples growled.

"Jerico thinks they comin' tonight," Fate said. "I think they comin' tonight. Now Jimmy's tellin' you they comin' tonight. Seems to me the only question is, what we goin' to do about it?"

"Radford gits here," Ples replied, "we'll let him decide."

"Radford don't know the country," Fate said. "Jerico do. You ought to go on what he says, and decide."

"Fate," Ples said patiently, "ain't neither one of us got to answer to the army. And this Wild Man here sho' as hell don't even answer to God. We'll wait and hear what

Radford's got to say. He's the one got to answer."

"Dead man no answer," Bowlegs said without concern. And got up, gathered up the reins to the other three saddled horses.

"We'll see," Ples replied, lifting his eyes to where Jerico and Radford were walking back toward them. "Army put him in charge, least we can do is let 'im be."

"Maybe he no look . . . no listen good," Bowlegs replied. And walked off, leading the horses over to where he'd seen Willie, Augie, and some others lolling around, listening to Battie telling high tales as he always did when there was a lull.

"Mr. Butler," Radford said, walking up, "we ain't s'posed to go to no Lone Jack."

"I told 'em already," Jerico said, looking innocently at Ples.

"Nobody said y'all had to," Ples stated to Radford.

"Lieutenant Badger said I was to git us to Sedalia and wait for the army. That's all. And stay out of trouble."

"Way I heard it," Ples said casually, "you had trouble already. Jerico killed a white man."

"Wadn't my doin'," Radford said. "Lieutenant Badger told us all not to git off that train. And I reminded 'em of it. We can't go off to Lone Jack. We got to go on."

"That's sound reasonin'," Ples replied. "That's what I'd do, was I you. But there's killin' afoot, boy," Ples said grimly. "This Lieutenant Badger ain't here now. Army ain't neither. You the one got to decide. Now, sit down and listen. Then make up your own mind."

"I thought you was in charge, anyhow," Radford said plaintively, ruefully.

"This's different," Ples replied. "Anybody git killed, you the one got to answer to the army. Not me."

"What about you?" Radford asked, looking at Fate. "You want to go into Lone Jack too?"

213

"I ain't in the army," Fate said. "I ain't got to answer to nobody . . . but myself."

"We ought to go into Lone Jack," Jerico stated. "Let 'em know there's tit-for-tat. Like we done before. They'd leave us alone then."

"This ain't before," Ples said, looking at Radford. "You got to do what's best for all of y'all," he added seriously, nodding toward the others.

"We make big fight," Bowlegs demanded.

"You got no say, Wild Man," Ples said. "Not in this."

"We make big fight there," Bowlegs said again, nodding toward Lone Jack, "or we make big fight there," he added, nodding out toward the prairie. "They come," he stated flatly. "Butler know."

"He's right," Ples said to Radford. "Out there or in Lone Jack, trouble is trouble. Only thing you got to consider is whether to wait for it or meet it head-on."

"You'd go in?" Radford asked.

"Yeah," Ples said deliberately. "If it was only me and Fate I had to worry about, I'd go in."

"I'd go too," said Fate.

"Me too," said Jerico.

"I make big fight too," said Bowlegs.

"We got more'n us to worry about though," Ples said pensively, looking around at the others. "Ain't no tellin' how many of 'em will turn out to be good soldiers, but I aim to see they all git the chance."

"Mr. Butler," Radford started, "we ought to—"

"We make big fight," Ples said, interrupting, looking at Bowlegs. "But not in Lone Jack. I gave myself a lot of argument but we got no fight in Lone Jack."

"Where, then?" Jerico asked.

"Out there," Ples said, nodding out across the dark, brooding prairie.

"Tonight?" Jerico asked.

"Tonight," Ples answered. "Right now."

"You sho'?" Radford asked. "We ain't never marched at night."

"You will tonight," Ples said firmly. "Git every man in rank . . . whether on foot or horseback. And tell every last one of 'em to stay in ranks where he's put. Last thing we want out there in the dark is broken ranks. Go tell 'em now . . . and let's move out."

"Now we make better fight!" Bowlegs stated fervently.

Bowlegs's life was all about chasing wild horses and shooting at white men crossing the plains and prairies that belonged to Indians, as he and other like-minded Indians saw it. Nothing else suited him better than to shoot at white men.

From over by the dying campfire where Radford was heading, and where Hezekiah was sitting in the dim glow of sputtering firewood sucking on his unlit corncob pipe, they heard Augie ask out loud of Fatback, "Ain't nothin' else to eat?"

"Hush up, Augie," Willie replied, "you et already. Let's go to sleep."

"Ain't nobody sleepin'," Radford spoke out loud from where he'd just walked up into the firelight.

"How come?" Hezekiah asked around his pipe.

"We movin' out," Radford said. "Mr. Butler thinks them white men comin' back."

"Let 'em come," Battie stated, sitting up close to the fire. He'd been telling tales of New Orleans, and every other place he'd been or imagined he'd been, to Willie, Augie, and anybody else who'd listen. "I'll kill another one," he added brashly.

"You ain't killed nobody," Hoby said derisively. "Only thing you killed was time."

"Ain't nobody talking to you!" Battie shot back. "Freeman," he added mockingly.

"Both of y'all shut up!" Radford snapped. "And git a move on . . . all of you. We movin' out in ranks. Fatback, put that fire out, and git that wagon ready to roll!"

Chapter Thirteen

A dozen or so miles north and a little bit east of Pardees Hollow, six men cantered their horses in off the moonlit prairie. At the edge of town they passed in front of a thriving wild apple grove, leaves trembling in the slight breeze. Checking their horses to a walk down the north-to-south-running main street, they ranged their eyes around the unlighted, war-ravaged town of Lone Jack.

Lone Jack and the surrounding country had been rabid secessionist country ever since 1854 when the Kansas-Missouri border war first kicked off. Twice Lone Jack had been burned. Once when a Union antislavery man had been hanged in the town square for making his sympathies known too vociferously and Doc Jennison and his Jayhawkers had ridden in and burned the town in retaliation; and once when Quantrill and his raiders set fire to the jail after outnumbered and surrounded Union troops had barracaded themselves inside. The fire had spread like a prairie fire, inadvertently burning the town. Quantrill hadn't batted an eyelash over the incident.

Now Lone Jack was mostly without population. Didn't even rate a federal patrol, let alone federal garrison troops, who were twenty-five miles north at Kansas City.

The six men riding in were all grim-faced, and trail weary. Led by a slight-built, one-armed man wearing a dingy Confederate gray colonel's uniform, a misshapen campaign felt hat pulled down tight on his head. Riding next to him was a shifty-eyed, hawk-nosed man wearing a flea-bitten, moth-eaten buckskin shirt, and had a turkey feather sticking in his wide-brimmed hatband.

None of them spoke; there was nothing to say. As returning beaten Confederate veterans, every man among them had seen perhaps hundreds of neglected, war-torn towns such as Lone Jack. And every man among them was bitter, revengeful. Laying blame for their own and their part of the country's wrecked condition to the Yankees and their nigger underlings. But that would change, would change real soon, ex-colonel of cavalry Peyton Long figured, riding ramrod straight in the saddle, empty coat sleeve jiggling with the motion of his horse.

They rode on. Running their eyes around the wasted town. Passing in front of what looked to be a newspaper office, or possible a dry goods store. Then next a two-story hotel on the right, two saloons and a trading house on the left.

Lone Jack was quiet. Nobody stirring this time of night. The only sounds they heard were dull thuds of their own horse's hoofs clip-clopping on hard-packed prairie sod.

A dog broke the silence, barking down at the end of town, drawing their attention. A light showed down there on the left.

Peyton Long led them out of the middle of the street, angling toward the dim light.

They reined up at a livery stable. The light they'd seen was a sooty lantern hanging over the door.

Out back a horse snorted, then again.

They sat in their saddles. Looking around for sign of human life.

Nobody.

Long twisted around in his saddle, looking back at the town they'd just ridden through.

Nothing. Just the loom of half a dozen, no more than eight, dark, huddled buildings.

"Town ain't much," Yoder said, bringing his eyes back around from where he'd looked at what Long had seen.

"I guess this's it," Long announced, wearily slumping forward in his saddle.

"I seen worse," Hollis retorted, his eyes inspecting the run-down livery barn. Dismounting, Hollis's eyes probed the livery stable even as the rest of them dismounted, stretching fatigued muscles. Hollis walked over, threw the latch on the barn door, and swung it open.

A swarm of startled bats fluttered to life, flapping out the rectangle of a window up in the loft; a scared wood rat took off like a scalded cat.

Hollis was startled, jumping into a fighting stance, his pistol leaping into his fist, his eyes darting around, looking for a target.

All he saw was a wide rectangle of moonlight streaming inside, casting weird shadows over the hay-strewn bare ground. Hollis stood braced there, eyes searching around, pistol leveled out.

"Anybody?" Long called out at him.

"Damn bats," Hollis said rudely, holstering his pistol.

Crossing over the threshhold, Hollis casually inspected the barn.

At Hollis's back, Long walked in, leading his horse. The others following suit, roaming their eyes around the barn, Frank Yoder disapprovingly. Yoder didn't like what he was looking at. He'd had his fill of sleeping in hay barns, bushes, and hollows. Eating when he could out of tin cans with fingers or sticks.

"Colonel," Yoder said grimly, "I say we roust the town. Git somethin' decent to eat, and a fit place to sleep."

"Wouldn't hurt my feelin's none," Joe Dockum said solemnly.

"I seen worse," Hollis said again, still roving his eyes over the barn.

"I bet you have," Yoder said scornfully. Yoder was grouchy, fed up with Hollis and his ways. "You bein' a Galvanized Yankee . . . a Cheyenne squaw man, and all."

Hollis went white at the lips and red around the ears. "Was I you," Hollis said gravely, "I'd leave it be. I done my Yankee killin'," he added, facing around deliberately.

"Some of Colonel Morgan's men made it back," Yoder said. "And that ain't the way they told it."

"Whoever told otherwise is a liar," Hollis answered threateningly, letting go of his reins, freeing up his gun hand.

"No use in bringin' up the past," Long said patiently. "We all done our duty . . . as best we saw it. Ain't none of us no worse . . . or better than the other. Let it lay. We got other business."

"Suits me," Hollis said grudgingly, going slack-legged where he'd been braced for action.

"Just you keep away from me," Yoder stated grimly.

"Colonel," Dockum said, relieving the tension, "Donnie here still needs seein' after. I'm with Frank. I say we wake up the town."

"Ain't no use in that," said a voice from behind them.

They all turned around. And saw a shabby-dressed, slack-jawed, played-out old man.

The old roustabout smiled weakly, showing bad teeth, then said pleasantly, "Name's Belch . . . Seth Belch. Y'all welcome to stable ya animals. If you be needin' somethin' else, just say so."

"A doctor," said Donnie Pence.

"Some vittles and a decent place for white men to sleep," Yoder added.

"Town's y'all's," Belch said, shrugging his slack shoulders indifferently. "Foller me." And Belch led out at a slouchy walk, store-bought pants too big for him switching from side to side around his loose hips.

Yoder looked inquiringly at Long; Long shrugged carelessly, and fell in step behind Belch. They walked out the barn door in a loose bunch. Belch talking over his shoulder even as he walked, asking, "Where you boys comin' from?"

"Sedalia," Long answered, knowing full well it was nobody's business where a man was from.

"Sedalia, huh?" Belch repeated with interest. "Heard the town was pickin' up some. Texas cowboys comin' in with beeves, and all. But then," Belch continued curiously, "just two days ago a feller rode in here said there was niggers sleepin' in the stock pens. Makes no sense to me," Belch added, wagging his head at the seeming contradiction. "Did y'all see 'em?"

"Not exactly," Long answered flatly. "But they was there, all right."

"Darnest thing I ever heard of," Belch said in wonder. "This feller said they was part of this new nigger outfit they puttin' together up there at Fort Leavenworth. That what you figger?"

"That ain't what we figger," Joe Shaler answered, "that's what we know. We run into 'em."

"Never expected to see it in my lifetime," Belch said, then added, "Lone Jack goes to sleep with the chickens but it's got most of what a man wants. Except a doctor," he added, looking back at Donnie's drooping shoulder. "Most anybody can treat a bullet wound though. How'd it happen?"

"One of them niggers what was in the stock pen," Shaler answered.

"Yankees got 'em armed already?" Belch asked, shocked.

"Somebody has," Dockum said. " 'Cause they sho' is."

"You don't say," Belch said, shaking his head in astonishment. "Like I always say, country's gone to hell now," Belch commented. Then continued talking conversationally, leading them up on the boardwalk: "I'm sort of the town's welcomin' committee. Course it ain't my concern when a man comes and goes less he needin' somethin'. And most men do . . . one thing or another," he added facetiously, grinning knowingly.

"We got business," Long answered. "And it ain't whore chasin'."

"Most men ain't chasin' 'em," Belch answered agreeably, then added sagely, "but somehow they seem to catch 'em anyhow.

"By the way," Belch added, clumping along the rotting plank boardwalk, "this business you got . . . important-lookin' feller rode in here with five others about sundown expectin' to meet somebody. Said I was to let him know . . . day or night, if anybody came askin'. You askin'?"

"Maybe," Long answered, glancing sideways at Yoder. "What sorta feller was he?"

"Decent enough. Tall, well-dressed, high-toned. Politician, I'd guess. He done most of the talkin'. A Yankee," Belch added sourly. "Wore a kid glove on his right hand. War wound, I 'speck. The other one who said anything at all was tall, lanky. Mean-looking. Had on a Reb cap and had a long scar along his jaw. The other four was just run-of-the-mill fellers. Neither one of 'em muttered a word."

"The man with the scar," Yoder said, looking across his shoulder at Long, "that'd be Woot."

"The man what done the talkin'," Long asked Belch, "he say anything worth repeatin'?"

"Just what I told you. Conversation I picked up, though, they come in to Kansas City by steamboat. Rented the horses they put up at the stable back there."

"Any one of 'em mention anything about organizin'?" Long asked.

"That Yankee-talkin' feller did. Left word I was to notify him if anybody's interested."

"He leave a name?" Long asked.

"Naw. And I didn't ask. He just said I'd know where to find him if anybody's interested."

"We interested," Long answered. "Where is he?"

"They put up here," Belch said, turning into the doorway of the Harris House hotel.

The Harris House hotel was a two-story, frame-fronted box of a structure. Had been the best hotel for miles around until Border Ruffians and Kansas Jayhawkers took turns abusing the place after pillaging and plundering the town. Now the whole building was shot up, rooms run down, furniture seedy. It had been headquarters, hideout, and whorehouse for Bill Quantrill, George Poole, Bloody Bill Anderson, and other guerrilla fighters when they chanced to come out of the Sni Hills after they'd been tipped off that the feds, or Doc Jennison's Jayhawkers, had vacated the town.

Belch simply turned the door lock and led them into the hotel lobby. Nobody bothered to lock up now that the war was over and ex-Confederates, guerrillas, and civilians too were displaced, on the move with little money in their pockets.

"Behind the desk," Belch said, jerking a thumb in that direction, "there's whiskey of a sort. Never touch the stuff myself, but you boys welcome. Make yo'self at home. I'll see if that feller's stirrin'."

Even as Belch hobbled up the rickety stairs leading up to the second floor, Long and the others were roaming their eyes over the lobby, sizing up the place.

The lobby was nothing more than a large saloon. Had a run-down settee and a shabby cowhide chair over next to the wall. Down in the far corner was a scattering of dusty tables, four backward-turned chairs leaning against each.

Hollis made the first move, heading over toward the desk, saying, more to himself than anybody else, "I'll have me that drink."

"Do you good too, Donnie," Shaler said, glancing at Donnie's limp shoulder.

"Do us all some good," Long stated, and they all headed toward the desk where Hollis was bent over, searching behind the counter. Directly, Hollis came out with a bottle that simply said WHISKEY. Uncorking the bottle, Hollis took a deep pull. And turned blue around the ears.

"Rotgut!" Hollis announced, wincing. "I had worse though," he added through puckered lips.

Clustered there around the desktop, they all took a drink of the fierce stuff. Shaler peeled back Donnie's shirt and poured a draft of whiskey onto the spot where the bullet had broke into his flesh.

Donnie screamed.

"Do it good," Shaler stated.

"The hell you say," Donnie retorted, wincing at the sting.

Just then Belch stepped out on the stair landing.

"Colonel, you can come on up," he announced.

Long made his way up the stairs, holding on to the banister with his one good hand.

"Room two-oh-one," Belch told Long when he reached the landing. "I'll see to the rest of 'em and the hosses," Belch added, descending the stairs.

At Room 201 a heavy, commanding voice announced, "It's open," when Long rapped on the door. Long pushed through and crossed over the threshhold. And came eye to eye with a tall, slim-chested man. Under a high forehead, he had a Roman nose, and below that thin sinister lips. He was sitting in a maroon satin night robe at a crude table in the middle of the room.

"Have a seat, Colonel," the heavy voice said. And the man behind the voice waved a kid-gloved hand at the empty chair across the table from him, his deep blue eyes shifting for a quick second at Long's empty coat sleeve.

Empty coat sleeves and pant legs were a common sight now. Yet Long's didn't go unnoticed.

Long pulled back a chair, and sat down, looking across the table strewn with a large map, some saddlebags, two books, and two bottles, one whiskey and one rye; both had been tapped some.

"Name's Bickley," the big man said. "William Bickley."

"Long . . . Colonel Peyton Long."

"I hear you're interested in joining us."

"I'm interested," Long answered. "Me and five more boys. We just come in. Word came to us General Forrest was organizin'."

"That he is," Bickley said, smiling thinly. "General Forrest Bedford is a true-blue Southern man. Realizes like we do that this's white man's country. And we aim to redeem it. This war ain't over yet. Not by a damn sight."

"What'd you have in mind?"

"You know what these are, Colonel?" Bickley asked, coming out of his robe pocket with an outstretched palm of coins.

"Yankee money," Long answered. "And not much of it."

"If that's all you think, Colonel," Bickley said, smiling cunningly, "you'd be wrong. See that?" he added, turning a coin. "Heads on both sides . . . copperheads." And Bickley let the words sink in, his eyes holding Long's, staring at the double-sided penny.

"Copperheads," Long said reflectively, thinking back on all he'd heard and read about the Confederacy's behind-the-lines allies, a sort of fifth column. Northern men with southern sympathies who encouraged and protected northern deserters, spurred on draft riots, and with Indiana as their home state, sought to establish a Northwest Confederacy in alliance with the Southern Confederacy. Their aim had been to draw off Yankee troops from southern battlefields.

"You a copperhead?" Long asked, struck by the remembrance of it all.

"True blue," Bickley answered profoundly. "Being up North among the Yankees, sometimes I think we raised more hob than you boys did down South," he added proudly.

"Except we done the sufferin' and dying," Long said solemnly.

"That's unfortunate," Bickley said seriously. "But we had casualties too. Lost some of our best men up there in New York City. We almost succeeded in burning down the place like we were sent to do except that damn Yankee who mixed the stuff for us didn't tell us exactly how to use that so-called Greek Fire concoction. I was there," Bickley added. "Got this to prove it." And Bickley brandished his gloved right hand that had been incinerated to a gnarl when the vile of sodium palmitate he was attempting to ignite the hotel room with went off prematurely in his hand. Bickley's trigger finger was still in working order though. That .32 Colt he carried in his left breast pocket wasn't just for show.

"But like I said . . . it ain't over with," Bickley added resolutely. "We've got plans, getting the right men in the right places all over the country. This time, when we strike, success will be ours."

"I got five men downstairs," Long said. "How do we fit in?"

"I don't know about the rest of them, Colonel, but you'll fit in nicely. General Forrest sent word about you. Feller named Tally . . . Woot Tally. He rode in this morning. The rest of them, I'll have to take your word on them."

"They all good men," Long said assuredly.

"They're the only kind we want. Fainthearted half measures won't do this time. We're going all out," Bickley said, a greedy glow in his eyes.

"Way I heard it, General Forrest only want to take care of the niggers," Long said. "Seems to me you got somethin' else in mind."

"The country, Colonel," Bickley said gravely. "The country's what we got in mind. We get the country, we got the niggers and everything else what's in it. Then we can do with them what we want."

"That's mighty ambitious," Long said doubtfully.

"That it is, Colonel. That's why we've got to have good men in the right places.

"Speaking of men," Bickley continued, "Tally's got some with him. You'll take command of them. I can't speak for a one of them, so it'll be your judgment. Once you're in operation, whatever you say goes."

William Franklin Bickley from Dayton, Ohio, and ex-Confederate Colonel Peyton Long from Pulaski, Tennessee, talked way into the night under the dim light of a coal-oil lamp and good whiskey before them.

Long came to find out that the man in his early forties talking glibly across the table from him was the nephew of George Bickley, the original founder back in 1863 of the Knights of the Golden Circle, the KGC, as they styled themselves. Back then, under the leadership of George, the KGC intended to overthrow all the countries running from the tip of Florida, around the shores of the Gulf of Mexico, to the Yucatán Peninsula. And then break up these vast tropical lands into twenty-four slaveholding states that would thrive on king cotton. And of course George had intended on getting the slaves to work the fields from the southern states. Lincoln's Emancipation Proclamations in '63 and '65 had shattered old man George's dream. But not William's. William had now revived the KGC, and had dusted off the old scheme he'd heard his uncle talk so much about. With the promised muscle-and-scare tactics of this new outfit General Forrest was bringing into being, the Ku Klux Klan, William intended to set the plan into motion again.

Now, William was telling Long, "Nothing will work unless we keep the niggers docile. Uneducated and unarmed. It's imperative that we put a stop to this idiotic army notion of arming niggers and training them to fight."

"How you figure on doin' that?" Long asked. "Army's already got 'em under arms and trainin'."

"There's ways, Colonel," Bickley said, smiling wickedly. "Colonel Hoffman of the United States Army at Fort Leavenworth is also General Hoffman in the KGC. That black regiment what's there at the fort, he's got orders to see that they don't measure up, see that the country come to scorn them. And believe me, Colonel, there's plenty more army men just like Hoffman who think like we do. Like I said, all we've got to do is get the right men in the right places, and success will be ours."

"There's more black recruits on the way," Long said.

"It'll be your duty to take care of them."

"It'll be a duty I relish. One of 'em shot Private Elmer Babcock, a decorated Confederate veteran who was travelin' with me."

"Where?" Bickley asked with keen interest.

"Back there in Jefferson City. A Yankee major . . . Major Holmes refused me the privilege of pressing court-martial charges."

"This's exactly the kind of incidents the KGC don't want. But maybe we can turn it to our advantage," Bickley said musingly. "In the morning I'm going to dispatch Colonel Hoffman out in the field. I'll let him know about this. That nigger what done the shooting, you get his name?"

"Jerico . . . just Jerico is all I heard him called."

"That's to be expected. Until recently most of 'em ain't had a last name. And don't care about one now," Bickley added carelessly. "I'll dispatch orders to Colonel Hoffman demanding he convene a court-martial. The whole country needs to hear about it when a nigger kills a white man. You'll get your court-martial, Colonel," Bickley said firmly. "But there's more to this than that. Right now we're settin' up headquarters over in Leavenworth City. Right outside the fort. That's where you'll take your men. You'll use that as a listening post. Keep your eyes and ears open. Notify me at the Trout House hotel if anything comes up. We'll turn any and every little incident or mistep to our advantage."

"When do we go?"

"Daybreak in the morning. On your way there you'll take care of that bunch that's heading to Fort Leavenworth. Your orders are to smash 'em, break 'em up. Scatter 'em to hell and back. Word gets out what happens to niggers who enlist, not another black soul will. Them that are already at the fort will be hounded and harassed day and night. They'll wish they hadn't come. And woe be unto any one of 'em who sets foot off that army post."

"General Forrest sent word no outright killin'," Long answered. "Seems he's afraid the federal government will step in."

"You and your men just take care of the ones on the way," Bickley said, more an order than anything else. "And report to me when and how it's done," he stated firmly. "As commanding general of the KGC I'll do the worrying about the federal government. Besides that, we've got men in high places too. Right at old Andy Johnson's elbow," Bickley added, smirking shrewdly.

"You mean the president? Andrew Johnson?" Long asked incredulously.

"The same," Bickley said. "The KGC has no fear of federal interference. There'll be no squeamishness in our methods this time. We'll do whatever we have to do. We mean to succeed.

"Now, Colonel," Bickley said dismissively, "it's getting late. I suggest we turn in. We both have a big day ahead of us tomorrow." Following Long's lead, Bickley rose to standing, saying all the while, "Rooms on the top floor reserved for the KGC. Put your men anywhere you like. Tally's got his down the hallway there. And, Colonel . . . don't worry about killin' niggers," Bickley added reassuringly. "There's casualties in every war. And we mean to war."

Ex-Confederate Colonel Peyton Long departed from Bickley's room with the bestowed rank of KGC Colonel Peyton Long. Making his way to the top of the stair landing, Long found Donnie Pence stretched out sound asleep on the settee, his wounded arm dangling over the edge. Joe Shaler snoring in the raggedy cowhide chair next to him, Hollis stretched out on the registration desktop, Yoder and Dockum alseep on tabletops down in the far corner.

Long stood for a long minute at the top of the landing, panning his eyes around, taking in the crude, ungentlemanly scene below, a scene he'd seen too much of during the war. Turning wearily in his steps, he headed slump-shouldered back down the hallway, going to find for himself more gentlemanly surroundings, if such there were, to get some much needed rest.

At this exact moment, six miles south of the Harris House hotel at Lone Jack, Jerico was piloting out of the breaks and hollows of Sni Hills a ragged column of twenty-six black cavalry recruits and three other black men without affiliation whatever. Jerico knew the lay of the land, and at Ples's direction, he was leading them toward the open prairie where chances were fewer of a sudden unseen attack.

Four hours ago back there at Pardees Hollow, two ranks had been formed and faced about, making a column. Ples

and Jerico in the lead. Next came recruits who had picked
a tame enough horse and chanced to ride it. There were
nine in all. Willie and Augie at the head of the mounted
column, riding side by side behind Ples and Jerico. Behind
the mounted men, Bosie had lined up those who had to
walk, whether out of fear of horseback or lack of a horse
tame enough, none of the eight was willing to admit. Kalem and Bobo were walking side by side in the lead of this
bunch behind the mounted recruits.

Next came the wagon. Hezekiah and Fatback riding the
wagon seat, Hezekiah handling the lines. Six recruits sitting their butts in the back of the wagon. Cecil and Deese
were with them. Bosie had told them all that in two hours
they would have to get out and walk some, let the others
now walking ride for two hours. They had already swapped
around twice.

Fate was riding behind the wagon where he didn't want
to be. As far as Fate was concerned, his place was at Ples's
side. But Ples had told him that the column needed a lookout and drag rider all in one: Somebody who could be
trusted to keep his eyes peeled on their back trail, and keep
the column moving. It didn't sit well with Fate but Ples
had told him, "We got to do what's best for us all. We got
to git through."

Bosie was riding on the column's right flank, the flank
next to settlements. Keeping an eye out toward Lone Jack,
and watching the column. Ples told him to put a boot toe
to anybody lagging behind, or lollygagging in ranks.

Where was Jimmy Bowlegs?

Only God knew. Ples had simply told him to scout ahead
of the column, "See what you can see and come a-runnin'
if you see men comin'." Willie and Augie had wanted to
go too. For the excitement of it all. Bowlegs had no ob-
jections because Willie and Augie were proving themselves
good riders. And because, for his own mysterious reasons,
Bowlegs had taken a liking to them. "They make good

ride," Bowlegs had said more than once. But Bosie didn't want them to go, and Ples was having none of it. He said as much. "Y'all hoss holders," Ples kept saying. "Ain't no hosses to hold out yonder." They didn't get to go.

Bowlegs had galloped out after tying his lead mares to the tailgate of the wagon, necking together his six remaining half-broken horses that nobody dared ride. The half-wild brutes would give no trouble following the lead mares. Trouble came when somebody tried to climb aboard. Bowlegs was working on this at every lull.

Two hours ago the column had crossed over Sni Creek, a hock-deep, stagnant, mosquito-infested ribbon of water lined by dark, suspicious-looking willows and oaks. Before they crossed over, Ples didn't have to say it twice when he galloped back from in the lead and told them to look alive, pay attention, and keep closed up. Nobody dared lag behind in this brooding country along the banks of Sni Creek where no doubt lay the shallow-buried bones of more than a few Border Ruffians, Jayhawkers, and civilians too. In the dim moonlight, it was a spooky-looking, dangerous place.

They got perky. Moving smartly, they crossed over Sni Creek without incident.

Now the plodding column was entering the country know ever since September 1863 as the Burnt District.

The Burnt District was a three-thousand-square-mile swath of land covering four counties: three south of the Missouri River running along the Kansas-Missouri border all the way down to the Osage River, and one county north of the Missouri. Bill Quantrill, freelance guerrillas, Southern sympathizers, bushwhackers, and anybody else who hated Yankees for whatever reason had infested these counties. Killing, burning, plundering. The law had no sway whatever. Yankee General Thomas Ewing from his headquarters at Kansas City had got thoroughly frustrated over his inability to punish lawlessness and disorder. When Quantrill struck Lawrence, Kansas, sacking and burning the town, General Ewing's patrols could catch not a single raider after showing up hours later and tracking the raiders for two days. Over the countryside his patrols scoured hills and hollows, looking, asking questions of farmers, ranchers, men, women, and children. Not a single one of Quantrill's sympathizers would admit seeing or hearing of Quantrill and the 150 raiders General Ewing knew had surely passed this way.

General Ewing had had enough. He came down hard, issuing Order Number 11. The effusive order was convuluted in its wording, but its meaning was plain enough: Every man, woman, and child living in the four counties where Quantrill and his raiders and other disloyal sympathizers took refuge had fifteen days to get out. Pack up and leave. Go south; go north; go any direction, General Ewing didn't care. Just git.

Fifteen days later, the general sent out squadrons to enforce Order Number 11. Their written orders were: (1)Chase out anybody who hadn't left voluntarily; (2)Drive off or shoot every horse, cow, hog, fowl; (3)Burn every house, barn, corncrib, haystack.

The officers and men who had to carry out these orders had been shot at and ridden to a frazzle by hard-riding, elusive guerrillas, and bushwhackers of one sort or another. And more than likely had had family members, friends, or comrades killed or robbed at one time or another.

They went about this duty with great gusto.

For three days rifle shots rang out, and smoke curled away, blackening the sky all the way to Kansas City. And from that day on, the area they desolated was known as the Burnt District. And it was said in all seriousness that if a crow had to fly over the area, it had better bring its own lunch because there was nothing out there.

And Jerico was leading the column into it.

He knew the country though. Knew it well. Riding with Doc Jennison's bunch back then, they had picked over the country even as the evacuation was going on. Waylaying evacuees, taking money and jewelry, freeing slaves, confiscating secreted-away valuable possessions the evacuees were trying to flee with.

Now, looking into the night out across the Burnt District, Jerico spoke, saying to Ples riding at his side, "Ain't much out there, but there's water. Little Blue Creek . . . 'bout a mile further. We can water the hosses, rest some."

"Might as well," Ples answered, glancing up at the moon hanging off to the west. "I'd guess it's well after midnight."

"Guess I was wrong," Jerico said, "about them white men attackin' us tonight. They ain't attacked by now, they ain't likely to."

"I 'speck not," Ples answered. "But a man can't always be right."

Ples turned in the saddle, and summoned Bosie Radford from where he was riding in the middle of the column.

"Water's yonder," Ples told Bosie, when he trotted his horse up. "Be as good a place as any to pitch camp, water the hosses."

"What 'bout them white men?" Bosie asked.

"They ain't likely to come tonight."

"You mean Jerico had us doin' all this night ridin' and walkin' for nothin'?" Bosie asked incredulously.

"Man can't always be right," Ples retorted, looking across his shoulder at Jerico. "Only thing you got to decide now," Ples added to Bosie, "is whether to pitch camp this side of the creek, or the other side." Ples knew perfectly well what he himself would do. He was just testing Bosie's knowledge again.

"I'd camp on the other side," Jerico said suggestively.

"Don't make no difference," Bosie said.

"It might," Ples answered.

"We was to camp on the other side and trouble came," Jerico said, "we wouldn't have no creek to cross at our back."

"I never thought of that," Bosie said.

"You better start thinkin'," Ples said bluntly, ". . . or we'll be buryin' somebody."

Chapter Fourteen

They crossed over Little Blue Creek. Bowlegs had already scouted ahead and had found the best place to cross. At a place where Fraziers Bridge used to be.

None of them knew it, but Frasiers Bridge was precisely the place where Confederate General Sterling Price, six feet four, weighing better than three hundred pounds, at the head of twelve thousand, ill-equipped, ill-trained Confederates, had fought his way across in his flight out of Missouri after suffering a severe defeat at the hands of the Yankees.

Back in 1864 General Price had marched his army from Arkansas into Missouri with the intent of conquering St. Louis, marching on to the state capital, Jefferson City, and installing as governor the pro-South lieutenant governor, Thomas Reynolds, now traveling with him. Missouri would then become a member state in the southern Confederacy.

Price's army fought its way north, defeating and scattering Yankee garrisons along the way. Nearing St. Louis,

Hiram King

Price got word that every Yankee within Missouri, and some without, namely Kansas and Illinois, was gathering against his army of invasion. Abandoning his grab for St. Louis, Price headed straight for Jefferson City. Closing in on Jefferson City, Price got word from General Jo Shelby, commanding his lead cavalry brigade, that the place was heavily defended. Price swung west along the line of the Missouri River. Yankee General Alfred Pleasonton and his hastily assembled army from St. Louis marched out after him.

By this time, Yankee General James Blunt with two thousand had crossed over from Kansas into Missouri to slow Price's advance. General Blunt took up a strong position at Frasiers Bridge, the most probable place where Price's army would cross.

Now Price's Confederate army was boxed in: Yankee General Alfred Pleasonton's seven thousand cavalrymen east of him, nipping at his rear; A. J. Smith's eight thousand infantrymen south of him, marching parallel to his route; and the Missouri River north of him. And Blunt's men holding Frasiers Bridge west of him.

Price's men stormed Frasiers Bridge even as the Yankees were burning it. Twelve thousand men, and wagons, caissons, horses, cattle, and everything else that an army carries with it, sloshed across to the west bank of the Little Blue.

This west bank is where Ples and his group pitched camp. On a long tongue of bare earth where Price's army and his pursuers had passed, leaving the earth yet nude of vegetation.

And like the rest of the Burnt District, there wasn't a stick of wood around for fuel or anything else. So the recruits sat talking around a fireless camp in a rude circle some thirty yards from the water's edge. Their mood was upbeat; conversations lighthearted, good-natured. Rafer D. was standing back slack-legged, listening, occasionally grinning sheepishly. Taking no offense at being made the butt of most jokes and gibes. They had been ribbing him unceasingly about how he'd come to worship his new rifle. Eating, drinking, sleeping with it, and all. Battie had said Rafer D. ought to marry the thing. Rafer D. had showed himself to be so caring about keeping his rifle to hand that Bowlegs had suggested that he use a length of rope to sling it over his shoulder, as he'd seen other yellowlegs do.

Now and again they'd hurl gibes at another man. But they all took it in stride as they all had done ever since coming together back there in St. Louis. All except Hoby. Nothing said or done brought a hint of smile to Hoby's lips. Battie had said that was because Hoby's lips were too heavy to draw back.

Now Battie was ragging somebody else besides Rafer D. and Hoby was saying, "Kalem, if them white men come, you goin' to shoot . . . or run? Like Rafer D. did?"

"Uh'm goin' to shoot," Kalem said in his slow, deliberate drawl.

"How you goin' to shoot?" Battie retorted, grinning impishly. "You ain't even got a gun."

"Uh'm goin' to git one," Kalem said. "When the army git here. Then uh'm goin' to show you how to shoot."

"That won't take much doin'," Ike said. "Battie couldn't hit his back pockets with both hands."

"I can shoot better'n you," Battie replied haughtily. "With my eyes closed. I shot one of them white men back yonder, didn't I?"

"You ain't shot nobody," Ike retorted. "Them squench eyes you got can't see nothin'. They said you was so scared you couldn't even hold your eyes open to see what you was shootin' at."

"That true?" Bobo asked, grinning, looking at Augie. "You was wid 'em."

"I wadn't lookin'," Augie said. "I was holdin' them wild hosses Jimmy turned over to us."

"Tell the truth, Augie," Deese said, smirking knowingly. "You saw it."

"I didn't neither," Augie blurted out.

"You wadn't holdin' them hosses with your eyes. You saw it . . . you just scared to tell the truth."

"He didn't see nothin'," Battie said. "He couldn't even hold them hosses right."

"I did too," Augie said. "Mr. Butler said we done all right. Didn't he, Willie?"

"Yeah," Willie answered without conviction.

"Mr. Butler's just sayin' that," Cecil said. "He didn't want to hurt y'all feelin's. Them hosses almost drug Augie to death, and them Willie was holdin' got clean away."

"We got 'em back," Willie said defensively.

"You ain't got nothin' back," Battie retorted. "Jimmy got 'em back. You was so scared your legs wouldn't move."

Bobo guffawed; Kalem hooted; another man roared; Rafer D. snickered.

Bang! A gun went off. Over near the wagon.

Every man among them was jolted where he sat or stood.

The half-wild horses tied to the tailgate of the wagon flinched in their hides, started rearing and snorting, straining against the tie rope. And suddenly they were free again. And they sensed it. Straining against each other in a wild, unruly bunch, they bolted and took off running in tandem, heading back across Little Blue Creek where they'd come from, as panicked horses will do.

The bunched-up recruits sitting and standing around shooting the bull in a rude circle were directly in their path.

But nothing was going to alter their course.

Through a scrambling melee of running, dodging, screaming recruits, the horses thundered. Kicking and buck-jumping, they kept on running. Straining against each other, they plunged into the Little Blue, hoofs thrashing wildly, noses distended, eyes walled. They careened together and went down in a wild tangle of splashing water and flailing hoofs. Fighting their way back up to standing, they stood there, trembling, whickering nervously, nostrils flared, ears pricked. Then as if nothing had happened, they trotted over to the east bank.

Behind them, the badly shaken recruits were gathering themselves. Asking each other across the dim light of moon what had happened. One man could neither ask the question nor answer it.

Hoby. He was dead. Life trampled out of him.

Hezekiah was the first to see Hoby's motionless body where he'd come running down from the wagon as soon as the horses had broken free.

"He's dead, Mr. Butler," Hezekiah said, looking up at Ples, who had just run up from where he'd been dozing off to the side out of earshot of their foolish talk, as he called it.

"Who shot?" Bosie asked, running his eyes around the rude circle of solemn-faced recruits arrayed around Hoby's dirt-caked body.

"Wadn't me," Rafer D. said firmly.

"I did," Jake said humbly, walking up, his carbine canted down to the ground.

All eyes came around as one pair, looking accusingly at Jake.

"What'd you shoot for?" Bosie demanded to know.

"I didn't mean to," Jake said defensively. "I was practicin' how to load and my finger slipped."

"Fate already showed you how," Battie said seriously. "He showed all of us."

"I was showin' him again," Fate said. "He had trouble loadin' back yonder."

"Did you tell 'im to keep his finger off the trigger?" Ples asked Fate.

"I told 'im," Fate said.

Ples ran his eyes around the whole bunch, his jaw rigid.

239

Kalem shuffled uneasily in his step, looking at the ground.

Battie, glaring out at Jake, started to say something.

"He didn't mean to pull the trigger," Fate said, breaking the moment. "It was an accident."

"It surely was," Hezekiah said. "I saw it."

Just then Bowlegs came splashing across Little Blue Creek from where he'd retrieved his runaway horses still tethered together.

"He no look . . . listen good," Bowlegs said without emotion, looking down at Hoby's crumpled body.

"It was an accident," Jake said again.

"On account of them wild hosses you ain't broke," Bosie said accusingly, looking at Bowlegs. "Like you was s'pose to."

"All right," Ples said patiently. "Ain't no use in blamin' nobody. We'll just go on."

"Jimmy," Bosie said solemnly, "don't tie them damn wild hosses to the wagon no more. Take 'em somewhere else."

"Or break 'em," Bobo said sullenly.

"You no like?" Bowlegs asked curtly, his eyes holding Bobo's.

"None of us do," Bosie answered. "Now take 'em somewhere else."

"Who say?" Bowlegs asked, lifting his chin defiantly.

"I say," Bosie answered sharply. "And I'm in charge. Ain't that right, Mr. Butler?"

"He's in charge, Jimmy," Ples said mildly. "Take 'em somewhere else."

"You no look . . . listen good," Bowlegs said, his eyes roving over Bosie's body. "But I take," he added carelessly, and heeled out with his horses.

"We got to bury Hoby," Bosie said, more to himself than to anybody else.

The frustration and disgust that had been on Ples's face had slowly drained away. Looking over at Hoby's body, he told them all, saying mildly, instructively, "Nothin' we can do about Hoby." Bringing his eyes around, he added sternly, "But from now on all of y'all better pay 'tention. And keep your finger off them triggers till you git ready to shoot." And Ples strode off, getting away from it all.

They all turned and watched him go. Then presently, Bosie called out, "Fatback!"

"Yeah, Sarge."

"See if there's a shovel in that wagon. We got to bury Hoby."

"There ain't," Hezekiah said, walking up from where he'd already looked.

"We got to find somethin' to dig with," Bosie said, looking around in the moonlight.

"There ain't nothin'," Fatback said. "I couldn't even find sticks to make a cook fire with."

"We got to find somethin'," Bosie said.

"Our hands," Rafer D. said. "We can dig with our hands."

"Not much, you won't," Jerico said, speaking for the first time. "Ground's too hard."

"You mean leave Hoby like he is?" Bosie asked.

"He's dead," Jerico said, more a statement than anything else. "He ain't the only one been left dead out here."

"He's dead, all right," Bosie retorted, ". . . and we goin' to bury him. Over yonder," Bosie added, pointing to a likely spot.

Jake was first to start digging. Then Battie, then Rafer D. Pretty soon a half dozen men were scratching at the earth. They clawed away at the topsoil, Rafer D. saying, "See, it ain't that hard." Then directly they struck black, hard-packed prairie sod.

Jerico stood there looking knowingly as they futilely clawed away at the hardpan, looking up at each other every now and again.

"Jefferson," Bosie said directly, "you got anything to dig with in that croker sack you been totin' around?"

"Nothin'. Just stuff for shoeing hosses."

"Sarge," Willie said anxiously, "there was two old shovels back yonder where we was. That was what me and Augie was shootin' at. Wadn't it, Augie?"

"It sho' was," Augie said reflectively.

"Me and Augie could go back and git 'em," Willie said.

"It's too far back there," Bosie answered.

"How we goin' to bury Hoby then?" Battie asked.

"We got to bury him," Jefferson said again. "Wouldn't be right to leave 'im like this."

"It's quite a ways back yonder," Bosie said thoughtfully.

"I'll go back," Jake said. "It was my fault."

"Wadn't nobody's fault," Bosie said. "It was an accident."

"I'll go back by myself," Jake said. "Or me and Willie could go."

"I can ride better'n Jake," Augie said. "Let me and Willie go back."

"Willie . . . ," Bosie said, "you think you and Augie can make it there and back tonight? We got to go on early in the morning."

"We can make it . . . can't we, Augie?"

"We can make it, Sarge," Augie said.

"All right," Bosie said firmly. "Git y'all's hosses."

"Just a minute!" a commanding voice rang out.

It was Ples. Coming back, striding purposefully.

"You younguns stay where you at," Ples said gravely. "Ain't nobody goin' back nowhere."

"Mr. Butler . . . ," Bosie said plainly, stalking toward Ples. "I'm in charge. These my men," he added emphatically. "And I got one dead. They goin' back and git them shovels so we can bury him."

Everybody was standing listening, looking as if they were seeing Bosie for the first time, standing up to Mr. Butler and all.

242

"You got one dead already," Ples said impatiently. "You send these younguns back alone you liable to have two more dead. Like Jerico told you, Hoby's dead. Ain't nothin' none of us can do about it. Except go on."

"There's somethin' we can do about it," Bosie said, bristling. "We can bury him. And that's what I aim to do."

"Ples," Fate said, cutting in, "I could go back wid 'em, if that's what you worried about."

Ples looked across his shoulder at Fate. Then panned his eyes around at them all. Ples could see it in their faces, could sense it in their mood. They all wanted Hoby buried. None of them could understand why he was objecting.

"Fate, you go wid 'em," Ples said resignedly.

"Fate ain't goin' nowhere," Bosie replied. "Like you said, y'all ain't in the army. Willie and Augie is. And they goin' back to git them shovels. We goin' to bury Hoby."

Ples kept silent for a long minute, his mind thinking on it, Bosie finally acting as though he was in charge and all. Directly Ples said, shrugging inoffensively, "Suit yo'self. Your doin'."

"Like you said, Mr. Butler," Bosie said, "I'm the one got to answer to the army. And turning away from Ples, Bosie called out loud, "Willie . . . Augie, go git y'all's hosses."

"I got 'em," Jefferson said, leading the handsome gray that Doyle Streight used to own and Willie had come to love, and the big-chested bay that Luman Bigelow had been riding before they both were shot from the saddle back yonder out on the prairie and Bowlegs had retrieved the horses and had given them to Willie and Augie.

Jefferson passed over the reins, saying, "These good hosses. Don't y'all kill 'em. You ride some and walk some."

"We will," Willie answered.

Willie and Augie stepped into the stirrups, and swung onto the saddle.

Bosie spoke, looking up at Willie, saying, "Y'all go straight there and straight back, you hear?"

"We hear," Willie answered.

"Sarge," Battie said, "they don't need to take them rifles."

"They ain't rifles!" Bosie said sharply. "They carbines."

"Whatever you call 'em," Jerico stated, "they ain't nothin' but dead weight. It'd be better to leave 'em here."

"They can't shoot nohow," Somebody said teasingly in low tones.

Bosie shot a dirty look in that direction.

Nobody so much as cracked a grin this time.

"Y'all right," Bosie said. "Gimme them carbines."

"Mr. Butler said we . . . ," Augie started.

"Hush up, Augie," Willie snapped. "Just give it to 'im."

Seeing the stern set to Bosie's face, Augie kept his mouth shut and passed over his carbine as Willie had already done.

"Now, y'all ride!" Bosie commanded. "And don't stop for nothin'. You run into them white men, you turn 'round and come back. You hear, Willie?"

"I hear," Willie said. And they spurred out, both low in the saddle, doing as best they could to ride the way Bowlegs had told them he'd ridden when Cheyennes up on the Platte River had chased after him for catching wild horses on their hunting grounds.

"Don't y'all kill them hosses!" Jefferson yelled again at their backs.

Ples had heard it all. He and Fate resting back in the crook of their saddles off from the wagon. Fate sorely wanted to go with Willie and Augie. And Ples knew it.

"You shoulda gone," Ples said casually. "They run into trouble, they'll likely need you."

"I ain't in the army," Fate retorted dryly.

"Be a good place for you," Ples replied, saying out loud something he'd been thinking for a time now.

Just at that moment, Bowlegs came up. Walking on quiet feet, his saddle blanket thrown over his shoulders. Dropping down to sitting cross-legged next to Ples, Bowlegs spoke, saying more to himself than to Ples and Fate, "Maybe now he look . . . listen good."

"Who?" Ples asked innocently, his eyes concealed beneath the hat covering his face.

"Bo-see," Bowlegs said.

"Maybe," Ples grunted. "Maybe not."

"I think maybe he make good yellowleg," Bowlegs said thoughtfully.

"Maybe," Ples grunted again. "Maybe not."

It was coming on to daylight when Ples's eyes fluttered open. Still concealed under his hat brim even though he'd shifted his position at least a half dozen times in his thought-filled sleep.

Ples lay there perfectly still, reaching his ears out into the lemon light of coming dawn. Hearing Fate snoring softly off to his side, horses stamping and milling about on the rude picket line Bowlegs had put them on.

Ples started thinking back, going over last night's events: crossing over the Little Blue; making camp on the dirt flats; the horses stampeding, running over Hoby, trampling him to death. Willie and Augie going back to get a shovel. Willie and Augie!

Ples sprang up to sitting, snatching his hat off his face even as he did so.

He panned bleary eyes around the camp. Seeing a haphazard jumble of recruits sleeping randomly about, probably where their mouths had stopped working, Ples was thinking.

Ples gathered himself, and rose to standing. Running his hands over his shoulders and arms, wiping the night chill from his old bones. Then started walking, in a hurry, heading west to the rise they were camped under. Reaching the crest of the rise, he looked back east to where Willie and Augie ought to be coming from.

Nothing.

Just a long sweep of prairie clear to the lemon-light horizon.

He swept the prairie all around with his eyes, just in case Willie and Augie had lost their direction.

Nothing.

He turned in his steps, concern etched on his black-leather face, and headed back, walking purposefully. His mind working at what sort of trouble, if any, the youngsters could have run into.

Those white men? Doubtful. But possible.

A lame horse? Maybe. But doubtful.

Lost? More'n likely, Ples guessed. He swore softly under his breath at Bosie for sending them.

And then Ples heard it. Grunts, groans, hoofs stabbing down on prairie sod. A great struggle going on.

Ples brought his eyes around. And saw it. Off to the north.

Bowlegs. Breaking one of those wild horses.

Ples stopped where he was. Watching Bowlegs in the pale light, clinging to a barebacked, seesawing, buck-jumping, end-swapping, back-kicking horse that didn't want anybody on his back.

Ples stood there watching this savage confrontation, smiling within himself at how good Bowlegs was at this violent work.

Presently the horse took off in a wild run. Bowlegs holding back on the bit ropes. And then the horse took on a steady gait, heading out across the prairie.

Ples turned in his steps, watching them go, wondering if this run was the horse's idea or Bowlegs's.

The horse ran in a wild, head-tossing unruly loop. Then headed back.

Ples smiled in spite of himself; he knew who had prevailed.

Fighting the horse up near Ples, Bowlegs slid down. Patting the horse's lathered shoulder, Bowlegs said, "He good horse . . . he make good ride."

"That's what you say about all of 'em," Ples answered, and started walking back down the rise toward the wagon and camp.

"I bring army only good horses," Bowlegs answered, falling in step with Ples, trailing the hang-necked, winded horse behind him. "Maybe you take," Bowlegs added, reaching the ropes across his body over to Ples.

"I like my own hoss," Ples answered.

"Suit yo'self," Jimmy said, mimicking Ples this time.

"Your doin'."

"My doin'," Ples retorted. Then added seriously, "Them younguns what rode out last night, they ain't back. You see anythin' of 'em out there?"

"I no see," Bowlegs answered. "I no look," he added, smiling wryly, brushing dirt from his backside where he'd been thrown twice by what he knew was one of the best horses, and guessed was one of the toughest to break in the string he had left.

"How many you got left?" Ples asked, as they descended the brow of the rise.

"Three."

"Job you got," Ples said, "I wouldn't want it."

"Butler scared," Bowlegs said chidingly.

Ples gave him a dirty look.

"Wil-lie, Aug-ie maybe lost," Bowlegs said, as they drew up to where Ples and Fate had slept, Fate still asleep there.

"Maybe," Ples answered. Maybe not," he added, nudging Fate awake with his boot toe.

"You go find," Bowlegs said and kept on walking. "I break one more, same same," he continued. Then added without care, "This good horse. I give to Bo-bo. He learn . . . he make good ride."

Fate rose to sitting, rubbing sleep from his eyes, seeing through the coming daylight Ples standing off from him. "They back?" Fate asked.

"They who?" Ples asked innocently.

"You know who," Fate answered. "Willie and Augie."

"Naw," Ples said. "They ain't back."

"Anybody go look for 'em?"

"Naw."

Fate jumped wide awake. Grabbing his hat next to him, saying excitedly, "We got to go look for 'em!"

"We is," Ples said casually.

"When?" Fate asked excitedly.

"Soon as I tell Bosie," Ples answered, heading in that direction. "Saddle our hosses."

Fate scrambled up to standing, grabbed up his blanket and saddle, saying behind Ples's back, "I shoulda went wid 'em."

"I told you that," Ples answered, walking on, heading toward Bosie and the others, standing, looking up the rise where Bobo was in the saddle they'd put on the horse Bowlegs had just turned over to him.

"Hold 'em tight!" Somebody yelled at Bobo.

"Pull back hard on them ropes!" Jake yelled out.

Ples shifted his eyes up the knoll. And saw Bobo. Hanging precariously in the saddle on the big horse that Bowlegs had just broken and given to him.

Suddenly Bobo was flung onto the horse's neck, his hands clutching a handful of mane, his eyes bucked wide.

The horse hunched its back, gave two quick buck-jumps, then plunged.

Bobo came clear of the horse's back. His right foot hanging in the stirrup, his body flailing back against the horse's flank.

The horse got scared. Started prancing away in a crazy circle like a drunk man. Every now and again kicking back, trying to get rid of the alien thing clinging against his flank.

Bobo screamed.

The horse plunged at the frightening sound.

Bobo's head smashed against the ground.

Bobo screamed again.

The horse trotted away panic-stricken, walleyed, nostrils distended. Then he stopped, neck craned back, eyes trying to see the strange thing hanging on to him.

Bowlegs took off running, heading toward them.

The horse smelled or sensed the human with whom he had struggled earlier, and took it for danger all over again. And trotted away.

From the way things had shaped up, Ples knew what had to be done. Looking back over his shoulder, he saw his Winchester way back there in his saddle boot where they'd slept.

"Rafer D.!" Ples yelled out, bringing his eyes over to where he'd earlier seen Rafer D. with his carbine strapped over his shoulder.

"Yeah, suh," Rafer D. answered.

"Shoot that hoss!" Ples commanded.

They all heard Ples when he said it. But none of them wanted to believe what they'd heard.

Bosie brought his eyes around, looking a queer look at Ples.

"Shoot that hoss! Rafer D.," Ples screamed again.

Rafer D. looked a question at Bosie even as he was un-slinging his carbine.

"Shoot 'im!" Bosie yelled out.

In one smooth motion, Rafer D. jerked up his carbine and fired.

A bullet broke into the horse's shoulder, knocking him wobbly on all four legs, staggering around in a distorted circle, dragging Bobo's head along the ground.

"Shoot 'im again!" Ples screamed, "in the head!"

Rafer D. fired again.

The horse's head exploded, his body hit the ground like a sack of dead weight.

They all started running that way, Bowlegs in the lead. Bowlegs bent down, felt of Bobo's grotesquely bent leg. Bobo screamed.

Bowlegs wrenched his twisted foot from the stirrup.

Bobo screamed again.

"He no die," Bowlegs said without emotion to Bosie when they all drew up around him, looking wide-eyed. And Bowlegs got up and walked off, as if nothing had happened.

"Take them wild horses away from here," Bosie said at Bowlegs's back, looking back over his shoulder from where he was stooped down, inspecting Bobo's leg. "We don't want no mo' of 'em!" he yelled at Bowlegs.

"You no like? Bo-see," Bowlegs asked, stopping dead in his steps where he was.

"Take 'em away from here!" Bosie screamed, his eyes blazing, looking back over his shoulder at Bowlegs.

"You take," Bowlegs said defiantly, facing around deliberately, his left hand hovering over his skinning knife.

"Jimmy," Ples said soothingly, "he's in charge. Take 'em away."

"Maybe me, Bo-see make good fight," Bowlegs said, his eyes flat, seemingly without meaning. Except to a knowing man.

And Ples was a knowing man.

"Nobody's goin' to make no fight," Ples said roughly. "Now go on, take 'em away."

"You dead already," Bowlegs said carelessly to Bosie. Then turned and strode off, his loincloth whipping against his butt.

Morning sunlight was pouring over the horizon when they got Bobo back down the rise to the wagon, Hoby's dead body under the wagon, a saddle blanket covering him at Hezekiah's insistence.

"What'd you try to ride that horse for?" Bosie asked scoldingly after they'd put Bobo down, his back leaning against the wagon wheel, a bloody bare spot on his head where his hair had been scoured away on the ground.

"Jimmy gave 'im to me and Battie said I couldn't ride 'im," Bobo replied, wincing back the pain. "So I was showin' him I could."

"You showed 'im, all right," somebody said.

"You let Battie put you up to ridin' that rank hoss," Jake said. "He can't ride hisself."

"I can ride better than him," Battie said indignantly. "And you too. At least I can stay on."

"Just barely," Deke said. "We seen ya."

"I didn't fall off," Battie said smugly.

"All y'all just shut up!" Bosie screamed exasperatedly. "Ain't none of us no expert. We all got to learn. So just shut up about it.

"Fatback!" Bosie continued, "you got somethin' to put on Bobo's head?"

"Cookin' grease is all," Fatback answered.

"Git it," Bosie said. "It'll have to do."

At the clatter of hoofbeats, they all turned, looked that way.

It was Ples and Fate. Splashing across Little Blue Creek.

"Where they goin'?" somebody asked.

"They goin' off and leave us!" another somebody said. "We done made Mr. Butler mad."

"They ain't leavin' us," Bosie said. "They goin' look for Willie and Augie. Mr. Butler's worried about 'em. Me too," he added. "They might be lost out there."

"Maybe them white men caught 'em," Cecil Hall said seriously.

"They shoulda took they rifles," Kalem drawled.

"Carbines," Bosie said exasperatedly. "I keep tellin' y'all, the army calls 'em carbines. We got to start callin' 'em

251

carbines too. Now, all y'all git ready. We got to be ready to go soon as Mr. Butler and Fate git back."

At something like a mile out across the prairie, Ples's eyes were still sweeping the country all around as they had been doing ever since they rode out.

Nothing. Except a pale, far-off horizon.

On they rode.

A mile, maybe a bit less, they gated along, looking; seeing nothing, listening; hearing nothing.

Ples's eyes swept across again. And something caught the tail end of them. Something out of place, a smudge on the horizon that didn't belong. Focusing his eyes that way, he made out what it was.

Willie and Augie. Walking. Leading their horses.

Ples looked at Fate and pointed that way even as he gigged his horse into a full-out gallop.

They clattered up where Willie and Augie had stopped, waiting.

Fate leaped from the saddle, his horse still on the move.

"What happened?" Fate asked excitedly.

"Nothin'," Willie answered. "We got the shovels." And Willie nodded toward where the shovels were tied to Augie's saddle on the other side.

Fate walked around, and lifted up the broken-handled, rusty things to Ples's eyes.

"They'll have to do," Ples said. "Y'all mount up and come on. They waitin' for us. We'll bury Hoby and move out." And Ples swung his horse away.

Chapter Fifteen

It was an hour past sunup by the time they had finished burying Hoby wrapped in a horse blanket in a picked spot some twenty yards west of where he'd been trampled to death. Nobody said any words over his body; nobody knew what to say. It was a silent, brooding ceremony, if such it could be called. Everybody's mind was somewhere else; they all just wanted to be off, to be away from this janky place, as Ike Peeler called it, holding his top hat reverently at his belt buckle. It had hit home to Ike that this cavalry stuff he'd been picked as a bugler for was a whole lot more dangerous than that traveling minstrel show he'd been making music in, and clowing around on the stage back there in Illinois. This was for real.

So they moved out. Each man in formation as they had come in. Except now there was one less man on horseback. And Bobo, with his bum leg and all, was riding in the wagon. As were Willie and Augie. Bosie had said they'd done well and needed some rest after riding all night. So into the wagon they went; and out of the wagon came Cecil Hall and John Deese. They had to walk even though Willie's and Augie's horses were available.

"Ain't nobody ridin' my hoss," Willie had said.

"Mine neither," Augie blurted out. "They played out like we is."

Bosie gave in. He knew there'd be no peace among them if anybody else rode Willie's gray and Augie's big-chested bay. So at Bosie's direction, Fatback tied them in back of the wagon.

Jerico led them out. West by a little north. Heading for Big Blue Creek just outside of the Burnt District on the Kansas line where he knew there was firewood, and maybe wild game for table meat.

Jimmy Bowlegs? Only God knew where he was. He'd galloped out with his two evil-eyed, unbroken horses. All Ples and Bosie, and anybody else for that matter, knew was that he was ranging out front. Keeping an eye out.

So the column moved on at a walk.

Back in charge now, Bosie had told them all, in the most commanding voice he could muster: Keep in ranks; keep closed up; and keep your finger off the trigger. Nobody snickered or grinned this time. Word had got around about what Jerico had told Bosie: We ain't out of trouble till we cross the line into Kansas. Jerico spoke from past experience. Doc Jennison and his raiders had gone into Missouri, taking what they wanted, then riding like the devils they were, daring not to slow down until they were safely back across the border into Kansas.

The Kansas line was at least twelve miles west, Lone Jack half that north. Jerico had warned Bosie this was no time to dillydally around, as Doc would have said.

Six miles north of them, eleven raw-edged white men clattered out of Lone Jack. They were all burdened, in mind and with weapons. A pistol belted around each man's waist and a long gun jiggling in everybody's saddle scabbard except one man. Anybody who had seen them ride out couldn't have mistaken them. They were killing men. Riding to kill.

The man without a saddle scabbard was riding in the lead. A former colonel of Confederate cavalry. Peyton Long. Had one arm. But that didn't matter. To a man they were all battle-tested fighters. Grim men who'd suffered their share of hard, desperate times. Times that had scarred their souls, had left them bitter, vengeful. As the Civil War, which took half a million lives on both sides, young and old, had left so many others who had come out on the losing end.

Four of the eleven were strangers to the others. And that worried Long some. He'd said as much to Bickley this morning back there at the Harris House hotel. And Woot Tally, the man who'd brought the other four along, was just as worried. But Woot was keeping his worry to himself; he had nobody he trusted to express his concerns to.

"They'll answer to your orders," Bickley had said reassuringly to Long.

But would they? Long's mind had asked the question back there at the stable when they were saddling up at sunup this morning under the inquisitive eyes of Seth Belch. And Long still yet didn't know the answer.

So they galloped along, Long's and Woot's minds dwelling on the strangers each was riding among. Long's mind started putting faces to the four names Woot had given him. As Long remembered them, they were: Shalor ... Shalor Broomfield. The one in the black-checked shirt. Heavy-set. Close to six feet tall, weighed at least two hundred. Broad shoulders, wide, square face. Had a scary silence about him that made a man wonder what he was thinking.

Archie Lee ... Archie Lee Bocock. The short, skinny one. An inch, maybe two, better than five feet tall.

Weighed maybe a hundred and ten, no more than a hundred and twenty soaking wet. Hook-nosed, weasel-eyed. Had a big Colt .45 hanging on his right side and at least an eighteen-inch Bowie knife on his left side.

Long didn't know it, but Archie Lee had ridden with Mosby's Rangers. That Bowie knife wasn't for show. Archie Lee had slit throats. And still would.

Conway ... Martin Conway. The one with the gray waist jacket on, and black striped pants. Looked to be about thirty. Talked like a Yankee.

Back in 1861 when Republican Abraham Lincoln had taken the presidency and the Civil War really busted loose, Conway's convictions had led him to the Confederacy's cause. Martin had felt then, and still did, that white people ought to be able to keep nigger slaves if they wanted to. And if South Carolina wanted out of the Union it ought to be able to go out, the same way it had come in. So Conway had joined the Copperhead movement. Twice, once in '63 and again in '64, his Copperhead unit in Illinois had had attention thrust on it when Ohio representative Clement Vallandigham had been too bold in his deeds and too explicit in his talk. Arrests had been make in Illinois and Ohio. Conway, Billy Southwick, John Thompson, and a dozen others in Illinois had been apprehended in the night by Yankee soldiers and locked up in Illinois' infamous state prison without benefit of habeas corpus at President Lincoln's expressed word. Conway was yet bitter over the way the Yankee guards had denegrated and humiliated him in prison for fourteen long months.

Lige ... Lige Green. Tall, lean. Had a wad of tobacco bulging in his left jaw. Uncouth-looking.

Lige had been a slave driver over in Tennessee and had been driven almost to mad-dog killing when he'd heard the Yankees had put guns in the hands of the very slaves he used to flog at will.

Strangers they were, but Peyton Long needn't worry. They were all of like mind. If the Civil War meant putting blacks on a level with white men, the war hadn't settled diddly-squat, as Archie Lee had said. And none of them could disagree.

So they rode. To organize. To redeem their wayward country. And they'd do whatever needed to be done along the way.

Their first order of business was to stop the niggers on the way to Fort Leavenworth to get Yankee guns and train to be fighting men.

They stopped to water their horses at the Little Blue. The morning sun starting to make its presence felt.

"Like that old man back yonder at the stables said," Hollis said, looking at the tracked-up earth at the water's edge, "they crossed over here."

"When you figure?" Long asked, lifting his horse's muzzle from the stagnant, unhealthy water.

"Six . . . seven hours ago," Hollis answered, looking at the tracks Ples and the others had left last night.

"That don't make no sense," Frank Yoder said scornfully, looking cat-eyed at Long. "Hollis here's been hangin' 'round them blanket-ass squaws so long he figures he can read sign like 'em."

"Any fool with half a brain could figure it out," Hollis said disdainfully.

"Watch your talk, squaw man," Yoder said rudely. "We got a long ride ahead of us . . . talk like that and you might not make it," he added threateningly.

"They right friendly, ain't they?' " Archie Lee said, grinning wickedly from where he was watering his horse next to Dockum. "They know each other?"

"They know each other," Joe said. "It's mostly talk."

"I'd kill a man for less," Archie Lee replied seriously.

Seeing the doubtful look to Long's gaze across to the other side, Hollis said reassuringly, "Colonel . . . they crossed over . . . camped on the other side."

"I'd say so, too," Woot Tally said agreeably, running his eyes over to the west bank.

They all lifted their eyes that way.

In the gathering morning they could make out chopped-up earth and vague wagon tracks.

"Let's move out," Long commanded, mounting up.

They ran their horses across Little Blue Creek, splashing green water everywhere. Came out on the other side, pulled to an abrupt halt, each pair of eyes inspecting the ground all around.

They saw what Hollis had told them.

"Them niggers been here and gone," Woot said, more to himself than anybody else.

"They ain't got far," Hollis replied, looking the way the fresh tracks led.

"Let's git after 'em!" Archie Lee replied.

"Let's ride," Long said with conviction.

They spurred out.

Long riding uneasy. So was Joe Dockum, Donnie Pence, and Joe Shaler. They'd already had a run-in with an old black man, a kid, and a breed back there at Sedalia. They knew, as they galloped along, it wasn't going to be as easy as Woot and Archie Lee had talked as though it would be. They knew, Long and his bunch did, that trouble was ahead if that old leather-faced man was still with them. Woot Tally and his bunch knew nothing of the kind; and wouldn't have believed it if they'd been told.

The rising sun moved inexorably up the high and wide prairie sky.

Fate was still riding at the tail end of the column, his eyes sweeping the prairie from left to right, now and again twisting around in his saddle, glancing back on their back trail.

Like the rest of them, Fate had heard Jerico say that he thought an attack would come before they reached the

Kansas line, four, no more than five, hours ride from here.

Now, two hours later, the sun had crept almost to overhead.

Fate's eyes swept the prairie again, as they had been doing all morning. Left to right, horizon to horizon. He twisted back, looking on their back trail.

Nothing. Just high, wide, clear blue endless sky.

On he rode. Eyes sweeping, probing.

Twisting around in his saddle once more, Fate glanced back. When he started to face back around, something caught in the corner of his eye. He whipped his head back around, coming up in his saddle, eyes focusing.

Riders!

Fate jerked up short. Faced his horse around. Unsheathing his Winchester even as he did so.

Narrowing his eyes, Fate made out at least a dozen riders. He triggered off one quick warning shot.

Up ahead, Ples snatched in his reins, jerking his horse to a halt in its tracks, and faced around; the moving column was rocked in its step, every man jolted to alertness. Everybody in the canvas-covered wagon, to a man, came tumbling out. Including Willie and Augie.

"They comin'!" they heard Fate yell out, pointing.

"Mr. Butler!" Bosie called out from where he was riding in the middle of the column.

Ples swung his horse that way, jabbed in his spurs, and was off. Jerking up next to Bosie, he reminded him, "You in charge! Keep 'em movin'! I'm goin' back there where Fate is!" And Ples dug out, leaving Bosie sitting there, eyes wide, mouth agape.

Directly Bosie gathered himself, yelling to the stalled column: "Keep movin'! And keep your eyes in front of you," he added without conviction, looking back himself, wondering what was going to happen next.

Galloping up next to Fate, Ples asked, "How many?"

"Ten . . . twelve."

Just at that instant they saw Bowlegs. Galloping toward them from the west, his two unbroken horses running at the end of a tether rope behind his long-legged pinto.

Coming to an abrupt stop, Bowlegs said flatly, "They come. We make good fight."

"We make good fight," Ples said agreeably. "Any cover out there?" he asked, looking the way Bowlegs had come.

"I no see," Bowlegs answered.

Ples panned his eyes around their surroundings. Seeing what he could see for cover.

Nothing. Not a thing growing higher than a horse's belly. A man could see unobstructed clear to the horizon.

Ples's mind got to working, fast. Directly, he said, "Fate . . . take our horses back . . . tell Bosie to halt the column and turn that wagon around broadsided. Git everybody behind it . . . or under it. Make sho' Willie and Augie git hold of them hosses."

"Okay," Fate answered, spurring out.

"Jimmy . . . ," Ples added, facing back around, "we got to make our own cover." Ples unholstered his pistol, looking at the two unbroken, walleyed horses Bowlegs had been leading.

Bowlegs knew right off what Ples was going to do even as Ples fired a pistol bullet into one of the horse's brain.

Bowlegs had already jumped out of his saddle, unsheathing his skinning knife all the while.

Now, with one quick uppercutting stroke, Bowlegs plunged his knife into the other horse's heart. The horse caved, screaming a death scream as he was going down.

Throwing themselves belly-flat behind the two dead horses, their Winchester barrels leveled out, Ples and Bowlegs lay there, sizing up the riders sitting their horses out there. A good two hundred yards off, maybe a little more.

Presently, Ples brought his head around at the sound of running footfalls behind him.

It was Battie. His horse on the dead run. Battie jouncing in the saddle.

Battie jumped out of the saddle, and dived in next to Ples, breathing hard.

"Where you think you goin'?" Ples asked, surprised.

"We make good fight," Battie answered, mimicking Bowlegs, leveling out his carbine. "Right, Jimmy?" he added, smiling handsomely at Bowlegs.

"You no shoot so good," Bowlegs said dryly.

"All right," Ples told Battie, "you want to make good fight, just keep down and see what you aimin' at. Maybe this time you'll hit somethin'."

Seconds wore on.

Presently, Ples twisted around and looked behind him. And saw the column some fifty yards back, a jumble of activity: Men scurrying about tugging on bridle reins, Bosie barking out directions; Hezekiah yelling at the top of his lungs, gee-hawing the wagon's mules into position; horses being gigged around; recruits dodging for cover, running around like disturbed ants.

"Rafer D.!" Ples yelled back into the bedlam of activity.

"Yeah, suh!" Rafer D. answered back above the din, his voice bringing a certain quiet over the others.

"You see that one-armed man out there?"

"Yeah, suh."

"I'm goin' to shoot at him. . . . You see that man with the black hat on . . . in the buckskin shirt?"

"Yeah, suh."

"Git your sights on him."

Rafer D. looked a question at Bosie standing off from him, now looking out over the wagon's tailgate.

"Do it," Bosie said gravely.

"Yeah, suh," Rafer D. yelled back to Ples.

"Aim to kill," Ples added. "They mean to."

"Yeah, suh," Rafer D. said, swallowing back the lump in his throat.

"Bosie!" Ples continued.

"Yeah, suh."

"You hear what I said?"

"Yeah, suh."

"You listen to Fate and Jerico . . . do what they tell ya. And tell everybody to keep they fingers off them triggers till I shoot."

"Yeah, suh."

So twenty-five half-armed, untrained, nervous, black recruits waited. Looking out apprehensively at eleven white men sitting in their saddles. Studying the black men's disposition, as Long had told the others when Long had lifted a halting hand at the sound of Fate's warning shot.

"Colonel . . . ," Woot called Long patronizingly. "Ain't no sense in makin' a big to-do about this," he added impatiently. "All we got to do is ride right over that rabble and be done with it."

"It ain't going to be that easy," Long answered. "There's somebody in that bunch who knows what for."

"They ain't nothin' but a witless mob," Woot said scornfully. "I seen 'em back there in St. Louis."

"A lot can happen between here and St. Louis," Long answered carelessly. "That right, Frank?"

"That's right, Woot," Frank answered. "There's two or three stand-up fighters with 'em now."

"The hell you say," Woot replied contemptuously. "Archie Lee . . . Shalor . . . maybe we got to show the colonel here how it's done. What you figger?"

"Could be we got to show 'em," Archie Lee answered. "They don't seem up to it," he added, grinning like the weasel he was.

"Whatever we goin' to do," Shalor said impatiently, "let's git on with it."

"Lige . . . Martin," Woot called back, unholstering his pistol. "We'll ride right over 'em and keep on goin'," Woot said when Lige and Martin had guided their horses up.

"Colonel," Woot added, a mocking sneer to his lips, "you and your boys can pick up what pieces we leave."

"I wouldn't take 'em lightly," Long said advisedly.

"I never do," Woot retorted confidently. "All right!" Woot yelled out to his four men, "spread out and let's hit 'em!"

And they dug out, each man's pistol at the ready.

Long had sensed there'd be no holding back Woot and his men. They wanted to attack this instant. Long also knew that like previous cavalry charges he'd been in on, it was tactically sound to attack as one solid, swift, hard-hitting body.

"Let's go!" Long yelled out to his men, bringing his pistol to bear.

In a ragged wave of a mounted skirmish line, eleven white men came thundering down on Ples and the others, closing the distance, the midmorning sun at their backs.

Like Long, they all had fought from horseback before. They all knew that a man's only salvation was to ride like hell and shoot as fast as he could work the trigger. And that's the way they came on. Knowing full well that a man on horseback was no easy target.

Lying belly-flat behind a dead horse, Ples could see that his first intent to shoot Long, and for Rafer D. to shoot Hollis, was out the window. Men he'd never seen before were riding directly at him. Closing the distance fast.

Ples picked out a target. A man with a Rebel kipi cap on, riding low in his saddle.

And fired.

Bowlegs fired on the instant; Battie fired; a racket of gunshots went off behind them from the wagon.

Not a rider left the saddle. And they were even closer now.

Ples fired again.

The man with the kipi cap left the saddle.

Bowlegs fired, then fired again.

The man in the black-checked shirt slumped in his saddle, then vacated it, landing clumsily.

Suddenly the attackers were up on Ples and them. Parting as if on signal, thundering by on both sides, firing furiously. Bullets digging up troughs of dirt all around them, Battie and everybody else, scrunched down in the dirt as far as they could get. Bullets thudding into the dead horseflesh they were scrunched down behind.

God alone knows why neither one of them was hit.

Ples and Bowlegs twisted around from where they were, and started triggering off shots as fast as they could work the lever. Battie stayed scrunched down.

And there went the one-armed man! Coat sleeve flapping like a broken wing on a chicken hit over the head.

Ples leaped to his feet, jacked a round into the chamber, and brought up his sights.

Then *whap!* A bullet made an ugly sound digging into the dirt right next to Ples's boot heel, whining off angrily into the unknown. Spoiling Ples's aim.

A rifle bullet!

Snapping his Winchester to his shoulder, Ples fired. An angry, disconcerted shot.

The one-armed rider kept on going, as did the rest of them.

Ples swore under his breath.

"Let's go!" he yelled out to Bowlegs and Battie. And Ples didn't have to say it twice to Battie. He was on his feet in a flash. And they started running toward the unbroken racket of pistol and rifle shots where Long and his men were smashing over, around, and through the recruits at the wagon.

Every recruit who had a trigger to pull was pulling it. Throwing wild shots at anything that moved in any direction. Curses, wild shouts, hysterical screams were all mixed in with a solid chain of gunfire.

Long and his riders swept by, blazing away, passing in front and in back of the wagon.

And just like that, it was suddenly over. The attackers had swept through and were away. Throwing back wild shots as if by afterthought.

Fate, Bosie, Jerico, and Rafer D. had moved away from cover of the wagon, popping off random shots at them.

Behind them the attackers had left chaos. A great confused jumble of men, horses, . . . and death.

Firing off a last shot even as he thought they were out of range, Jake spoke: "We done it! y'all," he shouted jubilantly. "They gone!" he added, looking the way the attackers had gone.

"Yeaaaaa!" Bobo yelled out exuberantly, waving his carbine overhead. "We whupped 'em!"

They all stood there, looking after the attackers. To a man they were smiling and grinning, overflowing with pride at what they had done and lived to tell about it.

"We showed 'em!" Deke said. "They ain't goin' to mess with us no mo'!"

On the instant Rafer D. fired again.

Everybody was jolted back to reality, looking the way the shot had come from, wondering what Rafer D. was shooting at.

At least three hundred yards away a man lurched in his saddle from a bullet between the shoulder blades.

They saw him slumped forward. So far away they could barely make him out.

"You hit 'im!" Bosie said in stunned disbelief.

"I hit 'im," Rafer D. said matter-of-factly. "But I was aimin' to kill 'im like Mr. Butler said."

"You see that, Willie?" Augie exclaimed at the tailgate of the wagon where he and Willie were being tugged around and dragged, each holding on to the reins of their own and a half dozen other horses while trying to keep from getting shot.

"I seen it," Willie answered. "You just hush up and hold on to them hosses."

"Well . . . they gone," Bosie said. "Thank God for that. Now we can go on to Fort Leavenworth in Peace."

"They gone, all right," Fate said solemnly. "But they left they mark," he added, looking back at the scene behind them where he knew at least two recruits had been killed, and possibly another, Kalem. Fate had seen Kalem sag down groaning there at the end.

"Sarge!" Cecil Hall called out.

Everybody brought their eyes to bear where Cecil was.

And they saw what Cecil was looking at.

Ike Peeler. Slumped lifeless against the tailgate of the wagon. A circle of blood had spread out from a ragged hole in his back where a bullet had passed through from the front. His bowler hat lying off to the side, trampled misshapen by the skittish horses Augie was still fighting to calm down.

"He's dead," Cecil said somberly to Bosie when Bosie, Fate, and Jerico drew up. Cecil lowered Ike by the shoulders from the tailgate to the ground.

"Hezekiah's dead too," Fatback announced gravely, leaning his head out from behind the canvas top at the wagon seat where he and Hezekiah had taken cover, Hezekiah holding on to the lines.

"Where's Kalem?" somebody asked out.

"He was up front," Deke answered. "Holdin' on to them mules."

"He's dead," somebody answered. "I seen 'im go down, right along with one of the mules."

Just at that time, Ples, Bowlegs, and Battie drew up, looking at Kalem's body mostly concealed under the dead mule.

"Battie," Ples said grimly, "cut that mule outa them traces and git Kalem from under there."

"I ain't got nothin' to cut with," Battie answered, "remember?"

"You got somethin' now," Ples stated, withdrawing his Bowie knife, flinging it at Battie's boot toe, Battie leaping wildly out of the way.

Battie retrieved the knife, turning it over in his hands, coldly eyeing Ples, who had turned away.

"How many mo'?" Ples asked Bosie where they all had gathered around, watching Battie cutting Kalem free, the other three mules straining against the dead weight.

"Three mo'," Bosie answered, knowing full well Ples was asking how many more had been killed.

"Did y'all git any of them?"

"Naw, suh," Bosie answered dejectedly. "It happened so fast."

"Ples," Fate said, "there's one layin' out yonder," And Fate nodded that way. "The one you told Rafer D. to shoot . . . I got 'im myself."

"It all happened so fast," Bosie said again wonderingly.

"It always do," Ples retorted, panning his eyes around at their wrecked surroundings.

"Rafer D. hit one of 'em," Bosie added.

"We seen it," Ples said, looking out at Rafer D., his rifle slung over his shoulder where it always was. "Best shot I ever witnessed," Ples added.

"Well . . . ," Ples continued, "at least we got three of 'em . . ."

"I make four," Bowlegs said without emotion, and walked off. Looking the way the attackers had gone, remembering the wounded man Rafer D. had slumped over in his saddle.

"Where you goin'?" Bosie asked, seeing Bowlegs retrieving his pinto from Augie.

"There," Bowlegs said, nodding out the way the attackers had gone.

"No need to go out there, Jimmy," Ples said. "He'll likely die on his own."

"I make sure," Jimmy said firmly, slapping heels to his pinto, taking off at a gallop. They stood there watching him go. Then directly Bosie spoke, saying firmly to Ples: "Mr. Butler . . . we got dead. I aim to bury 'em fo' we go a step further."

"Be the right thing to do," Ples said agreeably, walking away, remembering Hezekiah's words now that Hezekiah was among the dead.

Bosie looked a queer look at Fate standing next to him.

"Ples listens," Fate said, shrugging indifferently. ". . . Sometimes," he added, grinning wryly at Jerico.

Chapter Sixteen

The sun had dipped at least two hours past the overhead by the time Bosie had got the column organized and back in motion again. Much to his discomfort, John Deese had been ordered to ride Ike's horse; Bobo Jackson had volunteered to ride the extra mule that had had to be taken out of harness after the dead mule had been cut loose, the wagon being drawn by only a two-mule team instead of the standard army four-up.

Jerico and Ples were riding in the lead, heading for a ford of Big Blue Creek that Jerico knew of. It was on Bosie's mind to reach the Big Blue, cross over, and make camp before nightfall. He had no wish whatever to hear Ples's mouth again about camping with a stream at his back.

So they moved out. Every now and again somebody in the column would look back soberly, taking a last look at the three side-by-side mounds where they'd used the two broken shovels to dig three graves for Hezekiah, Ike, and Kalem. Fatback, Augie, and Willie had done most of the digging out of regard for Hezekiah, who had taught them to read, such as they could.

Now, under a high, wide, brassy sky, they moved on, frolicking indifferently, without care or vigil.

Scudding puffballs of fleecy clouds now and again blocked out the sun, throwing patches of shade upon the prairie. Giving the march an air of youthful romp. To Ples's chagrin. His age and temperament simply wouldn't allow him to indulge the friskiness of youth.

The attack they had expected had come and gone. And those who had survived had put behind them the dangers they faced out here. Just now, nobody cared. None of them, not even Ples, expected any more trouble.

Battie swung his horse out of the column, galloped up front, and falling in behind Ples and Fate, asked Jerico the question that was playing on everybody's mind: "How far's the fort from here?"

"We cross the Big Blue yonder," Jerico answered, nodding that way. "The fort's a day's ride north."

"The army was 'spose to come git us," Battie continued. "Where you reckon they at?"

"Ain't no tellin'," Fate answered. "Army's got they own ways. Ain't they, Ples?"

"That's fact," Ples answered. "Sometimes the army act like the right hand don't know what the left's doin', but they manage."

"Mr. Butler," Battie asked conversationally, "what you reckon they'll do with us when we git to the fort?"

"Was I them," Jake said, grinning, riding next to Battie, "first thing I'd do is stuff some old dirty rags in your mouth and shut you up."

Deke Poole, riding behind Jake, busted out laughing, then said, "He'd just swaller 'em and keep on talkin'."

Rafer D., riding next to Deke, smiled shyly.

"The army'll teach y'all how to march," Ples said seriously, ". . . how to ride, shoot, and such like. They'll keep you busy, all right."

"We seen it at Fort Scott," Fate added.

"I already know how to do all that stuff," Battie answered casually.

"Not the army's way," Ples retorted. "There's a whole lot more to solderin' you don't know . . . none of you do," Ples added, gigging his horse into a trot, getting away from the irksome bantering and badgering he'd heard so much of, and that was starting to wear on his nerves.

Just then Willie and Augie came into view, galloping toward the column from off to the west, riding in a blotch of shade cast by a scudding cloud blocking out the sun, throwing the land in shadow, where they happened to be riding.

Willie and Augie had ridden out to scout around, like Bowlegs, they had said; to get themselves in trouble, Ples had said; to kill good horses for no good reason, Jefferson had said; just being nosy youngsters, Bosie had said. But he had given them permission to go when Fatback had mentioned they could shoot some table meat, and Jerico had said they just might run across game since they were practically out of the Burnt District.

"Did y'all see Jimmy out there?" Bosie asked when Willie and Augie swung their lathered horses into the column, falling in behind Fate and Jerico.

"Naw," Willie answered. "We seen his tracks though."

"How you know they was Jimmy's tracks?" Battie asked rudely. "They coulda been anybody's."

"They was Jimmy's tracks," Augie answered brashly. "Jimmy's pinto ain't shoed and his right front hoof is chipped."

"How you know that?" Battie asked skeptically.

"Jimmy told us," Willie answered. "Told Jefferson too. Jefferson said when we git to the fort and he git a forge and some tools the first thing he's goin' to do is shoe all our horses real good."

"Jimmy told us how to read some other sign too," Augie added boastfully. "Didn't he, Willie?"

"Yep," Willie answered smugly. "Me and Augie can tell you about most anything out here."

"Yeah . . . ," Battie said dismissively, ". . . like you can tell most anything about that book Hezekiah was teachin' y'all how to read."

"We can read some," Augie said. "Can't we, Willie?"

"Yep," Willie answered. "Battie probably can't read none his own self. He can't do nothin' but talk. I betcha if Hoby was here, he'd . . ."

"Hoby's dead," Rafer D. said quietly. "Y'all leave him out of it."

"Yeah," Battie said agreeably. "And it wadn't my fault, neither."

"Nobody's sayin' it was yo' fault," Rafer D. answered mildly. "But Hoby's dead now. You oughta keep his name outa yo' mouth."

"It's my mouth," Battie answered. "I got a right—"

"Rafer D.'s right," Jefferson said frankly. "Hoby's dead. So's Hezekiah and Ike. Let 'em rest in peace," he added solemnly.

Riding casually at a walk out front where his eyes had been naturally sweeping ahead westward, Ples picked out Bowlegs riding toward them, leading three saddled horses. A man slung over the saddle of one of the led horses.

Ples jabbed heels to his horse, lifting him into a gallop, making a beeline for where Bowlegs was.

"What'd you bring him back here for?" Ples asked when he drew up.

"I make four," Jimmy said, nodding at the dead body of Archie Lee, whose name Bowlegs had no way of knowing.

"You make four, all right," Ples said agreeably. "But why'd you bring him back here?"

"I git big idea," Bowlegs answered.

"For you to haul him all the way back here, it must be a damn big idea," Ples answered. "What is it?"

"They no shoot so good," Bowlegs said, nodding toward the column, "because they scared white man. I teach them no more scared white man."

"How?" Ples asked.

"They shoot white man," Bowlegs said, nodding back at Archie Lee's body, "then they no scared no more."

"He's already dead," Ples replied.

"No matter," Bowlegs said, "he still white man."

"Damndest idea I ever heard of," Ples said. "But maybe you right," he added musingly.

"Butler know . . . ," Bowlegs said conversationally, "they talk like boy . . . play like boy. They must pass from boy to man, like you, like me."

"So you figure if they shoot into this white man's body, they'll pass from boys to men?"

"Man not made so easy," Bowlegs said sagely. "Butler know that. But we make try anyhow."

"You better tell him first," Ples said, looking back at Bosie riding toward them from where he'd stopped the column. He was riding forward now to find out if that was table meat, "a deer or somethin'," Fatback had said, that Jimmy had brought back slung over the saddle of one of the horses.

"You tell," Bowlegs answered. "He maybe no understand me. He look . . . listen good."

"What's wrong, Mr. Butler?" Bosie asked when he drew up, running his eyes over a dead body instead of the table meat they'd all been hoping for.

"Nothin's wrong," Ples answered. "Jimmy here's got an idea and I think it's worth a try."

"What is it?"

"That bunch of white men rode right through y'all back there and y'all didn't hit a one. . . ."

"It happened so fast," Bosie said again, ". . . and we ain't had much practice."

"That's fact," Ples said, "but mostly it was because they was scared. Ain't none of them boys ever raised a hand against a white man before. Every one of 'em is goin' to stay scared till they shoot they first white man. We figure to give 'em the chance. That way, they won't be scared no mo'. Sorta like 'nitiation," Ples added, seeing the cat-eyed way Bosie was looking at him.

"Shoot him?" Bosie asked incredulously, looking at Archie Lee's dead body. "He's dead already."

"Only white man we got to hand," Ples retorted.

"You think that'll work?" Bosie asked skeptically.

"Can't hurt none," Ples answered. "Like you said, he's dead already. March 'em by and let 'em see a dead white man close up, then stop 'em out yonder about a hunded yards or so and make every one of 'em shoot 'im."

"I fix," Bowlegs said, dismounting.

"Wouldn't hurt none if you was to tell 'em he's the one killed Hezekiah," Ples told Bosie, watching Bowlegs unstringing Archie Lee's body from the saddle.

"Was he the one for real?" Bosie asked.

"Don't matter," Ples said. "They all liked Hezekiah. That'll make 'em mad. Maybe make 'em shoot straighter."

"It might at that," Bosie said, turning the matter over in his head.

Ples and Bosie sat their saddles there, watching Bowlegs propping up Archie Lee's body in a sitting position in the crook of his saddle that he'd stripped off.

"He make good fight," Bowlegs said, looking at the gaping wound in Archie Lee's chest where he'd plunged in his skinning knife. Bowlegs had come up unsuspecting on Archie Lee, thinking Lee was dead from his wound. Lee, ever wiley, had been cunningly playing possum, and had summoned his last ounce of strength to spring at Bowlegs even though he knew he was mortally wounded and had been left on his own at the east bank of the Big Blue where Peyton Long and the others had crossed over.

"You want?" Bowlegs asked Ples, holding forth the holstered .45 and the big skinning knife on the same shell belt that Archie Lee had been wearing.

"Naw," Ples answered. "I like my own."

"Suit yo'self," Bowlegs answered, mimicking Ples. "I give to Je-ri-co," Jimmy said. "Maybe he kill more white men," he added, remembering that he'd heard Jerico had shot a white man already.

"Suit yo'self," Ples retorted.

"You take," Jimmy told Bosie, reaching up the reins of the three saddled horses he'd retrieved. "Now all have good horse," he added.

Bosie took the reins and wheeled out, heading back toward the column, meeting Fate along the way.

"Ples, Bosie said they goin' to shoot a dead man?" Fate asked disbelievingly when he galloped up and drew rein at Ples's side.

"Yeah," Ples replied casually. "Jimmy's idea."

"You goin' 'long with it? You all the time callin' him Wild Man . . . uncivilized and all. This sho' ain't civilized to me."

"I didn't say he was uncivilized. I said he was a wild man," Ples answered defensively. "There's a difference. Besides, this'll do 'em all some good. Sorta like 'nitiation.'"

"I heard of 'nitiation before," Fate said, "but nothin' like this."

"It won't hurt none," Ples said.

"Butler," Bowlegs called over from where he had propped up Archie Lee's body, "daylight maybe three hours more. I meet you there," and Bowlegs nodded toward the tree line marking the Big Blue.

"Bosie will want to camp on the other side," Ples told him.

275

"You tell Bo-see make hurry," Bowlegs replied. "Daytime no wait. Nighttime no good to cross river."

"He knows that, Wild Man," Ples said facetiously. "We'll be along directly."

Ples and Fate sat their horses there, watching the recruits file by, gawking at the dead white man, the first one they'd ever seen up close. All except Bosie and Jerico. They'd both seen dead white men; had killed a few themselves.

Willie and Augie were first to pass by, riding at the head of the column of twos.

"Jimmy killed him," Augie said in awe. "See where his knife went in?"

"I see, Augie," Willie answered. "Just like you do."

The wagon was last to parade by. Fatback riding the empty wagon's seat all alone now that Hezekiah was dead. The wagon empty because Bosie had made everybody get out and walk so they could get a close-up look at the dead man.

"Shootin' a dead man don't seem right," Jerico had said after Bosie had told them what they were going to do.

"He shot Hezekiah," Fatback had answered sullenly. "I'm goin' to shoot him."

And that's what he did. Hauling back hard on the lines, Fatback drew the wagon to a stop. Tightening his jaw in determination, he retrieved Hoby's carbine that he'd borrowed from Bobo Jackson and had propped on the wagon seat next to him. Deliberately bringing it to bear, he fired a bullet into Archie Lee's body. Calmly propping the weapon back against the seat, he took up the lines, shook the team into motion, and pulled off, to join the column that had moved on, his jaw still rigid.

Bosie halted the column in a slight undulation of the prairie some hundred yards west of where they'd left Archie Lee's body.

"We'll shoot from here," Bosie announced. "Rafer D., Jerico . . . ain't no need in y'all shootin'. I know y'all ain't scared to shoot white men."

"I ain't scared neither," Battie said. "I shot a white man back yonder."

"Nobody seen it," Bosie replied. "Now's your chance to prove it."

Under a high, wide, and cloud-studded prairie sky, twenty-one raw recruits walked up to where Bosie had stationed himself, took aim, and fired a shot at Archie Lee's body. Judging by the sneer on some lips, and the hard set to some jaws, not a few shots were fired in anger, as Ples had hoped. Only God knew how many bullets actually struck Archie Lee. But Bosie made anybody who was way off the mark shoot again.

Deke Poole was the last man to shoot. His first shot kicked up a trough of prairie sod at least twenty feet short of Archie Lee's body, now canted over from numerous hits.

Somebody snickered. Somebody on the rim of the rude horseshoe where they were all looking on in amusement.

"Shoot again," Bosie ordered Deke. "Aim higher this time."

Deke fired again. The result was no better.

"Bosie," Ples called out impatiently, "let it go. Jimmy's waitin'."

Just then a huddle of dark clouds moved over the sun, plunging the prairie where they were into shade. A stray raindrop spattered down. Then another, and another.

"You feel that, Sarge?" Deke asked Bosie, bringing his carbine around carelessly.

"Feel what?" Bosie asked back. "And keep that carbine pointed to the ground," he added rudely.

"Rain," Deke answered, looking up at the sky. "I felt raindrops," he added, ranging his eyes out at the gathering clouds looming off to the west.

"It ain't goin' to rain," Bosie said offhandedly. "Sky's mostly clear, sun's still out."

"Don't let that fool ya," Jerico said from off to the side where he was adjusting the swag on Archie Lee's gun belt that Bowlegs had given him. "Rain come up mighty quick out here," he added, looking at the gathering storm clouds that Deke had seen.

"Mr. Butler!" Jerico called ahead, gigging his horse into a trot, heading to where Ples was.

"Rain's comin'," Jerico said, reining his horse up next to Ples's.

"I wouldn't argue the point," Ples said, ranging his eyes west where the white puffballs of clouds that had been there ten minutes ago had now turned smut black, racing toward them. "Clouds startin' to git mean-lookin'," he added.

"Rain comes, it wudn't pay to be caught this side of the Big Blue," Jerico said. "Least little rain overflows the bottom land. No tellin' how long we'd have to wait to cross."

"Did you tell that to Bosie?" Ples asked.

"Naw. He was still hollerin' at Deke, tryin' to git him to shoot straighter."

"Maybe the rain'll go 'round," Ples said wishfully, lifting his eyes to the west again.

"Mr. Butler," Jerico said plainly, "I know this country. Them clouds rollin' in yonder . . . the wind's pushin' 'em and they full of water. They'll turned black and drop down some. It's goin' to rain," Jerico said definitely. "The only question is, how much?"

Presently, the wind stirred, tickling the prairie tufts. Stray raindrops increased to a patter.

"Guess you right," Ples said to Jerico. Turning in his saddle, he called back, "Bosie!"

"Yeah!"

"Rain's comin'! We intend to cross that creek, we better make haste!"

"I told you it was goin' to rain," Deke said to Bosie, lowering his carbine carelessly, glad to be doing anything except shooting at that white man, which he hadn't come close to hitting yet.

"Fatback!" Bosie called out, glancing up at the sky through slanting raindrops, "git that wagon movin'! The rest of y'all, mount up! Let's go!"

The recruits burst into motion: catching up bridle reins, clambering inexpertly into saddles. After a time, the column, such as it was, got into motion in a jouncing trot, heading into a drizzle of rain slanting down into their faces.

In less than half a mile they were all drenched to the skin, riding slumped forward in the saddle, faces turned aside or down against the rain.

The high, wide sky turned even darker, more ominous. The patter grew into a steady drizzle.

They plodded on.

The steady drizzle turned into a downpour. Big wind-driven torrents of raindrops whipping into their faces, and soaking the flat prairie earth. Their grass-fed horses moving heavy-legged, plodding along hang-necked in hock-deep mud, the wagon wheels cutting deep into the rain-sodden earth.

Yet the rain came down.

Twisting around in his saddle, looking from under his dripping pulled-down hat brim, Ples peered through the pelting rain at the column. And saw a jumbled-up mob, horses struggling to make headway, barely able to lift a foot out of the mire and place it ahead of the other, the wagon creeping along axle-deep in mud, Fatback lashing the lines against the mule's rumps.

Augie and Willie were walking, leading their horses. Augie had heard the labored breathing and had felt the panting sides of his gray, struggling to put a foot forward in the prairie mud and mire. "I rather walk myself," Augie had told Willie, "than see him hurt like this."

"Me too," Willie had said of his big bay horse. So they both had dismounted and were themselves slogging along through the quagmire to save the horses they'd come to love.

Ples's own heavy-hammed horse had been doing little better, and knowing the tree line marking the Big Blue was only something like half a mile away, Ples pulled up and dismounted, saying to Fate, whose own winded horse was struggling alongside him, "Best we walk some. We'll lame these horses we keep pushin' 'em like this."

Fate dismounted, started walking alongside Ples, leading his winded horse as Ples was doing.

"Mr. Butler!" Jerico called back from where his own horse was struggling along in front, leading them the way to the Big Blue, "we got to keep goin' till we git cross or we won't be able to."

"We don't give these hosses a rest," Ples yelled up through the wind and pouring rain, "we'll git there with dead hosses. We got to save our hosses and take our chances on crossin' the creek."

"We won't make it in time walkin'!" Jerico yelled back.

"No help for it," Ples answered.

Seeing Ples and Fate dismounted, Bosie dismounted the rest of the men, calling up to Ples, "Mr. Butler! What about this wagon?"

"It'll never make it," Ples yelled back, seeing the wagon axle deep in mud, the mules slipping and sliding trying to get a foothold. "Leave it!"

"Fatback!" Bosie yelled out when he struggled his horse over alongside the almost mired wagon, "can you ride one of them mules?"

"I rode a plenty befo'," Fatback answered.

"Let's unhitch 'em then," Bosie said, dismounting. "We leavin' the wagon here."

"What about that stuff in there?" Fatback asked.

"Take what you need and the bullets. Leave the rest," Bosie told him.

The whole column waited huddled against the wind and rain while Fatback and Bosie unhitched the team. Fatback slung his cooking tin and a sack of some small stuff onto one of the mules, tied the half-empty box of cartridges onto the other mule, then mounted one, the beasts still harnessed together.

"Ples!" Fate yelled out from where he was looking ahead. "There's Jimmy!"

They all looked that way. And saw Bowlegs standing in his stirrups off from the tree line a bit south of where they were headed, waving a beckoning hand, indicating the way they should come.

"Let's go!" Ples yelled out.

They moved out in a confused body, veering toward Bowlegs.

Bowlegs was waiting for them, standing slump-shouldered, dripping wet under a cluster of oak trees, the bark eaten away as high as Price's army horses' mouths could reach. This was Byrums Ford.

Byrums Ford was the best and safest crossing of the Big Blue for miles around. And it was exactly the crossing that Price's engineers had discovered when Price's eight thousand survivors of his twelve-thousand-man army had been whipped, and were fleeing from Missouri. Reaching the Big Blue after a day of marching in a torrential rainstorm, Price's engineers had had torn down in the surrounding counryside every house and barn, every corncrib and smokehouse, every gristmill and outhouse, to lay a plank road down to the water's edge for his wagons, caissons, and artillery pieces.

This corduroy road was still there, such as it was. And Bowlegs had found it.

"We cross here," Bowlegs told Ples and Jerico when they trudged up first in the lead. And Bowlegs indicated a dim, grown-over road that had been hacked out through the tree line, and leading down to the creek.

Ples led his dripping horse onto the plank road halfway through the tree line, looking through at the waters of the Big Blue.

"Jerico," Ples called back, "come look at this."

Jerico joined Ples, and they both stood there looking.

The sudden downpour had driven the Big Blue completely out of its banks. Foaming dirty water rushing by, carrying prairie sod, dead trees, and anything else that had got in its path on its headlong rush to join the Missouri River some twelve miles northeast.

"How deep you reckon it is?" Ples asked Jerico.

"I'd guess about six feet," Jerico answered. "How deep it is ain't the question though," Jerico continued. "How fast it's runnin' is the question."

"Jimmy!" Ples called back, "did you cross that?"

"I cross," Bowlegs said. "Maybe one hour ago."

"You think we can cross now?"

"We must cross," Bowlegs answered. "Food is there . . . for horses too. Here no food."

"We can cross," Ples answered. "But what about them?" he continued, nodding toward the recruits.

"I can cross," Jerico said. "Done it before when it was worse than this."

"We cross okay," Bowlegs said agreeably. "Maybe they not so okay."

"I seen the Big Blue like this before," Jerico said. "Sometimes it take three, four days for the water to go down."

Just then Bosie walked up, peering out at the rapidrunning, foaming water, eating at the tree-lined bank no more than twenty feet from where they stood.

"Jimmy says there's food and forage on the other side," Ples told Bosie. "And Jerico says if we don't cross now we'll have to wait here three, four days."

"What you think, Mr. Butler?" Bosie asked.

Off to the west, thunder muttered, then rumbled; lightning flashed.

"We cross," Ples said.

"Now," Jerico added. "Before it gits worse."

"We must go now," Bowlegs added positively, looking at the churning water, throwing up whitecaps. "Soon too late."

"Most of 'em scared, Mr. Butler," Bosie said, looking back over his shoulder at the water-logged recruits, standing hunkered, holding on to the reins of hung-necked, drenched horses. "You or Jimmy was to go first and show 'em, they'd foller."

"I show," Bowlegs said.

"I'll bring 'em," Bosie said, turning in his steps, heading back to bring up the huddled recruits.

"You wait," Bowlegs said, mounting up, calling out instructively at Bosie's back. "You look . . . listen good. Butler tell you when to come."

Ples, Jerico, and Fate sat their horses there, watching Bowlegs work his pinto across Blue Creek, following the plank road down to the water's edge, and keeping a direct line to where the planks began again on the other side. His pinto had obviously swum some, but how deep the rushing water was, nobody was prepared to say. But Bowlegs had kept his saddle, and had come out dripping wet on the other side. Turning in his saddle, he motioned Ples to send over the others now bunched up behind him.

"I ain't goin' cross there," somebody said. "I can't swim."

"You ain't got to swim," Bosie answered. "All you got to do is stay on your hoss. He'll do the swimmin'."

"We ought to go round," somebody else said.

"We ain't got time," Bosie answered. "We crossin' here. All of us," he added definitely.

"Fate and Jerico'll go first," Ples announced out loud to them all. "So you can see ain't nothin' to it. Like Bosie said, all you got to do is stay on your hoss and foller along.

"Bosie," Ples continued, "you go next and I'll send 'em cross one at a time. They git on the other side, keep 'em back from the water . . . and no horseplay!"

Fate led out, plunging his horse into the rushing water; Jerico and Bosie followed.

Sitting his horse on the upstream side, Ples prompted them across one at a time, using his judgment to send the least experienced riders first.

"You scared?" Battie called out to Rafer D. when Rafer D. tentatively guided his horse onto the planks.

"Battie!" Ples said testily, "shut your mouth and pay 'tention."

"I ain't scared," Rafer D. answered, more to himself than anybody else. Adjusting his carbine slung over his shoulder, he added confidently, "I can swim," and plunged his horse into the stream.

Nobody spoke a murmur after that. The stern set to Ples's face and the bark in his voice had let them all know that this was serious business. One by one they silently guided their horses into the water, each man keeping his own thoughts to himself, hearing Ples now and again yelling out instructions and encouragement.

A dozen men were strung out across the creek by the time Fate and Jerico were coming out on the west bank.

"Your turn," Ples told Battie. "You do this as good as you run your mouth and you'll make it."

"I ain't said a word, Mr. Butler," Battie answered, giving Ples a mock hurt look. "I'll make it," he added brashly and plunged his horse in.

"You'll make it," Ples said agreeably. "Just stay closed up and keep movin'."

The rain slackened.

Ples continued to feed them across without incident. Grinning, dripping wet recruits coming out on the west bank, proud that they'd made it.

"Fatback, you next," Ples said. "Keep that outside mule in line with the rest of 'em."

"I know," Fatback answered. "Back in Alabama I rode mules across the river more times than you can shake a stick at," he added haughtily.

"You ain't in Alabama now," Ples retorted. "So watch your step."

The rain slackened to a patter.

"Okay, you two," Ples said to Willie and Augie, the only ones left because they'd proven to be the best riders, "y'all come on."

Ples plunged his horse in, started splashing across. Willie and Augie did the same.

"Can you make it, Mr. Butler?" somebody yelled out facetiously from the west bank.

"Don't fall in!" Battie yelled chidingly.

They all started hooting and jeering, watching Ples's horse kicking up a spray of water, fighting its way across.

"Y'all shut up!" Bosie said admonishingly. "Mr. Butler don't like that kind of stuff."

"They just kiddin'," Jefferson said mildly. "We don't mean no harm."

"Mr. Butler ain't that mean nohow," Battie said agreeably. "He just want us to think he is."

"I wouldn't bet on it," Fate said seriously.

They kept on hooting and jeering even as Ples neared the west bank, Willie and Augie still out in the middle.

"There's a bunch of stuff comin'!" Jake yelled out, serious.

"Where?" Battie asked, looking where Ples's horse was swimming.

"Out in the middle, fool!" Jake yelled. "Headin' towards Willie and Augie!"

"It's a tree and stuff!" somebody cried out.

Ples looked downstream across his shoulder, and saw what they were alarmed about.

A huge tree that had been uprooted from the bank and cut adrift was hurdling along, its ball of tangled roots protruding out front, its branches bringing along other dead branches and all manner of drifting flotsam that they had collected.

"Augie!" Ples yelled back, "look out! Somethin' comin'!" Seeing that the flotilla of debris would intercept Augie, he screamed, "Stay where you at! Don't come no further!"

But it was too late.

Chapter Seventeen

Augie's big gray horse had just plunged into the deepest part of the creek and was now swimming furiously, making for the west bank as fast as his powerful legs could take him, Augie in the saddle holding on to the saddle horn.

"Come on! Augie," Willie yelled back from where his horse had already swum the ten or twelve yards of deep water and had struck bottom again.

"Come on, Augie!" they all started yelling and screaming from the bank, seeing that it was a race between Augie and the hurdling debris that would smash him if he didn't hurry.

Ples knew as soon as he splashed ashore and looked back that the race was lost. "Jimmy! Fate!" he yelled out, "ride upstream a ways. He might fetch up somewhere."

Bowlegs and Fate dug out, such as they could in the mud.

Augie had seen the floating raft of trees and trash coming at him, but there was nothing he could do. The gray simply wouldn't be turned back or stopped; all that horse wanted was to get to dry land on the other side.

They collided in midstream, the gray and the treetrunk, a knot of roots striking first. Smashing the gray alongside the head, knocking him silly, sending him floundering, thrashing about wildly without direction, Augie leaving the saddle. Disappearing in a foam of churning water and rushing debris.

"Augie!" Willie screamed, wheeling his horse back from where he was now only knee-deep, almost to the bank.

"Don't go back out there!" Ples yelled at Willie. "Ain't nothin' you can do."

Willie ignored him; kept on going. Splashing his horse back toward where Augie had gone down. "Augie!" he kept yelling out, turning his horse into the wake of the pile of drifting rubble that was hurtling on upstream.

"Augie's gone," somebody said sadly.

"Drowned under them logs," Cecil Hall added gravely.

"His horse's gone too," somebody added woefully.

"There's his hat!" Jake blurted out, pointing, seeing Augie's black flop hat that had surfaced some fifty yards upstream.

"Where?" asked Battie.

"Up in front of where Willie is," Jake answered.

Willie was on the near side of the creek, swimming his horse after the floating pile of junk, yelling "Augie!" at the top of his lungs.

Willie had seen the hat surface, and was now sailing along on the current. But Willie gave no thought whatever that Augie was gone. For good. Just like that. So he kept following the hat and the pile of debris, his horse swimming every now and again when he struck deep water.

"Damn fool youngster," Ples muttered helplessly, watching Willie go.

The patter of rain stopped.

"Mr. Butler . . . ," Jerico said solemnly, "there's a bend in the creek up yonder. Maybe he'll wash up to the bank there."

"Show me," Ples said abruptly. "Bosie," Ples continued, "y'all wait here. Keep 'em back from the water . . . and make 'em shut up!"

Jerico led Ples up the rise leading away from the water's edge, and they headed upstream, such as they could through clinging mud.

A quarter mile upstream, Willie was still wading and swimming his horse in the wake of the hat and the debris, steadily losing ground, his eyes fixed on the pile.

And then he thought he saw something move, something blue-looking in the tangle of green leaves and branches.

Willie fastened his eyes on the spot, looking intently.

The bluish something moved again.

Willie telescoped his eyes on the movement.

And saw that the movement was that oversize army shirt that Augie was wearing.

Presently a black head bobbed up, showing prominently among the green of leaves and branches.

Willie's heart leaped.

It was Augie! Clinging in the yoke of two branches, struggling to get a better hold in the lurching, tossing, pitching mass of heaped-up debris.

"Augie!" Willie screamed out at the top of his lungs, urging on his winded horse, such as he could.

Up ahead, Augie jacked himself around to a more secure position in his perch. Then glanced back the way he'd been carried. And saw Willie! Coming after him.

Clinging with one arm looped over a branch of the yoke, Augie waved frantically with the other hand, yelling as loud as he could: "Willie! . . . Willie! . . . I'm here!"

Sure that Willie had seen him, and possibly heard him, Augie twisted around, scouting his eyes ahead.

Seeing the bend of the creek up ahead, Augie concluded that he was about as close to the bank as he was likely to get.

Taking a deep breath, Augie let go of the yoke he had been suspended in, and dropping down through branches raking at his body and face, he took to the water under the debris. With a couple of kicks, and the debris moving away from him, Augie surfaced in the clear, sputtering water. A minute or two he swam, then stood up, and stumbled the rest of the way to the bank, sucking in great gulps of air.

Bowlegs had seen it all.

His eyes had been following that pile of floating debris ever since he and Fate had split up, Fate going farther upstream. He'd seen Willie futilely chasing after the pile of debris, and had also seen that blue shirt move just as Willie had.

Now sitting his horse up the rise of bank where Augie had slogged in, Bowlegs said without feeling, "You make good swim."

Augie was startled. His eyes found Bowlegs, and Augie blurted out: "My horse . . . did you see my horse?"

"I no see," Jimmy answered, his flat eyes holding on Augie dripping water from head to toe, his chest heaving for air.

"My horse . . . ," Augie shrieked, "I got to find my horse. . . ."

"Your friend . . . Wil-le come," Bowlegs told him. "He take you back. I find your horse." And Bowlegs was gone as suddenly as he'd come.

"Augie!" Willie called out happily, coming splashing along the water's edge. "You all right?"

"Yeah. I thought I was drowned for sho'."

"I thought you was too," Willie answered, dismounting.

"Gray Boy couldn't git out of the way," Augie said, using the name he'd come to calling his horse, a name only he and Willie knew about. Willie dubbing his own bay horse Brownie. "He's gone, Willie . . . did you see 'em?" Augie asked pleadingly.

"Naw," Willie answered. "He never came up like you did. He's drowned."

"Naw, he ain't," Augie said agonizingly "He ain't drowned," Augie added hopefully. "He's washed up some-where up yonder."

"He's dead," Ples said solemnly, sitting his horse up on top of the sloping bank.

"Is he for real?" Augie asked, dreading the answer.

"For real," Ples repeated. "Drowned."

"How you know?" Willie asked, remembering that he'd seen Jerico and Ples riding along the bank earlier, and they couldn't have gone farther upstream.

"Fate brought back his saddle," Ples said. "Jimmy was with him."

Augie's head dropped, his shoulders slumped, and his eyes welled over.

"Come on, Augie, let's go," Willie said quietly, taking him gently by the arm. "You can git another hoss," he added consolingly.

"Not like him," Augie said dejectedly, turning in his steps.

"Y'all come on," Ples said mildly. "It'll be dark soon." Ples watched them leading Willie's horse, working their way up the bank, slipping and sliding in their steps.

Ples turned his horse and walked him off, heading back to where the others were, his mind repelling the tender nature of youngsters: mooning like that over a dead horse.

It was coming on to sundown by the time Willie and Augie walked to where the others were on high ground some twenty yards up the rise from the rushing water. Wil-lie leading his horse. No more inclined to ride Brownie double through ankle-deep mud, as Augie would have been to ride Gray Boy under similar circumstances.

The westerly wind had driven away the water-laden storm clouds. Shoving them farther east to finish spilling what water they had left. Leaving a field of blue western sky shot through with crimson streaks of sun, its leading edge tingeing the far-off horizon purplish gold.

Everybody was waiting expectantly for Willie and Augie. Fatback off to the side, coaxing into flame damp leaves and broken branches to ignite the wet planks that Jerico had brought back from upstream where he'd ransacked an old barn he knew was still standing just outside the Burnt District.

They all had heard what had happened to Augie; had heard that Augie wasn't dead, hadn't drowned. Spirits had lifted, Battie's quips putting the whole bunch back into a light-hearted mood.

They all knew Augie, and Willie too for that matter, could take a ribbing as good as the next man.

Now Battie was asking, smiling disarmingly when Willie and Augie drew up to where they were gathered, "Augie, did you git your fill of water?"

"Yeah," Augie answered, grinning shamefacedly, "I got a good bellyful."

"Long as you live, Augie," Jake said, smiling broadly, coming forward, slapping Augie on the back, "you gonna git sick when you hear somebody say water."

"If that had a been ole big mouth Battie that fell in," Bobo said, grinning, "he'da drunk the creek dry."

Somebody laughed out loud.

Along with the rest of them, Fate grinned, in spite of himself, looking at Ples.

Ples shook his head in mock disgust, a hint of grin on his own lips.

"Augie's always wantin' to eat," Fatback said. "He ain' got no room in his belly to eat nothin' now. Is you, Augie?" Fatback asked facetiously, joining in the ribbing as he rarely did, speaking of the deer that Bowlegs had killed, had stashed away, and was now gone to bring in.

"Augie's always got room to eat. He ain' never gonna have no missed-meal cramps," said Jefferson.

"Soon's that deer meat's cooked," somebody else said, "Augie'll eat more'n any two of us put together."

"I didn't swaller all that much water," Augie said lamely. "For real," he added convincingly. "I was holdin' my breath mostly, swimmin' underwater."

"What about your hoss?" Deese asked curiously. "Did you see him at all?"

It got quiet; smiles and grins vanished. It was as if a skunk had dropped out of the sky and had landed in their midst.

"He never saw him," Willie said quietly, speaking for choked-up Augie. "Augie guess he was killed when that tree hit 'im."

"I bring him another horse," Bowlegs said, sitting his horse from where he'd quietly returned with the killed deer. "More better this time," he added, pitching the deer off from behind his saddle.

"Bosie!" Ples barked abruptly, breaking the moment, "we want to eat this meat 'fore it rot, you better git somebody else to skin him out . . . the way Fatback's foolin' 'round with that fire."

"I ain't foolin' 'round," Fatback answered grumpily, "this wet stuff ain't that easy to git burnin'."

"You just don't know what you doin'," Cecil Hall said mockingly.

"Why don't you do it, then?" Fatback said huffily.

"I do it," Bowlegs said, coming forward. "I make you good fire."

"Somebody ought to," Ples said. "He's been at it for a month of Sundays."

"I ain't neither," Fatback answered back.

"It ain't Fatback's fault," Fate said softly, trying to soothe Ples's impatience.

"Whose is it then?" Ples asked tersely, rising to standing. "Bosie . . . come mornin'," he added, "the ground's dry

293

enough, we'll move on to Fort Leavenworth." And Ples stalked off.

They all watched Ples march off, heading to higher ground.

"What's wrong with him?" Battie asked. Ples's words and actions had brought the question to all their minds.

"Nothin'," Fate answered, standing up, walking off after Ples. "He's just anxious to git goin'," Fate added, knowing full well Ples was in a huff because Deese had mentioned Augie's dead horse after Ples had told them all not to mention it and send Augie into a downcast.

"Jimmy's got the fire started now," Fatback said at Fate's back. "You ought to stay . . . git some meat," he added, ". . . take Mr. Butler some . . ."

"Meat can wait," Fate said curtly, and kept on walking.

"Mr. Butler's mad," somebody said. "He's leavin' us."

"Aww, that's just the way he is," Jake said. "He wouldn't go off and leave us. Would he, Sarge?"

"Leave it alone," Bosie answered ruefully.

"Is he leavin'?" Jefferson asked solemnly.

Jefferson was thirty-two, the oldest recruit there now that Hezekiah was dead. And like the rest of them, Bosie respected his age; owed him an answer.

"I don't know," Bosie answered earnestly. "I told him what you said about waitin' here till it dry out some or we'll lame these hosses."

"Only sensible thing to do," Jefferson said defensively. "I seen it happen a many times befo'."

"One more day . . . maybe a day and a half, we'll be at the fort," Jerico commented.

"Maybe not," Bosie replied. "Mud'll slow us down some. Anyhow, we'll see in the mornin'," Bosie added dismissively.

The flare of crimson sun disappeared behind the western rim of the horizon. Plunging into darkness the dripping trees they were camped under. The only relief from the utter black of night was the dancing flames of fire that Bowlegs had coaxed into being, and that Fatback had built up. Had the deer meat skewered over the fire on a fair-sized stick. Bowlegs had refused, for his own reasons, to skin and dress out the deer even though he knew perfectly well how to.

"I bring . . . you cook," Bowlegs had plainly said when he got the damp wood burning.

So Jake and Fatback had prepared the meat as best they could. Using Jake's Texas cow-skinning know-how and Fatback's Arkansas hog-killing skill, they had managed, but with considerable mutilation.

Nobody complained when the meat was cooked. They all came around, eating and bantering.

Time wore on. Talk died off; in groups of twos and threes they wandered off and turned in for the night.

A half dozen miles west and a little bit north of them, ex-Confederate Colonel Peyton Long and six other white men lay sleeping in their blankets under dripping oaks. Two hours ago they too had been huddled around a campfire. What they had eaten was meager, only what a man chanced to have in his saddlebags. And in Long's case it was jerked beef, washed down with coffee provided by Lige Green, a man who never traveled without it, so he said.

They had ridden in in brooding silence. Sitting off to the side drinking coffee, Peyton Long stretched his silence out to bitterness. Bitterness about the way Woot Tally's rashness had brought on a premature attack on the black recruits; and bitterness about the meager circumstances they now found themselves in. Meager circumstances Long had seen too much of during the war.

"Colonel," Lige Green said respectfully to Long now that his own leader Woot Tally was dead, "Mr. Bickley expect us to tackle that bunch again, we'll need more men."

"It didn't have to be this way," Long said solemnly. "We got four men dead . . . all for nothin'. That damn fool Woot," Long added bitterly.

"Woot's always been like that, Colonel," Frank Yoder said consolingly.

"Well, from now on we'll do things strictly my way," Long said solemnly. "You hear that, Lige . . . Martin?"

"I hear, Colonel," Lige replied agreeably.

"Okay by me," Martin answered.

"Maybe it wasn't all for nothin'," said Lige.

"How you figure?" Long asked innocently.

"The killin' wasn't just on our side," answered Lige. "We laid some of them to rest too."

"That's right," Martin stated. "Maybe they'll turn back."

"Not likely," Long said. "Not as long as that old black man's alive they won't turn back. I told Woot, now I'm tellin' you two . . . he's a stand-up fighter . . . don't scare easy. I don't know what his stake is in this but he's in it."

"I told Doyle we should'na took his wagon," Joe Shaler said. "That stuff what was in it wasn't worth much no how."

"That's water under the bridge," Long said dismissively. "We got him to deal with now."

"I still say we need more men," Martin stated.

"That'll be up to Mr. Bickley," Long replied, dashing out the leavings of his coffee. "I'll fill him in tomorrow when we git to Leavenworth City," Long added, reaching for his blanket roll. "We got a long ride ahead of us tomorrow," Long continued, unfurling his blanket roll. "I suggest you boys turn in too."

They did.

Morning came. Clear and hot. At their muddy camp on the west bank of the Big Blue, Fatback was first to stir. Had already poked into flames the smoldering coals he'd left last night. What little meat that had been left from last night was still there over the fire where the last man to eat his fill had left it.

Now, Fatback lifted his eyes at the sound of voices and saw Ples, Fate, and Bowlegs walking toward him, coming from up the rise where Ples and Fate had bedded down; only God knew where Bowlegs had slept, if he had at all.

"You got meat?" Bowlegs asked blandly when they drew up.

"Not much," Fatback answered. "Between Augie and the rest of 'em, ain't nothin' left but what you can pick off the bones. Anyhow, we goin' on to the fort this mornin' . . . ain't we, Mr. Butler?"

"It's up to Bosie," Ples said pleasantly, following Bowlegs's lead in twisting off a piece of meat from the carcass. "Jimmy here just come from out yonder. Figures it's dry enough to travel. But Bosie's in charge. . . . he'll have to decide."

"I go . . . git pay," Bowlegs said plainly. "Maybe I wait you at fort."

"Tell that to Bosie," Ples retorted. "I ain't in charge."

"I tell Bo-see," Bowlegs said between chews of the meat he'd pulled off.

"Tell me what?" Bosie asked, coming forward from where he'd slept, such as he could, burrowed in sedge grass and oak leaves, as they all had done.

"I go to fort," said Bowlegs.

"We all goin' to the fort," Bosie answered mildly.

"Wild Man here figures to go right now," Ples said good-naturedly. "Figures the ground's dry enough."

"It is," Jerico added, walking up from where he'd slept. "Before noon," he added, bending forward, picking at the carcass as the others had done, "it'll be so dry, you won't think it rained yesterday."

"I doubt that," Bosie said frankly, looking slant-eyed at Jerico.

By ones and twos the rest of them turned out, straggling down to the fire, each man picking at the carcass in his turn, searching for a morsel, such as he could find.

Augie got the brunt of ribbing when he and Willie walked up, Augie heading for the carcass picked to scabs now.

"Augie, much as you et last night . . . ," Deese said in mock anguish, "you oughta not want no mo'."

"Where you put so much food?" Battie asked, chewing on the tidbit of meat he'd managed to pick off.

"In my belly," Augie said flatly, roaming his eyes over the carcass, trying to spot some meat.

"Boy, you better tighten your belt some," Jefferson said. "Jimmy's gone. You ain't gittin' nothin' else to eat till we git to the fort."

"When we goin'?" Augie asked brightly.

"Yeah, when we goin'?" Willie repeated, looking at Ples.

"Ask him," Ples retorted, looking at Bosie.

"Soon as we eat," Bosie replied, his mind mostly made up now that Bowlegs had gone and the others had been prodding him ever since.

"Soon as we eat!" Jefferson repeated incredulously. "Ain't nothin' to eat. We might as well go now."

"All right," Bosie said in mock surrender. "Let's go," he added, standing up from where he had been squatting on his haunches.

"Let's go, y'all!" Bobo yelled out to all who hadn't heard.

The camp sprang into a burst of activity: men scrambling for loose-bunched horses, fitting on bridles, and slinging on saddles.

"I told you," Fate said knowingly to Ples over by the campfire where they were, watching the hive of activity.

"Told me what?" Ples asked innocently.

"Bosie would go if he figured you wanted to."

"His choice," Ples said contentedly.

"Didn't seem like it," Fate said smugly. "I'll git our horses," he added, grinning back at Ples.

"Augie!" Battie called out from where the horses had

been collected. "All that trouble you went through yesterday . . . almost drownin', losin' your hoss, and all . . . Sarge's got somethin' for you. . . . A present," he added slyly.

Augie looked a puzzled look at Willie; Willie shrugged unknowingly.

"What is it?" Augie asked skeptically.

"Rafer D.!" Jefferson called out. "Bring Augie's present out here."

"He's all your'n," Rafer D. said, leading forward the spare mule, passing Augie the reins. They'd put Augie's bridle and saddle on the big, hammerhead Missouri mule.

Augie looked a queer, almost hurtful look at Willie.

Willie grinned haltingly.

Doubtful smirks were on the faces of a few of them. Nobody quite sure if this was the right to do.

Seconds dragged by.

Then Battie smiled plainly; Jefferson's tentative grin spread into a wide smile.

"Go on, take him, Augie," Willie said encouragingly, smiling wider now.

"I bet this wadn't nobody's idea but Battie's," Augie said, taking hold of the reins, a smile playing on his lips in spite of himself.

"It was mine," Jefferson said, grinning. "I figured this mule just suit you."

"Till Jimmy git you another good horse," Willie said encouragingly.

"Beats walkin'," said John Deese.

"Let's go!" Bosie yelled out, seeing that Ples and Fate had taken to the prairie already. "Mount up!"

Across the prairie they went. Willie riding up front next to Augie jouncing along on the evil-gated mule. Augie had been more shamefaced than scared of riding the beast. The whole column leaving a swath of deep tracks in stiff mud. Ples and Fate in the lead, if you didn't count Bowlegs.

Nobody knew where he was out there now that his long-legged, fast-stepping pinto's tracks had disappeared from sight in front of them.

The sun climbed up the sky. Further drying out the prairie earth and anything else it touched.

At about noon they crossed over the Missouri-Kansas border. No more than a stone's throw from the main military road running from Fort Leavenworth, about twenty miles north, to Fort Scott, some fifteen miles south.

"Be a good place to noon down yonder," Ples said suggestively to Jerico riding next to him. And Ples nodded off to the right at a copse of trees situated in a shallow depression.

"It is," Jerico said agreeably. "People roundabouts call it Shady Grove. There's forage and water there . . . Brush Creek. Army stops there mostly."

"Mr. Butler!" Bosie called out, coming pounding up from the middle of the column where he'd been riding. "Be a good place to noon down yonder." And he drew up, pointing.

"Your choice," Ples said carelessly, looking cat-eyed at Jerico.

"As good a place as any," Jerico said. "Army uses it."

"We'll use it too, then," Bosie said, turning his horse.

"He's learnin'," Ples said, more to himself than to Jerico. And they swung their horses that way.

They nooned down in the shallow valley covered with perhaps two acres of oaks, Brush Creek running along the northern fringe. A circle of rocks, dead ashes, and sticks of half-burnt wood from previous campfires still there.

They didn't know it, but this was precisely the place where Long and his men had camped only hours ago.

Bowlegs had known it. And had quietly told Ples. And at Ples's direction had kept it to himself. Ples had figured there was no use in starting another panic among the recruits since Bowlegs had told him that the riders had headed north, obviously not planning another attack.

Augie had got down from his mule, stiff-backed and sore-butted. Right off they started giving him the business, instigated by Battie. Willie grinning and laughing right along with the rest of them now that he knew Augie had got over the loss of Gray Boy, or else had just put it to the back of his mind.

"You can keep that mule if you want to," Fatback was saying seriously.

"Not for nothin' in this world," Augie said, grinning good-naturedly. "I want another hoss as soon as Jimmy git me one."

"Where he goin' to git it?" Deese asked. "Ain't no wild hosses 'round here."

"I don't care where he git it," Augie answered, "as long as I git me another hoss."

"What about somethin' to eat, Augie?" Deke asked. "You want some more of that too?"

"You know we ain't got nothin' to eat," Fatback said scoldingly. "And ain't goin' to git nothin' till we git to the fort."

"What if we don't make it there today?" Augie asked.

"Then you ain't gittin' nothin' to eat today," Fatback answered rudely.

"First thing we do," Bosie announced to them all, "is see to these hosses. "Water 'em and tie 'em up somewhere."

"That don't go for you, Augie," Bobo said impishly. " 'Cause you ain't got no hoss," he added, grinning.

"You might as well not have one," Battie said, as they fell in behind Bosie, leading their horses down to the creek. "You can't ride nohow."

"I can ride better'n you," Bobo answered. "Shoot better'n you too," he added.

"How come you didn't hit none of them white men then?" Battie asked.

301

"You didn't hit one neither." Bobo answered back.

"I did too," Battie said seriously.

Somebody snickered in disbelief; Jake laughed out loud.

"What you laffin' at?" Battie asked. "You didn't hit one neither."

"At least I ain't lyin' about it," Jake said, grinning.

"What's Battie lyin' about now?" Bosie asked, overhearing the conversation from alongside the creek, his horse already taking its fill.

"Battie swears he hit one of them white men," Bobo answered. "Did he?"

"Did a man in the moon?" Bosie asked incredulously.

"Naw," Bobo answered.

"Well, Battie ain't hit nobody either," Bosie replied definitely. "Y'all finish waterin' your hosses, and come on back," Bosie told them, leading his horse away.

Meanwhile, under a spreading oak off to the side of the circle of rocks and dead ashes, Ples and Fate had been standing there watching the others leading their horses to water, bantering and kidding good-naturedly, Fate grinning as if he were right there along with them. And Ples knew he ought to be there. Wished he were, in a way. When they were out of earshot, Ples started stripping off his saddle gear, saying conversationally to Fate, "Why don't you go on down and join 'em? Your hoss needs waterin' too."

"Your'n do too," Fate answered.

"Mine can wait," Ples said, dragging off his saddle and blanket, tossing them against the treetrunk.

"Mine can too," Fate said, ripping off his saddle and gear.

"You gave any thought to what we talked on?" Ples asked casually.

"What?"

"Joinin' the cavalry," Ples said offhandedly. "Be a good thing for you."

"I thought we settled that," Fate replied dismissively.

"We ain't settled nothin'," Ples retorted.

"Well, I did," Fate said definitely, and walked off, heading to where Fatback was picking over the dead ashes, looking for half-burnt firewood he could use.

"Mr. Butler!" Bosie yelled from down by the creek, looking north, "Jimmy's comin'!"

Ples walked a dozen paces out into the open, then stopped, looking north. It was Bowlegs all right. Galloping his pinto toward them, obviously coming from the main road.

Bowlegs drew reins next to Ples and Bosie, who had joined Ples.

"Army come," Bowlegs said flatly, swinging down, walking his horse over to the fire that Fatback had got started.

Ples and Bosie glanced questioningly at each other, then followed Bowlegs.

"You seen the army yo'self?" Ples asked anxiously.

"I see," Bowlegs answered, looking askance at Ples for asking the question.

"How far off?" Bosie asked.

"Not far," Bowlegs answered blandly, unhooking from his saddle horn two rabbits he'd killed. Throwing the meat down next to the fire, saying brusquely to Fatback, "I bring . . . you cook."

"Hey, y'all!" Bosie called out down to the creek where the others were, "the army's comin'! Y'all come on!"

Exuberant yells went up from down by the creek, everybody glad the army was finally coming.

"Yeeaaa! The army's comin'!" Deke cried out jubilantly.

"What you hollerin' 'bout?" Battie said in mock derision. "They'll prob'ly send you back to the cotton fields," he added, grinning.

"Not me," Deke said assuredly. "I'm goin' to mind . . . do like they tell me to."

"How to shoot too?" Bobo asked.

"That too," Deke said confidently.

"Naw, you ain't," Battie said bluntly, leading his horse away, " 'cause you ain't got sense enough to." And Battie led his horse away from the creek, following after Willie, Augie, and some others, heading back.

Tying their horses wherever they could, scattered about the oaks, they gathered in twos and threes around the circle of campfire stones. Everybody apprehensive. Talking in low tones. Not knowing what to expect from the army. More than a few having already asked Bowlegs the same questions Willie was now asking, "How many of 'em was it, Jimmy?"

"Not many," Bowlegs said for at least the third time.

"How you know they the ones comin' to git us?" Battie asked.

"I know," Bowlegs repeated with certainty.

"You don't know everythin'," Battie said doubtfully, ". . . Wild Man."

"I know," Bowlegs repeated. "You look . . . you see."

They all looked the way Bowlegs had nodded his head.

And saw three wagons, two riders in front, snaking their way along the main road.

Presently, the procession turned off, heading toward them.

"How they know where we at?" Augie asked, more of himself than anybody else.

"I tell," Bowlegs said flatly.

"How'd you know we'd be here?" Augie asked, awed. "You was gone."

"I know," Bowlegs said plainly.

They all stood there watching the army wagons come on, a saddled horse tied behind each wagon.

"You know the captain?" Ples asked Bowlegs when they drew close enough for him to recognize that a captain was riding in the lead, and a black sergeant was riding next to him; all three drivers were black.

"I know," Bowlegs answered. "I see at fort. He buy horses."

"What about the sergeant with him?"

"I no see," Bowlegs answered.

It was Captain Dudley. From Fort Leavenworth.

Chapter Eighteen

Captain Gilford Dudley had left Fort Leavenworth before first light this morning with Sergeant Remus Brown and three wagons of supplies. Going out to locate a partial company of new recruits who hadn't been provided an escort, and consequently hadn't reported for training. Unforeseen and unimagined problems had prevented Colonel Grierson from sending out an escort days ago.

Problems had been thrown in Grierson's way by Lieutenant Spurlock, who had been left in command at Fort Leavenworth when Colonel Hoffman took to the field in search of promotion and glory with General Custer, himself ever in search of headlines and glory.

Lieutenant Spurlock had verbal orders to thoroughly obstruct Grierson—hold up supplies, discard or lose requisitions, deny rations—in any and every way possible. This colored regiment Grierson was putting together would never succeed if Colonel Hoffman had his way.

And Spurlock had succeeded beyond even what Hoffman had prayed for.

Grierson was thoroughly frustrated. And infuriated. Driven almost dog-mad. Grierson could see there was only one thing left he could do: relocate his regiment. Get out of Fort Leavenworth. Move farther west to Fort Riley. With or without army knowledge, certainly without army orders.

The only saving grace that Grierson had for this unauthorized transfer was that the army high command, General Grant in particular, expected him to succeed. Plus Grierson knew that Grant expected his subordinates to be resourceful, even unorthodox, in the face of daunting obstacles. As Grant himself was. Like the time back in '63 when he had been stymied in his effort to descend the Mississippi River and attack from the rear Vicksburg, the citadel of the Confederacy. For six months and with seven failed attempts, Grant had had his army digging canals, redirecting creeks to alter the flow of the mighty Mississippi, trying to leave Vicksburg up on the bluffs high and dry so that his army could come to grips with the high-sighted fort's defenders. The capricious, impetuous Mississippi River would not be redirected. But Grant had let the whole country know he was a man who would try anything to achieve his objective. Which he did on the eighth try.

Now Grierson was trying a wholly unorthodox method of his own to achieve his objective. Hoping Grant and the war department would understand. Knowing they would if he succeeded in turning ex-slaves into a fighting regiment.

So here was Captain Dudley. With orders to reroute these stragglers. Send them to Fort Riley rather than to Fort Leavenworth.

Dudley drew rein and for a long minute he sat in his saddle stiff-backed, perfectly silent, deliberately running his eyes over the recruits fanned out in a rude horseshoe around the stones of the campfire, Rafer D. standing prominently up front, his carbine slung over his shoulder. They were all looking him over with about as much apprehension of him as he had of them.

Nobody could say what the recruits were thinking. But Captain Dudley was thinking that what he was looking at was a motley bunch of mud-spattered, sloppy-looking, ill-dressed, partially clad recruits who'd need to be whipped into shape fast if they were to measure up to the nine hundred and fifty other recruits who had been rounded into right smart-looking troopers, as Grierson himself had pronounced them when they rode out last evening, heading for Fort Riley. But there was more training, much more training to be done. And Grierson knew it.

Dudley looked doubtfully across his shoulder at Sergeant Brown. And could read nothing in the sergeant's manner.

"Sergeant Radford?" Dudley finally asked out, looking for the recruit that Lieutenant Badger had put in charge.

"Yeah, suh," Bosie answered, shifting uneasily in his steps.

"I'm Captain Dudley," he stated firmly, running his eyes up and down Bosie's body, sizing him up. Exposing for the first time the southern lilting rhythm to his voice. The kind of voice these recruits had heard too much of from men they were trying to get away from.

"Is he the cavalry?" somebody asked in low tones.

Nobody answered but the question was on all their minds. They all had come from far and wide to join the cavalry. Now the cavalry was here. And they all were leery about the voice they'd heard, and the man behind the voice.

"Sergeant," Dudley continued, "I'm here to see that y'all git to camp. Fall in for roll call, and I'll explain it to all of y'all," he added.

"Yeah, suh," Bosie answered.

Dudley brought his eyes around to the older, well-armed man, with a youngster just as well armed standing next to him.

"Butler?" Dudley inquired.

Ples nodded affirmatively.

"Feller named Dinsmore's been to the fort askin' about you. Says he hired you to deliver supplies."

"He did," Ples said. "And I did."

Dudley nodded his head agreeably, asking casually, "Them carbines I see 'round, they what you delivered?"

"Part of it," Ples answered.

Dudley made no reply. Started roaming his eyes over the woods surrounding the camp, seeing slack-legged horses tethered about. Bringing his eyes around to Bowlegs, he said, "I see you delivered the horses."

"You pay now?" Bowlegs asked expectantly.

"I no pay . . . remember?" Dudley answered, recalling the same conversation he'd had with Bowlegs back at the fort. "Army pays," Dudley added, swinging down from his horse.

The sergeant sitting his horse next to Dudley swung down too. And Dudley told him, "Sergeant, have the teams unhitched and watered."

"Yeah, suh," came the reply.

Dudley fished around in his saddlebags for his muster roll, looking back over his shoulder even as Bosie was poking and prodding the recruits into a semblance of formation.

Everybody got serious-looking. The laughing and grinning put aside now. They all knew the army was finally here. This was serious business. Somebody could get sent packing, as Ples had told them he'd heard tell of. None of them wanted that. Not even after seeing that Captain Dudley was a Southerner.

Dudley walked up front and center of the solemn faces, the recruits standing in postures ranging from relaxed to exaggerated attention.

Dudley's eyes scanned his muster roll, which contained a crude description of each recruit that Lieutenant Badger had forwarded.

While Ples, Fate, and Bowlegs took their ease lying back in the crook of their saddle under a shade tree off to the side, looking on with mixed feelings, Captain Dudley called the roll, each recruit answering up according to his lights and disposition. Dudley giving each the once-over, comparing what Lieutenant Badger had written down with what he saw.

"Skidmore," Dudley was saying, ". . . Hezekiah."

No answer.

"He's dead," Bosie said.

Dudley looked across his shoulder at Bosie.

"Suh," Bosie added, catching himself.

"How?" Dudley asked.

"Shot, suh."

"Where?" Dudley asked.

"Back yonder, suh," Bosie answered.

"I'll want a written report, Sergeant," Dudley said with conviction. Then thinking twice, Dudley asked innocently, "You can write, can't you?"

"Yeah, suh."

Captain Dudley resumed calling the roll.

He looked twice when he called out Jerico's name, seeing Jerico the only recruit armed as he was with Archie Lee's big Colt .45 hanging low on his thigh and a big skinning knife on the other side.

Dudley and Grierson both had come to know that the country roundabouts was wrought up over the outcome of the late war between the states. Vengeance prevailed. Retaliation was ever looked for. Most nobody would pass up a good opportunity to shoot or hang a Yankee, or one of their lowlife, inferior niggers the Yankees protected.

Grierson and Dudley both had suspected that without a heavy escort the recruits would more than likely run into trouble. But Dudley was shocked to hear that three other recruits had been killed along the way. Recruits that must be accounted for on the army's rolls. Dudley demanded of Bosie a complete written report detailing the circumstances of each recruit's death, which would be forwarded to the war department.

"All right," Dudley said when he'd finished calling the roll, "there's been a change of plans. "Y'all goin' to Fort Riley instead of Fort Leavenworth," he added, roaming his eyes around, looking for a reaction.

He could discern nothing; there was none.

"In them wagons," Dudley continued, "there's provisions and supplies—uniforms, saddles, camp gear, weapons, ammunition . . . everything troopers need in the field. And enough rations to get you to Fort Riley."

At the mention of rations, taunting eyes came around to Augie.

But nobody dared say anything, or grin, or snicker.

"Right now," Dudley added, "y'all part of Company M. Just like them troopers you see over yonder." And Dudley nodded that way.

They all looked. And saw three well-tailored troopers standing tall next to a supply wagon.

"They been through most of what y'all got to go through. Private Ross there is goin' to stay with you . . . he's learned already. And he's goin' to teach you what he's learned . . . what he and the rest of Company M have already learned.

"By the time you get to Fort Riley, all of you better know what he's gonna teach you: how to wear your uniform properly . . . how to sit a saddle, how to shoot . . . march, follow orders. Any one of you who don't, Company M don't want you . . . the regiment don't want you . . . the cavalry don't want you." Dudley paused, letting his words sink in.

Silence reigned.

Nobody sure of what to expect; this sounded ominous. Nobody sure they could measure up.

"Fall 'em out, Sergeant," Dudley finally said to Bosie. "And have somebody break out some of them rations from that last wagon." Dudley faced away, started to walk off.

"Yeah, suh," Bosie answered, shaken by the suddenness and sweep of it all, just as the others were.

". . . And, Sergeant," Dudley added over his shoulder, "we got one hour to noon." And Dudley kept on walking, heading toward the inviting shade where Ples, Fate, and Bowlegs were.

These three had been listening with mixed thoughts while the captain had been talking. Now they saw him coming their way.

They all rose to standing.

Fate started walking toward the recruits, some clustered around Sergeant Remus Brown and Private Asa Ross, ogling their complete well-tailored uniforms, some others milling about in small clusters, talking in measured tones.

Bowlegs started walking toward his horse. Nobody could say whether because the captain was white-faced or whether because the captain was a yellowleg, as most Indians called cavalrymen.

Captain Dudley approached Ples, standing there alone now.

"You 'bout to leave too, Butler?" Dudley said amusingly.

"I wasn't fixin' to," Ples answered.

"You must be the only one then," Dudley said casually, taking a seat on one of the half dozen big logs scattered about that somebody had dragged up, and other campers had worn slick from sitting on. "I guess they wasn't expectin' the likes of me."

"Truth be told," Ples said, "none of 'em knowed what to expect."

"And you?" Dudley asked, looking across his shoulder at Ples as if he were seeing him for the first time. "You wonderin' what I'm doin' here?"

"It ain't no wonder to me," Ples answered, dropping back down, leaning back in the crook of his saddle. "I ain't in the army. I was hired to deliver supplies."

"So you was," Dudley answered resignedly. "This Dinsmore feller," he continued conversationally, "he spoke highly of you. Said you was one of the few colored men hereabouts who hadn't cowered down. Said you'd stand up for yo'self."

"Been my intention to," Ples answered dispassionately.

"What about them?" Dudley asked, nodding toward the recruits.

"What about 'em?" Ples asked innocently.

"You seen 'em," Dudley answered. "You been with 'em. You know what they like. I ain't convinced they can make it to Fort Riley on their own."

"How come you don't take 'em then?" Ples asked.

"I can't. There's more just like them comin' into Fort Leavenworth with no idea to go to Fort Riley. Believe me, Butler," Dudley said, chuckling at the thought, "before it's over with I'll have my share to take to Fort Riley.

"They'll need you, Butler," Dudley said soberly. "I got authority to hire a guide and a wrangler. I ain't much worried about a wrangler," Dudley added, smirking to himself.

"Bowlegs?" Ples asked. "Did he say he'd go?"

"He'll go," Dudley stated factually. "He got pay comin'. The paymaster's at Fort Riley."

"He'll go then," Ples said agreeably, amused at the fix Dudley had Bowlegs in.

"Butler," Dudley continued, "Dinsmore left me the impression you and that youngster was mostly footloose. Trying to make somethin' out of an old farm hereabouts that's got doubtful title to it."

"Intend to fix it up," Ples said confidently. "Make a go of it."

"What about him?" Dudley asked, looking out at Fate talking animatedly right along with the rest of them. "He seems to like the company he's keepin' now."

"We been together nigh on to four years now," Ples said, looking out thoughtfully at Fate. "He's kind of growed on me, but it's crossed my mind he ought to join up. I brought it up but he ain't willin' to listen."

"No offense to yo'self, Butler," Dudley said, looking cat-eyed at Ples, "but you ain't gittin' no younger. He ain't got no future knockin' 'round with you."

"He won't listen to me," Ples replied. "His thinkin' is he's lookin' after me. My thinkin' is the cavalry would be a good place for 'im."

"He looks strong and healthy enough," Dudley answered, looking again at Fate. "His mind ain't bad, is it?"

"Naw," Ples said, amused at the question. "Not if you don't count goin' off half cocked."

"This regiment's lookin' for colored men sound of body and mind. Seems like he'd do."

"That's my thinkin' too," Ples answered. "But he won't talk much on it."

"Well, keep at 'im," Dudley answered, looking out at Fate and the rest of the recruits, eating army rations, talking, and grinning.

"You want to know somethin', Butler?" Dudley continued directly. "You . . . and them neither," he added, nodding that way, "might not like the sound of my voice, or where I come from, but I believe there's a future in this regiment. Truth is, I'm stakin' my career on it."

"How come?" Ples asked.

"Let's just say I'm doin' it for my country, our country," Dudley said, looking squarely at Ples. "What about you? Maybe you don't figure you owe your country nothin'. That's all well and good. But you owe them somethin'." And Dudley nodded toward the recruits. ". . . Your own kind."

"I was hired to take 'em supplies," Ples said defensively, "and that's what I done. And brought 'em this far."

"Take 'em on to Fort Riley," Dudley said rudely, more an order than anything else. "You know, and I know, how the country is. Ain't a one of 'em know the way. And if trouble was to come, ain't a one of 'em can stand up to it.

"Except maybe him," Dudley added on second thought, looking at Jerico standing off to the side, looking the way he knew Fort Riley was.

"Maybe," Ples said agreeably. "From what I heard."

"You heard he killed a white man back in Jefferson City?"

"Yeah."

"He was also a Jayhawker," Dudley added distastefully. "The worst of thieves and murderers who took advantage of the war. Right along with Quantrill and his bunch. Quantrill's dead now, but there's a hew and cry for some of his men to answer to the law. Some Jayhawkers too."

"He included?" Ples asked, indicating Jerico.

"More'n likely. Colonel Hoffman wired a demand to the fort that he be held on court-martial charges of murder. Seems some prominent citizen named Bickley dispatched him about the killing. Once he's brought to trial ain't no tellin' what all he'll have to answer for."

"You takin' him back to Fort Leavenworth?"

"Not if you was to take him to Fort Riley," Dudley answered thoughtfully, looking slyly at Ples.

"I see," Ples said, catching the drift of the fix Dudley was trying to put him in. "Well . . . if you was to convince him"—and Ples nodded toward Fate—"to join up . . . I'd more'n likely want to ride along . . . see that he got to Fort Riley."

"If I can't convince him," Dudley said, smiling, "this regiment don't need 'im." And Dudley walked away from Ples, saying out loud: "Sergeant Radford! Noonin's over! Finish them rations . . . and fall 'em in. We got duty to perform!"

With a burst of motion under the captain's watchful eye, the recruits fell in in half the time it had taken before.

Dudley spoke, saying, "Private Ross, first thing we goin' to do is demonstrate how a trooper is expected to look in uniform. Take Fate here to the wagon, outfit him in a complete uniform so they can see."

Fate smiled at the prospect; Dudley looked knowingly at Ples; Ples didn't know what to do.

"Fit him good, Private Ross," Dudley added. "Carbine, side arm, campaign hat, everything."

"Yeah, suh," Private Asa Ross replied snappily.

When they were gone, Dudley continued in a voice of authority: "All of y'all that got carbines . . . they're unauthorized. As far as the cavalry's concerned, you stole 'em. Bring 'em all up here and pile 'em right here." And Dudley indicated the spot. "Sergeant Radford, see that they all git up here."

"Yeah, suh."

Every carbine that Ples had delivered was brought forward and dropped in a pile under Radford's watchful eye. Augie and Willie, behind Rafer D., were last to drop their carbines on the pile, Augie asking Willie in a low voice, "We ain't goin' to have no gun to protect ourself?"

"How I know?" Willie answered.

"Army's goin' to issue you one," Dudley replied, overhearing the question from off to the side.

Just at that time, Fate climbed over the tailgate of the covered wagon where he'd changed clothes. Gone were his faded Levi's jeans, black cotton shirt, and down-at-heel boots. He was now dressed out in a well-fitting blue cavalry uniform, yellow stripe running down the legs stuck inside high-topped cavalry boots. His own low-crowned hat had been replaced by a wide-brimmed campaign hat, crossed sabers on the front. Even his side pistol had been replaced with a flapped-over Army Colt.

Fate strutted forward beaming, first at Ples, then at the other recruits, who'd all shifted their attention on him.

Dudley smiled cunningly at Ples; Ples wagged his head at Dudley's craftiness.

"Fate . . . you look right smart," Dudley said, smiling, when Fate drew up in front of them. "Now this is the way a trooper is supposed to look," Dudley announced proudly. "The way you all have got to look by the time Mr. Butler git you to Fort Riley."

Fate jerked his eyes around at Ples, the beaming smile vanishing. This was the first time he'd heard of this.

Ples shrugged helplessly.

"For y'all's information," Dudley continued, "Mr. Butler has signed on as company guide. He's goin' to lead you to Fort Riley." And Dudley said it more to Ples than anybody else.

"Fate here," Dudley announced, bringing his eyes back around on Fate, "is fixin' to joining the cavalry, like Mr. Butler's been urgin' him to do."

They all cheered lustily.

"Yeeeaaahhh!" somebody yelled out exuberantly; "alll rriight!" another recruit said cheerfully.

Fate Jerked his eyes around at Ples again.

Ples shrugged defensively; wagging his head in distress at the way Dudley had put them both in a fix.

"All right!" Dudley called out sharply, "Private Ross is goin' to outfit the rest of y'all."

"Private Ross, take 'em in two at a time. Outfit 'em properly, and make sure every one of 'em sign for his side arm.

"Private Lamb . . . start issuing out them carbines. Every trooper is to sign for that too . . . by serial number.

"Fate," Dudley said finally, "you come with me. I need your name on an enlistment contract."

Fate was wide-eyed, looking powerlessly in Ples's direction; Ples nodded affirmatively.

It was in the shank of the afternoon when Captain Dudley finished doing cavalry business. Each recruit had been fitted with a complete, properly fitting uniform, including boots and spurs; had been issued a seven-shot Spencer carbine and Colt Army .45 flapped-down pistol; and twenty-two McClellan saddles with saddlebags, blankets, bridles, and lariats had been passed out. Last but not least, a guide had been hired, and one new recruit had been signed up. All in all, Captain Dudley was proud of his accomplishments. The only thing hanging fire now was the matter of a wrangler. Bowlegs was still out there.

Only God knew where.

"Huntin' for meat more'n likely," Ples said speculatively to Captain Dudley, who had resumed his seat on the log. "He'll be in round sunset."

"We don't have till sunset, Mr. Butler," Dudley said wearily.

"You pullin' out this evenin'?" Ples asked, surprised.

"That's right," Dudley answered. "The sooner I git back to Fort Leavenworth the better off we'll all be. As it is, ain't no tellin' what might've happened since I been gone."

"That bad?"

"That bad," Dudley repeated disgustedly. "Mr. Butler . . . ," Dudley continued, talking in confidential tones, "I know you hired on as a guide but I expect you to keep an eye out. General Custer's got every Cheyenne Indian between Smoky Hill River and Mexico stirred up. Colonel Grierson thinks they're gathering somewhere. Possibly on Walnut Creek. You run into any, stay clear of 'em. Git word to Fort Riley if you can.

"As far as your routine goes, Private Ross knows that. Daily drills, cavalry regulations, and all. Anything he can't remember, he's got a copy of *Hardee's Cavalry Tactics Manual*. So you'll have no trouble on that score."

"What else is there?"

"Sergeant Radford is who I'm concerned about. Lieutenant Badger picked him as sergeant because he had experience . . . was at Brice's Crossroads. Well . . . I told him I was at Brice's Crossroads too. Told him we licked 'em,

318

licked 'em good . . . pure and simple. And we licked 'em because they wasn't trained. And I told him that's what'll happen to them out there"—and Dudley nodded the way of Fort Riley—"if he don't see they git trained.

"He'll have to keep after 'em, day and night if it comes to that. Make 'em do their trainin'. What I said ain't no empty threat. I wadn't just spoutin' off when I said I'll send any one of 'em packin' who don't measure up . . . and you know perfectly well what I mean, Butler," Dudley added, looking squarely at Ples.

"Don't measure up to white troopers?" Ples asked.

"Exactly," Dudley stated. "That's Colonel Grierson's standin' order. And I aim to see it carried out. Even if I have to cashier Sergeant Radford . . . or the whole company."

"Well . . . he listens good," Ples said honestly. "He can't help but learn."

"He better," Dudley said. "I told him everything I just told you. Told him to listen to you and Private Ross. But in the end, it's his own common sense and judgment he'll have to look to and answer for.

"Well . . . ," Dudley said, catching himself for talking so openly, ". . . good luck, Mr. Butler," he added abruptly, standing up, reaching out a palm toward Ples.

"What about Jimmy?" Ples asked even as they were shaking hands.

"When he come in, you tell him for me . . . he wastin' good horseflesh ridin' to Fort Leavenworth. The paymaster's at Riley." And Dudley walked off, leaving Ples standing there searching for words.

Captain Dudley and Sergeant Brown rode out at the head of two empty wagons; the cook wagon had been turned over to Fatback.

A dozen or so yards away Dudley twisted around in his saddle and yelled back over his shoulder, struck by an afterthought, calling out, "Private Ross!"

"Yeah, suh," Ross answered up, standing near the fire with an iron triangle held in one hand, a piece of iron rod in the other. To serve as the bugle call. They had no bugle, and nobody to blow one even if they did since Ike Peeler was dead.

"See to your duty!" Dudley commanded a last time, then twisted around, touched spurs to his horse, and rode away.

"Yeah, suh," Ross said quietly at his back. Then started clanking on the triangle with the iron rod, yelling at the top of his lungs, "Suppertime! Suppertime!"

Fatback, standing over the fire frying salt pork, gave him a slant-eyed, dirty look. The same look he'd given him when Ross first told him how and at what time a company cook goes about his duties.

It was 1630 hours.

Chapter Nineteen

Jimmy Bowlegs rode into camp at sunset as Ples knew he always did. Ples was first to see him from where he was sitting off to the side drinking coffee for the first time in a long time. Talking with Fate about their futures, about the old Barlowe place they both knew they'd probably never fix up now.

"Just 'cause I'm in the cavalry, don't mean nothin'," Fate was saying. "We can still fix it up in my spare time."

"Ranchin' is a full-time job," Ples said, looking up to where Bowlegs was coming on. "So's solderin'," he added.

"I ain't so sho' how I got in the cavalry in the first place," Fate said petulantly.

"Best place for ya," Ples answered tersely. "Here comes Jimmy," he added, deliberately shifting the subject.

"He ain't goin' to like it when he finds out he's got to go to Fort Riley," Fate said, smiling at the prospect of the tantrum he knew Jimmy would pitch.

"He'll go," Ples said. "He ain't 'bout to miss out on cash money owed him."

They watched Bowlegs come on, holding the reins to a led horse.

"What's that he's got on the back of his saddle?" Fate asked, more to himself than to Ples.

"We'll both know soon enough," Ples replied. "But that ain't the worry. The worry is that black hoss he's leadin'."

"You think he stole 'im?"

"We'll both know that too soon enough," Ples said again.

They both rose to standing, watching Bowlegs cantering toward them.

Bowlegs walked his pinto in, roaming his eyes around the camp, seeing for the first time all of them in full uniform, sitting around talking, eating army rations, their eyes shifted on him. Except Jefferson's and Deke Poole's: they were down on the picket line doing stable duty that Bosie had assigned them to. Dressed in long white smocks, corn-feeding the company's horses from army nose bags.

"What you got, Wild Man?" Ples asked affably when Bowlegs drew up, sitting his saddle, looking out at the recruits as if he were seeing them for the first time.

"I bring meat," Bowlegs answered, looking back at at least three-quarters of a skinned carcass dangling in back of his saddle.

"What is it?" Fate asked.

"Where'd you git the hoss?" Ples asked curtly. Seeing the high breeding of the animal.

"I git . . . by and by," Bowlegs said evasively, throwing a leg over his saddle horn, sliding down easily. Staring at Fate, Bowlegs asked, "You yellowlegs now?"

"Yeah," Fate said, shifting uneasily in his steps, looking down at himself dressed in complete uniform. "How I look?"

"Like yellowlegs," Bowlegs said, running his eyes in mock disapproval over Fate's uniformed body. "Maybe I kill you too," Bowlegs added.

"He's gov'ment property now," Ples said, smiling as he rarely did. "You kill him you'd be in mighty big trouble."

"He look . . . listen good." Bowlegs said seriously. "He make good yellowlegs. Maybe I no kill."

"They all better make good yellowlegs," Ples said, looking out at the rest of them.

"Him maybe not so good," Bowlegs said, indicating Battie, standing off to the side talking as usual. "He no shoot so good . . . make too much big talk."

"He don't shoot so good," Ples said, "but he sho' ain't scared to try."

"I bring Au-gie good horse," Bowlegs stated, and walked off, leading his pinto and the led horse.

"Mr. Butler," Jerico said, walking up, "horse stealin' is about the worse thing to do hereabouts. They'll hang whoever's caught ridin' that hoss."

"I reckon," Ples said seriously, his mind working at what to do about it. "Keep it to yo'self for now," Ples added to Jerico.

At the cook fire where most of them were gathered eating, Bowlegs tossed Augie the reins to the led horse, saying, "You take. He good horse."

"He looks good," Augie said, catching the reins.

"He sho' do," Willie said, standing next to Augie. "Where'd you git him?"

"I git . . . by and by," Bowlegs said again, throwing the hunk of meat off the back of his own saddle. "I bring . . . you cook," he told Fatback standing over by the fire.

"That cow meat?" Fatback asked.

"Meat same same," Bowlegs said. "You cook."

"That's a beef," Jake said. "I'd know that meat anywhere."

"You cook," Bowlegs said again to Fatback.

"You killed somebody's cow," Bosie said rudely, overhearing the conversation, sitting next to Ross tediously writing out the reports on the deaths of Hezekiah and the others. "Stole that hoss from somebody too, didn't you?" Bosie continued accusingly, jumping to his feet, coming forward.

"Did you have to kill anybody?" Augie asked anxiously, wide-eyed at the implied danger of it all.

"I no kill," Bowlegs said flatly.

"You stole, though," Bosie stated.

"I no steal," Bowlegs said irritably. "I take."

"It's the same thing," Bosie replied. "We don't want no trouble."

"I no steal," Bowlegs repeated gravely, staring down Bosie. Then turning in his steps, he walked away.

"Jimmy," Ples said when Bowlegs drew up, "Bosie's got reasons for askin'. You didn't kill nobody for that horse, did you?"

"I no kill," Bowlegs said. "I make white man walk."

"Which way?" Ples asked.

"That way." And Bowlegs nodded north where the main road went.

"That's some better," Ples said. "We goin' a different way."

"I go that way," Bowlegs said. "Pretty damn quick. I no like Bo-see say I steal."

"You go that way," Ples said, stabbing a finger west, "to Fort Riley. If you want to git paid for them hosses," he added, smiling amusingly at Bowlegs.

"Who say?" Bowlegs asked testily.

"That Captain Dudley. Said he'd pay you for the hosses, and pay you wrangler wages . . . at Fort Riley."

"How much he pay?"

"He didn't tell me that," Ples said. "I guess he figured it wadn't my business."

"They go to Fort Riley too?" Bowlegs asked, looking at Fate, sitting there adjusting the stirrups on his McClellan saddle, which looked to be half the size of the western saddles they'd all have to give up now.

"We all goin'," Fate said. "Ples too. Army hired him on as guide."

"I no like," Bowlegs said. "But I go," he added tersely.

"Figured you would," Ples retorted.

"Maybe I kill yellowlegs captain," Bowlegs said musingly.

"Maybe you won't neither," Ples answered. "He's sho' 'nuff gov'ment property."

"Okay, everybody!" Bosie called out, interrupting their conversations. "Fall in!"

"Again!" Battie cried out. "For what?" he asked irritably from where he was sitting next to Deke going over their stocky, thirty-eight-inch-long cavalry carbines. Deke swearing he could have hit that white man back yonder if he'd had this gun.

"Yeah! What we fallin' in for, Sarge?" Cecil Hall asked out. "You know we all here."

"I told ya! . . . told all y'all!" Bosie shouted back acidly. "From now on, I'm Sergeant Radford . . . not no Sarge, not no Bosie. Sergeant Radford. Now fall in! And answer up like you been told to."

"You better git," Ples said to Fate. "Sounds like he means business."

"How'd I come to this?" Fate asked plaintively, walking off, Ples smirking at his back.

Radford called the roll, each man answering up according to his own feeling at the moment: some grudgingly, some sullenly, Jefferson cheerily.

"All right," Radford said, standing in front of them, Private Ross at his side where he always was, "from now on we got to fall in for muster every mornin', noon, and night just like we was at the fort. Drill every day too. We got to keep to a schedule Captain Dudley left, and Private Ross here got in his head.

"We travel in the morning, eat dinner, and drill in the afternoon. Captain Dudley said anybody don't measure up by the time we git to Fort Riley will be discharged . . . sent packin'. Tomorrow mornin' we git up at six o'clock . . ."

"Oh-six-hunded," Private Ross said quietly at Radford's ear.

"We git up at oh-six-hunded," Radford repeated, ". . . and git started. Fall out!"

"What we do next?" somebody asked facetiously.

"Have another muster," Battie answered, smiling mischievously at Radford.

"You can do whatever you want to," said Radford. "But come nine-thirty . . . twenty-one-thirty hours all of y'all got to shut up and turn in. That goes for you 'specially, Battie," Radford added sternly.

"That's too early for my bedtime," Battie said, smiling handsomely. "But I'll go just for you."

"I know you will," Radford said. " 'Cause I'm goin' to see that you do."

"Willie . . . you and Augie better turn in now," Battie continued playfully. "It's way pass y'all's bedtime already."

"I ain't turnin' in now," Willie said. "I'm goin' see after Brownie."

"I'm goin' see after my hoss too," Augie said, and took off after Willie.

"Did you give him a name yet?" somebody asked playfully.

"Not yet. But I will," Augie answered.

"Them old hosses ain't nothin' special," Jake said teasingly. "They ain't nothin' but sway backed old bones."

"Willie hear you say that 'bout Brownie," Bobo said, smiling, "he'll jump on you."

"That little runt," Jake said, pooh-poohing the notion. "He'll jump off too."

Ples and Bowlegs had been standing there looking on ever since muster, Ples with renewed interest. Remembering years gone by when he had been in a regime of the sort back in the Texas State Police. And had listened on while his own men had bantered, badgered, and ragged each other good-naturedly like this. Ples knew it was a sign of good fighting morale . . . or latent fear that might surface at the first sign of danger.

Ples turned aside, a look of deep yearning on his face. Had in his hands Fate's pistol belt and Winchester that Fate would have to give up now. Ples hefted the pistol belt, looking at it like he was already missing the kid at his side who had worn it for so long.

"Butler," Bowlegs said, breaking into Ples's thoughts, ". . . maybe you, me join yellowlegs."

"I'm too old," Ples stated. ". . . And you too wild," he added, smiling wanly at Bowlegs.

It was 1830 hours.

The first peep of daybreak came at 0545 hours. By the clock in Private Ross's head.

Shady Grove where they were was calm, but not quiet. Men snoring, tossing, and turning over, horses stamping and blowing.

Two men were already awake.

Fatback. Thirty minutes ago he'd been rolled out of his blanket by Private Ross's nudge, and had already fanned the cook fire's smoldering embers into glowing coals.

Now he was moving in and out of moonlight shadows like a ghost in the night, getting stuff from the wagon to cook breakfast: fried salt pork, hardtack soaked in salt pork grease, and coffee.

The other man awake was Private Ross. Sitting on his blanket, going over in his mind the coming day's activities, occasionally lifting his eyes to where Fatback was.

Presently, Ross got up out of his blanket, went over, and nudged Radford awake, saying, "Sergeant Radford . . . it's time."

Radford jerked awake, coming up in his blanket.

"Time to git up," Ross said.

Radford rubbed sleep from his eyes, then panned them around the sleeping camp, the smell of fried salt pork and coffee invading his nostrils.

"You takes ten minutes to git yo' uniform on right," Ross said instructively, "then we wake the rest of 'em up ... reveille ... oh-six-hunded hours."

"Then we see after the hosses." Radford said drowsily, more to check his own memory than anything else.

"Dat's right," Ross answered. "And you got to volunteer two mo' stable hands for today. Stable duty only for twenty-four hours."

"I forgot about that," Radford said.

"Anything you forgit, I remind you," Ross said flatly.

"And after reveille, we muster, have roll call, then eat, right?"

"Dat's right," Ross said, agreeable. "You say somethin' to the men after roll call ... if you got anything to say."

"Like what?"

"Anythin' you want to. They can't do nothin' but stand there and listen nohow. Sergeant Baggs, he was always talkin' 'bout who done what wrong, and if they did it again how he was goin' to hang 'em up."

"Did he ever?" Radford asked.

"Lotsa times."

Radford looked slant-eyed at Ross.

"So they won't forgit next time," said Ross.

Radford pulled on his boots, then stood up, looking around for his shirt.

Ross tossed it to him, saying, "I sewed on yo' stripes for you last night while you was sleep."

Radford looked bleary-eyed at him again.

"So they don't forgit you the big boss," Ross said, smiling into the dawn.

It was 0600 hours.

Reveille was held. Ross moving among the sleeping troopers, clanking on the triangle with the iron rod.

"What's all the racket 'bout?" Cecil Hall asked indignantly, startled awake by Ross's clanking in his ears.

"Time to git up!" Radford yelled over.

". . . Like somebody's deef," Cecil muttered, rubbing sleep from his eyes.

"Some of y'all act like it," Radford said. "Now git up outa that blanket."

With Sergeant Radford's nudging and prodding, they turned out of their blankets in various moods, mostly ugly, and states of attire as they'd fallen asleep in last night. Ross moving through them, showing troopers this or that way to properly put on an article of his uniform, or how his side arm was supposed to be worn butt forward.

With Ross's patient help and prompting, they all got in uniform for the day. Bobo Jackson and John Deese involuntarily volunteering for stable duty. And with Ross listening in, Radford told them what their duties were, as Ross had told them to him: Feed each horse individually a nose bag of grain, water each one, then tie it to the picket line.

It was 0630 hours.

"Fall in for muster!" Sergeant Radford yelled out.

They came up for muster in groups of twos and threes, hitching up pants, tugging at shirttails, adjusting pistol belts.

"*At-ten-shun!*" Sergeant Radford barked out.

They got that way.

Sergeant Radford started talking, saying, "When I call your name, fall out and go git yo'self a hoss. Bobo and Deese down there now feedin' and waterin' them all and puttin' them on the picket line. No matter which one it is, you git the first one on the picket line. Go saddle up, then come back and eat."

Radford called the roll. Which was in no particular order except how Lieutenant Badger had chanced to put it down. Each trooper in turn fell out and walked off, going to pick a horse.

Afterward they ate breakfast of Fatback's making: fried salt pork, hardtack, and coffee. Willie and Augie ate standing off to the side away from the rest of them, talking in low tones, looking long faces.

"What ails them?" Deke asked around a mouthful of meat and bread.

"They mad 'cause they didn't git they own hosses."

Willie's Brownie and Augie's highbred black horse had both been already picked by the time their names were called.

"Who got 'em?" Cecil asked.

"Jake got Brownie," Battie said. "And Deke got Augie's."

"Sergeant Radford said to git the first one on the line," Jake said defensively. "That's what I done."

"Nobody said you done nothin' wrong," Jefferson replied. "He just said you got Brownie."

"Well, he sounded like I done somethin' wrong," Jake said testily.

"I can sound any way I want to," Battie said. "It's my mouth."

"One of these days somebody's goin' to shut it for ya," Jake said.

"It won't be this day," Battie replied, smiling broadly. ". . . And it won't be you neither," he added, dashing out the leavings of his coffee, walking off.

"All right!" Sergeant Radford's voice rang out, "breakfast is over. Stand to hoss!"

"What he talkin' 'bout?" Deese asked around a mouthful of food.

"Go stand next to yo' hoss, fool," Deke Poole said, smirking. Pitching his cleaned plate and empty coffee cup into a big washtub Fatback had there.

"All right," Radford told them when they'd finished breakfast, "when I say *stand to hoss* that means you stop what you doin' and run to the picket line, untie yo' hoss, and stand there on the left side. When everybody's standin' next to a hoss, I calls you to 'tention. All y'all know what 'tention mean, right?" Radford asked sarcastically.

Then he reminded them what it meant: " 'Tention means you stand up straight, chest out on a line with yo' hoss's mouth. Hold the reins in yo' right hand . . . six inches down from yo' hoss's mouth.

"See Private Ross there?" added Radford, indicating Ross off to the side posing as an example. ". . . That's the way you 'spose to look."

They all looked at Ross.

Radford spoke again, saying: "Every time we git ready to move out we goin' to practice doin' it. Everybody got to know how by the time we git to Fort Riley. Less you want to git sent packin'," he added, looking a warning at Deese.

Twice they practiced the mechanics of *stand to horse*. Each time Radford calling out the command, and Private Ross moving down the line, showing each recruit that needed showing how it was done correctly. Ross knew there was more showing to be done, but Radford said that that was enough for now.

"Mount up!" Sergeant Radford finally commanded them. Then stood there watching them swing disjointedly onto their saddles. Nobody in step.

"Next time we practice how to mount up too," he told them out loud, walking off, going to mount up himself.

The morning was clear and bright. They moved out in columns of twos. Heading west out across the prairie, going to Fort Riley. None of them knew the way; Ples had only vague knowledge, plus Captain Dudley's general direction: Follow the line of the Kansas River until you strike the Smoky Hill Trail. Follow it west and you'll come to Fort Riley.

Ples was riding in the lead. Behind him was Fate and Private Ross on the right, carrying the company's guidon, a square flag with a field of blue broken by a big gold M in the middle.

Hiram King

Augie and Willie were riding side by side next in the column. Still long-faced, but silent now. Hadn't uttered a word since they started out. Ples had heard about what was the matter with them, and had shaken his head woefully, struck by the fickle nature of both youngsters over their horses.

Sergeant Radford still rode off to the side of the column, now and again gigging his horse up or dropping back, yelling at somebody: "Keep in line! Guide right! Look to yo' right!"

The wagon came last in the column. Two mules hitched behind it. Private Ross had told Sergeant Radford, "You oughter turn them mules loose. Company wagon don't look good with civilian mules tied behind it."

"They ain't civilian mules," Fatback had said. "They good mules," he added plainly. "Ain't no sense in turnin' loose good mules."

"Sho' ain't," Jefferson had added with conviction.

Sergeant Radford had seen it Fatback's and Jefferson's way: The mules were along.

Where was Bowlegs?

Nobody knew. He'd quietly ridden out an hour ago while they were eating breakfast.

It was 0800 hours.

Westward Ples led the column. Traveling at a walk under thin clouds stretching like gauze across a clear blue sky. Sergeant Radford gigging his horse up and checking him down, riding the length of the column, keeping an eye on its alignment. Yelling out praises and reprimands, mostly reprimands. Radford had warned them as Captain Dudley had warned him: Any man who can't hold formation in the saddle will be dismissed. Sent packin'. Radford knew that meant him too.

Not a one of them was anxious to get sent packing, sent back to where he'd come from: Jake to the slaughter pens back in Texas; Augie back to dockside beatings; Jefferson

332

back to that hovel of a blacksmith shop he'd had.

Now they all paid more attention to Sergeant Radford and to Private Ross. No more laughing and grinning in ranks. It was as if the complete uniforms they all now wore had transformed them all, stamped into each man's mind that this was serious business now. Captain Dudley's words of warning constantly hurled at them by Sergeant Radford helped a lot too.

Now Sergeant Radford was yelling out rudely, "Willie, hold that hoss back! Can't you see straight! Keep in line with Augie. Guide right!"

"It's this dumb hoss!" Willie said irritably. "He won't act right. I want my own hoss."

"You ain't got yo' own hoss!" Radford shot back. "Now hold that hoss back . . . guide right!" Radford added, spurring off ahead.

Radford checked his horse down to a walk next to Ross: "I'd guess noontime, ain't it?" Radford asked, looking up at the sun.

"Noontime is when you say it is, Sergeant," Ross answered across his shoulder. "You the boss."

"Way you been tellin' me what time it is, I thought you had a clock in yo' head," Radford said facetiously.

"I mostly do," Ross said honestly, "but I ain't the boss."

Radford looked a look at Ross, then gigged his horse ahead to where the guide was, saying, "Mr. Butler, it's noontime. Pick a spot."

"One spot's as good as another," Ples answered, panning his eyes around, seeing not a tree or a rock, not a hill or a gully. Just the same trackless prairie, rising gradually, flattening out into great plains of short grass all around.

They nooned under the sun. Eating standing up or squatting on their haunches.

It didn't make much difference though. They had no wood to build a cook fire with. There wasn't a stick or twig in sight. What they ate was only hardtack, a waferlike unleavened piece of bread that would test a man's teeth. Nobody, not even Augie, would chance eating fat, uncooked chunks of salt pork.

Fatback took a ragging for it all. Not thinking to put wood in the wagon. All Fatback could do was shrug helplessly, and say plaintively, "I didn't know we was comin' way out here to nowhere."

"If Mr. Butler was leadin' us to nowhere, this sho' is it," Battie said, panning his eyes around to the four winds, seeing nothing but prairie horizon. "Ain't nothin' out here," he added, and champed down on a piece of hard bread.

"You still wishin' for a whorehouse?" Jake asked.

"Don't hurt to wish," Battie answered, grinning.

"There's somethin' out here," Jake said seriously, munching.

"What?" asked Deke innocently.

"We out here," Jake retorted, and guffawed. Sly snickers and knowing grins broke out.

"You sho' stupid," said Battie, grinning, "fallin' for that."

"All right!" Sergeant Radford called out, coming toward them. "Noon's over. Fall in!"

"I'm sick of hearin' Sergeant Radford's big mouth," Battie said in low tones.

"Tell 'em to shut up, then," Cecil Hall said, smiling at the thought.

"I ain't that sick," Battie answered, rising from his haunches to standing. "I ain't anxious to git sent packin'."

"You was to git sent packin'," Bobo said teasingly, "you could find a whorehouse on the way." And Bobo fell in step with Battie and Jake.

"I can do without one a while longer," Battie answered, smiling sheepishly.

"That while longer might turn out to be a whole lot longer than you think," Cecil said sagely.

They fell in promptly without fuss or incident.

"At-ten-shun!" Radford called out.

They got that way.

"We goin' to have target practice," Sergeant Radford announced. "When I call yo' name, you fall out and git your piece. . . ."

"Git yo' what?" Deese asked innocently, looking stupidly at Jake.

"Deese!" Radford screamed out, ". . . you at attention! Keep yo' mouth shut!

"Now . . . like I was sayin', you fall out and git your piece . . . your carbine . . . and ten cartridges. Then we goin' down yonder where Mr. Butler and Private Ross at"—and Radford nodded that way—"and practice shootin'."

Under a wide blue prairie sky out in the middle of nowhere, they took target practice. The target was about a four-foot square of rolled saddle blanket that Ples and Ross had stretched over the mess kettle's forked iron stakes driven into the ground out across the prairie some hundred yards, as Ross judged it.

The recruits were lined up, and Radford gave out instructions: "When it's your turn, you come over in front of the target. When I tell you to shoot, you git to shoot ten times. Private Ross will signal when you hit the target.

"You hit the target six times, you first class; you hit the target four times, you second class; you hit the target three times, you third class. If you can't hit the target at least three times by the time we git to Fort Riley, you git sent packin'," Ross added plainly, looking cat-eyed along the line.

Deke Poole got worried, shuffling in his steps, his eyes studying the ground. "You hear that, Willie?" Deke asked in low tones.

"I heard," Willie answered. "We can do it," he added encouragingly.

"That go for me too?" Jefferson asked seriously. "I'm 'spose to be the blacksmith."

"Everybody," Radford answered. "Captain Dudley said the cavalry don't care what you is, you got to qualify in everything just like everybody else."

"Blacksmiths git killed too," Battie said snidely, repeating what Ples had told Jefferson before.

"Shut up, bigmouth!" Jefferson retorted.

"Bobo!" Radford called out, "you first."

Bobo walked over in front of the target, shouldered his carbine, and fired. His eyes naturally shifted to where Ross was positioned, hoping for a signal that he'd scored a hit.

Nothing.

"Shoot again," Radford told him. "Keep your elbow up, look through both sights."

Bobo fired again.

Ross's hand went up.

"He hit it!" somebody exclaimed.

Bobo grinned. Stiffening his jaw and squinting down the barrel, Bobo fired again.

Nothing. Ross standing as fixed as the sphinx.

All afternoon they blazed away at the target. Radford correcting each man's technique as he saw fit and writing down the score next to each man's name. Ples off to the side, a detached observer until it was Fate's turn. Ples knew what Fate could do but his interest was piqued anyhow. Fate put eight of ten shots through the target. As did Jerico. But Ples, just like the rest of them, was shocked at what Rafer D. did. Rafer D. put nine of ten shots right square in the middle of the target, the other shot nicking the corner.

Results were mixed for the others; appalling in Deke's case. One bullet nicked the corner. That was it. No amount of coaching and encouragement helped his aim.

"We work on it some mo'," Sergeant Radford said consolingly to Deke.

"Battie, you next!" Radford called out.

"I'll show you how to shoot," Battie said boastfully when Deke passed by, his head hanging down dejectedly.

Battie shouldered his carbine and fired even as he was approaching the firing position.

A spout of dirt lifted up two feet wide of the target.

Ross's hand stayed at his side.

"He ain't killed no white man shootin' like that," somebody said in low tones.

"Battie!" Segeant Radford screamed, "you deef? I told you don't shoot till I tell you to."

"That don't count, then," Battie said innocently.

"It counts all right," Radford said. "You missed.

"Now . . . fire!"

Battie fired again.

Ross's hand went up.

Battie grinned back over his shoulder at the others. "That's what I was intendin' to do the first time," he said proudly.

Battie went on to put five of ten shots through the target.

"I thought you could shoot real good," Jake said tauntingly when Battie walked up from in front of the target.

"I can," Battie answered, smiling confidently.

"How come you didn't then?" Jake asked. "Five out of ten ain't all that good."

"I shoot better at real targets," Battie answered, smiling handsomely.

"Yeah . . . so nobody'll know you missed," Cecil Hall retorted, grinning.

"What you grinnin' 'bout?" Battie asked haughtily. "You didn't do no better."

"I hit it six times," Cecil said proudly. "Me, Augie, and Willie hit it six times. We all beat you."

"Them two runts!" Battie said disdainfully. "I can beat them shootin' any day."

"Well, you didn't," Radford commented, overhearing the conversation as he walked up.

"Most of y'all done all right," Radford continued, "but some of you didn't," he added, his eyes studying the score sheet. "Deke, Bobo, Fatback, Jefferson . . . y'all got to do better. Tomorrow we practice some more."

"All of us?" Rafer D. asked quietly, knowing he'd put nine out of ten shots in the target.

"All of us," Radford said. "We goin' to do this every day till we git to Fort Riley.

"We done for now," Radford continued. "Fatback . . . go git supper started." And Radford walked off, heading out to where Ross was, picking up the target.

"Hey, Fatback," Battie said teasingly as Fatback walked off, "you can't shoot . . . you might as well go cook."

"I'm goin' to make somethin' special for you," Fatback answered. "Poison!"

"I take it back," Battie said in mock apology. "You can shoot good."

"Naw . . . ," Fatback said disdainfully, "you meant it, and I meant it too."

"You goin' to poison him for real?" Jack asked in mock sincerity, goading Fatback on.

"Sho is," Fatback said seriously. "Goin' to kill 'im deader than a doorknob."

"Battie, I guess you seen yo' last whorehouse," Jake said sadly.

"Battie was to die, they'll have whorehouses where he's goin'," Sergeant Radford said seriously, and kept on walking.

It was 1630 hours.

Chapter Twenty

A dozen or so miles north of where the recruits' target practice shots had been racketing away across the prairie, Peyton Long and six men were trotting their horses along a prairie trail of their own making. They rode with no urgency, yet there was purpose in their gait. None of them knew what to expect when they got there, but they were heading for Leavenworth City. To report back to William Bickley.

They had broken camp and ridden north away from Shady Grove at sunup yesterday. They had no way of knowing that the black recruits they'd attacked and had hoped to scatter to hell and back, as Bickley had ordered, were doing nothing of the sort. Fact was, the recruits were still coming on, themselves breaking camp at Shady Grove at about the same time, getting more organized and trained with each passing hour.

Now, about mid-morning Long led them down a hump-backed prairie ridge and they struck the north-to-south-running main road between Fort Leavenworth and Fort Scott.

An hour or more they had galloped along the well-traveled road. Presently Frank Yoder spurred his horse up next to Long's, and yelled into the wind, saying, "Colonel, there's a man afoot ahead of us." And Yoder pointed off to the side at the dim boot tracks running along the edge of the dirt road.

Long nodded acknowledgment. His mind working at what it could mean. One thing they all knew was that a man afoot in this country had trouble; the only question was what kind.

They galloped on. Peering ahead, occasionally glancing aside at the boot prints, making sure they were still there.

Presently, Yoder pointed ahead.

And they saw a man standing at the edge of the road, saddle and blanket dropped at his feet. Holding in his right hand a Winchester he'd unsheathed from the saddle scabbard.

He was a medium-sized man. Looked to be in his mid-thirties. Had a sun-reddened square face, plainly visibly under his tipped-back wide-brimmed hat. Was wearing store-bought black wool trousers and a blue cotton shirt.

They checked their horses down to a walk, then drew up. Looking the man over. But not quite as intently as the man was looking them over. Suspiciously, and warily. Especially Peyton Long, obviously the leader of the bunch.

"Name's Daniel," the man said conversationally. ". . . Boyd Daniel."

"Lose your horse?" Long asked right off, skipping the introduction.

"You could say that," Boyd said inoffensively, smiling naturally.

"It ain't what we say, mister," Yoder said bluntly, "it's what you say that matters. What happened to your hoss?"

"Stole," Boyd stated, his Winchester held carelessly alongside his leg, his eyes holding Yoder's.

"How'd it happen?" asked Long.

"Some breed jumped me. Came out of nowhere," Boyd said, his eyes still locked with Yoder's.

"Where?" Long asked.

"Four . . . five miles yonder side of Shady Grove," Boyd answered, shifting his eyes to Long.

"This breed . . . what he look like?" Long asked.

"Dark-complected, 'bout six feet tall, well set up. Ridin' a pinto hoss."

Long exchanged knowing glances with Yoder.

"You know 'im?" asked Boyd.

"Maybe," Long said carelessly. "Where you headed?"

"Town up ahead between here and Leavenworth City . . . Johnny Cake," Boyd answered. "Less than two miles," he added.

"Shaler," Long called back, picking the smallest man in the bunch, "put him up behind you."

"What about my saddle?" Boyd asked.

"You want it, you carry it," Shaler replied from where he'd gigged his horse up alongside Boyd. Shaler removed a boot toe from the stirrup and sat there.

Boyd slid his Winchester back into the saddle scabbard, shouldered his saddle and blanket, stuck a boot toe into the stirrup, and with his left hand, grabbed ahold of Shaler's arm and swung aboard.

Off they rode.

They hadn't gone fifty paces before Yoder spoke, bringing up something that was already eating at Long's mind: "Colonel, that breed, he's—"

"I know," Long said, interrupting. "He's the one that was with them nigger recruits."

"If he's this far west stealin' hosses . . ."

"They ain't turned back," Long finished.

"I thought you said, General Bickley said—"

"I know what General Bickley said," Long cut in.

"What we goin' to do about it, then?"

"What we set out to do," Long stated testily. "Report back to General Bickley at Leavenworth City."

"He ain't goin' to like it," Yoder retorted.

"I don't neither," Long replied flatly.

They rode on.

It was a little bit past noon when Peyton Long and his men rode into the rude settlement of Johnny Cake. Drawing stares from the only three people out on the boardwalk.

"Where's your hoss, Boyd?" a tall, well-dressed man asked out from where he was standing in front of the Hester House hotel.

"Stole," Boyd yelled back. "Some damned nigger Indian."

"Nigger Indian . . . ," the man repeated under his breath, and stood there, staring after them, wondering what to make of it.

Everybody roundabout had heard that General Custer had the Cheyennes scattered and riled up. Everybody was wary. Men chopped wood with a rifle close to hand; women milked cows with a shotgun propped nearby. On the alert in case a dispersed bunch of fleeing Cheyennes mistakenly turned up close to Johnny Cake.

Johnny Cake was nothing more than a way station on the main road to Leavenworth City. It had started out as a lone cabin where travelers could stop and have a meal inside rather than make the long jump to Shady Grove only to eat outside. Word got around about the Arkansas white woman, Ellie Mae Tuttle, who made real tasty skillet-fried cornbread at her hewn-log cabin. Soon more travelers started stopping. Including Yankee soldiers moving back and forth between forts.

Seeing the woman, hearing her talk, and calling Confederate soldiers Rebs and Johnnies, the Yankees started calling the matronly woman's southern-style bread johnny cake.

The lone eating house sitting alongside the main road gradually drew other businesses to it—two saloons, a two-story hotel, a stable and wagon yard, and a hardware store—and became a town that took over the name Johnny Cake, the good eating place just Ellie Mae's now. Eating, drinking, and gambling were Johnny Cake's main attractions, plus discreet whoring on the top floor of the hotel, the Hester House.

Long swung his horse in next to three horses standing slack-legged at the hitch rail in front of Renner's Saloon. The others following suit, scattering their horses along and beyond the hitch rail.

Boyd Daniel slid down from Shaler's horse, saying, "Much obliged to you, mister."

Shaler nodded acknowledgment.

"I'll stand you a drink soon's I stow my gear down to the stable," Boyd added.

"Suits me," Shaler answered.

"Good place to eat . . . Ellie Mae's up the street there," Boyd continued, talking over to where Long was sitting his horse.

"We'll be needin' one," Long answered, swinging down, looking the way Boyd had nodded.

"Where's ya hoss, Boyd?" Glenn Harmony asked, just stepping out of the batwings of Yeager's Saloon next door, seeing Boyd standing there, his saddle slung over his shoulder.

"Some nigger breed put a Winchester on me and took 'im," Boyd answered.

"You don't say," Glenn retorted, surprised.

"I do say," Boyd answered. "I run into that bastard again I'll put a bullet in his brains, no questions asked," Boyd continued, asking, "Riley and them in there?"

"Riley and Pete is."

"What about Will and Sam?"

"Over to the hotel . . . talkin' to Mr. Belmont."

Boyd nodded acknowledgement, then said thoughtfully, "Mr. Belmont makes a lot of sense about redeemin' the country."

"You figure to join 'im?" asked Glenn.

"Dunno yet. You talk to him any more?" Boyd asked.

"Naw. I been waitin' for you, Will, and them to show up."

"I'll be back directly," Boyd said, and turning in his steps, walked off, lugging his saddle.

"You git back . . . we'll be sittin' over drinks," Glenn yelled at his back. "The boy's wanna hear what happened."

"It'll have to be Renner's then," Boyd answered, twisted back in his steps. "I owe a drink to that feller what rode me in."

"One place's as good as the other," Long said to Glenn, hearing the exchange. "We'll join you in Yeager's."

"You boys welcome," Glenn said. And stood there on the boardwalk, waiting for them to dismount and tie up their horses.

Glenn Harmony was thirty years old. Six feet tall. Solid-built. Square-jawed, and wide-mouthed. Had on faded jeans and a black shirt. And like everybody else, was armed. Had a Colt Army .44 swinging at his hip.

Long and his men filed through the batwings behind Glenn, panning their eyes around the dimly lit place.

Yeager's was a long shotgun affair of a saloon. Bare-topped plank tables crowding each other from front to back. Tom Yeager was bartending.

"Some breed stole Boyd's hoss, huh?" Yeager asked, lifting his eyes to where Glenn, Long, and the others were filing through the batwings.

"That's what he said," Glenn answered carelessly.

"That's scary," Yeager said ominously. "What'll you boys have?" he continued, looking along the bar where Long and the others were scattered out.

"Beer," Long answered, looking inquisitively down the bar at the rest of them. ". . . Round?" Long added, more a question than anything else.

"Make mine whiskey," said Yoder.

"Mine too," Lige Green stated.

"Whiskey it is," Yeager answered, and continued talking, asking Glenn, "You reckon Indian trouble's comin' our way?" And Yeager shoved Glenn a whiskey that he knew Glenn always drank.

"Hard to tell," Glenn answered, taking up his whiskey even as Yeager poured for Yoder and Green. "One stole hoss don't make no Indian uprisin'," Glenn said facetiously.

"Yet and still," Yeager said thoughtfully, "it's scary. Don't set right. Hoss stealin' is what we don't need started again round here. That's 'bout the best way I know of to set off a hangin' spree," Yeager added from over where he was drawing the beers.

"You worry too much," Glenn said dismissively. "You boys welcome to join us," Glenn added to Long, nodding over to the table where two men sat. "Yeager ain't much comp'ny nohow," he added playfully.

"I'd just as soon sit," Frank Yoder said, heading toward a table.

"We all might as well," said Long, taking up a beer, walking off toward the table.

"This here's Riley McCoy," Glenn said when Long walked up and pulled back a chair at the table where they were, and sat down as he'd been invited to do. ". . . And this's Pete Cooney."

"Long . . . Peyton Long."

Both Riley and Pete nodded affably at Long, Cooney saying respectfully, "Colonel, I see."

"General Forrest's Tennessee Cavalry Volunteers," Long answered.

"General Forrest, huh?" Cooney repeated, lifting his eyebrows with interest. Remembering wild stories he'd heard

345

and admired about General Forrest's unorthodox tactics, his daring attacks, and his improbable victories against long odds over the Yankee cavalry.

"Me and Cooney was infantry . . . Second Texas," said Riley.

"Started out as cavalry, though," Cooney said, smiling at the memory. "We left home as cavalry . . . ridin' our own hosses, but they took 'em from us as soon as we got to camp over in Louisiana . . . appropriated 'em," Cooney added, grinning now about the slick way their own horses had been taken, almost provoking a revolt, every volunteer among them threatening to go back home if he couldn't go to glorious war riding his trusted steed.

"Yeah," Riley said amusingly, "and every time there was a big fight comin' on, General Taylor would throw us in afoot."

"The boys started callin' us foot cavalry," Cooney added, grinning.

"Colonel . . . ," Riley said seriously, "me, Cooney, Boyd, and some more of the enlisted boys who's Holdouts come in to talk over the proposition of joinin' General Price, General Shelby, and them down in Mexico. Havin' an officer along sure would make me and some of the other boys feel better. You inter'sted?"

"I've already gave that considerable thought," Long said. "It's thought out now. I ain't interested."

"Ain't inter'sted in what?" Boyd asked innocently, just walking up, coming from the stable where he'd put his saddle on a borrowed horse tied up outside.

"Me and Cooney's been tryin' to convince the colonel here to go wid us to Mexico," Riley answered.

"He ain't inter'sted," Cooney added.

"Sounds to me like he's a Submissionist," Riley said, disappointment in his voice.

"Every man to his choosin'," Boyd said honestly.

"I ain't hightailin' it to Mexico," Long stated. "But that don't make me no Submissionist neither. Not by a damn sight," Long added, and brought his beer mug up to his lips, and took a deep swallow.

"I guess they told you how come we here?" Boyd asked.

"Some of it," Long answered.

"If you ain't a Submissionist . . . and you lookin' to join up . . . organize," Boyd said, "there's a feller . . . Mr. Belmont, over to the hotel. He's lookin' for Holdouts who intend to fight on . . . redeem the country, he calls it. Me and the boys been thinkin' it over. Could be you ought to talk to him, hear what he's got to say."

"Maybe," Long answered noncommittally.

"Like I said," Boyd continued, "every man to his choosin' but you bein' an officer and all . . . He says he's got authority to enlist and promote good men."

"Meanin' officers," commented Riley.

"I'd guess so," Boyd answered.

"This Mr. Belmont, where'd he git his authority?" Long asked.

"He said from a General Bickley up at Leavenworth City."

"Where's this Mr. Belmont?" Long asked, coming upright in his chair, his interest suddenly piquing at the mention of Bickley's name.

"Hotel lobby," Boyd answered. "Will and Sam over there now talkin' to him."

"Maybe I will hear what he's got to say," Long said, pushing back his chair, rising to standing.

Off to the Hester House hotel Long went. Striding purposefully. At the door he met two men coming out, two big, tough-looking men.

Will Helvie and Sam Biddle. The two men Riley had spoken of.

Long politely turned sideways, letting them pass out, his eyes sizing them up as they went by. Presently, Long crossed over the threshhold, ranging his eyes around the hotel lobby.

Down in the far corner, Long saw an expansive mahogany desk, obviously out of place, apparently just recently put there. A lone man, important-looking, sitting behind the desk, blowing blue smoke from an expensive cigar.

It was Lewton Belmont.

Lewton Belmont was thirty-eight years old. Tall, slight-built. Smooth-complected with a keen nose, and deep blue sinister eyes that forever hinted at deviltry. Had on black pants and a black striped scissor-tailed coat. A white linen shirt ruffled at the cuffs. Plain-grained Wellington boots polished to a high gloss.

Smooth of voice and ever ready to talk, Lewton had within him at any given time a full two hours of talk about how ex-Confederate President Jefferson Davis had lost the country, and the KGC was duty-bound to redeem it.

"Name's Long," Peyton said, walking up in front of the desk, facing Belmont.

"Colonel Peyton Long?" Lewton asked, lifting inquisitive eyebrows.

"That's right."

"Belmont . . . Lewton Belmont," said the man graciously, importantly. And Lewton rose to standing, smiling cordially, thrusting out a palm of handshake. "Have a seat, Colonel," he added, nodding toward the settee, even as he was pumping Long's good arm.

Peyton Long seated himself, crossing one leg over the other.

"General Bickley said to expect you . . . be on the lookout for you," Lewton said, his eyes straying to Long's empty coat sleeve.

"I was to report back to him," Long said, "but word came to me over at the saloon that General Bickley had a man here in Johnny Cake. I thought I'd stop by."

"Good thing you did," Lewton said seriously. "Something unexpected has come up and we intend to turn it to our advantage. Something General Bickley wants you and your boys to tend to."

"Maybe General Bickley ought to hear what I've got to say first," Long answered.

"That can wait," Lewton said dismissively. "Right now our good fortune has got to be pushed to advantage. I don't reckon you heard, but that nigger regiment at Fort Leavenworth's been completely drove off."

"You mean disbanded?"

"Not yet they haven't, but that'll come soon enough," Lewton answered confidently. "Just drove somewhere else for now. They're retreatin', so to speak. To Fort Riley. We intend to drive 'em out of Riley too. It's only a matter of time till we get the right man over there too."

"What about the ones on the way?"

"General Bickley's concerned about that. One of our men at Leavenworth, Lieutenant Spurlock, brought word that they've already been redirected to Fort Riley. That's what concerns the general. But the solution is right here in our hands, Colonel," Lewton said positively.

"How's that?" Long asked innocently.

"Can't you see, Colonel? For public consumption we needed an alibi . . . an excuse. And Boyd Daniel has just given it to us. Coming in here saying that a nigger breed stole his horse. Everybody knows horse thieving is a hanging offense."

"He's not one of them," Long said. "So we gather some men and hang a breed. What then?"

"Not some men," Lewton said, smiling cunningly. "Our men . . . your men."

"Six men?" Long answered. "We'll need more'n that."

"There'll be more," Lewton said. "You leave that to me. When I git done working up Johnny Cake and the people hereabouts, I'll have every white man in the county ready to ride with you to hang that nigger horse thief."

"We go after him to hang him, the recruits get caught up in it . . ."

"Who's to say whether they get caught up in it or not? All the army'll know is they've got a bunch of dead nigger recruits on their hands. . . . Besides that, the army's already got their hands full with Black Kettle's Cheyennes."

"I thought General Forrest said no outright killin'?"

"Come now, Colonel," Lewton said, smiling wryly. "Surely you know how rank works. General Bickley is commanding out here."

"When do we act?"

"Soon. It'll take me some time to get the town worked up enough to join your posse. You'll get your orders."

"What about my men?"

"The town's yours, Colonel," Lewton said slyly. "The KGC takes care of its own."

Lewton Belmont spent hours on end talking in his hotel office or on the street, with any and every white man of fighting age. Agitating and exaggerating about how deplorable the country had become for white men under Yankee and nigger rule; about how niggers were being promoted by Yankees over whites; about how niggers were overrunning the country, taking up dubious land deeds, and holding prominent positions. And stealing stock with impunity. White men had to fight back. Stand up . . . redeem the country.

Every white man who rode out of Johnny Cake took this message with him. And some of them rode out on fast horses, spreading the word.

Lewton Belmont kept up his talking. Smoking fine cigars and blowing blue smoke. During lulls, he holed up in his hotel room, waiting for his words to strike pay dirt, swell the tide of resentment against blacks that he knew lay just under the surface.

Broken Ranks

* * *

West and south of Johnny Cake, Ples was piloting the recruits toward Fort Riley. Under the leadership of Sergeant Radford, who'd taken to his duty with added zeal imposed on him by circumstances and Captain Dudley's threat of sending him packing.

They all made steady progress in their movement and training. From the first sound of Private Ross's triangle gong at 0600 hours until they turned in at 2130 hours, Radford prodded and pushed, harangued and scolded the recruits. Going through cavalry drills as Private Ross had gone through them. And what Ross didn't remember or hadn't learned, he and Radford gleaned from Captain Dudley's copy of *Hardee's Cavalry Tactics Manual* that Ross carried with him all the time.

Their daily drills, done according to a clock in Ross's head, became routine: reveille; dress properly; stable call; muster for roll call; take a horse from the picket line; saddle up; come back and eat breakfast.

After breakfast they'd stand to horse, mount up, and move out westward in formation until dinnertime, advancing ten, maybe twelve miles each morning.

Somehow Jimmy Bowlegs turned up wherever they stopped for dinner; no longer waiting for sunset before riding in. Twice he had brought back buffalo meat, and once the column had come in plain sight of thousands of buffalo of the southern herd that were just now starting to be slaughtered wantonly by white buffalo hunters. None of them knew it but Bowlegs would take annoying potshots at the white hunters, as was his wont, then quietly ride away.

Willie and Augie were no longer moody each morning at breakfast. No longer irritating everybody about not getting their own horse. Sergeant Radford had finally given in. While passing along instructions to the two assigned stable hands, Radford also told them to have Willie's

351

Brownie and Augie's handsome black horse put on the picket line ninth and tenth, where their names appeared on the muster roll. Now, each day Willie and Augie got their own horse, making their day and everybody else's less sour.

Target practice went on each day at 1300 hours. Almost everybody qualifying, hitting the target at least three times at a hundred yards.

Rafer D. was by far the best shot. His, Fate's, and Jerico's target had been moved back to four hundred yards, as Ross calculated it.

Deke Poole and Jefferson were by far the worse shots. Neither had qualified at a hundred yards. They kept practicing and Deke kept anxiously asking Radford, "How many mo' days befo' we git to Fort Riley?"

"How many mo' days befo' you stop shootin' like a blind man?" was all Radford would answer. None of them knew how many more days before they reached Fort Riley. Not even Ples.

Nobody ragged or chided Deke and Jefferson for their ineptness on the firing line. Not even Battie. Surprisingly, Battie was most encouraging. Giving out helpful hints such as he thought he could. None of them wanted to see Deke and Jefferson get sent packing.

It was in the heat of the afternoon when a lone buckboard turned in off the prairie and entered the main road leading into Johnny Cake. The driver had the team at a trot, obviously in a hurry to get where he was going.

Lewton Belmont leaning against a pillar of the Hester House hotel, his vantage point for initiating conversation, was first to see the wagon coming in.

Lewton could tell from the haste the wagon made that something was up. He drew himself upright, narrowing his eyes attentively.

The wagon lumbered on.

"What's your hurry, Plunk?" Lewton asked out when the wagon got within hailing distance.

"Trouble," Plunk answered, hauling back on the lines at the hitch rail by Yeager's Saloon.

"What kinda trouble?" Lewton asked even as Plunk was jumping down from the wagon seat.

"Dead man," Plunk yelled out, coming around to the tailgate of the wagon.

Lewton came down off the boardwalk, heading toward the wagon.

Peyton Long, Frank Yoder, Lige Green, and some others—Riley McCoy, Glenn Harmony, Sam Biddle—came spilling out of Yeager's Saloon at the mention of a dead man.

Plunk threw back the tarpaulin, revealing a dead body, saying soberly, "Whoever killed 'im meant for him to stay killed."

It was Archie Lee Bocock. His body punctured by a dozen or more bullets from where the recruits had avenged, and nerved themselves by firing into a white man's body.

They all stood there looking at the hideous sight.

"Anybody know him?" Lewton asked.

"I knowed 'im," Martin Conway said, "knowed 'im well," he added, tightening his jaw, going red around the mouth.

"He was one of us," Long added, casting a disdainful glance at Lige Green.

"Like I told you, Colonel," Lige said defensively, "he was dead when I got back to 'im."

"Who did this then?" Long asked.

"Only savages would do a thing like this," Lewton said sagely.

"Like I told you," Lige said, looking at Long, "when I last seen him, that nigger breed was skulking around. Maybe he done it."

"Where I found him," Plunk said, "I seen lots of tracks. It was done a'purpose, all right," Plunk added with certainty.

Plunk Murray was thirty-five. Six feet tall, powerfully built, and square-jawed. Had on homespun trousers held up by suspenders and stuffed down inside high-topped boots. And a blue flannel shirt, with a big ten-gallon hat flopped down at the brim. Plunk was a mule trader. Known hereabout as a brutally honest man. And like the rest of them, he was well armed. Belted around his waist was a Walker Colt .44 and on the other side a big Bowie knife.

"Anybody who'd do a thing like this," Plunk said soberly, "oughta be hunted down and killed like a mad dog."

"Colonel," Yoder said grimly, "it was them niggers. If that breed was 'round, they was too."

Lewton Belmont looked a cunning look at Long. Then added solemnly, "Riley, Glenn, Will . . . this's what I been preachin' to you about. Country's gone to hell in a handbasket. That nigger breed horse-thieving, niggers killin' white men. Mutilating the body. It's about time you boys get your heads out of the sand and do somethin'. Put a stop to these outrages."

"Mr. Belmont's right," Riley said somberly to the others. "Things gittin' worse by the day."

"And they ain't going to get no better unless white men make it better," said Lewton. "The colonel here's the right man to make it better," he added, brightening up. "Put him in charge of a posse, head off them niggers . . . hang that horse thief, and make the rest of 'em answer for killing and mutilating a white man."

"I'd go along," said Will Helvie. "I got family and stock to protect."

"I'd ride with you, Colonel," Sam Biddle said. "Like Will here, I got family and stock out there too. Plunk here knows the country. He could lead us to where he found the body."

"Wouldn't do no good to go there," Lewton said. "They headin' to Fort Riley. Once they get there, the army'll protect 'em. Your best bet would be to head 'em off. Catch 'em strung out on the prairie."

"I was thinkin' on notifyin' the army up at Leavenworth," Plunk said honestly. "Let them handle it.

"Don't be a fool!" Lewton said contemptuously. "Army ain't goin' to handle it," Lewton added disdainfully. "They protectin' 'em. We want to put a stop to these outrages, we got to do it ourselves! Tomorrow morning! Every man among you that's got family, property, and stock to protect, meet me in front of the hotel. We'll settle this our way! And I'll see that the right word gets to Leavenworth."

It didn't take smooth-talking Lewton Belmont long to get every man in Johnny Cake to see things his way. Get them stirred up. Ready to act.

They broke up into small parties, each party going its own way, talking in low, portentous tones. All of them feeling duty-bound by Lewton's cutting words that immediate degradation was the white man's lot if they didn't act. Not a man among them felt he could in good conscience fail to appear.

It was midmorning the next day when they roared out of Johnny Cake, twenty strong, ex-Confederate Peyton Long and Plunk Murray riding in the lead; Plunk knew the country well. Behind them, strung out in a rude column of twos, were eighteen other tough frontier men that Lewton Belmont's smooth talk had riled up to a killing pitch. Frank Yoder, Joe Dockum, Donnie Pence were there; so was Pete Cooney, Glenn Harmony, Tom Lykins, Will Helvie. To a man they were all experienced fighters of one sort or another: Confederate soldier; Border Ruffian; guerrilla raider; and just plain outlaw as was Charlie Twoshirts. Killing would turn none of their stomachs.

They had come into Johnny Cake this morning in groups of twos and threes, mustering in front of the Hester House as Lewton had told them to do yesterday. They had listened again to a rousing speech by Lewton Belmont, glorifying in the rightness of their cause. And they had got a stern lecture from Peyton Long, stressing the necessity of following his orders and maintaining discipline.

Two miles south of Johnny Cake they had turned off the main road, striking the wide open prairie sweeping away toward the Smoky Hill Trail and Fort Riley beyond.

They rode on. At a steady, ground-eating lope.

Plunk Murray knew every hill and hollow, every mott of trees and scrub oaks, every creek, slough, and ditch between here and Fort Riley. Knew where the recruits would most likely be at this stage in their travel.

It was coming on to noontime when they struck the back trail of the recruits. Plunk pointing to the trail of trampled prairie grass just as Long spotted it. Long swung the column that way and they fell in with the trail.

After three miles, maybe four, Long lifted a hand, calling a halt to rest the horses.

They gathered in little knots, some silent in grim thought, others talking in low ominous tones; all of them deadly serious in the task they'd set out to do.

"I figure they'll be at Bull Creek," Plunk Murray announced to Long, Frank Yoder, and some others standing near him. "If they got any sense atall," he added reflectively.

"How far's Bull Creek?" Long asked.

"Hour . . . hour and a half's ride," Plunk said, munching on jerked beef he'd lifted from his saddlebag.

Bull Creek was precisely the place where back in '56 Missouri Senator David Atchison at the head of three hundred pro-slavery Border Ruffians had launched an attack on old man John Brown's hangout at Osawatomie, killing a dozen of John Brown's so-called Liberty Guards, a ragtag bunch of antislavery Kansans. Bull Creek had a lot of half-buried dead bodies along its shallow banks, both pro- and antislavery men.

And if Peyton Long and his posse had any say in the matter, Bull Creek was soon going to be holding to its bosom some more dead bodies, dead nigger bodies.

Chapter Twenty-one

Three miles ahead of Peyton Long and his grim-faced posse, Sergeant Radford and the column were advancing at a walk across the monotonous, trackless prairie.

Sergeant Radford had little to do in keeping discipline within the column now. Had very little yelling and screaming to do about this and that: Things had shaped up to that extent. The great worry for each of them now was whether he was good enough to stick, good enough not to get sent packing when they reached Fort Riley and joined the rest of Company M.

Everybody but Deke Poole had been "marked down" as they came to calling it when a man qualified on the shooting range. Deke was a problem. And it was a thing that baffled Radford, chagrined Ples, and played on the minds of the others.

"What ails him?" Bobo had asked disgustedly, more to himself than anybody else, after they all had had to stand out there, muttering in low tones, watching Deke firing away, hitting nothing.

"Ain't nothin' ails him," Cecil Hall had answered.

"Maybe he's just nervous," Augie answered.

"Awww, hush up, Augie," Willie had said. "What he got to be nervous 'bout?"

"Well, it's somethin'," Bobo said lamely.

"Maybe Rafer D. can help him like he helped me," Jefferson said suggestively.

"Somebody ought to . . . somebody besides Sergeant Radford."

"He got good sense, ain't he?" Jake had asked honestly.

"Yeah, he got good sense," Battie answered. "But you don't shoot wid yo' sense, you shoot wid yo' eyes."

"Yo' sense tells yo' eyes to hit what they lookin' at," Jake said positively.

"Everybody miss sometime," Battie answered. "That mean they ain't got good sense when you miss?"

"You know somethin', Battie?" Jake said reflectively, "you ain't got good sense no time. You sho' Sergeant Radford marked you down?"

"I'm marked down," Battie answered.

"Well, Jefferson got marked down yesterday," Jake stated. "Maybe Deke'll git marked down today."

"I'd hate to see him git sent packin'," Battie said seriously.

Now, Deke riding in the lead next to Ples, his ineptness had moved back into Sergeant Radford's mind. "Mr. Butler," Radford was saying conversationally, breaking the silence, "for the life of me, I can't figger out what's wrong wid Deke . . . how come he can't shoot straight . . . what he doin' wrong?"

"He can see good, can't he?" Ples asked.

"Yeah, suh. He says he can see the target. But he just can't hit it."

"If he can see it, he can hit it," Ples answered tersely.

Radford looked a queer look across his shoulder at Ples, saying, "You sound mighty sho'."

"Nothin's for sho'," Ples answered. "But there's mo' ways than one to skin a cat."

Radford chuckled at the saying. Then said: "I tried all the ways I know. You got any?"

"Maybe," Ples said. "But I'd have to do it my way."

"Like you done Battie back there?" Radford asked.

"Sort of," Ples answered.

"Mr. Butler, I ain't lookin' to make out no mo' reports," Radford said seriously. "Captain Dudley left me a lifetime of reports he said I got to fill out when somethin' unusual happen . . . comp'ny reports he calls 'em. I already filled out six . . . four for dead men and two for accidents. Bobo gittin' dragged by that hoss and Augie almost drownin'."

"You don't see it, you don't have to report it," Ples said suggestively.

Radford fell silent, leaving Ples's words hanging there.

On they rode.

Directly, Ples said offhandedly, "Jimmy's comin' in."

"Must be comin' on to noontime," Radford said, twisting around in his saddle, looking back at the column where the unofficial timekeeper, Private Ross, was riding with the guidon.

Ross gave no indication whatever.

"Seems a mite early for dinner," Ples said carelessly, looking up at the sun.

Bowlegs cantered up, swung his horse in stride with Ples's and Radford's, Ples saying facetiously, "You lost track of time, Wild Man? It ain't noontime."

"I no lose track," Bowlegs said. "Water is there," and he nodded dead ahead.

"A river?" asked Radford.

"No river. Only small water."

"A creek," Ples said. "Bull Creek . . . as I remember."

"How far?" Radford asked.

"Not so far," Bowlegs answered.

"We'll noon on the other side," Radford stated.

"He's learnin'," Ples said, looking cat-eyed at Bowlegs. "You think he'll make a good yellowlegs?"

"He no make good yellowlegs," Bowlegs said without emotion, "I kill. Give to coyote."

"He's gov'ment property," Ples said, smirking amusedly.

"I no care," Bowlegs answered. "Coyotes no care either."

Without incident they crossed over Bull Creek. A shallow, mostly south-flowing stream that regularly overflowed its banks, running out of its channel, leaving steep-cut banks at the outer edges of a swath of black prairie sod. Less than a dozen miles south it fed into the Osage River right along with Pottawattamie Creek, along whose banks old John Brown had launched his claim to martyrdom by broadswording to death five pro-slavery Missourians he knew had settled there.

The dinner that Fatback dished up was salt pork, hardtack, and beans that he'd soaked overnight and started cooking yesterday.

Each trooper filled his plate and moved off, joining groups of twos and threes, eating and talking: Ragging each other about something or other, or arguing over how a particular drill was done.

Time flew by.

"All right! Dinner's over!" Radford screamed out. "Put them plates down and fall in for muster and target practice!"

They fell in.

Radford deliberately took out his muster roll, looking it over carefully.

Just at that time Ples came cantering up from down the creek bed, saying to Radford, loud enough for them all to hear, "Jimmy's spotted Indians out there! You better go!"

"Indians!" somebody repeated.

"Where?" Radford asked anxiously.

"Up yonder," Ples said, pointing that way. "You better git! Take my hoss," he added, swinging down.

Radford swung onto Ples's saddle, then passed down the muster roll to Ples, saying out loud so they all could hear, "Git 'em started at target practice. Mark down the scores." And Radford spurred off.

Ples stood there a long minute, watching Radford's back move away from them. Presently he turned in his steps, studiously looking at the muster roll.

"Jefferson, you first," Ples announced.

Jefferson came forward to the firing line even as Ples spoke, saying, "I see you been marked down already."

"I hit it three times yesterday," Jefferson answered.

"Well, this time try for four. Fire!"

Jefferson blazed away at the target, the others looking on, shifting their eyes out to Ross each time he fired.

Three in the target were all Jefferson could manage.

"Deke, you next," Ples said.

Deke came up to the firing line, Ples asking innocently of him, "You ain't marked down, is you?"

"Naw, suh. But I been tryin'"

"Well, you gonna try harder," Ples answered tersely, looking cat-eyed at Deke.

"I been tryin'. . . ."

"Fire!" Ples screamed.

Deke threw his carbine up to his shoulder, and fired.

Ross stayed motionless.

"Take yo' time," Ples told Deke. "Put the target in both sights, take a deep breath, hold it, then squeeze."

"Dat's what I been tryin' . . ."

"Fire!" Ples screamed.

Deke fired off another shot.

Ross stayed motionless.

Ples gave Deke a dirty look; Cecil Hall and Bobo shifted uneasily in their steps.

"What in hell you seein'?" Ples roared angrily, snatching the carbine from Deke's hands. Throwing the carbine up to his own shoulder, Ples fired off a shot.

Ross's hand went up.

Ples lowered the weapon, giving Deke a dirty look all the while.

"I been . . . ," Deke started.

Ples rudely thrust the carbine back into Deke's hands, the sudden impact cutting off his speech.

"Now," Ples said solemnly, "sight that rifle in, squeeze the trigger slowly, and hit that blanket the same way I did. Now fire!"

Deke fired.

Ross's hand stayed down to his side.

"Goddamnit!" Ples screamed. Turning in his steps, Ples ran his eyes over the rest of them, standing back not knowing what to say or do. They all just knew that Ples had gone off again. And they all were scared for Deke of what Ples might do next.

Nobody said a word.

"Fate," Ples said quietly, a deep scowl on his face.

"Yeah?" Fate answered.

"Go out yonder where Ross is."

None of them knew what to expect. Not even Fate. Walking out the hundred yards or so where Ross was, looking curiously back in his steps at Ples, who had turned his whole attention back to Deke, saying solemnly in Deke's face, "You see that boy walkin' out there?"

"Yeah, suh," Deke answered, perplexed at the question. "That's Fate."

"You heard how long me and Fate been together?"

"Yeah, suh," Deke answered.

"You heard about some of what we been through together?"

"Yeah, suh."

"You know I mean what I say when I say it, don't you?"

362

"Yeah, suh."

"Fate!" Ples yelled out. "Pick up that target and hold it up!"

Fate picket up the target sheet, and held it out at arm's length from his body.

Ples deliberately pulled his pistol, leveled it at Deke's ear, and said gravely, "Now, you hit that target, you hear me?"

"Yeah, suh," Deke said, swallowing back his tongue.

"You miss and hit Fate, I'm gonna blow yo' brains out. You hear me?"

"Yeah, suh," Deke answered, a quaver in his voice.

"You sight down that gun barrel and shoot whenever you git ready. Just make sho' it ain't yo' last."

Deke went blue at the lips. He glanced back at the rest of them looking at him.

Nobody said a word. Deke knew he was all on his own.

Bringing his eyes back around to the target, he swallowed hard, wiped his face.

"You ain't got all day," Ples said solemnly, cocking his pistol in Deke's ear. The hammer click heard by the farthest man away, it was so quiet.

Deke squinted through the sights, then looked off and squinted again.

Seconds went by. Everybody watching Deke's trigger finger.

Deke fired. Jolting everybody like a thunderclap out of a clear blue sky.

Ross's hand shot up.

"He hit it!" somebody exclaimed in shocked relief.

"Shoot again!" Ples yelled at Deke even as the smoke was wafting away.

Deke raked a tongue over his dry lips. Then fired again.

Ross's hand shot up again.

Deke took a quick sideways glance at the rest of them, obvious relief in his face.

Nobody even twitched; it was as if they were awestruck at Deke's success, and how he'd come into it.

"Shoot again!" Ples roared.

Deke squeezed off another shot.

Ross's hand went up.

Ples took his pistol out of Deke's ear, holstering it, and relaxing his stance.

Deke lowered his rifle barrel, tension draining away from his body.

"He done it!" Augie blurted out. "He git marked down."

"Hush up, Augie," Willie said. "He ain't finished yet."

"Fate!" Ples called out, "put that target down and come on back here!"

"I'm done?" Deke asked anxiously.

"You is as far as I'm concerned," Ples said, and walked off, heading back up the creek to his seat on a deadfall.

Just at that time, Sergeant Radford came cantering up from where he'd intentionally been out of sight.

"Mark him down," Ples said when Radford walked his horse up.

"For real?" Radford asked.

"For real," Ples said, a hint of smile on his lips. "Some of the best shootin' you ever seen."

"How'd you do it?"

"Told him I was goin' to blow his brains out."

"Shit!" Radford said exasperatedly, "I told him that . . . more'n once."

"I guess he didn't believe you," Ples said, and walked off.

Radford walked his horse up to where they were, Radford looking a queer look at Deke. Deke standing there, a foolish grin on his face.

"Sergeant Radford," Battie said happily, "you can mark down Deke. He qualified."

"Mr. Butler told me," Radford answered, dismounting. Scowling at Deke. "I oughta not mark nothin' down," Radford said in mock disdain. "He coulda hit that target long ago."

"I was tryin'," Deke said defensively.

"Since everybody's qualified," Jake said, "what we goin' to do now?"

"Muster and have roll call," Battie said facetiously.

"You can do whatever you want to," Radford said. "I got comp'ny reports to work on." And Radford walked off, heading to where Ples and Fate were sitting on the deadfall, talking. Fate saying, "At least you could'a told me. What if he'da shot me?"

"I woulda shot him," Ples replied carelessly.

"That would'na done me no good," Fate said testily.

"Would'na done me no good neither," Ples said, "but I still woulda shot 'em."

"Mr. Butler," Radford said, walking up, interrupting the conversation, "everybody's qualified so I'm givin' the men the rest of the afternoon off."

"They deserve it," Ples answered, watching Fate walk off, heading to where the others were clustered around Deke, laughing and grinning now. "Fort Riley ain't goin' nowhere. Won't matter if we git there a day early or a day late."

"I guess not," Radford said. "Cap'n Dudley didn't say when we had to be there."

"He didn't say 'cause he didn't know," Ples said casually. "He likely ain't been to Fort Riley hisself."

"You?" Radford asked.

"Naw," Ples answered. "But when you seen one army post, you seen 'em all."

"You been to army posts before," Radford said thoughtfully. "When we git to Fort Riley and join up with the rest of Comp'ny M, you think we'll all be able to stick? Nobody'll git sent packin'?"

"I don't reckon the rest of Company M is any different from this bunch you got. They'll have some that catch on quicker than the others, and they'll have some that's slow-witted too, same as you got. Only thing you can do is help 'em along.

"Course you'll have to worry 'bout yo'self too," Ples added, meeting Radford's questioning glance.

"This Sergeant Baggs Ross is always talkin' 'bout," Ples stated, "sounds to me like he's well thought of."

"So?" Radford said carelessly.

"When you git to Fort Riley only one of you'll run Company M," Ples stated, and paused, letting his meaning sink in.

"One of you'll be put in ranks," Ples added, looking across his shoulder at Radford.

"I been in ranks befo'," Radford said tersely. And got up and walked away, heading over toward the cook fire where the rest of them had gathered, talking, eating up what food had been left over from dinner.

None of them knew it but at this very moment they were being watched. Plunk Murray had led Peyton Long and the rest of them to Bull Creek. And here were the recruits, just as Plunk had figured.

Now, from the east bank Peyton Long sat his saddle, studying through his field glasses the layout of their camp.

And what Long saw didn't bring to his mind a military camp. It was more a carnival atmosphere than anything else: troopers standing around slack-legged, talking, plates in their hands; sitting around on drift logs, talking and laughing. No sentry in sight. Horses unattended on the picket line.

But Long's military mind gave them credit for one thing: putting the creek between themselves and Long's bunch.

Long swung his glasses off to the side of the camp, up the rise there. And a lone figure came into focus. Sitting on a deadfall, a cup of coffee in hand, Winchester propped at his side. Long didn't know the man's name, but right off he recognized who it was.

Ples Butler.

Long lowered his field glasses, and passed them over to Plunk, his lips puckered in studied thought. There was one man he hadn't seen. That nigger breed. And that worried Long some. He knew that breed was there. Somewhere.

Plunk had the glasses up to his eyes, studying the camp for himself. Lowering the glasses, he passed them back to Long, saying arrogantly, "This oughta be easy."

"Did you see that old man up the rise there?" Long asked.

"Yeah, I seen 'im," Plunk answered.

"Nothin's been easy with him around," Long retorted, panning his eyes around their surroundings, his mind working at a plan of attack.

"I say we ride right in on 'em," Plunk said suggestively.

"That'd be a fool thing to do," Long replied. "Whether by accident or on purpose, they got the creek between us. I'd guess it was that old man's doin'. They'd pick us off like sittin' ducks crossin' that creek."

"It'd take us at least two more hours to head this creek and come up on 'em," Plunk said advisedly.

"I'd rather take two hours than eternity," Long retorted. "We got time," he added, swinging his horse away, saying to Plunk, "Lead out."

What Long, Plunk Murray, and the rest of them didn't know was that they too were being watched. By that nigger breed, as Long had called him.

Bowlegs was sitting on his haunches, unmoving as a stone, eyes steady, watching them from over by the horse herd. Bowlegs was never far from the horses when he was in camp. Especially now that Captain Dudley had warned them that fleeing Cheyennes were about. Bowlegs knew that even squaws and old men would steal horses at a time such as Captain Dudley described.

Now Bowlegs quietly rose to standing, and mounted up. Cantering his pinto out some distance on the open prairie, he looked after the way the riders had gone. And there before him Bowlegs saw Long and them, riding hard, strung out along the rise of the creek bank, heading north.

Bowlegs swung his horse, and cantered back to camp. Reining up next to where Ples was sitting on the log, Bowlegs slid down, Ples watching him with interest all the time.

"Butler," Bowlegs said without emotion, "white men come back. They make big fight again."

"Where?" Ples asked anxiously, looking the way Bowlegs had ridden in.

"They come there," Bowlegs said, nodding across the creek.

"You seen 'em?" Ples asked, jumping to his feet.

"I see," Bowlegs answered. "They watch camp . . . then go that way."

"How many?" Ples asked, looking north where Bowlegs had indicated.

"Many," Bowlegs stated.

"How many's many, Wild Man?" Ples asked. "Twenty . . . thirty?"

"Maybe twenty . . . no thirty," Bowlegs said.

"That one-armed man . . . he wid 'em?"

"He is there," Bowlegs answered.

Ples swore under his breath, then yelled out, "Radford!"

"Yeah, suh?" Radford answered from over by the cook fire where he was talking to Deke, Fate, Jerico, and some others.

"You better come hear what Jimmy's got to say," Ples told him.

At Ples's words the whole camp got attentive. They all knew something was up. The only question was what.

"White men come back," Bowlegs said to Radford even as he was walking up.

"Where?" Radford asked.

"There," Bowlegs said, nodding north. "Or maybe they come that way," he added, nodding out across the prairie the way they were headed. "By and by they come," he stated definitely.

"You seen 'em?" Radford asked.

"I see," Bowlegs answered for the second time.

"What he's tellin' you is, he seen white men comin'," Ples said. "At least twenty."

"Maybe they ain't after us," Radford said hopefully.

"They is," Ples said. "Anytime you see that many men ridin' together, they after somethin' or somebody," Ples added sagely. "Besides that, Jimmy seen the one-armed man wid 'em."

Radford looked behind him at their leisurely camp, men standing around in clusters, watching them, listening for a word or hint of what was up.

Radford roved his eyes around their surroundings, gathering his thoughts. Figuring out what to do next.

"You got the creek behind you, like you wanted," Ples said encouragingly. "But Jimmy figures right now they skirtin' the creek, comin' up on us from the north . . . or west," Ples added, looking out across the prairie.

Radford looked a questioning look at Ples.

Ples said suggestively, "You could stay here and fight with the creek at yo' back like you didn't want to . . . or you could meet 'em head on out there." And Ples nodded west.

"Maybe they ain't after us," Radford said again.

"They after us, all right," Ples said definitely. "The only question is, what you goin' to do about it? You got the rest of these men . . . your men, to look after . . . Sergeant Radford," Ples added rudely.

Radford shifted in his steps, his eyes studying the ground.

"You ain't got but two choices," Ples stated. "Fight right where you at . . . or out there."

"Maybe he no make good yellowlegs," Bowlegs said. "Maybe he scared of white man," he added disdainfully, goading Radford, which he never did before.

Radford stiffened at the notion, giving Bowlegs a dirty look.

"I no scared, Wild Man," Radford said, mimicking Bowlegs. "We make big fight."

"Where?" Ples asked.

"Right here," Radford said firmly.

"Creek at yo' back," Ples said as a reminder. "You got no place to maneuver."

"You mean no place to run, don't you, Mr. Butler?" Radford asked, bristling at the suggestion.

"That's what I mean," Ples answered.

"Well, we ain't intendin' to run," Radford said firmly. "Not none of us.

"I'll go tell the men," Radford continued. "Jimmy . . . you go out there and keep watch. Let us know when they comin'." And Radford walked off, walking with a purpose.

"He's learnin'," Ples said to Bowlegs, both standing there watching Radford walk off.

"Maybe he make good yellowlegs," Bowlegs said. "Maybe I no kill."

"Just remember he's gov'ment property," Ples retorted even as Bowlegs was mounting up.

They were all standing there, waiting anxiously, watching Radford come on toward them. Expecting him to tell them what was the matter.

"All right!" Sergeant Radford yelled out, walking up, "fall in!"

"Fall in!" Battie repeated exasperatedly. "That all?"

"That ain't all," Sergeant Radford said. "Just shut yo' mouth and fall in," he added curtly.

They fell in. Muttering in low tones.

"We got trouble," Sergeant Radford stated. "Them white men done come back." And Radford stood there, panning his eyes around, letting his words sink in.

"We got our backs to the creek, but we gonna fight 'em right here," Sergeant Radford continued. "Jimmy don't know which way they comin' from . . . but it don't matter.

"We ain't goin' back cross that creek. This's Comp'ny M. And Comp'ny M is goin' to Fort Riley. If we have to fight our way there, we will.

"Anything happens to me, Mr. Butler'll see that you git there," Sergeant Radford added, glancing off to the side where Ples was standing, listening to his talk.

"Willie . . . you and Augie git down to the picket line and watch them hosses. Don't let none of 'em break away and don't let nobody take none of 'em. Go now!

"Fatback . . . you and Jefferson git that wagon further back from the water. " 'Bout middle way to the bank. Don't worry 'bout puttin' no cooking gear in it 'cause we ain't goin' nowhere. Git goin'!

"Battie, Rafer D., Jake, y'all go up this creek bank 'bout a hundred yards or so, find a good spot where you can see out. You see 'em comin', one of you come back here and let me know. You got that, Battie?" Sergeant Radford asked.

"I got it, Sergeant Radford," Battie answered.

"Y'all go on down there then," Radford told them. "Git down out of sight under the bank and stay there.

"Cecil, Bobo, Deese . . . y'all go out there in front of the wagon. Pick a spot under the bank where you can see everything. You see 'em comin', start shootin'.

"Fate . . . keep half of these men back here wid you so y'all can help Battie and them if they come that way. Jerico, you take the other half and help Bobo and them. Deke . . . you stay wid me."

"I'm marked down," Deke said. "I can shoot too."

"I know you can," Sergeant Radford said. "You'll git yo' chance. But for now I need you as a runner. Go git yo' hoss and keep 'im handy.

"You got anythin' to say, Mr. Butler?" Radford asked, walking over to Ples, even as Fate and Jerico were picking out their half of the rest of the men.

"Seems you said it all," Ples answered, standing there slack-legged, his Winchester in his right hand. "Except . . ."

" 'Cept what?" Radford asked.

"You got two, maybe three men . . . Rafer D., Fate, Jerico . . . who was hittin' that target at three . . . four hunded yards. I'd put 'em out there." And Ples nodded west toward the steep bank where the prairie started. "Let 'em start shootin' as soon as they come in sight. Put somethin' on they minds even before they git in shootin' distance."

"Fate! Jerico!" Radford called abruptly. "Y'all forgit what I said befo'. Both of you go wid Mr. Butler. Fate, send the men you had up the creek where Battie and Jake at . . . Jerico, take yo' men wid Mr. Butler and spread 'em out along the bank.

"I'll send Rafer D. on later," Radford told Ples. "Anything else?" he asked, looking cat-eyed at Ples.

"Naw," Ples said. "Nothin' we can do now but wait."

"What about me?" Private Ross asked, standing there looking useless.

"You go to the wagon," Radford said.

"I'm qualified," Ross said, protesting. "I been marked down."

"Maybe so," Radford answered, "but I don't want my timepiece killed. Go to the wagon . . . and keep yo' head down."

Time moved slowly.

They waited.

Battie and his group watching the north approach; Fate, Jerico, Rafer D., and the others lying belly-flat under the lip of the creek bank, watching the west approach, ready to shoot at the first sight of anything that moved; Willie and Augie guarding the horses at the picket line; Fatback, Jefferson, and Private Ross in the canvas-covered wagon.

Time passed.

Radford making the rounds, checking with everybody.

Now he was saying to Ples, "Mr. Butler, I hope this works."

"It will," Ples answered, "if they go 'bout it with a will."

"They better," Radford answered. "I told 'em all . . . Comp'ny M goin' to Fort Riley . . . not back cross that creek. I told 'em I'd shoot any one of 'em that try."

"Ain't nothin' to do then, but wait," Ples said.

Chapter Twenty-two

They came riding out of the west. Twenty strong. Ex-Confederate Colonel Peyton Long and mule trader Plunk Murray riding in the lead, eighteen other disgruntled, negligent white men riding at their backs. Each man riding for his own reasons and some that had been exaggerated and overstated by smooth-talking Lewton Belmont. All of them bent on killing or maiming for life black recruits going to make a life for themselves.

None of them knew what manner of men they faced. Not one of them much cared. All they knew was that they were riding to attack black men. Men who would run at the crack of a rifle shot, as they'd heard.

Peyton Long knew better. But somehow he couldn't tell the rest of them. Somehow he knew they wouldn't listen, wouldn't believe him. But they hadn't been there at Brice's Crossroads, hadn't heard about Forts Pillow and Wagner, knew nothing about Milliken's Bend. All great Civil War battles where black men had taken white lives, spilling their own blood in the doing.

But Long kept quiet. Grimly silent. Culture and pride pulling him on beyond turning back.

On they came. Long in studied doubt even as they galloped to battle. In the back of his mind, Long knew this wasn't going to be as easy as Plunk and the rest of them thought.

They topped the rise looking down on Bull Creek, Long checking his horse down, then drawing up to a halt.

Sitting his horse, his eyes inspecting the terrain ahead, Long pondered the situation. Looking it over carefully.

And Long got wary. Something in the back of his military mind making him think twice. It was too quiet down there. Not like before.

"Plunk, how far is it from that creek bank to the water's edge?" Long asked.

"Fifty . . . sixty yards," Plunk answered. "Water's down some now."

"I figure that breed's seen us," Long said. "They waitin' for us. Likely hid down under that creek bank somewhere."

"Don't matter," Plunk said heedlessly. "We was to go in shootin' they'd run. And they ain't got nowhere to run to 'cept that creek behind 'em."

"Like I told you," Long said, ". . . like I told the rest of them . . . it ain't gonna be as easy as that. Not as long as that old man and that breed's wid 'em."

"Maybe you did have a run-in wid 'em before," Plunk said dismissively, "but you overratin' 'em, Colonel. Ain't a nigger I seen yet got sand."

"That's 'cause you ain't seen many," Long said rudely, swinging his horse away.

Long rode back to the middle of the column of waiting men, and announced: "They down there. With their backs to the creek. We'll sweep right over 'em. Shoot anything that moves. We git down to the water's edge, we'll double back, shoot anything that's left alive."

Long swung his horse, heading up to the lead of the column, and that's when he saw the rider. His pinto horse in a full-out gallop, heading toward the creek.

It was Bowlegs.

Racing back to where Ples and the recruits were.

"Colonel, that's the one what stole my hoss!" Riley McCoy called up to Long.

"I told you he'd be 'round somewhere," Long answered.

"Colonel, we can handle this," Riley said respectfully, whether in deference to Long's missing arm or for the fact that Long had been an officer, nobody could say.

"Yeah, Colonel," Pete Cooney added. "In case you change yo' mind about goin' to Mexico wid us."

"Was I you, Colonel, I'd listen to 'em," Frank Yoder said. "When this over wid, we gonna need you."

"All right," Long said reluctantly. "Frank, you lead the attack just like I said. Sweep down to the water, wheel around, and come back, killin' all you can comin' and goin'. Then come on back here. We'll ride back to Johnny Cake and tell Mr. Belmont, and Mr. Belmont can git word to General Bickley."

"Don't you worry, Colonel," Frank Yoder said reassuringly. "Won't be a nigger left worth mentionin' when we git back."

Bowlegs leaped his horse down the low creek bank. Weaving in and out of stunted willows and second-growth small stuff, he worked his way along the dirt flat to where he knew Ples and the men were.

"They come," Bowlegs announced to Ples and Radford, concealed belly-flat under the lip of the cut bank.

"This the way you wanted it?" Ples said, looking across his shoulder at Radford, sprawled out next to him.

"This the way I wanted it," Radford said resolutely.

"Rafer D.! Fate! Jerico! Y'all git ready! They comin'!" Radford announced. "Start shootin' as soon as you see 'em. Bobo! Deese! The rest of y'all, don't start shootin' till they git in close.

"Mr. Butler," Radford continued, "I'm goin' to git the rest of the men hid in the wagon. When they come by, we ain't goin' to shoot. We goin' to wait till they git all the way down to the water, then we goin' to jump out and let 'em have it."

And Radford slithered away from the bank, jumped to his feet, and took off running low, going to get the rest of the men into the wagon.

"It might work," Ples said, looking up at Bowlegs in the saddle.

"We make it work," Bowlegs said, dismounting, Winchester in hand.

They waited. Minutes passed. Tension rose. Palms got sweaty on carbine barrels.

At something like 1600 hours Frank Yoder and his men struck.

Nineteen horsemen charging in a solid, close-packed bunch.

Pounding hoofs shaking the very earth they rode on.

Rafer D. fired; on the instant Jerico and Fate fired.

A man in the middle of the bunch left his saddle, the riderless horse running along with the rest of them.

Frank Yoder and the rest came charging on, closing the distance, firing their saddle guns at vanishing black heads popping up and down, and at puffs of smoke wafting up from the creek bank.

At something like two hundred yards away, Ples and Bowlegs opened up on them, joining their rifle fire with that of Rafer D.'s, Jerico's, and Fate's.

Two more horses were suddenly riderless.

At about a hundred yards away, Cecil Hall, Deese, and Bobo joined in the shooting. Laying down a continuous racket of gunfire.

Another man left his saddle.

Suddenly the mounted attackers were upon them, no more than fifty or sixty yards away. Every man among them firing his rifle as fast as he could work the lever from the saddle. Their bullets pocking the prairie out in front of Ples and them, lifting up troughs of dirt all along the lip of the creek bank.

Bobo lifted his head to fire. And that was the last thing he ever did. A bullet exploded his face.

Deese took a bullet through the lungs from somewhere off to the left, his lifeless body going stiff at the shock, sliding back down the low embankment.

And then Frank Yoder and his men leaped their horses down the bank, kicking back dirt from the flats, firing left and right as they went.

Cecil Hall went down. Shot through the belly as he tried to wheel around into firing position.

And then they were past Ples and them, heading toward the water's edge. Two more riderless horses, Will Helvie's and Joe Shaler's, galloping along with them.

On Yoder and the rest rode, twisted around in their saddles, firing back. Nobody paying much notice to the seemingly empty wagon left parked there.

At the water's edge, they jerked up to a thunderous halt and wheeled their mounts around, preparing for a return assault.

And right before their eyes the innocent-looking wagon's canvas-cover blossomed off. And from point-blank range a dozen rifles started spitting flame at them.

Donnie Pence and Martin Conway left their saddles; Sam Biddle's horse went down, screaming. Biddle no sooner got clear of the downed horse when he too was cut down. Struck from off to the right by Ples's bullet from where Ples was running down with half of the men who had been under the lip of the bank.

Glenn Harmony and Joe Dockum were instantly shot from the saddle. Both cut down by rifle fire from off to the left where Fate and Jerico had come running up with the other half of the men that had been with Ples.

Frank Yoder could see that they were in a fix: their own backs to the water, flying lead zinging in on three sides. And his ranks greatly thinned.

They were in a fix all right. Their chances slim to none. And Ples knew it.

Ples stopped firing, looking a doubtful look at Radford.

"Hold yo' fire! Stop shootin'!" Radford yelled out to the rest of them.

Firing tapered off, then died out.

Frank Yoder and the rest of them, their horses under rein now, sat their horses, guns at the ready, Yoder making up his mind what to do.

Yoder didn't want to give it up. He'd come here, like the rest of them, with a purpose in mind. It wasn't in him to concede victory to black men. Somehow he had to come out on top.

Yoder panned his eyes around, looking at the guns arrayed against them. And there on the left, he saw Ples. The old black man that was the source of this belittling put-down, as he reasoned it. And Yoder sensed a chance to come out on top after all. In spite of being boxed in like this.

Yoder started to bring his rifle around to the left from his own right . . .

And Fate shot him. From over on the right where he was first to see Yoder's gun move.

The rest of the men mistook Fate's provoked shot for a renewal of the gun battle.

Everything turned haywire: Lead started flying; horses started snorting and rearing; men started screaming.

Riley McCoy swung his rifle and fired at a man at the wagon directly in front of him.

A bullet broke into Deke Poole's chest, dropping him instantly against the wagon wheel.

Ples's bullet swept McCoy from the saddle.

Bowlegs shot Boyd Daniel from his horse.

Plunk Murray snapped off a quick shot at Bowlegs, and screamed, "Let's git outa here!" Wheeling his horse, he dug in his spurs, heading toward the water.

Plunk didn't have to tell the rest of them twice. They wheeled their horses in behind Plunk's, firing back as they went.

Pete Cooney threw back a shot. And that was the last trigger he ever pulled. Rafer D. drilled him between the shoulder blades, dropping his body in midstream.

"Let 'em go!" Radford told the recruits when they went running down to the water's edge, firing out across at the fleeing men.

"Mr. Butler!" Radford yelled out, seeing Ples running for his horse, ". . . let 'em go!"

Ples jumped in the saddle, and wheeled his horse away from next to the picket line. Digging in his spurs, he came galloping down the creek bank. And wheeled his horse west. Away from where Plunk and the others had gone.

"Where's he goin'?" Radford asked, more to himself than anybody else.

"The one-armed man," Bowlegs said without emotion. "He is there. Butler know."

"He's gone," Jerico said. "Rafer D. shot at 'im, and he rode off."

"Butler no care. He follow," Bowlegs said.

"Where?" Radford asked, looking at Jerico, who knew the country.

"Closest town is Johnny Cake," Jerico said. "Used to be full of secesh and Border Ruffians. Didn't allow blacks in town. Mr. Butler go in there, they'll kill 'im on sight," Jerico said definitely.

At those words, Fate took off running, heading for the wagon.

"Where you goin'!" Radford asked.

"Wid Ples!" Fate yelled back from the tailgate of the wagon where he was unbuckling his service revolver. Tossing the awkward weapon over into the wagon, Fate reached over the tailgate and retrieved his own shell belt and six-shooter that he knew Ples had stashed there.

"Fate!" Radford screamed again. "You in the army now! You can't go to that town! I'm orderin' you not to!"

"Only way I don't, you'll shoot me first," Fate said, buckling on his own gun.

Just at that time, Bowlegs came riding up, leading Fate's horse. Passing Fate the reins, Bowlegs looked out at Radford, and said plainly, "I go too. Help Butler. We make big fight."

Fate swung onto his saddle, and he and Bowlegs dug out. Radford and the others standing there in their tracks, watching them go. They watched until Fate and Bowlegs jumped their horses up over the creek bank, striking open prairie.

They all brought their eyes back on Radford. Wondering what he was going to do.

Radford knew they were watching him; could feel their eyes boring into his body. He knew they all wanted to go into Johnny Cake to help Mr. Butler. And they expected him to lead them there.

"Fatback! Jefferson!" Radford called out, "y'all stay wid this wagon. . . . The rest of y'all, stand to hoss!"

It was as if a silent cheer went up. Every man among them broke, dashing for a horse. Willie and Augie untying their own horses from the picket line even as they came running.

When Sergeant Radford walked up in front of them, every trooper was standing at attention next to a horse. Even Private Ross.

"Where you goin'?" Radford asked him.

"I'm marked down," Ross stated tersely.

Radford left it at that.

"We goin' into that town," Radford announced to them out loud, "and we goin' as United States cavalry troopers. "Comp'ny M," he added proudly. "We ain't goin' to bother nothin' or nobody . . . unless they mess wid Mr. Butler.

"When Mr. Butler git done with his business, we done wid ours too. Jerico . . . you ride up wid me and show us the way. Mount up!"

They all stuck a toe in the stirrup, and as a unit swung into saddles.

"Column right . . . by the right flank, at a walk! March!" Radford commanded.

They walked their horses up to and over the creek bank, striking open prairie.

"Forward at a gallop! March!" Radford commanded.

On they went. At a full-out gallop.

By this time, Fate and Bowlegs had caught up to Ples.

Ples had been galloping along at a steady gait trailing Long. Ples knew there was no great hurry to overtake Long. It was set in Ples's mind once and for all to put a stop to this one-armed man's attacks. It didn't much matter where he caught up with him. He was going to put an end to the matter.

All this had been on Ples's mind when he chanced to look on his back trail, as he often did.

And Ples saw riders.

Recognizing who they were, Ples checked his horse down to a lope, not bothering even to look back again. Ples had had a feeling that Fate wouldn't let it go at that. Had kind of suspected that Fate would be along, in uniform or out. Seeing him ride off on his own and all.

Fate and Bowlegs joined on either side of Ples, putting their horses in gait with Ples's.

"Where you goin', Wild Man?" Ples asked Bowlegs.

"With you," Bowlegs answered. "We make big fight."

"Not so big this time," Ples answered. "Only one man." And Ples nodded out front where Long's back was barely visible.

"We kill . . . I give to coyotes," Bowlegs said.

"Your doin'," Ples said carelessly, lifting his horse's gait a notch.

Conversation ended. Ples didn't say anything to Fate; Fate didn't say anything to Ples.

There was nothing to say between the two.

On they rode.

It was 1700 hours when Ples, Fate, and Bowlegs struck the main road leading into Johnny Cake. The tracks of the lone rider ahead of them plainly visible in the dirt.

Falling in with the tracks, they galloped on.

At the edge of town, Ples drew up, Fate and Bowlegs following suit. They sat in their saddles, looking the town over: nobody in sight; a lathered horse standing slack-legged in front of the Hester House hotel; four more wet horses standing head down at the hitch rail in front of Yeager's Saloon; a hay wagon standing empty down in front of the stable.

"Y'all don't have to come," Ples said to them. "You gov'ment property now," he added, looking across his shoulder at Fate.

"I know that," Fate said. "I'm comin' anyhow."

"I nobody's property," Bowlegs said without emotion.

Ples nudged his horse out.

Fate and Bowlegs did the same.

"Y'all wait here," Ples said, swinging his horse in next to the lathered horse there.

Swinging down, his Winchester in his right hand, Ples stepped up on the boardwalk, and paused. Panning his eyes along the street.

Nobody in sight.

383

Momentarily, Ples turned in his steps, and crossed through the doors.

"You ain't s'pose to be in here!" a tall, bushy-browed man said from behind the desk counter.

"The man ridin' that lathered hoss outside . . . he in here?" Ples said grimly.

"Nobody's here but who you see," answered a deep voice from down in the corner of the lobby.

Ples focused his eyes in the direction the voice had come from. And saw a man sitting behind a desk, fingering a deck of cards.

It was Lewton Belmont.

"Fact is," Lewton continued affably, "you ain't got no business bein' in here yo'self."

"I got business," Ples answered solemnly. "With the man ridin' that lathered hoss outside."

"Only business you got is to turn around and go back out that door the way you came," Lewton said, laying the deck of cards aside. "Join that lathered hoss outside," he added contemptuously.

Ples's Winchester came around carelessly, the barrel pointing in Lewton's general direction.

Lewton smiled disarmingly. His left hand innocently falling away from the table, his right hand harmlessly moving up to his coat pocket, toward the pocket gun Ples knew men like him preferred to carry.

Ples shot him. The Winchester's explosion rocking the hotel.

Lewton was smashed back in his chair, his body slamming against the wall at his back. The hotel clerk started to reach for a shotgun behind the counter.

Ples swung his Winchester that way.

The clerks eyes went big; then both hands shot skyward. "I don't want no trouble, mister," the clerk said anxiously.

"The one-armed man . . . where is he?" Ples asked.

"Honest, mister," the clerk said, red around the lips, "I don't know."

The clerk's words betrayed his eyes. Eyes that had involuntarily shifted up to the bannister running along the second floor behind Ples.

Ples whirled and fired up.

The bullet clipped wood from the six-inch bannister there, and dug into Long's body, stiffening him upright from the shock, exposing his full body.

Ples triggered off more shots. Working the Winchester's action as fast as humanly possible. A steady stream of searching bullets. Not even he was prepared to say exactly how many.

Long's body teetered there for a long minute, then plunged over the side rail, bringing the bannister with it, crashing down to the floor.

Outside, Fate and Bowlegs had heard the spate of gunshots. So had everybody else in Johnny Cake that evening.

Fate kept his eyes focused on the doors, watching for Ples to come out, if he ever did. Bowlegs gigged his pinto around, watching the entire street.

Two men came running out the batwings of Renner's Saloon; four came scrambling out of Yeager's: Plunk Murray, Lige Green, Tom Lykins, and Nathan Bell. Had two more men with them, Emmett Goss and York Johnson. Plunk and the others had been inside telling the story their own way of what had happened out there at Bull Creek.

They came to an abrupt halt on the boardwalk when they saw Fate and Bowlegs, two black men they recognized from the earlier gun battle. Both sitting their horses up there where the shots had come from, Ples backing out of the Hester House hotel. His eyes sweeping the street, his Winchester in his hands.

None of them expected black men to ride into Johnny Cake. Starting trouble. In broad daylight like this.

Plunk Murray got it in his mind to do something about it. Plunk wanted to make up for the way they had been rudely handled out there at Bull Creek.

". . . That damned hoss-thievin' breed again," Plunk said, and his gun hand started to reach for his pistol. . . .

And that's when they heard hoof-falls at their backs.

They all twisted around where they were, looking south down the main road.

It was Sergeant Radford. At the head of Company M.

Plunk's gun hand went slack where it was; the others froze right where they were. Looking in awestruck disbelief.

Company M came on at a walk down the middle of the street. Passing in front of Ellie Mae's, Ellie Mae peeping out the window around drawn curtains.

In front of Yeager's, Sergeant Radford barked out the command: "Comp'ny, by the right flank! March!"

As a unit, they all swung their horses right.

"Comp'ny, halt!" Radford called out.

They all drew rein. Sitting in their saddles ramrod straight, eyes straight ahead. Arrayed in front of Yeager's. In front of where Plunk and the rest of them were standing on the boardwalk.

Nobody spoke. Both sides looking each other over in stone silence.

"Mr. Butler!" Radford finally called down the street where Ples was out on the boardwalk, ". . . you done?"

"I'm done!" Ples answered back, sheathing his Winchester, mounting up.

"Fate!" Radford continued, "you in the cavalry now. Git back in ranks where you 'spose to be!"

Fate trotted his horse up to the formation, and swung into ranks.

"What about that hoss thief?" Plunk Murray asked lamely, looking at Radford.

"And that nigg . . . ," the clerk who'd just rushed up started, ". . . that one," he continued, catching himself, pointing at Ples, "shot Mr. Belmont and Colonel Long over to the hotel."

"Anybody got a complaint," Sergeant Radford answered, "take it to Fort Riley. That's where we'll be."

The clerk looked a helpless look at Plunk Murray; Plunk looked a powerless look at York Johnson; York stayed grimly silent.

"Mr. Butler," Radford continued, talking to Ples, who had ridden up with Bowlegs, "let's go to Fort Riley. Lead out."

Ples swung his horse, and led out.

"Comp'ny, by the left flank! March!" Radford barked out.

They swung their horses and rode out of Johnny Cake. It was 1730 hours.

On a July morning Sergeant Radford and his remnant of Company M reached Fort Riley. Captain Dudley was first to get word of their coming from Bowlegs, who had ridden on ahead as he had always done.

Captain Dudley had passed the word on to Colonel Grierson, adding hopefully, "They're the men scheduled to fill out my Company M."

"If they don't measure up, Company M will stay under-manned the way it is," Grierson said. "My orders are to have this regiment in the field next month. We don't have time to start recruit trainin' all over again."

"We won't have to, sir," Dudley stated.

"I'll be the judge of that, Captain," Grierson answered. "March 'em in and let's see if your idea of trainin' them on the way here worked . . . see if this Sergeant Radford and Private Ross taught 'em anything all this time they been out there, God knows where."

Captain Dudley rode out and stopped the column some fifty yards from the main gate.

"Mr. Butler," Dudley said. Turning his eyes to Radford, he continued, "I see you made it, Sergeant Radford." And Dudley ran his eyes down the column, mentally counting heads.

"Yeah, suh," Radford answered. "We had some trouble though."

"Four more missin' men," Dudley said solemnly. "Whatever the trouble was, I hope your judgment and common sense measured up, Sergeant. You got some explainin' to do."

"I can, suh."

"Comp'ny reports filled out?"

"Yeah, suh."

"Very well, Sergeant," Dudley answered.

Dudley gigged his horse past Radford and Ples, and rode back to the middle of the column.

"Inside that gate," Dudley announced to them all out loud, "the commanding officer . . . Colonel Grierson, will be standing in front of headquarters watchin' you when you ride in.

"If you want to stick, if you don't want to git sent packin', you better look sharp when you ride through that gate. Keep yo' head up, yo' eyes straight ahead. Keep yo' back straight, and yo' butt down! Show 'em you United States cavalry troopers. Show 'em you want to stick!

"Sergeant Radford . . . march 'em in!"

Captain Dudley wheeled his horse, and rode back to the fort, and was standing at Grierson's side when they rode in.

Company M rode in in splendid fashion, guidon fluttering in the slight breeze, ranks perfectly aligned, troopers holding their saddles in good order.

Colonel Grierson had been standing there looking, not knowing what to expect. When the last rank rode by, Grierson said dispassionately, "Captain Dudley, looks like they'll do. You got the rest of Company M."

"Yes, sir," Dudley answered.

"For now at least...," Grierson added cautiously. "There's more to a good trooper besides paradin'."

"They'll measure up to the rest of it too, sir," Dudley answered.

"They better," Grierson retorted, turning in his steps, heading back inside headquarters.

Epilogue

Every recruit that had survived the trip from St. Louis stuck with Company M. Company M joined other colored companies made up of men who had come from all over the United States, and they were designated the tenth Cavalry Regiment by the war department.

The tenth rode into distinguished history, gaining fame as Buffalo Soldiers.

Sergeant Bosie Radford became Company M's first sergeant over Sergeant Biggs.

In '70, Jerico Walker was discharged. He was summoned back to Fort Leavenworth to stand court-martial for murder at Jefferson City, Missouri. Sergeant Radford and Battie were detailed by Captain Dudley to take him back to Fort Leavenworth. The trial lasted four days. Peyton Long wasn't there as a witness for the murder charge, but a prominent citizen, William Bickley, turned up information and a witness who testified that Jerico had been a Redleg. Had participated in killings, horse stealing, and robbery. Doc

Jennison, on his death bed, his own reputation ruined, sent Jack Dinsmore to speak on Jerico's behalf. But it did no good. Out of the cavalry Jerico went. The last anybody of Company M heard of Jerico, he was riding with Bowlegs, selling horses and doing odd jobs for the army.

Rafer D. Turner was killed two months after Jerico was discharged. The cavalry was looking for sharpshooters. General Custer had every Indian on the continent in an uproar over his mistaken attack on Black Kettle's Cheyennes on their way to the reservation as they had been ordered to do. On the southern plains Cheyennes, Sioux, Kiowas, and Apaches started making hit-and-run raids, taking concealed long-range shots at army patrols. To combat this the army was going to put in every company a crackshot rifleman with the latest model long-range weapon. Rafer D. went off to Fort Laramie, Wyoming, to participate in the shooting contest that would select these sharpshooters. Rafer D. won first prize, a telescoped British Whitworth rifle.

On the way back to join company M, Rafer D. was waylaid and shot dead. Nobody could say whether because he had won the shooting contest against white men or because somebody wanted the rifle. Rafer D.'s body was recovered but the rifle he'd ridden out of Fort Laramie with was missing.

Augie Lincoln froze to death in the severe southern plains winter of '70. He had become the company's dispatch/mail rider. Crossing the Arkansas River that winter, that handsome black horse he was still riding stepped in a sinkhole at a place called The Caches. In spite of Company M's disagreement, the cavalry carried Augie on the rolls as a deserter. The next spring when the river thawed, Augie's body turned up, the mail pouch somehow still clutched in his fist.

In '71 Antoine Battie was knifed to death in a whorehouse, or hog ranch, as they were called at Fort Union, New Mexico, where Company M got sent.

Hiram King

In '72 Fate Elder was awarded personal honor. Comanches and Kiowas had been put on a reservation at Fort Sill, Oklahoma. However, they continued raiding across Red River into Texas and Mexico, then scurrying back to safety on the reservation. Big Tree, Lone Wolf, Kicking Bird, Stumbling Bear, and some other principal chiefs were summoned by Colonel Grierson to the fort supposedly for a big powwow about these raids. When the chiefs assembled, Grierson promptly commanded Company M from concealment, rifles at the ready, and put under arrest Big Tree and Lone Wolf as the ringleaders of the raiding. Angry over this treachery, Stumbling Bear promptly notched an arrow to his bow, and let fly at Grierson. Fate leaped in front of Grierson, taking the arrow in the arm even as he triggered off a shot into Stumbling Bear's chest, killing him. Big Tree and Lone Wolf were promptly loaded into separate wagons, and transported back to Texas to stand trial for twelve murders committed on Salt Creek.

On the way to Texas, Lone Wolf was shot to death by one of his guards, supposedly for trying to escape; Big Tree was convicted of the murders and sentenced to hang. For saving his life, Grierson recommended Fate for the Congressional Medal of Honor and the Army Department awarded it.

Ples Butler never went back to fix up the old Barlowe place. He continued working in and around army posts. Wherever Company M and Fate went, Ples turned up sooner or later. Ostensibly looking for work. Mostly he wangled his way to serving as guide for Captain Dudley, whether Dudley needed a guide or not.

Jimmy Bowlegs? He continued to roam the plains in search of wild horses. From time to time Jerico would be seen with him. Bringing in horses to sell, whether stolen or caught. Now and again an army patrol or supply train would report being shot at by somebody riding a pinto horse.

Broken Ranks

The KGC got absorbed by General Forrest's Ku Klux Klan. The Klan came up through years of ugly, bloody covert war of a sort. Terrorizing, beating, and lynching colored folks. Having members in high places in the government, the Klan acted with something close to impunity.

DARK TRAIL
Hiram King

When the War Between the States was finally over, many men returned from battle only to find their homes destroyed and their families scattered to the wind. Bodie Johnson is one of those men. But while some families fled before advancing armies, the Johnson family was packed up like cattle and shipped west—on a slave train. With only that information to go on, Bodie sets out to find whatever remains of his family. And he will do it. Because no matter how vast the West is, no matter what stands in his way, Bodie knows one thing—the Johnsons will survive.

___4418-8 $5.50 US/$6.50 CAN

Dorchester Publishing Co., Inc.
P.O. Box 6640
Wayne, PA 19087-8640

Please add $1.75 for shipping and handling for the first book and $.50 for each book thereafter. NY, NYC, and PA residents, please add appropriate sales tax. No cash, stamps, or C.O.D.s. All orders shipped within 6 weeks via postal service book rate. Canadian orders require $2.00 extra postage and must be paid in U.S. dollars through a U.S. banking facility.

Name_____
Address_____
City_____State_____Zip_____
I have enclosed $_____ in payment for the checked book(s).
Payment <u>must</u> accompany all orders. ❏ Please send a free catalog.
   CHECK OUT OUR WEBSITE! www.dorchesterpub.com

BENEATH A WHISKEY SKY
TRACY KNIGHT

Escaping the past is no easy feat. Just ask Sim McCracken. Sim is a jaded, weary gunslinger with a whole packsaddle worth of secrets and shame, who wants nothing more than to forge a new life. That's why he spared the life of the young pastor he was hired to kill. But that hasn't made the land baron who hired him for the job too happy. Before Sim has a chance to make a clean escape, another secret from his past catches up with him—a retarded brother named Charles, whom Sim hasn't seen since they were children. Sim has to travel across Missouri to escort Charles to a hospital, with his past breathing down his neck the whole way—and with murderous pursuers just one step behind him.

___4883-3 $4.50 US/$5.50 CAN

DEATH RIDES THE DENVER STAGE
LEWIS B. PATTEN

Clee Fahr has just arrived by stage in Denver City, Colorado. It is 1861 and the War Between the States has broken out back in the East. Torn apart by opposing military and political sympathies, the town is a tinderbox of treachery and suspicion. Eames Jeffords, an old enemy of Clee's from the South, is buying arms for the Confederate cause. Sam Massey, a mine owner, is raising a company of volunteers to march east and join the Union forces. Although he was born in the North, Clee has divided sympathies. But he's caught in the middle, and both sides see him as a threat—a threat that needs to be removed.

___4885-X $3.99 US/$4.99 CAN

MORGETTE IN THE YUKON
G. G. BOYER

Dolf Morgette is determined to head west, as far west as a man can go—to the wilds of Alaska to join the great gold rush. He's charged with the responsibility of protecting Jack Quillen, the only man alive who can locate the vast goldfields of Lost Sky Pilot Fork. For Morgette, the assignment also holds the possibility of a new life for him and his pregnant wife, and perhaps a chance to settle a score with Rudy Dwan, a gunslinging fugitive working for the competition. But a new life doesn't come without risk. Morgette's journey has barely begun before he's ambushed. Soon he's beset at every turn by gunfighters, thieves and saboteurs. If he's not careful, Morgette may not have to worry about a new life— he may not survive his old one.

___4886-8 $3.99 US/$4.99 CAN

Man From Wolf River

John D. Nesbitt

Owen Felver is just passing through. He is on his way from the Wolf River down to the Laramie Mountains for some summer wages. He makes his camp outside of Cameron, Wyoming, and rides in for a quick beer. But it isn't quick enough. While he is there he sees pretty, young Jenny—and the puffed-up gent trying to get rude with her. What else can he do but step in and defend her? Right after that some pretty tough thugs start to make it clear Felver isn't all too welcome around town. Trouble is, the more they tell him to move on—and the more he sees of Jenny—the more he wants to stay. He knows they have something to hide, but he has no idea just how awful it is—or how far they will go to keep it hidden.

___4871-X $4.50 US/$5.50 CAN

TRAIL TO VICKSBURG

LEWIS B. PATTEN

Lewis B. Patten is truly a master of Western fiction. He received three Spur Awards from the Western Writers of America and was awarded the Golden Saddleman Award for lifetime achievement. Here, for the first time in paperback, are two of his finest short novels, restored to their original glory. "The Golden Magnet," a tale of murder and sabotage set in the boomtown of Denver City during the Gold Rush, presents Norah Forrest, a young woman who becomes the owner of a stagecoach line when her father is killed. In "Trail to Vicksburg," Jeff Hueston yearns to join his brothers in the Confederate Army, but instead must drive his family's cattle to New Orleans, a city recently occupied—by Union troops!

___4700-4 $4.50 US/$5.50 CAN